The Birth

of an
Island

François Clément

Translated from the French by Helen Weaver

Simon and Schuster · New York

DESIGNED BY ELIZABETH WOLL
MANUFACTURED IN THE UNITED STATES OF AMERICA

1   2   3   4   5   6   7   8   9   10

LIBRARY OF CONGRESS CATALOGING IN PUBLICATION DATA

CLÉMENT, FRANÇOIS, 1925–
THE BIRTH OF AN ISLAND.

TRANSLATION OF NAISSANCE D'UNE ÎLE.
I. TITLE.
PZ4.C6256BI3   [PQ2605.L422]   843'.9'14   74-19100
ISBN 0-671-21924-3

TO NICOLE

It was the Abbé de Montesquiou who, while walking in the country one day at Val, near Saint-Germain, is supposed to have commented to his admirers: "The life we lead is not a natural one. Natural man lived in his fortress, surrounded by his retainers."

—CONDORCET, *Mémoires*

1

AFTER THINKING IT over, I have decided to tell you the real story of my life.

Don't misunderstand my reasons for addressing myself to you. I don't think of you as the son of my son, as that child who has grown up in my shadow, who is at once my only future and the sum of my whole past, but as that young stranger who came to visit me last year after eight years of absence, whom I found to be free, ambitious, without plans, and who pleased me.

As for my decision to talk at all, that is more difficult to explain. I have several very different reasons for doing so. The first is a respect for the truth. For over thirty years I have been the life blood of an entire race. Along with my people, but more fully than they, I have lived through an extraordinary adventure. After all, I am the last survivor of the Old World.

It is natural that a great deal has been written about me. For a very long time now, my life has been inseparable from history. In the beginning I accepted these reflections, these reports, these analyses of my personality and my work. I regarded them as useful and even necessary. Perhaps they were merely flattering. One day I realized that they were only the materials that were being used to construct an official version of the truth that bore no relation to the reality I have known.

I don't blame anyone for anything. In order to tell a story, one must choose. And whoever listens to the storyteller chooses too. This alone distorts many things. In order to be understood, one must be clear and simple. And nothing is simple except syntheses constructed after the fact. After all, there is everything that historians do not know, everything that must be concealed from them to prevent a scandal, and which is nevertheless indispensable to an understanding of events.

It isn't easy to govern. It's a strange task, rather close, in its essence, to making love: all-consuming, uncompromising, and

9

ultimately disillusioning, for the best leader is in reality only the least bad one.

It is, I think, impossible to achieve anything solid without first deciding upon certain rules, without defining what might be called a morality. The great statesmen all had their own morality, and they were so convinced of its excellence that they strove to transform their fellow citizens in accordance with it. Revolutionaries tried to make new men, conservatives tried to make perfect men, but the impulse was the same.

It's an ambitious project. All those who have formulated it have, without exception, been led to commit, in order to achieve it, one or more of those actions which men without responsibilities call crimes. Some who had at first been compelled to perform these actions by the force of circumstances found them convenient, looked for justifications, and became tyrants. Others lost confidence in their fellow men because they no longer believed in themselves, and tolerated the worst vices in those around them. Still others, the rarest, ordered certain necessary actions without denying what they were, or their own responsibility. These, I believe, were good statesmen. But how is one to admit this? The people have always recoiled in horror from this obvious fact: The wisest government, the regime most concerned about the public welfare, and the lowest police state are in fact one and the same phenomenon.

After having concealed what must be concealed one must then, believe me, fabricate a great deal in order to explain what continues to show through.

By telling you the story of my life as it really was and not as historians have reconstructed it, I can serve the truth and help you, for I know that you respect me, and I am afraid that my official image might mislead you.

For over thirty years I have been the one to whom people have turned. Some men have learned how to breathe through my mouth. They think they have rights over me. This is natural. They love me. But because of this they think I belong to them, and they use me to build something which is no longer me. By retiring from power, by removing myself from their sight, by returning here to my island, I abandoned my memory to them, thinking that this would be enough, and that now they would leave me in peace. But it wasn't enough. In spite of the distance and against my will they continue to make inquiries, to watch me. They are afraid I might suddenly cease to resemble the creature whom they have invented and to whom they have given my name. In short, out of affection, they have killed me.

This is another reason to restore the true image, to peel away this insipid layer of paint with which they've whitewashed me. It's true that I'm old, extraordinarily old, if you please, but believe me, I'm not dead yet.

I'm lucky. I read somewhere that the exercise of power wounds the soul like a hairshirt, lacerates the penitent at every step. The image is striking. For a long time I have expected these wounds. I haven't received them. I have saved the world, I have remade it, I have governed it. I have had more responsibilities than any man has ever had. And yet today I still like to laugh. I have no wounds, other than those inflicted by old age.

When I want to forget them, I have only to relax. I read, I go for a walk, I look at the women, the children, the trees, I soak up the sun, I inhale the smell of the sea, I enjoy life as much and perhaps more than I did in my youth. I like to have fun. What better way could there be than to tell you, in spite of the respect with which I am surrounded, how stupid I was at times?

I'm going to die soon. In an hour, tonight, tomorrow . . . I'm eighty-nine. It doesn't bother me. I think about it rarely, without fear. I'm even curious to find out . . . I have arranged that if death should overtake me suddenly, these pages will be turned over to you in whatever state they are in at the time.

Will they interest you? Will you understand me? I shall tell you the truth, which is not always easy to hear; I shall describe for you my island as it was when, for a brief and uncertain time, it became the raft on which the human race took refuge; and above all, myself, the last witness of the Other World. I shall tell you in my own words about a society which I saw, a world of which you can find nothing in books but a cold and lifeless image.

How can a free child of the New World begin to suspect

all the complications, all the follies of the Other World? My misgivings about this came close to ruining my plan. And then I realized that I was, in the most ordinary sense, in the same situation as all old men and, if you'll excuse me, of all writers. I had to try to bring back to life people and events that have disappeared without knowing whether anyone would listen to me, or understand me, or be interested in what I was saying.

Well, I've made up my mind. I shall write to you as if you were going to understand everything. I shall tell you too much, so that you will understand a little. I shall enjoy myself, at the risk of boring you. And I shall be truthful, at the risk of misleading you.

Listen to me, my friend, listen to the old witness.

2

FIRST I MUST tell you why and how I arrived at Raevavae. No one has ever had any precise information on these points. It's not really important, of course. But it will be interesting to you. The facts and the dates are known. But no one has dared to interpret them. In this case, it is respect for me that has militated against the truth.

Because no one, I believe, has ever dared to face the fact that when I landed at Raevavae, I was a failure. A good-for-nothing. I knew it. I had admitted it to myself. And I had no intention of changing.

I was born September 6, 1944, in Paris. The war was not yet over. My parents were already living behind the Église Sainte-Clotilde in the ministerial quarter, in the enormous and gloomy apartment that I came to know later. During the war, it must have been very cold there in the winter. My father was not sensitive to cold. He wore an overcoat only on formal occasions, for the sake of correctness. At the ministry, the window in his office was open in all weathers. He closed it only when he was receiving superiors. He had been raised in the Military

School of La Flèche, just after the First World War. La Flèche was an institution which you cannot imagine, in spite of everything you may have read about the Old World. In it, adults forced children to live a very hard life in order to prepare them for self-sacrifice and glory. My father was an orphan. His parents had died in a railway accident. His guardian was an uncle, a general who may have been a swine. I never knew him. He died around 1930.

My father never hesitated or doubted. He was pious, hardworking, scrupulously honest, and followed a regime of extreme austerity. He never gave in, either to himself or to others. If a problem arose, he always chose the most disagreeable solution. He was occasionally known to complain, with a bitter satisfaction, but it was an affectation. I don't know why he didn't go into the army. He didn't tell me. He never talked about himself. And he had no friends. He studied law, alone, in Paris, and alone he prepared himself for an inspectorship of finance. One of his uncles who frequented what was then known as society, gave him an entrée. I think he felt sorry for this silent, respectful nephew who never asked for anything and led a miserably unhappy life. He invited him to his home, introduced him to people. It was through him that my father met my mother.

Her name was Monique Gerzat. She was born in 1916 after the death of her father, a captain who was killed at the front. I still have some photographs of her, now faded, worn, and cracked. I kept them in my wallet for years. For me they were like a proof of identity. In school I was always showing them to my classmates. Perhaps I wanted to take advantage of the prestige conferred by a dead mother. I think that above all I wanted to show that I was like everyone else, that I, too, had a mother.

She was a tall, slender young woman with pretty eyes and a gay smile. In spite of her smile I thought I sensed something sad in her, for which I held my father responsible. But for years I was totally preoccupied with accumulating evidence against my father.

In any case, he loved my mother, insofar as he was capable

13

of it. He loved her for herself, but also for everything she brought him. He had never known gentleness. She introduced it to him—too late, no doubt. And yet soon enough to make an impression. She taught him the meaning of relaxation, comfort, luxury. If he did not make use of these things for himself—this important official, this rich man, worked every day of his life until eleven o'clock at night, except on days when he dined out, and then he worked until two in the morning, and never wore anything under his well-cut but somber suits but the coarse underwear he bought at a shop for noncommissioned officers near the military school—if, then, he did not indulge himself, he was able to appreciate and to admire.

For him, I think, my mother came from another planet.

In spite of all his love, he did not allow himself to be corrupted. During the war he was detached from Vichy to Paris to fill a difficult post with many responsibilities. He did not avoid them, although he did not believe in the victory of the Germans and was sure from the outset that some day he would have to answer for his actions. He brought my mother to Paris at the beginning of the winter of '42 and requested my grandmother not to send them food packages. He lived on, and made my mother live on, the rations allocated by the Department of Food Control.

This probably explains why my mother died on September 29, 1944, three weeks after my birth. It is true that everything was scarce and that the doctors were unable to check the infection that had broken out. But I have always felt that if my mother had been stronger and better nourished, and if the apartment had been better heated, she would have survived.

Did my father think so too? It's possible. He must have suspected it, and forgotten it very quickly. Otherwise I cannot explain a remark he made to me one day, which I shall repeat to you in a moment.

This remark came from either stupidity or malice. But my father was not stupid. Lonely and inhuman, but not stupid.

If he suspected what I think he did, all is explained. For he suffered a great deal, in his own way. He loved my mother as

14

much as it was possible for him to love. To admit a share of responsibility in her death was impossible. Instead, he chose to accuse me.

I had just turned ten. It was during school vacation. My report card had not been very good. He looked at it and said, "If something is the matter, if you are unhappy, tell me. We don't know each other very well, but you are my son, and I have forgiven you for killing your mother . . ."

I hated him from that moment. Even today, as I write those words, the back of my neck tingles. And yet perhaps in his own bizarre way he was trying to help me, comparing my loneliness at boarding school with the loneliness he had known at La Flèche.

It was true that we didn't know each other very well. When I was born it was my grandmother Gerzat who took charge of me. There was nothing else to be done. She was my grandmother, everything was scarce in Paris, and she was living in Berry on a piece of property called La Brissonnerie.

I lived there until 1953.

My grandmother respected nothing except her own inclinations. Neither elegant nor attractive, she wore what she pleased and dressed up only for her friends. She was not very old at the time, but her old-fashioned clothes and antiquated hair styles made her look older. She had ceased to be a woman on the day she had learned of her husband's death and had transferred all her devotion to my mother. She loved me passionately, in memory of her.

She lived alone, doing exactly as she pleased, with a pair of old servants. Bernard looked after the vegetable garden and Stephanie did the cooking. We ate only home-grown food. My grandmother set aside the overripe fruits for herself. But when a sheep was killed she took only one chop and a slice of the leg, and forced the servants and myself to finish the rest, at every meal, in every form, to the point of nausea, for the next month.

She argued with me often, but forgave me for everything. She scorned ambition, respected honor, and loved wit. As soon as I could talk she treated me as an equal, consulting me on everything, telling me everything, and encouraging me to read the books she liked.

Very active, she read, knitted, gave orders without stopping. In spite of her independence she had many friends, in Berry and elsewhere. Every day she wrote ten letters and received an equal number. Passing on one person's news to another, she served as a connecting link between old people who had not seen each other for years.

She was a small woman with very white hair and a quick ironic expression. She had a large nose and thin lips that were perpetually drawn to the right in a half-smile. Her hands were very soft, with dark veins and brown spots. She walked with difficulty, leaning on an ebony cane. Around her neck she wore a ribbon of white faille which she replaced on special occasions with a sort of cravat of tulle. She smelled of Guerlain powder and ate hard candies.

She died suddenly in her bed one night in March, 1953.

I was nine years old. I was vaguely attending the local elementary school, and knew no discipline except what my grandmother referred to pompously, with her eternal smile, as the discretion of a gentleman, that is, pleasure tempered by reason. My father took me back to his apartment in Paris. I didn't know him. My grandmother had always made fun of him. He lived alone with a very old housekeeper. He never smiled. His only distractions were walking, church, and charities.

I believe he honestly tried to take an interest in me. He enrolled me in a little school near the house. The housekeeper took me there and called for me in the afternoon. I became stupid from unhappiness. I kept my mouth shut to keep from crying. I understood nothing because I heard nothing, preoccupied as I was with my own misery.

I must have been depressing. I was sent away to boarding school. Before I left, my father made the remark I just told you about.

He helped me without knowing it. From that moment I hated him so much that I did not become stupid: I became perverse. I was the adolescent that everyone is afraid of. I wasn't violent or loud. I was an incurable nonconformist.

Naturally, in class I did nothing. I was punished, but I didn't care. My classmates didn't like me. They didn't know how to approach me. And beneath my silence, I despised them as much as I did my professors and my father. The little I learned was from private reading, done at random after school or during vacations. These I spent at the home of some distant cousins of my father, or with him. I may also have remained at school.

At the age of fifteen I had a love affair with one of my cousins. We were discovered. Everyone was horrified. My father came to get me. He took me back to Paris and locked me in my room for the rest of the vacation. It happened quietly. Considering the nature of the offense, my father showed restraint. I think he was secretly satisfied to see his worst predictions come true. In fact he made it clear that he was punishing me to be at peace with his conscience, and not to cure me, for he did not believe I was capable of mending my ways.

Growing accustomed to disgrace, I completely stopped working and from then on was interested only in women. I had an enormous number of them. I am not boasting. I pursued them all, and no rejection discouraged me. I loved them all, less for their bodies, which I also needed, than for themselves, their wit, their personalities. Until I was twenty-five, they helped me to live, in every way.

My father was also helping me to live this way. We hardly spoke to each other anymore. I rarely saw him. I stole a few things from him now and then: an old book or a pair of candlesticks, which I would immediately sell . . . I would do it when he wasn't around, but without concealing my theft. Between us there was a kind of war. He regarded me with a bitter satisfaction. One day, after an absence of several weeks, we met in the hall as I was getting some fresh linen. He asked me in a tone of voice which I can still hear and which he must have thought was bantering, "Well, how many beds have you been in since I last saw you?"

He paralyzed me. As usual, I did not reply. But I lowered out the window into the courtyard, at the end of the pull-cords which I had cut off the drapes, a little Louis XVI bedside table which I sold for a bad price and which I often missed afterward.

It was my way of defending myself, of saving myself. It will never be sufficiently realized to what extent children are at the mercy of their parents. Until the age of twenty-five, I was entirely dependent on my father: I lived only to displease him. It can be just as absorbing as pleasing.

I did my military service in a cavalry regiment in Germany. My father had pulled strings to get me into an elite unit, as active as it was well-disciplined. He must have hoped, without really believing it, that this would form my character. I completed my training without complaining, then I was assigned to a tank. It was dirty, tedious, and a little frightening. I was often punished; all the dirty jobs were given to me. One day I had a pain in my chest. They called it a sore throat and gave me some pills, I don't know what they were. I had a fever of a hundred and four. I couldn't eat a thing. When I was sent to unload a truck full of military supplies, I refused. I was put in prison, after a sergeant had insulted me. I didn't give a damn. Live and let live, that was my motto. At that time military methods seemed to me particularly stupid. This is what I told the lieutenant who came to question me.

I remember that conversation very clearly. I spoke in a friendly, persuasive tone. I knew the risk I was taking, but I didn't care: I was fed up with military academies, with all the loyal soldiers in the world.

The lieutenant who was listening to me was young. He had probably served in Algeria. He had the bitter expression of the disappointed idealist.

He sent me to the hospital. Perhaps because he wanted to be liked; perhaps because, since I spoke to him in a tone of complete equality, he had recognized me as a man of his background; perhaps because underneath he agreed with me. A nurse took me under her wing. I was excused with honor from all the tests, all the examinations. In other words, I received a medical discharge.

My father was very upset. Nevertheless, he offered to help me find a position. I accepted, for the first time in my life. I was a little ashamed of my act of rebellion.

For a short time I was secretary to a romantic businessman

18

who was always poised between fortune and disaster because he relied too much on luck in exploiting his talents. My reputation as a black sheep, which my father had not concealed from him, interested him for a while, until he discovered that I was not extravagant. For my part, I found him amusing to watch, for he put as much ruthlessness into ruining his chances as he did into restoring them. But he was too predictable. We soon became bored with each other. We parted company quietly, like well-bred gentlemen.

I had in fact just been put in possession by my father of my inheritances from my mother and my grandmother. My father had sold La Brissonnerie without even informing me. So there was nothing left but some very choice stocks. I sold them one by one, calmly. It was natural: I needed money and I was having trouble earning my living.

And yet I was working. I did just about everything one can do without a degree. I was a good salesman, people liked me; but I wasn't interested. Each new job fascinated me. As soon as I had acquired its technique, as soon as I was in a position to profit from my work, it ceased to amuse me. It was the same way with women: I wanted only to win them, to discover them, and then phfft! on to the next. They didn't hold it against me. I instinctively avoided the jealous ones, the troublemakers, and I promised nothing.

As might be expected, it was a woman who rescued me from boyhood, that is, from my father. My mistresses were usually only shopkeepers, businesswomen, secretaries. This one happened to be a middle-class woman. She was my age, twenty-six. She was married to a manufacturer from Reims and her name was Claude. Like me, she was slightly mad. Why? I don't know. She never talked about herself and she often lied. I really loved her. Perhaps she was for me what my mother was for my father: the discovery of a certain refinement, combined with that independence, that *quality* that a certain kind of education provides. I wanted her to get a divorce, I wanted to marry her. She couldn't make up her mind. She never said no. Or yes. Her husband was older than herself. She loved and feared him like a father. He was shrewd. We were always having to hide.

Eventually I gave her a child, a boy who had my eyes. It estranged us, inexplicably. It was as if we had loved each other only to produce this child. Now that he was there, we no longer had anything to say to each other.

I became friends with the husband. He was interesting.

Whenever I was in Reims, I went to see them. The little boy really had my eyes. He looked like his mother. I had no rights over him. He barely knew me. He didn't interest me much.

It was at this point that I went back to my father.

All of a sudden he had ceased to frighten me. I had nothing left for him but pity. The memory of the past prevented us from loving each other, but we were father and son. And alone.

He had aged, lost some of his rigidity. I made an effort to see him often, but briefly: after an hour, we would start tearing each other apart again. When I had run through the money I had inherited from my mother, I told him so. He already knew it. He offered to help me again. I refused. I didn't want some quiet little job in an organization subsidized by the state. I had wasted my youth fighting someone whom I no longer hated. I felt a need to lose myself, to change my life. I was sorry that we no longer had colonies.

"I'll help you anyway," said my father, with a timid half smile.

Six months later I was appointed administrator of the Station for the Study of Citrus Fruits in Raevavae.

My father saw me off on the boat. As he wished me goodbye he seemed pacified, rejuvenated. And I felt lighter than I had ever felt before.

This is how I came to Raevavae. I've told you all this at some length, and perhaps you won't understand everything. What can you imagine of the relationship between father and son in a traditional French family? And what image can you form of the places I have talked about?

But all this had to be said and I was the only one who could say it. Thinking back on this time that had vanished has moved me. And wasn't it amusing to find out exactly what I was, knowing what I was going to become?

3

THE FIRST TIME I saw Raevavae, it was five o'clock in the morning. It was on the 14th of July, as you know. For three weeks I had been in Papeete, waiting for transportation. The night before, the young government attaché who was vaguely responsible for me had come to inform me that the Navy was sending a Catalina to the island of Rapa, where a ceremony was to take place the next day.

Rapa is very isolated, the southernmost of the Polynesians, but at that time about forty French people were living there permanently because preparations were being made for some atomic explosions in the Tuamotus. In any case, the hydroplane would stop at Raevavae and would let me off there. Departure was scheduled for one o'clock in the morning.

I was glad to be leaving. Tahiti was only a stopping off place for me. What could I find there? The fashionable life toward which the government attaché was trying to draw me? It interested me no more than it had in France. The natives? I suspected them of being rather slow. Besides, they weren't *my* natives.

The crew of the Catalina acted abused. In the cockpit, we hardly spoke. Having to get up in the middle of the night had depressed us. The cabin was perfunctorily furnished. The motors made a great deal of noise. The air was cold as we gained altitude.

Around four o'clock we were caught in the light of the sun, but the sea beneath us was still black. Little by little, however, it became grey, and then pink. It was at this moment that the pilot tapped me on the arm.

"There it is," he said, pointing to something in front of us.

At first I didn't see anything. Then—well, it looked the way it had in the atlas: a black dot surrounded by empty space. Only this time the empty space was the ocean.

I was really looking forward to arriving at Raevavae. I had an image of it that was very vague and very precise at the same time. I had thought about it a great deal. I judged myself without indulgence. I knew that I was a failure, or more accurately, that I was a kind of cripple, a man who was lacking something that set him apart from everyone else. This made me neither regretful nor ambitious. But I had had enough of it. I thought of Raevavae as a kind of monastery. In going there I was giving up everything in the hope of finding something. I had told myself all kinds of stories, no doubt. I was going to find the state of nature, and if not happiness—I had already stopped believing in that—at least peace.

But when I saw at the tip of my pilot's finger that tiny little piece of dark land fringed with foam in the middle of an empty immensity that seemed to contain no other island, no continent, at that moment I truly felt what it was to enter a monastery.

I remember everything the way one sometimes remembers certain scenes from one's childhood in full detail, including colors and smells. It is true that those days were the infancy of my new life.

I think the pilot felt a little sorry for me. We had met two or three times in Papeete. We had hit it off. He was my age. Imagine Raevavae, this little dot lost in the ocean, and me with my steamer trunk and my five suitcases.

If I had said that I didn't want to get off, we would probably have gone on to Rapa, and then . . . but it wasn't possible. Not for me. I'm not sentimental, and in those days I wasn't given to reflection. But I've always had an instinct about things. Raevavae was serious. You arrived, you closed the door behind you, and you never went back. I knew it. And because it was serious, I had no choice.

It's funny—at the same time, I detested heroes, self-righteousness, morality, rules . . . I smiled.

Very quickly, we began to lose altitude. Then we were over the island. It wasn't so small after all.

"Eleven kilometers by four," shouted the pilot.

I asked him if he could fly around it before landing. We lost more altitude. Then we flew along the reefs, remaining outside the lagoon. Next, we did the same thing along the land. The island was beautiful. It lay against the calm lagoon, protected by the white ring of waves that broke against the reefs. I remember two things: the color of the lagoon, and the shape of the tiny islands that formed the outside barrier. They looked like little bones strung on a necklace.

The pilot looked at me. I nodded.

He maneuvered the plane so it was headed into the wind. While he banked, the plane leaned forward sharply. Below me I saw a whole fleet of canoes. All of a sudden, I was happy.

We alighted in front of Tuamora, narrowly missing the men in the canoes, which made the pilot furious. He must have been expected at a certain time in Rapa. He didn't want to land on the ground. As soon as the motorboat arrived he unloaded my steamer trunk and my five suitcases, shook my hand, and slammed the door while I was still on the float. Then he went back to the controls, signaled through the window to the canoes to make way, and flew off, passing close over the reefs of the big motu.

The motorboat in which I had seated myself was grey and dirty, but official. There was a native at the helm, and another guarding my baggage in the front. On my right and left, near the motor, were two white men. One wore the uniform of a policeman with a kepi, a shoulder belt, and a revolver. I had been told of his existence in Papeete. But I didn't know who the other one was. My ears were stopped up, probably from the landing. Since the motor was very loud, I couldn't understand anything that was said to me. I shook the hands that were offered to me, smiled, and nodded at random. My stomach was upset from lack of sleep. In the airplane I had almost forgotten about it. Now, the waves created by the departure of the Catalina shook the boat, and I was nauseated.

Fortunately, there was the scenery. I looked at everything without seeing anything, but I was happy. Around us about thirty canoes, manned by laughing natives, were escorting us to shore. I started thinking about the state of nature again, in spite of my nausea.

We docked at Matotea. I learned later that it was the only

port that had a landing pier. It was more convenient for the baggage, I suppose. But I was disappointed. This famous pier was miserable, grey with age, half fallen into the water at the outermost end. As for the village that lay along the shore at the foot of a wooded hill, it consisted only of some rather squalid cottages made of parpen and covered with corrugated iron.

As soon as I set foot on land, the natives crowded around me. Once again, I was happy. And then the "Marseillaise" broke out.

Everyone made way for me. The policeman gave the military salute. Many of the natives, both men and women, imitated him. It was then that I noticed the little flags hanging from the coconut palms. And from behind one of the houses ten or twelve small boys, marching in step, led by an adult who was beating time, arrived, playing—very badly—on various wind instruments.

They stopped in front of us, marked time until the end of the national anthem, then fell silent.

Next, a young girl in a red dress with a red flower in her hair walked up to me shyly and placed a wreath of flowers around my neck, stammering out something like, "Welcome to Raevavae, Mr. Administrator."

Her mission accomplished, she put her hands over her mouth, burst out laughing, and disappeared among the spectators.

The policeman turned to me and asked whether I wanted to make a speech. He, too, called me Mr. Administrator. I was extremely tired, and the heavy, intense heat was overwhelming. I shook my head.

"No," I said. "I'd rather take a shower."

That's how I arrived at Raevavae.

4

I AM NOW going to ask you to forget everything you know. The *tsunami* has been described, analyzed, painted, and sung hundreds of times. You must forget all that. It's not *the* cyclone that I want to talk to you about, but *my* cyclone, the one I went through—lost, uprooted, disappointed, with my trousers wilted by the damp air we were breathing and my shirt drenched with perspiration.

I was very hot. Hotter than I've ever been since. Not a leaf stirred. Even the natives were perspiring, that oily perspiration that you know.

The policeman—his name was Peyrole, as you know—had a jeep. He offered to drive me to the "residence" that had been prepared for me. I accepted. The white man who had been in the motor boat sat in the back seat. The natives had already loaded my baggage into some incredible-looking carts drawn by some wretched animals I hadn't gotten a good look at but which I assumed to be donkeys.

At this time there weren't any roads in Raevavae. Besides the native paths, there were only two trails. One of these, which was simply the top of the beach, ran all the way around the island. The other connected Anatonu to Matotea, cutting across the island between Mount Taraia and Mount Hiro. Peyrole took the second. He hoped that by going higher, we would find a breath of air. Besides, from the side of Taraia there is a pretty view of the bay of Rairua.

Until then I had had very little contact with policemen. Like everyone else, I had been stopped by them a few times on the road. I had found them coarse, suspicious, honest, and over-fed. Except for his shorts, Peyrole was like any other policeman. He was about my age, but he was much heavier than me. He was of medium height, dark-haired and redfaced. He spoke little, with a strong southern accent which was new to me, and when you asked him a question he knitted his brows before replying.

The jeep drove slowly over a footpath washed by the rain, between two walls of foliage which often met over our heads.

The air was sticky. At first our passenger in the back seat tried to make conversation. Peyrole was concentrating on his driving, and did not respond. Still feeling queasy, with sweat dripping into my eyes, I sat there wondering how I could get people to stop calling me Mr. Administrator. I had nothing but an orange grove to administer, and in Paris they hadn't concealed the fact that nobody really knew whether it still existed. I wasn't even an official. Barely under contract. And here, they were treating me as if I were the governor of the Pacific.

I was going to live with these people. I didn't want to start out by displeasing them. Nor did I want to be taken for something I was not. It was essential that from the beginning our relations be straightforward and natural. The falsity of the situation was bothering me.

I was thinking about all this when Peyrole turned left off the trail and parked the jeep on a grassy esplanade that overlooked the whole bay of Rairua.

After leaving Matotea we had climbed rather high without my noticing it because the trail wound back and forth. Now we were about six hundred feet above the sea, which gleamed like molten tin.

Peyrole took off his kepi and mopped his head lengthily with his handkerchief. He seemed to be suffering from the heat, much more so than the other passenger, whose name and business I still didn't know. Around his waist, across his chest, under his shoulder belt, and under his arms, the shirt of his uniform was dark with perspiration. He sighed.

"Been here for two years, never seen a day like this. Am I right, Doctor?"

"Excuse me," I said, "I didn't catch your name . . ."

The other smiled. He was a tall man, very thin, with those empty blue eyes that you sometimes see in blind people or alcoholics. He was very wrinkled, very tan, and his white-blond hair was too long. I thought he looked between fifty and sixty.

"Dubois," he said, "former navy doctor."

"And a good one," put in Peyrole in the accents of the Midi.

I smiled, embarrassed. I am not, and never have been, shy, but perhaps because I was tired, or perhaps because I had some rather exaggerated ideas about Raevavae and its community, I hardly dared to say the simplest things. Also, I wanted to get things out into the open regarding my title of administrator.

I didn't have time. Suddenly, while we were looking at the

26

blinding sea under the grey sky, the universe shuddered. I've looked for a better expression, a less theatrical one, but I haven't found one. Nothing happened, really. Not a leaf moved, not a blade of grass. But something suddenly changed, so unmistakably that we looked at each other, all three of us. I think it was only a sudden change in atmospheric pressure. But we suspected nothing. We all thought of an earthquake. We looked at the summit of Hiro behind us, but there, too, nothing was moving. And then, all of a sudden, the sky began to move. Without our feeling a thing, the clouds that had been gathering over the island since morning broke up and rolled away like handfuls of dust toward the southwest, that is, from where we were, out to sea. In an instant, the sky cleared. Then from behind Hiro there arrived other clouds, driven even more quickly by a wind we still did not feel.

Dubois was the first to react. He made a little grimace and said, "At this time of the year it's unlikely, and it never happens in Raevavae. But . . . we may very well be in for the tail of a cyclone."

We didn't answer. Peyrole walked back to the jeep. We followed him. He was about to start the motor when Dubois placed his hand on his shoulder. "Listen!"

We heard the wind before we felt it. We saw it rushing toward us full speed from the top of Mount Hiro, first like a gust that turned up the leaves at the tops of the trees, then suddenly like an enormous tidal wave laden with branches, roofs, and other things which we could not distinguish.

"Take cover!" shouted Peyrole, jumping out of the car and running toward a very large rock that stood at the edge of the woods.

We followed him. I can still see him, running as hard as he could on his short fat legs, one hand on his kepi to keep it from flying away.

We still weren't in the wind. But the air was dense, almost palpable. We reached the rock. It was a good shelter. It was between Mount Hiro and us, and it leaned toward the sea, protecting two or three square yards of ground like a roof.

We reached the rock and leaned against it, and suddenly the air changed again, becoming light and cool. We looked at each other; we didn't have time to speak. This lasted maybe two seconds. Immediately afterward the first leaves passed over us, then the first branches, while all around us came the loud reports of palm trees breaking in two.

We lay down with our heads against the rock, which was trembling, and we waited. I don't know what the others did. I shielded my face with my arms, my mouth was pressed against a rich black soil that smelled of humus, I was having trouble breathing, my whole body was being buffeted and beaten by projectiles I could not identify. I waited. I believe, though I'm not sure of it, that it was dark around us. I know that the noise was so tremendous that it had gone beyond our senses and that we no longer heard it. I was clinging to the warm earth, my mind was blank. I almost felt sleepy. The others had ceased to exist, as had Raevavae and even myself.

Then the wind let up a little, and we heard it roaring again. It was then that the rain began. Like everything else, it arrived without warning. At first there was only the wind, and then all at once it was raining in cataracts, so heavily that I thought it was the sea. I licked my lips, but it wasn't salty.

Soon streams formed to the right and to the left of our rock, and began invading the little basin where we had taken refuge. We had to get up and lean against the rock, which was still trembling. The sky was grey-green, and the light was the same light you get thirty feet below sea level when you dive into a bed of algae. At first we leaned our faces against the side of the rock to protect them from the sand and brush that was still whirling around, but soon the water dominated everything else. We turned around. We were up to our knees in a kind of torrent that was digging out the ground under our feet. Beyond the shelter of the rock there was only the grey curtain of the rain and a few dark, indistinct shapes that were moving around frighteningly.

I looked at my companions. Both of their faces were bloody, so I ran my hand over my forehead and discovered that I was bleeding too. Later we found that we had been polished by the sand as if by sandpaper. Peyrole had, of course, lost his kepi. Dubois, with his long hair twisted into irregular locks, resembled an old woman who was slightly mad. I don't know how I looked.

Very soon, we began to shiver. This went on for over two hours before we could hope to do anything. At a certain point Dubois sat down in the water. It came up to his shoulders. Peyrole and I pulled him to his feet and held him up against the rock. It was impossible to talk. Then the wind dropped. The rain was only a very violent rain. We were drenched and frozen.

We waited a little while longer, then we went to look for the jeep. It had disappeared along with everything else. It was found several days later, wedged between some trees on the slope leading to the beach. It was still very difficult to see, but daylight had returned. Mount Hiro was covered with clouds, but from its summit was falling a large fresh flow of orange-red lava, no doubt caused by a landslide. Around us, the landscape made no sense. There were nothing but tree trunks broken off in the middle, roots pointing toward the sky, foundations swept clean with maniacal care or, on the contrary, incomprehensible piles of rubble. Peyrole leaned toward me:

"Look after the doctor," he shouted.

"Where are you going?"

He knitted his brows. "My wife, my children, the villages . . ."

He shouted with concentration. He looked serious and responsible.

"What happened?"

He threw up his hands and made a face. "Look after the doctor," he repeated. "I'll send someone to help you. Don't go away. The danger is over."

Then he walked off with a waddling gait, stepping over the fallen tree trunks.

We stayed there another three hours. Dubois very skillfully arranged a roof of leaves over a spot in the middle of a pile of branches that was almost dry. We huddled in there and waited in silence, shoulder to shoulder, shivering.

The rain finally stopped. The sun came out, the sky became very blue, and everything began to steam. Then we heard shouts. Three natives had come to get us. They had brought two of those little horses that I had mistaken at a distance for donkeys. We mounted them without protest and arrived at Anatonu without further incident.

The village was full of men and women running around and screaming. I couldn't understand what they were saying. Here, too, many trees had fallen, and almost all the houses were without roofs. In what could be called the streets, which were merely irregular spaces between buildings, the wind had constructed barricades. The steeple of the church was half demolished but the bell was still in place and was ringing constantly.

Dubois dismounted slowly. Like me, he seemed exhausted, but he managed a little smile.

"I'm going to see what I can do in this mess . . ."

"Can I help you?"

He hesitated. "I don't think so. It would be best if you went home. These men will show you the way. I think your baggage has arrived. Change your clothes, get some sleep . . . oh, and if you have tincture of iodine or eau de cologne, wash your scratches. I have all the help I need here . . ."

He walked off, limping a little, his shoulders round and his hair too long.

I was taken to what Peyrole had called my residence. You know it, it's the present museum. Actually, this house had been built for the policeman and his family. But during the war the navy or the marines, I don't remember which, had installed a much more comfortable post a little higher up, on the side of the mountain. After the war, the policeman had moved there. For me, there was a little rectangular house made completely of stone, with a roof of fibro-cement painted red to resemble tile and bars on the windows.

Over the door, inscribed on a stonework scroll, you could still read the words, "Liberty, Equality, Fraternity."

It was rather funny, but I didn't feel like laughing. I went inside. The room was in order. There was a bed, a table, two chairs. My suitcases were piled in the middle. A native was sitting on them. He smiled at me. I wanted to wash, to change my clothes, to be alone. I had to make an effort not to lose my temper. I made conversation for a quarter of an hour with my guides and my caretaker. I offered them cigarettes. They explained to me why the hurricane hadn't been able to get at my new house. To do this, they referred to places I didn't know. They tired me. I finally had to ask them politely to leave. It was my first lesson in Islander patience.

5

IT'S VERY DIFFICULT for me to tell you all this the way it happened. In the first place, because I haven't thought about it for a long time, and my memories come back in fragments which I must constantly rearrange and verify. But above all, because I am telling you about my first contact with a land that has since become my own. How am I to show you Peyrole as he appeared to me that first day, how am I to describe Dubois, whom I didn't know and who was later to become more than a father to me?

I don't know whether I'm right or wrong. If I am to succeed in saying what I want to say, I must go at my own pace. The pace of an old man mulling over the years of his youth, no doubt, but I think it will be useful to you, who have always known us flamboyant, in all our glory. It's important to know where we came from . . .

When I awoke in that strange room, the three open windows were lined with brown faces watching me through the bars. I felt as if I were in a cage. It was another lesson in Island ways. Here, private life did not exist.

I took a shower, dressed, and asked for directions to Peyrole's house. It was the middle of the afternoon, and much less hot. The sky was clear. The verdure, washed by the hurricane, glistened with youth. In spite of the scattered branches and broken tree trunks, one had the impression that the whole thing hadn't been that bad, that soon it wouldn't even show.

Peyrole lived in a long, rather well-constructed building, half barracks, half colonial villa, with a projecting roof that rested on wooden pillars. The only trouble was, there was no more roof. The little lawn in front of the house was covered with natives sitting or lying down, weeping and wailing. A jumble of broken trees in the back must have been a woods.

Even today I can't bear the sight of unhappiness. The suffering of other people makes me very uncomfortable. It's probably a sign of selfishness. I can't help it. At the time I'm talking about, the sight of a woman in tears would put me to flight. I almost ran away when I saw this mass of lamenting people.

If I didn't leave, it was because I didn't know where else to go. Besides, when they saw me the natives suddenly fell silent. Attracted by the silence, no doubt, a European woman came out of the house. It was Odile Peyrole. She was short, brunette, and pale, she was wearing a flowered apron, and she looked like every housewife in France.

She invited me in, inquired about my new quarters, and gave me lunch, although it was late afternoon, without making a fuss or asking unnecessary questions.

Like her husband, she spoke with the accent of the southwest. For this reason you expected to hear her talk in a loud voice, but in fact you had to listen carefully to catch what she was saying. She was the soul of discretion. At the same time, she was sensible and a woman of character, as I found out later. But she belonged to that provincial petite bourgeoisie very close to the peasantry which, although it had lost all religious belief, still retained, at this time in France, the discipline of the classical religious education and the firm conviction that man is not in this world to enjoy himself, but to advance.

Her husband wasn't home. He was making a tour of the island to assess the damage. The house was full of injured people whom Dubois was taking care of with the help of Odile Peyrole and the Tahitian schoolmaster. I offered my services, was accepted, and worked almost without stopping until midnight, when Peyrole returned from his inspection. His wife, who was waiting for him, served him dinner and invited us to come and have sandwiches and beer.

We were more interested in sleep, but we accepted in order to hear the news, and to have a few moments to ourselves. Besides, Dubois had just finished his work and there was nothing further for us to do but bring water to the feverish and keep them from getting up or taking off their bandages. Tekao, the schoolmaster, promised to keep watch until we returned.

Peyrole's house, the "Navy House," as it was called, was the only one on the whole island that had an attic. It consisted of boards laid across the rafters and deliberately not joined. This attic had not prevented the rain from coming into the house after the roof had blown off, but it had pretty well protected the interior from other damage. The kitchen, which had been cleared out, swept, and dried, was almost impeccable. Only the broken panes in the windows and the stars, which you could see through the ceiling, recalled what had happened.

Peyrole was sitting at the table with a reflecting lamp in front of him. His back expressed both great strength and great fatigue. He was slowly eating a thick vegetable soup into which he was dipping chunks of bread. He was knitting his brows. His face was covered with stubble, and there were dark circles under his eyes.

"Well?" asked Dubois.

Peyrole finished his soup, lifting the edge of the plate to get the last spoonful, took a swallow of wine, and wiped his mouth.

"Well . . . ?"

His voice was bitter with fatigue.

"Well, half the island is in a shambles. The east side got the worst of it. Fortunately, there aren't any villages over there. There was a tidal wave, no doubt about that. The big motu is completely stripped. Not a tree left, not a branch, nothing. At the Cape of Haratai, there's over three feet of wet sand in the middle of the woods, two hundred yards from the shore. Everywhere, it's a mess. I looked for your plantations (he nodded in my direction). You'll have to clear away tons of branches, tree trunks as

33

big around as that, to find them again, assuming they still exist . . ."

"What about the people?" asked Dubois.

"Don't know. Impossible to tell. I tried to see all the councils of elders; I asked them to count how many are missing in their villages. I'll know tomorrow . . . approximately, because they don't stay in one place. They're running in all directions to find out who is dead. Since everyone is doing the same thing, they find nothing but empty houses, and then they start to cry . . . Even allowing for this, there must be at least a hundred dead. At Rairua and Matotea, the waves carried away everything. In other places, there are injuries, people crushed by trees. But on the coast . . . The ones who came out of it best are the people in Vaiuru. It came from the northeast, that filthy business. In Vaiuru, they were protected."

"That's what I don't understand," Dubois broke in. "We've never had a cyclone come from the east. For that matter, we've never had a cyclone in July, and we've almost never had a cyclone in Raevavae. The last one was in 1906, I believe. It was nothing like this one. And anyway it passed between Rurutu and Tubuai. We only felt the wake. Yes, it was in January, 1906. And it came from the northwest, not from the northeast."

"I don't know," said Peyrole. "But I do know that this morning it was blowing from the northeast. Actually, it was a good thing it did, if I may say so. Hiro acted as a screen. If it had come from the west, it would have been worse . . ."

I listened to them and was amazed that they could sit there and talk about the direction of the wind.

6

THE DAYS IMMEDIATELY following the catastrophe have not left a very clear memory in my mind. We were constantly moving around, trying to round up the injured, get the dead buried in order to prevent infection, and help the living.

The living had very little need of our help. In forty-eight hours they had replaced their roofs of palm leaves, repaired their houses, and collected their black pigs, which had run off into the brush, and they sat in front of their doors, watching us go by.

This was my first contact with the island. It was a bad start, because I was exhausted and didn't seem to be communicating very well with the natives, but it did help me to familiarize myself with the place at once. Even in the state it was in then, it seemed to me to possess a beauty and diversity that were extraordinary. Everything pleased me: the little huts clinging to the sides of the mountains, the tormented rocks, indented as if by bullets, the mangrove forest to the south, so rich and seductive seen from a distance, with its tall emerald-green vegetation, so treacherous as you approached, with its shifting ground, its swamps and its canals; the beaches of grey sand, the lagoon, the hibiscus plants, the mangrove trees, the great columnar pines, and the tree ferns . . .

Everything was new to me. I was always taking pictures. I would photograph a scene, a detail of the landscape, I'd tell myself, "I'll come back," and I'd smile at the natives. They wouldn't look at me. They who were so trusting, so friendly with Peyrole and Dubois, put on blank faces when they looked at me. They never spoke to me directly. They avoided contact with me. I couldn't understand why. I've always gotten along well with peasants, and I treated them like the peasants of Berry. I could see that the situation was bothering my two companions. But we were too absorbed in our work to talk about it.

On the other hand, something they worried about a great deal as soon as we were alone, was the death of the radio. There was a broadcasting and receiving station on Raevavae, run by Peyrole, which had two scheduled contacts a week with Papeete. In case of emergency, Peyrole could call them outside of these biweekly sessions. He had tried to do this immediately and had received no response. He had checked his equipment and tried again, without success. He didn't know how to explain this silence.

It was Odile Peyrole who informed us that every radio sta-

35

tion was dead. Odile Peyrole was a good housewife. She never left the house without her husband. The natives brought her whatever she needed and she spent her time washing, sewing, and cooking, just as she would have done in Mont-de-Marsan. But she liked to work to music. Her husband had connected a loudspeaker to the radio in the police station and had placed it in the kitchen. This way she could easily pick up stations in the western United States, Hawaii, and New Zealand. But since the catastrophe, she could no longer get them. Everything was dead, everywhere.

Peyrole took this news as a personal challenge. He had taken courses in radio broadcasting and he knew how to use his equipment. For one whole day he left Dubois and me to undertake what he called a serious overhauling.

That evening when we got back—at the time we were taking all our meals at the Navy House—we looked at him questioningly. His brow was more furrowed than ever, and his expression was unhappy.

"Nothing," he said. "I took the whole thing apart, one piece at a time, I checked everything, everything works, and it's no good. And yet the equipment is working perfectly: I took the receiving set to Matotea to see what would happen. My wife talked to me from here; I could hear her perfectly."

"It couldn't be a power failure?" asked Dubois cautiously.

Peyrole shook his head. "I tested everything, checked everything. The antenna, the generator, everything. I reread my manual from cover to cover. I can only think of one thing . . ."

"Yes . . ."

"Some magnetic or atmospheric phenomenon that I don't understand."

He was pathetic.

"See here," said Dubois, "isn't it possible that something got damaged without your noticing it? Perhaps they can hear you in Papeete. Perhaps they're talking to you but you can't pick them up . . . Think about it: If you could still get one or two stations, it would be different. But not one? It's impossible. In a few days, in a few weeks at the latest, they'll send someone from Papeete, and you'll see. I say a few weeks, because it's possible that they were as hard hit as we were, and then . . ."

For the first time since the cataclysm, I thought of my Catalina and its crew. I mentioned it. Nobody answered. What could they say? In Raevavae alone, we were having trouble counting all our dead. We stopped talking about the radio. I think Odile Peyrole was the only person who really missed it.

There was almost nothing left for me to do. As I said, Raevavae was recovering extraordinarily quickly, as if this island had been created to endure and absorb catastrophes. I took the opportunity to return to my house. I wanted to unpack my bags and see what could be done with this official building I was living in. In addition to my clothes and my books, I had brought a battery-operated phonograph, some records, some photographs, a few modern prints and a small number of objects that had always followed me in my peregrinations. The most important of these was an ivory hairbrush and comb set which I had inherited from my mother, which I didn't use but was fond of. I was just hanging my prints when Peyrole and Dubois appeared. They were walking slowly up the slope that led to my house. I saw them coming from a distance, just as I was admiring the valley below them, which the evening was just starting to cover with mist. I called out to them. They looked up and nodded, but said nothing until they had sat down. I had given them the chairs and I was on the bed. I can still see the scene very clearly.

They seemed upset and almost solemn. Peyrole asked me, however, whether I was satisfied with my lodgings, and whether I needed anything. I replied, somewhat surprised, that everything was perfect, and that as soon as I had found a maid . . .

At this point, Dubois interrupted me.

"You won't find one. As a matter of fact, that's why we came to see you."

"Because I don't have a maid?"

Peyrole gave a flick of the head, as if he were chasing away a fly.

"No. Because . . . well, because the natives think you have the evil eye, that's why."

37

I had to digest that information. It sounded so meaningless and so unexpected, delivered by a policeman from Tarn . . . after a moment, I started to laugh. Dubois cut me off.

"It's not funny. In fact, it's a serious problem. I know these people well. I've been in Raevavae for six years now. They're all baptized, they all go to church, they know their prayers, but . . . but they also believe in *tupapaus,* and ghosts. There are two *marae** on the island, falling apart, of course, but from time to time you find animals there with their throats cut, or blood . . . and one mustn't inquire too deeply, you know. And the unfortunate part is that if they don't accept you, you'll have problems."

"What do you advise me to do? Swim for it?"

Peyrole shook his head. "That won't be necessary. In any case, you are under the protection of the authorities. But the doctor is right. These people all think the same thing at the same time. They are all cut out of the same cloth. They don't have to talk in order to understand each other. If they put you in quarantine, it could become difficult for you. In fact, you're in quarantine already."

"But that's ridiculous! Why?"

"Try to understand them," said Peyrole, who seemed very upset. "There has never been a cyclone in July in the whole history of Raevavae. We aren't even on the path of the cyclones. You get off the plane, and an hour later there's a hurricane that kills one inhabitant out of eight. Put yourself in their place . . ."

Now I was upset. "What's to be done?"

"Well, it's this way . . ."

Dubois looked slightly amused; Peyrole couldn't have been more serious.

"We may have one chance of getting you out of this. The people here change their minds quickly. But our remedy isn't very pleasant, and it may not work. Up there in the jungle, there's an old fellow named Maono who's regarded as a great sage. I think that above all he is very old and that in his youth he may really

---

* A Tahitian word meaning a temple enclosure used for worship, sacrifice, and other sacred ceremonies.

have belonged to a sect or school of *harepos*—priests, that is. Peyrole went to see him this morning . . ."

"Yes, he's very old and rather tired. But he has agreed to keep you with him for three days. We think that will be enough . . ."

I was dumbfounded. It was my third lesson in island ways. "How will that change anything?"

"It won't. But it will look as if you were going on a retreat, as if you were going to confess . . ."

"And that will be enough?"

"Perhaps."

"When must I go there?"

Peyrole nodded his head. "The sooner the better. Tomorrow morning . . . No, leave all that. There are bars on the windows and doors close tightly. You won't be robbed . . ."

It was true that Maono was very old. He was also very dirty. Without taking a back way, but without particularly attracting attention, as if it were something simple and normal, Peyrole had conducted me to his hut, bent down toward the hole that served as its door, touched his cap, and left.

I was left standing alone in front of this hollow mound of leaves which was the home of Maono, waiting for him to make some sign, or summon me inside.

After several minutes had passed without anything happening, I began to feel embarrassed. Don't forget that a month before I was still in Paris. I think I coughed and shuffled my feet. Nothing. In the end I bent down myself and looked inside the hut.

It smelled very bad and you could see almost nothing, because a little fire that had been lighted in the middle of the hut was filling it with an acrid blue smoke that rose and leaked out through the leaves. Nevertheless, I finally managed to make out Maono. He was sitting at the back of his house, leaning against the wall, covered with rags. He was a tiny little man, almost a dwarf, with a thick head of greasy, yellowish-white hair that fell to his shoulders. He had a flat nose and the thick lips that surrounded his toothless mouth kept smacking together in a continual wet muttering. His face was covered with wrinkles and grime. He was revolting.

We looked at each other for a moment without speaking. Remembering the recommendations that Peyrole had given me, I didn't dare ask him any questions. As for him, he scarcely seemed to see me. He sat there immobile, bundled up in his foul and stinking wrappings, now and then stretching out his hand from under the blanket lying around his shoulders to throw a handful of leaves on the fire. Uncomfortable from the odor and the smoke, but vaguely hypnotized by this monument of age and filth, I finally sat down cross-legged in front of the door and smiled. I said something like, "Well, Maono, may I stay here with you for a few days?"

The old man did not reply. I didn't even know whether he spoke French. I kept on speaking, slowly, articulating my words carefully, as if I were talking to a child. I said that I had taken a great voyage to come to Raevavae, that I liked Raevavae, that it was beautiful, in short, whatever came into my head so I could go on smiling and acting friendly.

All of a sudden, Maono raised his hand and, in a conversational tone, said something like, "KéKéKéKéKé."

Naturally, I understand nothing. He repeated this gurgling sound several times, while gesturing with his hand. Then I got an idea. Peyrole had given me some canned food and had told me that Maono was fond of preserved fruit. I opened a can of peaches in syrup and handed it to him. He emptied it with relish, then settled back contentedly and went to sleep. I got up.

Maono's hut was almost at the foot of a steep cliff of glossy black lava. From this rock there trickled a spring that formed a little pool of clear water on the ground and then disappeared in the moss. The area around it was occupied by a jumble of tree fern, bourao, and pandanus so dense and vigorous that it almost made one uncomfortable. In front of the hole which served as Maono's door there was a strip of grassy ground about thirty feet long, and then the ground seemed to leave off suddenly in the middle of the sky. Since I had nothing else to do, I walked to the edge of the grass. There wasn't any break in the ground, but a steep slope that extended down to the ocean.

The latter, a thousand feet below, lay like a calm and perfect lake. In this place the reefs were barely visible above the surface and created only a light foam. Green in the lagoon, almost black in the open sea, the water was blue only at the horizon. It was the triumphant domain of sun, space, and peace.

I looked at all this for a while, and then I began to get bored. Peyrole had given me some supplies and a bush knife, and I had brought cigarettes, but I had forgotten to bring books. Actually, it seems to me that I had thought of it and that I purposely hadn't brought any, out of concern for authenticity or something like that. I was sorry I hadn't. Maono was still asleep.

Then I went and cut some branches and attempted to make a little hut for myself. It wasn't very successful and I was glad that it wasn't raining, but it kept me busy for quite a while. Next, I opened a can for lunch. Maono woke up and called me: "Tané."

I peered inside. He hadn't moved. He looked at me and smiled, exposing all his withered gums. He made that sound again: "KéKéKéKé."

I didn't give him anything. He began to laugh and very cautiously he emerged, all bent over, walking on his heels with his knees wide apart. He remained in his doorway a moment, as if dazed, then he straightened up and began to laugh. "Me, Papeete," he told me. "Work-port-cinema. Me Papeete. Many-many."

He laughed, drank a little water from the pool, spat into it. Then he came over to inspect my hut and he laughed again. Very skillfully he smoothed out my tangle, added a few leaves, shifted a few branches, and this pile of brush became a shelter.

He was a good-natured old soul. He ate all my canned fruit, and he tried once or twice to tell me about his trip or trips to Tahiti, but he had forgotten almost all his French. In any case, he slept half the time.

I was very bored. I tried to recite poetry to myself, and discovered that I knew nothing by heart except a few stanzas of *Le Cid*. I promised myself that when I returned to Anatonu I would learn my favorite poems, which I had brought with me.

It also bothered me that I had nothing to sit on. Since I wasn't used to sitting on the ground, I soon had pains in my thighs and lower back. But that was nothing. What overwhelmed me was the sense of being completely alone and having nothing to do. This impression was so strong that in the end I started enjoying it. Maono was a hideous old man, but he was overflowing with local color. I should have been happy . . .

After three days, at dawn, a dozen natives came to get me, sent by Peyrole. They greeted Maono with considerable respect and tried to converse with him. I gave him my last can of cherries. He thanked me. We parted very good friends. The natives seemed very pleased. All during the trip down they gave me their arms and hovered over me as if I were convalescent or as if they wanted to be forgiven for something.

Peyrole was at his desk. He was wearing his eternal shorts and a tee shirt, and he hadn't shaved yet. He looked at me, looked at the natives, then he smiled at me.

"Enjoy yourself?"

I was about to tell him about Maono, but he cut me off.

"There's been a new development. A life raft has just been found at sea with three people in it, Europeans. They're in an isolated cottage on the coast, not far from here. I haven't seen them. It was this man who came and told me."

He indicated a native sitting on the ground, who smiled and said, "It is true. It is Tapoua who says so. It was Mai, my cousin, who found the *tanés*. Mai is a great fisherman."

Peyrole smiled briefly. "Maono may have improved your status, but he wasn't the only thing. Since the wind storm the other day, the fishing has been extraordinary. Every able-bodied fisherman is at sea. They're catching fish by the bucketful. They're starting to say that you bring good luck."

His face was very expressive. Then he knitted his brows again.

"The jeep has been found. A little battered, but it runs. Would you mind picking up Dubois and driving him to Mai's place? From what I hear, these people aren't in such great shape. That's not surprising, after five days in the sun."

I agreed. Dubois lived in a large *faré*, the traditional island house covered with pandanus leaves, on the west side of the Tuamora.

When we arrived he was standing up drinking coffee, wearing only a red and white sarong. He smiled that slightly oriental smile I was beginning to know. "I have my little idiosyncrasies. In a few months, you'll have yours."

When I had told him the news, he picked up his bag and came with us as he was, leaving everything open behind him. We were being escorted by three natives, including Tapoua, the messenger. While they were getting into the car, I asked the doctor in an undertone, "Aren't you afraid of being robbed?"

Dubois shrugged his shoulders. "They like me. And anyway, they could always make a hole in the roof."

7

MAI'S HOUSE WAS a very simple little fisherman's cottage, open on three sides, with a framework of palm tree trunks and a roof of pandanus leaves. At first I was amazed that it was still in good condition, but then I noticed that many fresh leaves had recently been slipped in among the old ones, and that its situation at the foot of a cliff and at least a hundred yards above the sea must have protected it from the wind as well as from the waves.

Dubois must have guessed what I was thinking, because he said, "This is Mai's vacation house. He had another one over there on the bay, which, of course, was carried away. Mai must have felt the hurricane. He must have been up there with his family. You'll meet Mai—he's the best fisherman on the island, and he's a poet. Some people say he's a clown, but I don't agree with them. Mai is a man with an extraordinary love of life . . ."

"You know them all, then?"

Dubois shrugged. "I'm a doctor. I've been here for six years. There are—or were—eight hundred inhabitants on the island. I paint watercolors and practice archery. How on earth could I not know them all?"

Mai was a lean, wrinkled man with a little beard and very intelligent eyes. He received us warmly, with an ease that was all the more remarkable in that he wore only a pair of khaki undershorts tied in front with a shoelace and stamped on the left buttock in big, thick letters: French Navy.

After Tapoua had introduced me rather ceremoniously, we went to see the survivors. They were in the back of the cottage, in the coolest part. I did not go into the room, but strolled around admiring the landscape while Dubois examined them.

He stayed in the room for over an hour and when he came out he seemed preoccupied.

When I asked him who the shipwrecked people were, he replied briefly that there were two men and a woman. He seemed to be thinking about something else.

He added, "We can't take proper care of them here. They're exhausted, of course, and have second-degree burns from the sun. The woman is in particularly bad shape. We'll have to transfer them to the Navy House."

He gave me a quick look. "Can you drive very slowly?"

With the help of Mai, Tapoua, and some women, we filled the back of the jeep with leaves and moss. Then on this bed we laid out, as carefully as we could, three mummies swathed in bandages, who moaned. And very slowly we drove back to the Navy House, as Dubois had requested.

The doctor was completely engrossed in his patients. It was, in fact, a distinguishing trait of his character that he concentrated all his attention on whatever he was doing and for this reason he was, unlike most people, incapable of carrying on two activities at the same time. This gave him depth but it also isolated him from other people and sometimes made him ridiculous. He was this way about everything: At a party or during a general conversation if he poured himself a drink, he didn't hear what was said to him during this interval and would ask to have it repeated, gazing at the speaker with his blue-green eyes. This weakness, or strength, as you prefer, may have been the cause of his behavior later. In any case, it was a trait of his character which we should not have overlooked.

Once we had arrived at Peyrole's house, Dubois carefully installed his patients and explained to Odile Peyrole how to take care of them. Then he accepted the *pastis,* a liqueur of the Midi, which Peyrole offered us.

We sat in the kitchen. Odile Peyrole brought us glasses, fresh water, and the bottle, and disappeared. It wasn't too hot. Everything was in order. The furniture was ugly but pleasant. We were comfortable. I began to relax.

"It's a little early in the day, isn't it?"

Peyrole nodded. "Exceptional circumstances."

For these two men I was doubly young because of my ignorance of Raevavae. They treated me politely, but as a nonentity. I sensed this and held my tongue.

"Well, Doctor," asked Peyrole, "tell us about your patients. Where are they from?"

Dubois raised his eyebrows. "I haven't had much conversation with them, you know. They're still in shock, and feverish . . . Anyway, they were all three on the *Galliffet,* that combination passenger boat and steamer that we had heard about, let's see, when was it? Oh, yes! Last week, the day before your arrival," he told me. "It was a boat that was making a cruise and was to have stopped at Auckland, then Melbourne, then . . . it was going around the world."

"What happened?"

"Oh, the *tsunami,* or the cyclone . . ."

Once again Dubois seemed preoccupied, ill at ease. Finally he made up his mind.

"I don't know if this makes sense, or if it's a hallucination caused by fever. But . . . well, one of them told me that an atomic war had broken out just before their boat went down."

We didn't react or protest. In my opinion this is the proof that each of us had privately been thinking of something of the kind. This business of radio communications being cut off had been running through our minds. At any rate, we sat there in silence looking at the table, as if what Dubois had just said were written on it.

Finally Peyrole said hopefully, "He was delirious, wasn't he?"

"Not exactly; he was exhausted and confused. But he wasn't

delirious. He gave coherent answers to my questions about his condition. No, he wasn't delirious. But bear in mind that it was very hard for him to speak. From what I could understand, he's an ordinary seaman. How could he have known? What distorted information could he have picked up?"

"True," said Peyrole. "Well. When will we be able to question them?"

"Tomorrow, perhaps."

The men were well enough to be interviewed the next day. Their names were Leguen and Bourdaroux. The one who was in better condition was Leguen, although he appeared to be the weaker of the two. Bourdaroux was a steward, Leguen an ordinary seaman. They had indeed been on board the *Galliffet,* which was making a round-the-world cruise. The woman was an Australian or English passenger whom they had not met and whose name they did not know. The ship had gone down in a few seconds, submerged by an enormous wave. It was Bourdaroux who had thrown the inflatable life raft overboard and who had picked up the other two. But about twenty minutes before the disaster, the ship's radio had picked up a message to the effect that a conflict had just erupted, or was about to erupt, between Russia and China. The captain had summoned all the officers. Bourdaroux had served the drinks. He was sure he had heard them talking about an atomic war. That was all he knew.

There were the facts, as precise and complete as possible. We certainly should have verified them, or tried to. At the very least we should have arrived at some conclusion, even a tentative one, taken steps, done something.

We did nothing. Not only did we refuse to draw conclusions, but we tacitly decided to forget the whole thing. We had a little difficulty convincing our three survivors, but we succeeded.

No doubt this attitude seems incomprehensible. But we weren't ready. And then, islands are islands.

All of Raevavae, inhabitants, animals, vegetation, set the example for us: only the present existed. The past was no more, and only a crazy person would worry about the future.

During the three days I had spent with Maono, the population had mourned and buried the last of the dead, repaired the cottages that were still inhabited, and torn down those that no longer were. New couples were forming, new families were being organized. The rain that had followed the cyclone, unhoped for in the middle of the dry season, had caused a new growth of vegetation. Even the landslide on Hiro was being erased by the grass. Without any kind of conspiracy, but with a common enthusiasm, everything that lived on Raevavae was working together to deny the calamity by reconstructing, very quickly and very carefully, a world where, once again, it was good to be alive.

8

FOR ME, THERE had never been any question of bothering with the plantation of orange trees. I went once to inspect it, realized that to restore it to order would require formidable resources of manpower and equipment which I did not possess, and abandoned it forever.

This did not prevent the trees from producing in the years that followed some excellent oranges which the natives, for some reason, refused to touch.

So I was free, and, for the first time in my life, without worries. I was drunk with independence. My only concerns were to make myself comfortable and to enjoy the moment. For the rest, I had privately decided to put off thinking about it until the arrival of the boat or airplane that would eventually appear.

I had a little money, and life on the island cost nothing. So I finished unpacking, and since I no longer had the evil eye, started looking for a maid. I was in a hurry to arrange my domestic life so that I would no longer have to depend on the Peyroles.

To my great surprise, I couldn't find a maid. Domestic help did not exist in Raevavae. The idea of spending one's life working for someone else struck the natives as ridiculous. All of them knew how to do whatever was necessary for their subsistence and fished, hunted, or gardened when they needed to. The rest of the time they slept or enjoyed themselves. Sometimes they enjoyed themselves by working, either to earn money, when they wanted to buy something, or to help out a friend. But this did not last very long.

So I was in an embarrassing position. I could have resorted to the classic solution: I could have taken a mistress so I'd have someone to cook for me. I didn't think of it. Fortunately Tapoua, the native who had conducted us to the home of Mai, the fisherman, took me under his wing. He had helped me with my unpacking and was protecting me from the curiosity of the inhabitants, for I still couldn't speak Tahitian. One day I saw him stacking some poles against one of the outside walls of my house.

"I'm going to build a little lean-to here," he told me. "It will be more convenient than coming every morning . . ."

He did so, and brought his wife, who immediately took charge of me.

This problem solved, I began to get settled. In the meantime, Dubois invited me to dinner. I accepted. He took me on a detailed tour of inspection of his house. It was an artful interpretation of the traditional Polynesian cottage, or *faré*. The materials were the same, the ventilation was just as good, and the rooms were the same size. The only difference was that there were more of them and they were much better furnished. The house was very well integrated with the landscape. It was much cooler than my house. Dubois told me that it had been built twice, and that it hadn't cost much.

So there was nothing to prevent me from imitating him. I mentioned the idea to Tapoua, who began by telling me that I was crazy, that Dubois was completely crazy, and that when one was lucky enough to live in a police station with real words written over the doorway, one didn't go and move into a common *faré*. I replied that in Raevavae, the *farés* were more comfortable and more attractive than the police stations. He shrugged his shoulders. But when I added that I wanted to have a new *faré* because I would build it wherever I liked instead of living in a house built for someone else, he understood me perfectly and threw himself into the adventure with enthusiasm.

After looking around, I chose a site on the north side of the island in a well-sheltered little hollow, close to a spring and not far from the sea.

Tapoua approved my choice and disappeared.

The next day at dawn he woke me up and asked me to come to the site and draw the floor plan of the *faré* on the ground, because, as he said, "My cousins are there, and they want to get to work."

When we arrived at the spot I had chosen the day before, I found about thirty men and a pile of freshly cut palm tree trunks. I gave my instructions and went home to shave.

These people, who have a reputation for being lazy, worked quickly and very well. Sometimes in their great enthusiasm they made mistakes, and after starting a framework from two sides at once, would set it up all lopsided. All you had to do was point this out to them, and they would cheerfully dismantle what they had just finished and immediately start again, laughing at themselves.

My new house was finished in ten days.

To thank the workmen, who asked for nothing, I gave a party. I paid for the beer, the candles, and the canned fruit, of which they were very fond. They brought everything else.

Since some men had left the job before it was finished and had been replaced by others, about forty men had worked for me, all told. Over three hundred people came to my party. It took place on the beach, right below my new house. Early in the day, an unknown number of people arrived with fruit, live animals, and utensils. The beach was cleared of all the debris that the wind and the sea had left there, raked, swept, and washed down. The people dug pits in which to cook the meat. They lighted fires. They slaughtered the animals and caught fish. When darkness fell they lighted the candles, which danced in the breeze, and brought out the meat, which had been braised under hot rocks. While we ate dinner, some of the people sang and danced. I was drunk with exoticism. I made a speech which

49

was enthusiastically applauded. Tapoua told me afterward that it was a small party, because they hadn't had time to tell everyone, but that it was a good party, anyway, the first one since the great storm. Indeed, it had been a month since an eighth of the population of Raevavae had disappeared.

In my brand-new cottage, I worked hard on the furnishings. I wanted to finish everything before inviting Dubois and Peyrole. I moved so many times when I was living in France that I'm not a bad amateur carpenter. I made shelves, armchairs, a table—whatever I needed. I had to have tools, lumber, fabric. I bought everything from Simon, the catechist. The inhabitants of Raevavae were Baptists. They had a church in Anatonu, and attended services very regularly. On Sunday they did nothing, but sat in front of their houses and stared. They did this very seriously. They were undoubtedly acting out of conviction. But it seemed to me also that this weekly day of rest, which they found foolish, took on a sacred quality for them for this very reason. Well, at any rate, they had a catechist. He was a boy from Rurutu who had been raised in Tahiti by the Protestant missionaries and then sent to Raevavae. Since there was no bank on the island, since the government had forbidden the Chinese to settle there, and since none of the natives was interested in business, Simon had decided, as much to keep himself occupied as to be of service, it seemed, to become the representative of a company in Tahiti, and had opened a store.

It was an ugly shed set up next to the church. In it you could find almost everything that the natives needed: material for making *paréos,* or sarongs, and dresses, tools, nails, corrugated iron, dishes, blankets, canned goods, tobacco, lamps, kerosene.

Simon was a young man, a little shorter than myself, with a nice face. He looked much like the other natives, except that he was heavier. He was always very correctly dressed, and he had a sweet voice, big blue eyes that stared at you, and skin that was much smoother than that of the other islanders.

He was very careful about everything, for he was afraid of not understanding your question immediately and missing the point in his answer, and this gave him a slightly startled expression. In his store, he was very obliging. In church, he shone. Peyrole thought him a good man. Odile Peyrole didn't like him. Dubois had no opinion. But then, Dubois never judged anyone.

Simon sold me the tools and lumber that I needed. There was only one thing he didn't have: small nails. He was well supplied with large nails, the kind everyone used for building *farés*, but he wasn't interested in woodwork.

Once again, it was Peyrole who came to my rescue. He was in charge of a large military warehouse which in theory was intended to supply fresh provisions to ships in distress. This warehouse was never used. Peyrole dipped into it in small doses, for the good of all, and kept an exact account of the "depreciated" items, whose replacement he requested at regular intervals. He had nails. I used more than I had anticipated. I asked him for more. He gave them to me again, but said, "Be careful. Don't waste them. I don't know when I'll be able to get more."

Thus, a shadow would occasionally pass over our timeless existence.

All this absorbed my attention. I kept rather apart from Dubois and Peyrole. I didn't avoid them, but neither did I seek them out. As for the three survivors of the *Galliffet,* it was they who had disappeared.

The woman I had only caught sight of once. She had turned out to be a New Zealander who was returning home after three years in Europe when her ship had gone down. She spoke French well, with a slightly harsh, but pleasing accent. But I hadn't seen her face. She was a redhead, and during the days on the life raft, her delicate skin had been deeply burned by the sun. In spite of Dubois' attentions, she was taking a long time to heal. When I had seen her, she was still partially bandaged. Her condition had improved since then but she still had scars or scabs, I don't remember, and she didn't want to be seen. She lived in seclusion with the Peyroles and I heard very little about her.

Her two companions had recovered much more quickly. Bourdaroux, the steward, was from Bordeaux. He was a very tense man, red-faced, with thick black hair that was straight and shiny, black eyes, and a perpetual look of indignation. At first he had forced himself on Peyrole because they were both from the southwest, then had fallen out with him and his wife, and had gone to live on the coast of Matotea with a native woman. Leguen, a skinny young man with protruding ears and little mouse eyes, was nicer, but even more independent. As soon as he was on his feet again he had thanked the Peyroles and disappeared into the island. I found out through Tapoua that he had made friends with some fishermen who were taking him to sea. All this was of no concern to me. I didn't need company, and my life pleased me very much.

I had brought from France a suitcase full of books. They fell into two categories: those I had read and liked, and those I hadn't read yet but wanted to read. Remember that I had hated most of the courses I had taken in school. As a result my education was a hit-or-miss affair, full of gaps and inconsistencies.

Until my arrival in Raevavae, I had never gone into anything in depth. I liked history, but I knew it only from biographies. I had never read a serious and complete study. I enjoyed literature, but it was not until Raevavae that I first read the *Odyssey*. I could give you a dozen examples of this kind. I was having a wonderful time with my books.

I was also enjoying the island. Everything about it was beautiful and interesting. The natives, with their indolence, their hospitality, and their love of fun and pleasure were charming. Raevavae was a miniature continent. The Hiro mountain chain, running east and west, cut it in two. The northern, more heavily populated part was cooler and pleasanter, although less beautiful. The southern part, more extensive and almost uninhabited, was very heavily wooded. On the steepest slopes there were nothing but bushes, but as you went toward the coast you came upon real forests with very tall trees which were unfamiliar to me. Almost everywhere there were unusual plants and dazzling flowers. I decided to use them to embellish the land around my house. This gave me an excuse for hikes and expeditions to the remotest parts of the island. I usually went with Tapoua, whose company I enjoyed. Sometimes we would catch sight of Dubois in his red and white *paréo*, painting or hunting with a bow and arrow. We would greet each other with a wave of the hand and continue on our way. He valued his freedom as much as I did mine.

During one of these hikes I happened upon the *faré* of a large family whom I did not know. At least twenty people were living in it. Among them was a rather light-skinned young girl, solidly built, like all the natives, but slender and very graceful. Her name was Naia. I came back several times. As soon as I would appear, the youngest children, the ones who barely knew how to talk, would shout, "Naia, Naia, it's your *tané.*" The adults would laugh behind their hands, not from shame, but out of politeness. I didn't want to look ridiculous. I asked the girl if she would like to come and live with me. She accepted. She wasn't a virgin, but in this country I've never met a virgin. She got along very well with Tapoua's wife. And so I ended where another man would have begun.

Don't think, in spite of all this, that I never felt any anxiety. Like all the Europeans in Raevavae, I believe, I thought about what had happened to us. The radio was still silent, no boat or airplane had arrived, and in the backs of our minds we remembered what Leguen and Bourdaroux had told us.

I couldn't bring myself to believe that it was true. But neither could I succeed in explaining our situation. Since this situation was, after all, very pleasant, I didn't worry about it very much. But since one can't help thinking, I had several times engaged in reflections that led me to an impasse. If a war was the cause of our isolation, I reasoned, it would have to have been very sudden and very violent to explain the silence of Papeete. In order for Papeete to have been directly involved on the first day of hostilities—the day before, I was certain, no one had suspected anything in Tahiti—one had to consider the possibility of a planetary conflagration. This made Bourdaroux's announcement about an atomic war plausible and even probable. But in that case one had to face the possibility that the radio stations that were no longer being picked up had been reduced to silence, destroyed. This meant, in short, that all the coasts of the Pacific had been devastated. Obviously, that was impossible . . .

I looked at my gushing spring, my trees with their delicate

foliage, the cloudless sky, the tranquil sea, and shook my head. It didn't make sense.

One day, however, while I was listening to César Franck's Symphony in D Minor on my battery-run phonograph, these ideas returned and became so insistent that I decided to discuss them with Dubois.

Thinking it over today, I'm sure it was Franck's music that precipitated everything. That symphony was so reflective, so well-wrought, so different from the natural life of the natives and from my own life that suddenly it seemed to be the very voice of civilization, and I was terrified at the idea that this civilization might have been destroyed.

Yes, what made me act, what may have put everything in motion, was neither concern for myself nor worry about the fate of those I had left in France, but that music.

Two days later, I went to see Dubois.

9

IT WAS EVENING but there was still some light, perhaps because of the last rays of the setting sun, perhaps because of the moon; I don't remember. But I remember clearly that when I had reached Dubois' house I turned around and gazed in the twilight at the vast expanse of verdure, at once powerful and indolent, that stretched down and disappeared against the silken shimmer of the sea.

Dubois was half lying in a hammock that hung between two trees next to his house. I didn't see him at first, then he called out to me. He had made a hole in a coconut and was sipping the milk through a pink plastic straw. Very pleasantly, he offered to make me one: "With a little rum, it's delicious . . ."

I declined. He asked if I would like to come inside. Again I declined. The air in this spot was as soft as silk. Dubois went back to his hammock, and I sat on the ground, leaning against one of the posts that supported the porch roof.

My host inquired about my new house and I answered briefly. There followed a rather long silence.

From that moment, I am sure that Dubois knew why I had come to see him. But he said nothing. I was free to speak or to keep still. It was his way of respecting people. At last I asked: "These stories about an atomic war—do you believe them?"

There was another silence, a very short one. Then Dubois replied, choosing his words carefully and pronouncing them very correctly, as if he were examining a matter of considerable intellectual interest, but of little practical consequence:

"A possibility of the kind is by no means absurd. For several years now I have ceased to have any interest in these questions, but when I was still in the Navy, I often heard specialists describe a hypothetical situation which corresponds rather closely to the one that presently appears to be ours."

It was only half an answer, and I couldn't let it go at that. So I pressed him. "Do you assume . . ."

He interrupted me. "I assume nothing. I have simply tried to construct a theory that accounts for all the facts that we know. What are these facts? First, the *tsunami*. Completely abnormal, that *tsunami*: the wrong time, the wrong place, and coming from a region where no cyclone has ever originated before. Next, the death of the radio. I have great confidence in Peyrole. He's a simple man, but calm, full of common sense and authority. He has theoretical knowledge—the police training schools are good —but that's not all. He knows how to think. In a sense he's the king here, you know. He administers justice, manages the villages, keeps order, supervises public health and records. He does his job very well. A man who simply goes by the book couldn't do what he does. I respect him very much. Now, what does he say? That his equipment is working. I believe him. If it's not picking up anything it must be because nothing is being broadcast. And that is serious, perhaps even more serious than the *tsunami*. All this checks out rather well with the wild, incredible information we then get from two sailors of rather limited intelligence. I don't think they're lying. They may, of course, have misunderstood or misinterpreted an altogether different piece of

55

news, but what could it have been? What could have been the reason for suddenly summoning all the officers on the ship that way, without any warning? If these men were lying they would be more precise, would offer more details. But what do they say? Almost nothing. An atomic war broke out. They don't even know exactly between whom. No, on the whole, it all hangs together."

"Do you mean . . ."

I still didn't know Dubois at all. His tone was very detached, very scientific. I wasn't absolutely sure that he was serious. I must have looked a little dazed, because he smiled kindly.

"Honestly, I'm in exactly the same state as you. I can't come to any conclusion. But honestly, too, I think something has happened and I am not far from thinking that we are alone in the world. There you are."

"And that's all the effect it has on you?"

He replied very quietly and firmly. "You can't possibly know what effect it has on me."

You never knew Dubois, of course. He was a very distinguished man, one of the most interesting I have ever known. He spoke little and never put himself forward, but was full of a calm integrity that made him a fascinating person. I think that beneath his appearance of an old Englishman in retirement, he took life very seriously. Later, when I knew him better, he told me certain things that helped me to understand him better. In fact, he was serious and concerned about all of humanity. In certain respects, he was very much like Toutepo. But what in Toutepo is a natural disposition was in him only the result of a bitter experience which had left him scarred and empty. I hoped for a while that Dubois would become what Toutepo has become for us. For a brief moment, he did. But he was too tired. At heart, he was an opium smoker who didn't need opium. There are things that certain men should not see, on pain of death. Dubois was almost dead.

All this I learned much later. At the time of our conversation I didn't have an inkling of it. Not that it would have changed anything if I had. But now there were two of us in Raevavae who shared the same fears. I asked him, "Don't you think we should do something?"

I can see him so clearly as he was at that moment, tall, thin, a little round-shouldered, with his tanned face, his white locks that fluttered in the slightest breeze, his blue-green eyes and that Chinese manner, both serene and unassuming, that he always had except when caring for the sick. He gave me an answer that was very like him. With his hand he indicated the hazy landscape in front of him.

"All islands," he said, "are self-contained. That's why I like them. That's why I chose Raevavae. I chose to die here. And to die in Raevavae or to die with Raevavae, what's the difference? So it's possible, yes, it's quite possible that I should tell you to do nothing. You know, I'm inclined to think that it is better to die than to run . . . And then islands, by their very nature, are unjust. Why do people drown themselves in the sea that surrounds them, and not on the islands? Why are they a refuge? Why do they exist? Even so, it seems to me that we should, indeed, do something. But what?"

"I've thought about it," I said. "If, as you say, we are alone in the world, it is possible that even here things may begin to change. We might have an epidemic, a rebellion, anything. I'm not completely serious, but we have to think about it. Above all, above all, we must know where we stand. And there's only one way to do that . . . Wait, I brought a map, just in case. The nearest land is Tubuai. From what I have heard about the abilities of the natives as sailors, it should not be difficult to reach it. We may be able to find out something down there. And if not, well, to the north, there's Tahiti."

I had unfolded my map, but by now it was too dark to be able to read it. Dubois didn't even look at it.

"It's possible," he said at last. "Risky, but possible. These people have a feeling for the sea . . . and the weather will be good until the end of October. This is the nineteenth of August . . ."

Suddenly his tone changed. "But what will it accomplish? Will the people you send be able to interpret what they find?

And don't forget the other risks: If there really has been an atomic explosion, something will be left. Do you think . . ."

"I'll go," I said. "We'll have to talk to Peyrole."

We went to see Peyrole the next day at his place. He listened to us almost in silence, knitting his brows. It was obvious that he had already thought of everything we were saying. He hardly reacted to my idea of a voyage. He sat there, very calm, very solid, with his arms on the kitchen table, listening. Only his wrinkled brow and his pursed lips showed that he was thinking.

"We'll have to inform the others," he said at last.

"Who?" I asked, astonished.

"Well, Bourdaroux, Leguen, Mademoiselle Binzer, and I think, my wife. It would be more correct. We might also discuss it with Simon and Tekao."

Dubois smiled. I was astonished.

"That's fine with me, but why?"

Peyrole made a vague gesture. "I don't know. It seems to me that it would be better. After all, this concerns all of us. And then . . . and then, I don't know. It would be more correct, that's all."

"But in that case shouldn't we also inform the representatives of the population, the heads of the villages, or whatever?"

Peyrole immediately became precise again.

"That's a little different. The natives are at home here, and in the end all this does not have much importance for them. Besides, we have the system of direct administration. There are no elections. The population is represented, officially speaking, by the councils of elders formed in each village by the oldest representatives of the families, but only in an advisory capacity. Anyway . . ."

He hesitated for a moment. "I don't want to be unpleasant, but these councils of elders, you know, aside from property rights and fishing rights . . ."

"I understand," I said. "Can you easily contact Bourdaroux and Leguen? If you can, I invite you all to dinner tomorrow evening. It will be a housewarming for my new *faré*. I'll take care of Simon and Tekao."

58

10

WHEN I GOT home I called in Naia and Tapoua's wife and asked them to prepare a big dinner for the next evening. I gave them money to buy what they needed at Simon's, instructing them to invite him and telling each of them to buy herself a new dress for the party.

Tapoua, who was never far away, broke in to help with the menu. He suggested some dishes based on pork and fish which I found very appropriate. In any case, these were the only dishes the women knew how to cook.

After Naia and her companion had left, I had a discussion with Tapoua about the decorations and seating arrangements. We didn't have a large enough table, so he offered to make one out of woven palm leaves stretched over stakes driven into the ground. For the seats, he suggested that we borrow two pews from the church.

I liked Tapoua. He was more active than most of the natives, because he was more curious. He was interested in everything. He was always listening, looking, appraising, and he was never at a loss. In spite of his torn trousers, his pink shirt, and his big nose, he was the incarnation of the valet of classical comedy. Like him, he was shrewd, inventive, and free. We got along famously.

While we were arranging the details of my party it occurred to me to sound him out about any voyages between islands that had been made in the past by the natives and to inquire about any boats in Raevavae that would be capable of withstanding such long crossings.

He listened attentively and answered my questions obligingly. Then suddenly he interrupted me, his eyes shining with excitement.

"*Tané*," he said, pointing at me, "you want to go to Papeete to see how it is after the great storm. Is this so?"

For a moment I was dumbfounded, then I smiled back at him. "Yes," I said. "But it's a secret."

His face was illuminated with joy. "You want a *pahi*—a boat—and you want good sailors to go to Papeete, no? My cousin Mai is the best sailor in Raevavae, and his *pahi* is the best of all. So I will go with him—and you. No? Because I speak *farani* and he does not. And I am a good sailor too, me, Tapoua. So we will go, no? And you will see the *pahi*. That one is not good. Not big enough. But my cousin Mai, he knows how to make *pahis*. We will make a big *pahi*, one as big as that. And you will come on it. No?"

He was stammering with excitement.

After this, the dinner the next day was a rather tedious formality. Bourdaroux criticized the native cuisine in front of the women, who fortunately did not understand very much French, and went on at great length, in a self-pitying tone, about the "negroes" with whom he was obliged to live. He intended to build himself a house out of stone, and when he learned that I wasn't doing anything with the former police station, he asked for permission to live in it, which Peyrole granted.

Leguen was of a very different cut. He had a kind of innocent mischievousness which gave him charm. Everything about Raevavae enchanted him. At the moment he was fishing with, as he put it, "some fellows who were good guys," but his real passion was the soil. "The richness of it, Monsieur—have you seen this black soil? It's all humus, light, rich, good enough to eat, Monsieur." He soon became slightly drunk. I enjoyed hearing him talk. He was the son of some poor Breton farmers from Morbihan and had five brothers who were half farmers, half sailors. As soon as he had left school, he had gone to sea. In almost all the great ports he knew a bar across from the entrance to the docks. But his first love was agriculture. He had been saving up part of his pay to buy a little farm in his part of the country. He was very gay and very likeable.

Simon, the catechist, hardly opened his mouth except to bless the meal and say grace. He lacked naturalness and hid behind his dignity to maintain some sort of composure. Tekao, the schoolmaster, on the other hand, was very amusing. He told a lot of incredible stories about things that had happened in Papeete and sang several songs in Tahitian which my women listened to with rapture. In this they were joined by twenty-odd friends and relations whose delighted faces appeared at all the doors and windows and whom we eventually invited to share the feast.

At dessert Dubois asked me to speak, and I explained, as undramatically as I could, because of the natives, the conclusions we had arrived at and the reasons why I wanted to undertake this voyage to Tubuai and possibly to Tahiti.

I was listened to without surprise and apparently without great interest. It's possible that those present had already reached the same conclusions in private, but that they were in no great hurry to hear them confirmed. Only Leguen offered to come with me, and only he seemed suddenly worried about his family in Brittany, when he saw that we believed Bourdaroux's statements to be possible. I thanked him and talked him out of coming along, pointing out that he had suffered enough from the sun on the life raft and inviting him to stay in my house while I was away and look after my garden.

Finally, I consulted Peyrole and Dubois about the abilities of Mai and Tapoua as sailors. They praised them without reservation.

So it was a useful gathering, after all.

I almost forgot to note that this was my first real opportunity to see Katherine Binzer. She sat on my left, and Odile Peyrole on my right. I judged her age to be between twenty-eight and thirty-five. Her hair wasn't red, as I had been told, but a dark auburn. The skin of her typically Anglo-Saxon face was still quite damaged; there were large pink patches where she had been burned. She said very little and drank my whisky like a man. Out of courtesy, and because she seemed very lonely, I tried to amuse her and bring her out, but I didn't have much success. She didn't attract me at all. I found in her a kind of hardness which is the quality I find least appealing in a woman.

However, I invited her to make use of my books and records while I was away.

To tell the truth, I couldn't think about anything but my voyage.

11

WE SET SAIL a few days later from Matotea. I had anticipated complicated preparations, discussions, delays, I don't know what, but I hadn't allowed for the enthusiasm of the natives.

The broken-off trunks of palm trees sticking up here and there like the columns of a ruined temple were the only traces of the typhoon.

Several families had gathered pieces of corrugated iron that had been scattered in the bush and on the reefs, and had reconstructed houses very much like the old ones. And so that everything would be as it had been before, the logs washed up by the sea had been used to rebuild a little pier which might never be used for anything.

At least half the population had come to help with preparations for our departure. All along the beach there were fires, temporary shelters, families sitting around boiling pots.

The lagoon was constantly filled with canoes, full to bursting, carrying visitors back and forth, for this population was not stable. The outriggers would collide, the paddlers would shout, and everyone would laugh.

The big problem was the *pahi*. Mai and Tapoua had found one somewhere that was larger than the customary fishing canoes but capable of being maneuvered by three men. The only trouble was, as Tapoua said with comical gestures, that it wasn't a very good *pahi*. If they had asked me, I would have burned it on the spot. It was dried out and cracked and rotten in several places, and there were holes all over the bottom. Mai, on the other hand, thought it only needed to be repaired. In his youth, apparently, this *pahi* had been a champion of speed and stability.

I looked inquiringly at Peyrole, who had come with me. But he looked glum and said nothing, so I kept my mouth shut, too.

Mai had had twenty men carry the *pahi* up onto the beach to a certain spot which, in fact, he had not found on the first try. With his shoulders hunched, his arms apart, and an air of intense concentration, he would walk back and forth, around the ailing hull, then suddenly he would shout, "No! Over there . . ."

And the twenty men, jostling each other, would again lift up their burden and carry it a little further up, or back down again, according to the whim of Mai.

Finally, the spot was declared to be good. Next came the ceremony of the materials. Mai walked around the hull very slowly, counting on his fingers and saying things which I couldn't understand and which Tapoua, behind him, repeated. This went on for over an hour. Then without warning, Mai walked off and dove into the lagoon, while Tapoua recapitulated for me: "We need two planks of canoe wood, eight planks of *buni* this long, and some French oak and some pine and nails and rope and canvas for the sail and needles, and . . ."

I told him to go and get everything for me at Simon's. Next came the ceremony of ship breaking. Amid the shouting, laughter, and confusion that reigned on the beach, Mai began to dismantle the old *pahi*. He was assisted by a large crew whose members changed constantly but obeyed his slightest whim. I had the impression, and I'm not sure it was wrong, that every man who passed in the vicinity of the construction site and had nothing better to do came by to give a hand, pulling, tearing, unnailing for a few minutes, and then having paid his respects, left to be replaced immediately by someone else. Soon the *pahi* had ceased to exist and the various elements that had composed it were scattered on the ground like old driftwood. Convinced that we would have to build a new boat, I went home.

The next day I didn't go down to the beach until late morning. The keel, reinforced with new planks bought from Simon, was in position. Around it, a few men were calmly puttering about with pieces of wood, seemingly at random. Mai was directing the work. Lean, black, always smiling, his eyes shining and his big white teeth gleaming between their shrunken gums, he walked around the group, tossing out jokes here and there.

When his companions began to mend the keel, he came over and placed himself in the axis of the boat, leaning forward with his elbows and knees apart. Then he began barking out orders and the work became organized.

It was marvelous to watch the boat take shape. Mai seemed under a spell. He laughed and chattered incessantly, circling the workers with a sideways motion, like a crab. He saw everything. From time to time he would stop, point to an imperfect joint, push away a worker whose work did not please him, demonstrate how to go about it, then resume his dance, which was both limber and spasmodic, without interrupting his flow of laughter and chatter.

It wasn't finished until the next day around noon. They had worked with torches almost all night. I had gone to bed. When I returned the hull had been caulked, the mast was in place, and they were putting in the outriggers.

No sooner was it finished than the boat was seized by fifty people, men, women, and children, who carried it, running and shouting, to the sea, into which they flung themselves fully dressed with their burden.

I had jumped in too, for fun and because the launching of a boat, however small, is always exciting. When Mai and Tapoua, who were already on board, saw me in the water, they grabbed me and helped me clamber up beside them. Then, after unfurling the brand-new sail, Mai gave the onlookers a demonstration of his ability.

He certainly was very skillful, and the boat responded well. We headed straight for the reefs at top speed, then came about at a sharp angle.

A fleet of canoes with paddles tried to catch up with us, and Mai had a fine time dodging them. Except for the shouts of our pursuers, we heard nothing but the squeak of the pulley and the rush of the water against the hull.

I was rather moved. At a certain point Tapoua turned to me and said, "*This* is a boat. And *that* is a sailor."

64

After I had jumped ashore, I examined the boat. With her hull of old grey planks patched with new reddish wood, she wasn't much to look at. She measured about thirty feet long by six feet wide and wasn't more than three feet deep. Almost all deck except for the helmsman's seat and in the middle, where a rectangular hole covered with a roof of leaves attached to wooden arches formed a kind of cabin, she had a short mast rigged out with a kind of lateen sail of red canvas.

It all looked fragile and precarious. But I had confidence. In fact the race we had just run had given me such a strong sense of security and skill that I said stupidly to Tapoua, "We should call her 'the Invincible.' "

"Invincible?"

"Yes, that means that nothing can destroy her."

Tapoua made a face. "The sea can destroy anything. And the reefs. That is not a very good name . . . I would rather call her 'Fouatoua.' It means in French 'Save me.' That is a good name."

In the meantime Bourdaroux had appeared, looking furious, as usual. He said mockingly, looking at Tapoua, "While you're at it, you should call it 'The City of Paris,' your ocean liner."

Tapoua's face lit up. "That is a good idea . . ."

He turned to Mai and quickly explained in Tahitian what it was all about. Mai and the natives who were standing around him laughed and clapped their hands. Bourdaroux looked at me contemptuously. "They'll laugh at anything, these Kanakas," he said.

After that things happened very fast. Mai and his companions had finished playing. It was as if suddenly they needed a change, they had had enough of the *pahi* party. They loaded and unloaded the boat three times, however, before the provisions were placed in the best possible way.

On the eve of our departure Peyrole gave me a sealed envelope for the chief of police of Papeete and an American army pistol with both cartridges loaded.

"It's mine," he said. "Take it, you never know."

Dubois had prepared for me—with the help of Odile Peyrole and Katherine Binzer, I believe—a sort of Martian outfit which he showed me and asked me to take along.

"I don't know if it will do any good," he said. "It's almost watertight, but of course, I don't know if it is proof against radiation. Don't put too much faith in it. But use it anyway . . ."

He gave me a slow, sad smile. "In my profession, the only thing I've learned is that you have to try everything, even if it seems ridiculous."

I thanked him.

The last night I slept on the beach, for Mai wanted to leave early. He woke me before dawn. Only natives were present. I had said my goodbyes to the Europeans the night before. I've always hated ceremonious departures. I was taking with me a small bag Odile Peyrole had made for me out of oilcloth. It contained Dubois' equipment and a suit of city clothes, in case we encountered civilized beings.

I also had a toilet kit which contained Peyrole's pistol and cigarettes. No books. I was leaving for a month and didn't want to damage them.

12

THE VOYAGE WAS long. On Tubuai we found no one. Not a human being, not an animal, nothing. The vegetation, on the other hand, was as beautiful as in Raevavae. But layers of sand and pieces of coral scattered almost everywhere, even in the most elevated sections of the island, indicated what had occurred. Tubuai was situated further to the west than Raevavae and must have been directly in the path of the hurricane, whereas we were only on its fringes. The water must have broken over the eastern face of the island and covered all the inhabited regions. Enormous gullies, very recently made, confirmed this hypothesis. It had all happened too suddenly to carry away all the soil, but no living creature had survived. The rain, coming next, had washed away the salt, and once again, the vegetation had taken over.

We spent two days on Tubuai, then I decided that we would go on to Papeete, as originally planned, although I was not very optimistic, since Tahiti lay due north of Tubuai and thus had probably been right in the eye of the storm.

It was a crossing of six hundred knots, but I wasn't worried. During the last nine days at sea, I had been completely won over by Mai and Tapoua.

They were quiet, easy-going men. On board, they chatted calmly in subdued voices, taking pleasure in small things. They behaved toward me with perfect courtesy and naturalness. To pass the time, I had decided to learn Tahitian. They taught me day and night, with patience and good humor. Nothing bothered them.

Their only time schedule was the whim of the moment. Sometimes after waking me up in the middle of the night because it was too rough on deck or because a particularly powerful wave had hit the *pahi* broadside, I would hear them whispering or laughing that soft little laugh that was so characteristic of them. During the day they would take turns at the bar, fish, eat a bite when they were hungry, and fall asleep at once when they were sleepy.

They were extraordinary sailors. Mai was by far the more experienced, but both of them had a relationship to the sea that was as familiar and intimate as that of a peasant with his land. In this immensity without landmarks in which one wave looked just like another, they seemed to be able to find their bearings as easily as on a road. I tried to understand how they did it. They couldn't explain it to me. It was all so natural for them that they hadn't the slightest idea what it was that I didn't know and that they knew so well.

Several times we met with squalls. Some of them were severe. Our little boat, caught up in a whole system of waves higher than she was long, took it well. But the sea, black and streaked with veins like marble, was there within arm's reach. I was sick a few times. They weren't, of course. And the curious thing was that they didn't seem aware of any danger. In the worst waves, when we clung to the gunwale or huddled in the ridiculous cabin, drenched and freezing, they continued to chatter unperturbedly or to laugh their curious laugh.

It took us seventeen days to come within sight of Tahiti. Mai and Tapoua had pointed the island out to me the evening before, although I myself saw nothing. They laughed and pointed to the sky, which was yellow in the setting sun.

"Look, you can see the reflection . . ."

Perhaps the clouds did have a slightly different color in that particular place. In any case, I could see nothing else. And yet when the sun rose, there before me was Tahiti, lost in the mist.

The rest you know. There was no port, no docks, nothing. Several large cargo boats were wedged between houses, far up on the land, on the hill that overlooked the port. All this had an air of desolation much greater than in Tubuai, for the ruins were too numerous to be hidden by the vegetation. We hesitated for a long time before landing. My companions, who were afraid, wanted to start for home immediately. I was anxious not to expose them any more than necessary. But I wanted evidence. Besides, what we could see from shore could still have been caused by a particularly violent tidal wave. If this were the case we would encounter survivors in the hills, for it was impossible that the sea could have submerged, even for an instant, the nine thousand feet of Mount Orohena.

Before my departure Dubois, Peyrole, and I had tried to pool our recollection of everything we had read here and there about the atomic bomb. All three of us seemed to remember that water was the best medium for carrying away radioactive particles. So after the torrential rains that had followed the hurricane, I probably wasn't in any great danger. Assuming that our memories were accurate, that is . . .

In the end we landed cautiously. I tried to prevent Tapoua and Mai from getting out of the boat, and explained the dangers that might have been awaiting us. They calmly refused to be separated from me.

"You die here, and we go back to Raevavae, and we say what?" Tapoua replied simply.

I gave in.

In fact, I was rather glad to have them with me.

What had once been the loading pier was covered with a thick layer of seashells and dried mud into which was mixed a thousand pieces of debris impossible to identify.

But it was not until we saw the first houses that we were able to estimate the force of the cataclysm that had struck Tahiti. The entire contents of the port had been flung there. In addition to the boats that I already mentioned, there were enormous anchor buoys embedded in the façades of houses like bullets in the walls of a fort, loading cranes twisted, torn, and crushed almost beyond recognition, a sea anchor, barges, landing stages . . .

We walked silently through this immense yard of scrap-iron which here, too, the vegetation was beginning to cover over. A species of soft, pale creeper was shooting up everywhere, and with its head lifted like a snake's, was attacking the most enormous piles of rubble. I asked Tapoua what its name was, but he didn't know.

For over an hour we walked through this nightmare land-scape. And then all at once we came to a line beyond which the water had not reached. It was a long way, a very long way from the shore, but in comparison with the total area of Tahiti, it was nothing. Mai noticed it at once.

"Now we will find people," he said.

We continued, however, to walk for a rather long time through a universe that was absolutely empty—no people, no birds, no chickens, no dogs, nothing. Only some huge albatrosses passed over our heads from time to time, making their rusty cry. Then all at once I saw what I had been looking for. On our left was a small suburban house, amusing because it was surrounded by palm trees, laurel, and hibiscus, but aside from that, rather ridiculous. On the side of the house facing the street a large French door was open, so that you could see to the back of the room. In an armchair, someone dressed in blue velvet was sitting.

I walked as far as the entrance gate and called out. There was no answer. I called again, then walked into the garden and approached the house. In the armchair was the dead body of a man in pajamas. His skin was completely dried out, like parchment, and was the color of tobacco.

My two companions made exclamations of disgust in Tahi-tian. I looked as hard as I could. It could be an accident. Cautiously I walked around the house, looking in the windows whenever I could. I saw no other bodies. Perhaps I should have gone inside, but I didn't dare. I was sorry now that I hadn't worn Dubois' outfit, but I had decided not to use it, partly out of respect for any survivors, partly because it didn't seem fair to my friends.

Just then Tapoua called me in a low voice. The silence was so profound that I heard him at once. In the garden of the house next door there was a sand pile, and on this sand pile were two children five or six years old, in the same state as the first corpse. The little boy wore red overalls and a white shirt. The little girl was in bluejeans and a yellow sweater. They were both blond. They looked like a Peruvian mummy I had once seen in the Musée de l'Homme. I looked at them for a moment, then I motioned to Tapoua.

"Let's go home," I said.

We returned to our *pahi* without looking back. As soon as we had reached the open sea I insisted that each of us in turn soak himself completely in the ocean, including all the clothes he was wearing on shore. Then, with a bucket, we washed down the *pahi* thoroughly. At last I said to Mai, "Let's go home. Let's go back to Raevavae."

He looked at me anxiously. "We can eat fish, and there is still a little *popoi* left. But what shall we drink? There is no more water, no more coconuts, nothing."

"But I told you . . ."

He cut me off with a weary gesture. "You told me, yes. But I did not believe you. Tahiti is a big island. I did not believe that the great storm had covered Tahiti. But we found this . . . and you did not give us time to look for coconuts . . ."

I explained to them again the risks we ran if we ate anything from Tahiti. They listened to me seriously. Then Mai said, "Very good, you do not wish it. But now what do we do?"

We did the only thing possible. We went in search of those little flat and uninhabited atolls on the southern border of the archipelago of the Touamotus. But neither Mai nor Tapoua knew this region well. In addition, the winds were against us most of the time. We were completely dehydrated. Mai had exaggerated when he had said that there was nothing left to drink in our *pahi*. There was still a little stale water and some coconuts. We wanted to keep them as long as possible. My companions constantly chewed on the flesh of raw fish. I imitated them. You could get a little liquid that way. But the many days at sea, combined with the privations, were causing me considerable suffering. I was covered with enormous and painful carbuncles. Tapoua lanced them for me with his knife. The seawater got inside them. They didn't heal.

I spent my time dozing. The other two held out better. They continued to chat politely, but I heard them laugh less and less often.

Nineteen days after we left Tahiti we landed on a little atoll that had been covered by the storm. We found no trace of a habitation on it. It didn't have a spring. But we found some clams and crayfish which had a little fresh water inside their shells. We found only half a dozen coconuts buried in the sand. Two were overripe, dried out. The others still contained a little milk.

We stayed there two days. Then, with our bodies crying out in every muscle that they would rather stay there and die on the spot, we got back into our foul, salt-incrusted *pahi* and went on.

Eventually we found another atoll which was also deserted, but which had water and coconuts in abundance. We spent a week there, repaired the boat, loaded it to capacity, and set off on a due southerly course for Raevavae, which we reached in one month without touching land.

These were days that weighed heavily on me. Physically, first. But also psychologically. Solitude and intimacy at the same time, as in prison. I liked my companions, but they were so different from me. Never to be able to go off by yourself, to be alone and undisturbed. Always to have someone looking at you, no matter what you're doing. And to have no way of knowing how long it would last.

At the end I was very weak, and because of this I was afraid of losing control over my nerves, of cracking. For me it had become a fixed idea, a reason for living: I had to remain as calm and agreeable as Mai and Tapoua.

I made it—barely.

It was dawn when we came within sight of our island. An hour later we were surrounded with canoes, greeted, acclaimed. It had been, it turned out, exactly three months since we had left Raevavae. My comrades got off the boat unaided, a little thinner, but in good form. I was taken to the Navy House on a stretcher.

Dubois took care of me for three days, with the help of Odile Peyrole. After that I wanted to go home. I wanted to be alone.

It wasn't until two weeks later that I was allowed to tell what I had seen.

13

NOT THAT MY telling changed anything. Everybody had already heard about our trip, for Mai and Tapoua had talked. But what did they know that they hadn't known before? Apparently nothing. Bourdaroux hadn't lied or misunderstood, and we had to prepare ourselves to live for a very long time, perhaps forever, without expecting any outside help.

Otherwise, everything was still the same in Raevavae. There were just as many shrimp in the lagoon, just as many fish in the sea, just as many wild boars in the forests, just as many papayas, guavas, yams, faros, and coconut trees. The air was as sweet as ever, and the people just as gay . . .

There were a few changes, however. Bourdaroux had permanently moved into the former police station, put a hedge around it, and planted a vegetable garden. Leguen had built himself a little *faré* not far from my house and had started clearing the land around it. He said he was going to turn it into a farm. Katherine Binzer had moved in with Dubois. Finally, Odile Peyrole was expecting a second child.

All these things were unimportant, but they were the only events that marked that year. Each of us, without admitting it, closed his eyes and ears and wrapped himself as tightly as he could in a soft little cocoon.

Until now all of us—even Dubois, who had come to Raevavae to die, even Peyrole, who had been sent here officially, even the survivors of the *Galliffet*—had been tourists. Suddenly, we had become exiles. We withdrew into ourselves. With one accord, we broke off the relationships that had been forming between us. When we ran into each other we said hello and exchanged a few words, but we didn't talk to each other. What could we have said? As the days and weeks went by, each of us was assimilating the reality of what had happened, was beginning to believe what he already knew, and to imagine. We had all left friends and relatives somewhere. What had become of them? Would we ever know?

To avoid answering these questions we numbed ourselves by various means, according to our temperaments. Each of us had his mania, which amused the others. But we respected each other's privacy. Indeed, how could we have done otherwise? By what right? Bourdaroux foresaw an uprising of the natives and was preparing to withstand a siege. Leguen was wearing himself out clearing several acres of forest alone. It was still only a vague clearing bristling with rocks and tree stumps but he would show you around, pointing out in dead earnest the site of the future pig sty, the future cornfield, the future orchard, and I don't know what else. Dubois was more himself than ever, and Katherine, who had also started cultivating a garden near his house, was taking up watercolors.

Only Peyrole hadn't changed. He continued to make his rounds, settle disputes, and register births and deaths, as if nothing had happened. But I wonder if this wasn't the worst affectation of all. To render justice in the name of the French Republic when you don't even know if there's still a Frenchman alive outside of Raevavae . . .

No, the only person who never changed was Odile Peyrole. Before the hurricane, she lived in Raevavae just as she had lived

73

in Mont-de-Marsan, in Tulle, in all the other places to which she had followed her husband. After the hurricane, she continued to live for her husband in the same way.

She had a little boy three years old, Daniel, born in Papeete. She was expecting another child, and that was good. She had common sense and character, but was not, perhaps, very intelligent. Anything she did not see did not exist. And anything that did not affect her family was of no importance.

As for myself, I had woven my cocoon out of women and the arts of leisure. When I returned from my voyage I had not found Naia, who was now living with a young native. I didn't hold it against her. I could never feel ill will toward a woman who left me. Besides, in Raevavae there were at least a hundred women for whom I was a curiosity. I had only to choose at random, and I did not deprive myself.

In those days, in spite of the police, who stayed out of such matters, and the missionaries, who couldn't do anything about it, relations between the sexes in Raevavae were governed solely by desire and whim. In each village the people were so in harmony, their instinctive reactions were so similar, and problems were so rare, that families virtually did not exist. Children lived in the village under the protection of the community. They usually lived with the people who liked them best, who were rarely their parents. Within the solid structure of the village, they were completely free. So what need was there for indissoluble partnerships, or strong families? You made love while the sun shone, you said goodbye when it rained, and there were never any scenes. The natives had a sixth sense in these matters: They never pursued someone who was happy with another lover. As long as the affair lasted, it was as if she were invisible. But as soon as boredom or satiety set in—and I've already said that in Raevavae it was impossible to conceal anything—admirers immediately appeared at a run. Yes, everything went very well and I had only to let nature take its course. But of course this state of things divested lovemaking of much of its importance. It has never been very important in my life, and with one exception all my relationships with women have been either for pleasure or for friendship. But in Europe there was the chase before the surrender, the desire to please afterward. Here, none of that existed. So I had to have other distractions. I found myself one that was quite ridiculous and very demanding. But before telling you about it, I must give you a bit of background.

A few years before my arrival, someone in Paris had a brainstorm. He must have been one of those civil servants who, in order to reach the next highest level, has to give evidence of a certain number of projects. Thank God, that race of men no longer exists. But it could easily reappear. Be careful: you ran across them most often in politics and administration. These were the two big areas of activity in which the criterion was not efficiency, but intelligence. When I left France, they had just added character to intelligence, but I doubt that this could have been a wise reform. A man of character who doesn't have to be efficient simply turns into a fanatic.

At any rate, someone who may have passed through here on official business took it into his head one day to create in Raevavae the French Institute of the South Pacific. On an island where by the admission of Tekao the schoolmaster himself, barely seven or eight percent of the population even knew the alphabet, it was admirable.

Nothing came of it, however. But the author of this idea had had time to send twenty thousand volumes here, for a library that did not exist. That's right, twenty thousand. What's more, they were rather well chosen. There was a substantial number of books on the South Sea islands, but also a good selection of general literature and history, and some good popular works on scientific and technological subjects. The packing cases had arrived at great expense, Peyrole's predecessor had signed for them, and they had never been opened. They were taking up a lot of room in a shed, and ever so often they were counted to see if any were missing. I cannot imagine what would have become of us all if those boxes had disappeared, or had not existed.

It was Peyrole who told me all this. I had some trouble persuading him that we had a right to make use of these books before they turned to dust, but with the help of Dubois and

Tekao (although lazy, he had a real reverence for the written word), I finally succeeded.

So we opened the packing cases. They were lined with tin and paper. On the whole the books had stood up well. I was beside myself with joy, and for a while, I read just about everything that fell into my hands. When these first hunger pains were appeased I was a little ashamed of my solitary binge and I decided to organize a kind of public library for those who would be interested. Peyrole, who in his own way also respected knowledge, gave me permission to use the shed in which the packing cases were being stored, and a few of those carpenter's nails that he was guarding so jealously.

Bourdaroux helped me a great deal. I never liked the man, and he caused us some problems whose consequences could have been dramatic. But I must admit that he was a skillful and inventive person. Indeed, there was something almost magical about his relationship with raw materials. You'd have to see him examine a piece of wood or turn a stone over in his hands to know what I mean. I could never understand why he had become a steward, and I'm sorry I didn't ask him. There was nothing in his physical or psychological make-up that predisposed him for the job. He was a man of strong constitution, proud and very much of a conformist. His skill and resourcefulness in handling material things was matched by a total inability to get along with people. He was extremely suspicious. Every new face was the face of an enemy. Yes, he was a strange man. He built me, with considerable skill, all the bookshelves I needed. And I began the job of arranging the books.

I needn't tell you that I didn't have the slightest notion of what the work of a librarian entails.

So I invented my own classification, by subject, and alphabetically within each subject.

In order to do this I had to leaf through almost all the books. And this is how I ran across the library of equitation.

There's no other word for it. Our inspired benefactor had sent here to Raevavae, in the heart of the subtropics, all the great classics on equitation, from La Guérinière to Baucher, by way of Lenoble du Theil and Faverot de Kerbrech, and including some moderns like Licart.

I have always instinctively liked horses. There weren't any at my grandmother's, and my father was as far removed as possible from this kind of activity, which he must have considered pointless and pretentious. The way I was brought up in Paris and in those depressing provincial schools gave me no opportunity to take riding lessons. Nevertheless, I like horses. I find them beautiful, I like their smell, and I've never been afraid of them. Every time I'd had an opportunity, and they had come at random, and at long intervals, I had tried mounting, jumping, and walking. I think I had shown some natural aptitude for riding, but I never had a chance to find out if this was true. Out of curiosity, then, I took home a pile of treatises so I could look through them at my leisure.

All these authors have in common a precision and discretion in their writing which often invites comparison with the best writers of prose. The practice of that particular form of asceticism involved in training a horse, when it reaches a certain level, the close contact with nature and the necessity of coming to terms with brute force, also gives them a kind of philosophy which, though limited, is vigorous and full-bodied. I was very quickly won over.

But to study a science without practicing it can end only in regret, or daydreams. I was still too young to daydream. This explains how I happened to get a ridiculous idea, but one that indicates rather clearly what we were all going through. I told you that when I first arrived at Raevavae I had noticed some rather sorry-looking beasts of burden whom I had mistaken for donkeys and who were in fact very small horses.

These small horses were domesticated, which means that they had a very bad life. When they weren't working, they wandered around the natives' shacks with their feet tied, looking for something to eat.

But they weren't the only horses in Raevavae. In the savannah that lies in the middle of the island and on the southern slopes of Hiro there were wild horses whose herds I had already seen on several occasions. They were also small animals, but stronger than the domestic horses, and they were generally in much better condition.

I decided, in short, to select one of these, catch it, and train it.

I made several excursions to the places frequented by these horses. After a few unsuccessful attempts I found them, began to identify herds, and then individuals. Among the latter I noticed in two different herds a very sturdy mare and a colt who promised to be taller than his fellows.

With the help of Tapoua, I organized a hunting party. It was very ingenious, with corrals, beaters, and doors that could be closed from a distance. As always when something new was happening, I had far too many well-meaning collaborators. But just then I had a little misadventure that gave me reason to think.

I wanted to be ready to receive my horses when they were captured, so I built a stable which I placed inside a solid enclosure. Unfortunately, we miscalculated on our materials, and while Tapoua was making preparations for the hunt for the next day and I was finishing driving in the stakes for the enclosure, I realized that I wasn't going to have enough stakes. It was tiresome—without a fence, the stable wasn't secure. I'd have to postpone the hunt, lose the momentum of the project, and run the risk of not being able to get the natives together again for a long time.

Just then I caught sight of a man who was looking at me. I motioned to him to come over, and with a brand of innocent offhandedness which I put on with the natives and which had always worked for me, I told him, "I need stakes, and I need them right away. Run and get some pals and come back quick. I want you to cut me five or six trees back there."

The man smiled and shook his head. I was astonished.

"But I'll pay you," I said.

He shook his head again and smiled more broadly.

"It's not worth it; there is nothing more to buy here," he replied. Then he strolled off calmly with his hands behind his back.

I was surprised but not as surprised as I should have been. This was partly because of Leguen, who paid me a neighborly call, and came to my rescue.

In the days that followed, we captured my two horses. I called them, for some reason, Philemon and Baucis. It didn't make any sense, for the mare was much older than the colt, and I intended to geld him.

Before starting to train them I built, again with the help of Leguen and Tapoua, a little riding ring which was really just a very large lean-to. Leguen was accommodating by nature, but in this particular case he also had a personal interest. As soon as he had got wind of my project, he confessed his desire to imitate me so that he could have some horses at his farm to help him with the plowing. I had promised him that as soon as one horse had been trained, we would go and look for more.

I told you that I had been on a horse only on a few rare occasions. So I wasn't a rider, not even an amateur one. In the beginning I had a lot of problems. In spite of all my reading, I didn't know where to begin. I had neither saddle nor bridle. The responsibility I had assumed for the mare and the colt made me nervous.

Leguen, who had been brought up with horses all around him, helped me again. Between the two of us we succeeded rather easily in winning the animals' confidence and in feeding them correctly.

After that, I was on my own. Relying on my authors, I put together a bridle, reins, and a whip. A piece of rope borrowed from Peyrole served as my lunging rein.

I will admit that I felt very awkward with all these instruments when, after leading Baucis to the beach, I tried, as my authors instructed, to make her turn in a circle. I was surrounded by natives who howled with laughter, jostled each other, came close enough to touch us, or scattered like sparrows, depending on whether the mare seemed about to obey or to rebel.

She was completely panic-stricken, and the first day I couldn't get anything out of her. The next day, learning from the previous day's failure, I worked with her at dawn, when the two of us could be alone. She had a few flashes of comprehension. I could ask for no more. In the days that followed I repeated the experiment with all the patience counseled by my authors, who were unanimous, for once, on that point.

Little by little, a round track hardened on the beach, was carved out of the sand. The natives forgot about us, or got bored. We made great progress. It was an absurd experiment, but an all-absorbing one. My mare and I began to understand each other very well. I gave her more attention than I ever gave to anyone, even my children. I observed her and studied her until I could read her like a book. Whenever she made a step forward, it was a victory for me.

After two weeks, with Leguen's help I got into the saddle. It went well. Baucis and I learned a lot about horsemanship, each of us teaching the other, and I keenly regretted that I couldn't find a large mirror anywhere on the island. I would have hung it on my palm-tree fence, and I could have checked my position in it as I passed, as the best manuals recommend.

In spite of this, I enjoyed myself thoroughly. Timidly, for it isn't always easy to make the transition from a printed textbook to the handling of an animal who weighs several times your weight and is not without ideas of her own, I made progress with the training of Baucis. Once I had won her confidence, she turned out to be intelligent and relatively docile. Although no taller than a polo pony, she was solid and well-built. I often regretted having no other saddle and bridle than the strange contraptions made of rope, straw, wood, and carpeting that I had had to put together myself. With a good English saddle, she would have made a pretty cavalry horse.

She wasn't very patient. When training her, I had to constantly vary the exercises, give in, let her rest. Certain things pleased her. She liked to jump and gallop, but turns, figure eights, and changes of lead bored her, perhaps because of my inexperience.

After a few weeks I tried going for a ride. Everything went so well that I began doing it every morning.

One day I ran into Katherine Binzer, whom I had not seen

in a long time. Dressed in slacks and a cut-down man's shirt that must have belonged to Dubois, she had a clean, athletic quality that I hadn't noticed before. Her hair, which was straight but very long, was gathered into a thick braid. The skin on her face no longer bore any trace of the burns. She greeted me and motioned for me to stop. From her questions, and the way she petted Baucis, I could see that she wanted to mount her. I offered to let her take a trial ride. As soon as she had gotten used to my tack she took off down the road at a gallop, her hand high, but her position perfect and her leg secure. After a few minutes she came back, flushed, her eyes shining, looking as I had never seen her before. She jumped down, handed me the reins, and thanked me in the same movement. Then she picked up the gourd full of laundry that she had dropped and walked off through the bushes.

Because of this incident, and to keep the promise I had made to Leguen, I organized another expedition to hunt wild horses. Baucis participated in it eagerly. We captured three horses. I gave two animals to Leguen and trained the third for Katherine.

I felt sorry for the girl. Of all the Europeans, the only person she really got along with was Odile Peyrole, but she had nothing in common with her. Whereas the other woman lived only for her family and knew nothing except cooking, sewing, and housekeeping, she had had a good education, supplemented by travel. Of all of us, she was perhaps the most cultivated. But being accustomed to a fashionable life, she was lost in Raevavae. She was one of those Anglo-Saxons for whom success is a drug, an indispensable stimulant. She had suffered for a long time from her disfigurement, from having to wear the ugly dresses of Odile Peyrole, from being alone and surrounded by men who were not of her background and whom she intimidated. Dubois had helped her as much as he could, but it wasn't enough. If he had asked her for something in return, she probably would not have given it to him, but it was humiliating to have nothing to refuse, and she felt that he had taken her in only out of charity, which was partly true. So she had made herself a stupid life, like the rest of us, with her gardening and water colors, a life that she could stand, nothing more.

But unlike the rest of us, she had a real problem to contend with: She was afraid of the natives.

They, who knew everything, were not unaware that there was nothing between her and Dubois. Amazed to see this woman without a man, they were always watching her curiously. She knew what they were thinking, and feeling their eyes on her made her sick.

I gave her a little piebald horse, very spirited, which she decided to take care of herself. We often went riding together. She was good company and she wasn't afraid. But our relationship wasn't simple. I didn't try to make love to her, not wanting to take advantage of the state of dependence in which she found herself. She refused to make the advances, dreading that I might respond out of pity. Our encounters were sometimes a little strained. Then I decided to treat her like a pal, and things became more relaxed between us.

One year and six days after the hurricane, Odile Peyrole gave birth to a boy whom she called Claude. Katherine was the godmother and Dubois the godfather. We weren't hurting anyone. But when I think of myself now, riding around my manège on Baucis with my heels twenty inches from the ground, trying to reproduce the paces invented a hundred years ago by Baucher, I want to laugh.

I almost forgot to mention that when I wasn't practicing equitation, I was involved in local archeology, and traded the natives eau de Cologne or canned goods in exchange for all the stone or wooden carvings they brought me. In this way I acquired a rather fine collection which included two primitive axes, a very beautiful paddle, several carved clubs and bludgeons, some nasal flutes, some sculptured planks and beams, fishhooks, breastplates, and various other objects. It was a mistake to bring these things together, as you will see later.

But it must also be acknowledged that my collection made it possible much later, to open an interesting museum in Raevavae.

14

So WE WERE recovering—foolishly, perhaps, but rather well. The natives, on the other hand, experienced no apparent change in their way of life. But there were two individuals who were not adjusting well to the new situation.

These were Tekao the schoolteacher and Simon the catechist.

Tekao, as I said, was lazy. But he was an intelligent and agreeable man who enjoyed his life and deeply respected his calling. The son of a fisherman, he had risen through his own efforts to an enviable social position, was an official of the French government, looked forward to a pension, and was confident that whenever he wanted to, he could establish himself in Papeete by marrying the daughter of a tradesman or restaurateur. The news which I brought of the destruction of Tahiti affected him very profoundly. I think he was more upset about that than we were grieved by the disappearance of Europe of which we were not certain, and which we had great trouble imagining.

Tekao kept his unhappiness to himself, with that discretion which is the great charm of the Tahitians. We didn't pay enough attention to him. It was also true that being neither of French blood nor a native of Raevavae, he was somewhat isolated. So he pined away, stopped laughing with the girls, who found him very attractive, neglected himself, and treated his students, who did not complain, with greater and greater laxity.

Little by little, he left them completely to themselves, and you'd see him from time to time walking alone on the beach in an old faded *paréo*. Casually, for in those days I had no respect for the education of children, I mentioned it to Peyrole.

"Yes," he said, "it worries me. "We have a school; it should function. If Tekao is sick, he should say so. We'll close the school for vacation. But this lack of discipline makes no sense."

Legally, he had no power over the schoolteacher. They were

both civil servants with approximately the same rank. But he felt responsible for the welfare of the island, and his professional discretion was in conflict with his sense of order. He asked me to go with him to see Tekao. We found the teacher in the little house adjoining the school in which he lived. He was alone. It was obvious that no woman had been in there for a long time. Everything was very dirty, and the room that we entered was in a state of great disorder. Tekao, who was sitting on the edge of his canvas bed, did not get up. There was something dejected and heavy about him that astonished me. He had put on weight; his face looked puffy and grey. His eyes were swollen and blood-shot.

In France, in the course of all my various jobs and travels, I had encountered many misfits and loners. Among these there had been alcoholics. I suddenly had the feeling that Tekao was drinking, but since there hadn't been any beer at Simon's for a long time, I wondered where he was managing to find alcohol.

"Say there," Peyrole said to him, "not feeling so well? We came to see if you were sick . . ."

Tekao made a long face. "Sick, yes. Very . . ."

And to prove it to us, he belched. He was pitiful.

"Well," Peyrole went on nervously, "you must see the doctor, take care of yourself, do something. You must clean up this mess, pull yourself together, my friend. The school is waiting. And besides, it's not healthy . . ."

Tekao seemed to retreat into himself.

"School, school, who wants a school here? Nobody studies. And they are right. Why go to school? To learn the alphabet? To read what? The newspaper? There is no newspaper. Books? What do they talk about? The Champs-Elysées, Nôtre Dame de Paris, the Palais Royal . . . and now all that is dust, dust, dust."

"Tekao, I'm thirsty," I said suddenly. "Do you have anything to drink?"

It was so incongruous that he lifted his head, looked at me, and stood up. "I have a little palm wine . . ."

It had a sort of sweet-sour taste. Peyrole had some too. I sat down on the edge of a table.

"Listen here," I said, "I don't know whether the cathedral of Nôtre Dame has been reduced to dust. Maybe yes, maybe no. But I am certain that that doesn't change anything. Think about it: to read, to write, to count, isn't that the beginning of progress? Why are you what you are? Because you are educated, cultivated. So we may be alone in the world? So what! In the first place it's not certain, and some morning we may be very surprised to see a boat anchored in front of the Channel of Teaverua. And even if it's true, what does it mean? It means that there are five or six of us here in Raevavae who are holding onto a fragment of all that human beings since the beginning of time have dreamed, thought, invented. If it's true, the library there in the shed represents the memory of the universe. And you think it's useless to teach children to read? Come, now! You have the necessary knowledge. You are irreplaceable. Do you realize that you may be one of the ten civilized beings left in the world? And you want to keep your knowledge to yourself? Why, you'll be cursed for it someday. Go on, professor, teach; we all need you."

As we left, Peyrole remarked in his restrained way, "That was good, what you just said. The memory of the universe . . . I hadn't thought of that."

I swear to you by all that I love that I didn't believe a word of what I had said. I felt I had been pompous and ridiculous. I only said it to rouse the poor devil out of his depression, because I felt sorry for him, because I didn't want to wake up some morning and hear that he had committed suicide or gone mad. That was all, absolutely all. Not a word that I said that day was spoken with conviction. I had only one idea in mind: to get to Tekao, and I chose my words for the sole purpose of achieving that end. As soon as we were outside I quickly forgot my speech. It wasn't my fault if the whole thing backfired on me.

But it was because of me that the school reopened, and that Tekao recovered his spirits.

With Simon the catechist, I was less fortunate.

Simon was a strange man. Like Tekao, he was ill at ease, between two worlds. But this was complicated by the fact that he regarded himself as the minister of God and that in his heart he looked on us as heretics. In this sense, he felt he was very superior to us, but this superiority was in no way visible. In the old days, the occasional visits of missionaries on tours of inspection and instruction gave him enough luster to leave him satisfied. Now, left to himself, he was at a loss. Like Tekao, he lived only for his job and suddenly that job seemed to him to have lost its meaning.

Perhaps because his superiors had given him instructions to this effect, he had never made friends with any of us. He lived alone with his wife in his little house near the church and saw no one outside of his ministry or his store. We had no idea how he lived or what he thought. Always giving a performance, knowing his two roles to the letter, he stuck to the texts of the perfect catechist and the perfect storekeeper. He irritated us a little, and we were inclined to make fun of him, but I must admit that in his actions, too, he was true to his part. He took good care of the church, preached proper sermons, was a devoted teacher, and looked after the old, the sick, and the crippled. He never looked at another woman besides his wife, he never got drunk, he was always correctly dressed and freshly shaven, and always gave you good weight on the merchandise he sold at fair prices.

Yes, that was it: He was honestly trying to play the role that had been assigned to him.

And then suddenly he was no longer really sure he had a role, and must even have wondered if the play was really going on somewhere. I'm not certain that he believed in God. He probably was more inclined to trust in his bishop, like so many of the clergy. I don't say this to make fun of him, or of them. The majority of people are incapable of experiencing passion. This does not prevent them from marrying, from going through the motions, from repeating words of love. It does not prevent them from honestly believing themselves to be the equals of the few great lovers they have heard about. In the same way, the churches include in their ranks a few mystics and a great many servants who believe what is told them, who obey, who act in good faith, but who do not *feel*. Woe to these people when they are no longer guided.

Simon said nothing, withdrew into his nest, and turned around in circles, like a dog in his basket. But unlike Tekao, he did not give up. Perhaps he did believe in God after all.

Then one Sunday, he made up his own sermon. I never went to church, any more than the other French people did. It was Tapoua who told me about it. He had been informed by one of his cousins, who didn't take the thing that seriously. The Sunday closest to the anniversary of the catastrophe, Simon gave an extraordinary sermon in which he explained to his congregation that God the all-powerful had sent this calamity to the earth to punish the sinners, particularly the European Catholics. Most of them were now roasting in hell, and that was only justice. But the men and women of Raevavae must be on their guard: Through the fault of a few unconscious persons who respected neither the Lord nor his ministers, the calamity would strike again. And if some innocents were chastised, they could only blame themselves, and recognize that they were not altogether innocent, since they tolerated those who were responsible for the scandal.

His delivery had been fiery, and the natives had been very much impressed. Pleased with the artistic emotion they had been given, the little thrill they had felt, they calmly went about their business, retaining nothing but a little astonished admiration. I didn't take the thing very seriously either. But whether he was annoyed at not being obeyed, or intoxicated by the unusually large number of people who turned up in church the following Sunday, Simon repeated his sermon with still greater violence and precision. He went so far as to threaten that if the scandal continued he would stop ringing the church bell and forbid the singing of hymns.

I don't think for a moment that he wished our deaths. He must have believed what he said, and he certainly would have been happy if someone had brought us to him to be converted.

He succeeded only in puzzling his parishioners and in making them talk a lot. At least six of them came to ask my opinion.

I replied with a smile that Katherine, Leguen, and Bourdaroux, who had been saved from the waters by a miracle, must in that case be very holy. They smiled, too, and were content with that.

But Bourdaroux, whom they also questioned, came to the worst possible conclusions. As I told you, for months he had been expecting to be massacred. He thought the time had come and ran to complain to Peyrole.

Peyrole must have known about it for a long time, for his intelligence service was good, and though he may not have been as well-informed as the natives, he was much better informed than us. Cleverly, he let Bourdaroux talk without trying to calm him down, and curtly refused to give him the rifle he asked for "to defend himself." Bourdaroux walked into the trap. He called Peyrole an idiot and an ass, in the southern French dialect they both understood.

Getting up, Peyrole said very coldly, "I don't care if you are French, and a southwesterner; I only respect the law. If you ever again insult an agent of the government in the exercise of his duties, I'll throw you in jail until an examining magistrate rules on your case. And if the examining magistrate takes his time, so much the worse for you."

Bourdaroux, dumbfounded, said nothing.

Then Peyrole changed into long trousers, put on the jacket of his uniform and his kepi, and drove the jeep to the mission. The use of the jeep was particularly remarkable, for there were only two thousand liters of gas left in Raevavae, and they were being reserved for emergencies.

I didn't find out what he said to Simon until much later. At the time the conversation was a well-kept secret, which only called more attention to his action.

In substance, he had said to Simon: "You have made seditious statements in public tending to disturb the public order. I could put you in prison. I will not do so, because I respect religion. You have told your congregation that if they do not obey you, you will stop ringing the bell. To spare you any inner struggles, I am confiscating the bell. I will return it to you in three months, if you behave correctly between now and then. Now I must inform you that all places of worship are defined as public places under French law. They fall, therefore, under my jurisdiction. In the event that I should ever decide that you were losing your reason, I might find you unfit to perform your functions, and be forced to dismiss you. Your residence is in effect an adjunct of the church. Now, help me take the bell down from the steeple. You will call your congregation to church services by banging on an oil drum, like everyone else."

The mission is due east of the Navy House. With the bell resting on a blanket in the back seat of the jeep, Peyrole continued to drive east. Very slowly, he drove all the way around the island, stopping everywhere and saying that the bell had been damaged and was going to be repaired. Then he returned home from the west.

He said nothing to any of us. But the following Sunday he went to church, sat in the first pew, and listened to Simon's sermon, which was quite harmless and quite disconnected. As soon as the sermon was over he got up and left, saying pleasantly, "Sing well."

"And the best part," added Peyrole when he told me the story, "is that I come from a long line of Protestants."

The situation might have been handled differently. I doubt it. Simon grew thin and yellowish, reduced his ministry to a service conducted without passion, trained a young man named Léné, that is, Réné, and gradually turned the responsibility for the church over to him.

We couldn't do anything for him. He tried to win Tekao over by arguing that they were both cultivated Tahitians, but he had no success. Tekao had almost lost himself by losing Europe. He wasn't going to start all over again by abandoning us.

So Simon disappeared from our lives. I would catch sight of him from time to time when I rode around the island. He would be alone, or talking with some old men. I didn't pay any attention to him. But I'm sure Peyrole was keeping an eye on him. Otherwise he wouldn't have been able to act as quickly as he did when the Poumi business came to light. But I'll come back to that.

15

WE MIGHT HAVE gone on living this way, perpetually on vacation, like country landowners who are short of cash and can afford neither the pleasures of town nor travel abroad, but who remain at home and allow themselves the luxury of doing exactly as they please. We might have become a stifling little provincial capital with its petty quarrels aggravated by boredom, its brewing dramas, its communal joys, and its fundamental equilibrium. But there was Katherine Binzer.

I told you that she was in a peculiar position, partly of her own making, partly the result of circumstances. She was fond of Dubois, who was very kind to her. But Dubois was only a camouflage. She knew this, and knew that nobody was fooled. She felt it as a humiliation. It drove her to acts of rebellion. For instance, she was afraid of the natives. But she'd be damned if she'd allow this fear to guide her behavior. She went out alone, sometimes very far, and never asked anyone for help or advice, not even Dubois. She was a responsible adult, and refused to believe that she could be treated, or that she ought to behave, otherwise.

I had warned her. But it had only made her angry. She thought I had appointed myself her protector, that I wanted to run her life. She was hard to get along with in those days. I was sorry, because she had charm, but what could I do? Unhappy love affairs have never appealed to me, for I have never pursued a woman who didn't surrender at the first attempt. Perhaps that's not very romantic, but that's the way I am. As a matter of fact, I still believe it's the only way to proceed.

But let's get back to Katherine Binzer. Tapoua was completely free. There was no agreement between him and myself, no master-servant relationship, no material compensation. But he was fond of me. He had adopted me. Our voyage to Tahiti had created a bond between us. I treated him as an equal, and made it my policy never to expect anything from him. From the first, he made it a point of honor to be my interpreter on behalf of the entire island. Besides, I amused him. At that time I was thin, but pretty strong, and always ready for anything. I was never sick. In spite of my laziness, any opportunity to move around, to do something new, was welcome. At heart, I was something of a Polynesian myself. A few years ago I was discussing all this with a little old man you don't know, and I asked him why we got along so well together, the natives and I. He replied, "Because you were the only one who laughed with us." Maybe that's why Tapoua liked me. He extended his affection to all my friends, particularly to Katherine. I suspected that he was keeping an eye on her. Not only didn't I tell him not to—how could I have prevented it?—but I encouraged him to do it. I had complete confidence in him, and I was right.

One afternoon I was home having a siesta with my lady of the day—I've completely forgotten her name—when Tapoua burst into my bedroom, out of breath. Given the circumstances, it was rather embarrassing. The natives weren't prudish and I liked them for that, but all the same, there were times . . . I was about to say this to Tapoua when he shouted at me, "Come quick, they are taking away the *vahiné* Katéléné."

I leaped out of bed and put on my pants.

"Where? Who? What happened?"

"Quick," said Tapoua, stamping with impatience, "quick, I know where they are going."

We took two horses from the corral and rode off at a gallop, without saddles. Just from watching me, and without being particularly interested in the matter, Tapoua rode as well as I did. Before we left I had grabbed an ax and he a hammer.

We rode straight uphill through the woods until we reached the first slopes of Mount Hiro, which we went around. Then we went downhill again toward the east, and across some fields of frightening loose rock, still at a gallop. At a certain point Tapoua stopped and listened, then nodded his head as if satisfied. More cautiously, we continued riding downhill toward the shore.

I knew now where we were going. Down this way there was

an old ruined *marae* whose reputation was not very good. Some said that it was haunted by *tupapaous* of former times, others told you that young people gathered there to "play," as the *arioi* used to do in the old days. I had gone there several times in broad daylight without noticing anything in particular.

Thanks to the horses and to Tapoua's quickness, we got there first. Tapoua made me hide behind a screen of bamboo cane, and placed himself next to me. Soon I heard shouts and laughter. Then three boys appeared, carrying Katherine in their arms.

We fell on them without warning. I used the flat part of my ax. Tapoua did not have the same scruples, and I heard a shoulder blade crunch beneath his hammer. It was all over in a few seconds.

The aggressors fled at once, leaving Katherine unconscious on the ground. I wanted to examine her, but Tapoua wouldn't let me.

"Later," he said, looking around nervously.

With considerable difficulty, I lifted Katherine and laid her across Baucis' withers, and started for my house at the fastest trot I could manage.

Katherine was still unconscious. She had received a violent blow on the forehead and half of her face was covered with dried blood. Her clothes were torn and muddy. Her man's shirt had lost all its buttons and with every jolt one of her breasts, firm and full, appeared practically under my nose.

What with my uneasiness and the discomfort of my position, I was very glad to get back.

I laid her on my bed and asked Tapoua, "Where is the doctor?"

Tapoua lifted his eyebrows and flung up his hands.

"Don't know. Left this morning with his bow . . ."

I shrugged my shoulders, exasperated by this doctor who was never at home, and who wasn't even capable of protecting his guests.

"Try to find him. Send the women to look for him. Go and tell Peyrole."

Then I got up to get water and some clean rags. I didn't know what should be done, but at least I could wash Katherine's face. Tapoua hadn't moved.

"Well?" I asked him.

He shifted from one foot to the other. "The doctor, yes, I will go. But Officer Peyrole . . ."

"What about him?"

He gave me a very knowing, very familiar smile.

"He is a policeman, that one, you know. Policeman say, this is the law, and they put people in jail. Here, jail is not good . . ."

"But after all," I said, surprised and angry, "you wouldn't want them to go free. They knocked her out, and after all . . ."

"Oh," said Tapoua, "I saw it. They felt good, they came to have some fun. She is a woman who belongs to no one, you know. So they wanted to have some fun. No harm, just fun. She did not want to. That is her right. But she does not speak Tahitian well, that woman. She said some very bad words, and besides, she hit one of them here—" he pointed to his cheek, as if ashamed—"she hit one of them here. Well . . ."

I understood. In the old days, in the South Sea islands, the head was sacred. There was no longer anything sacred in the islands, and there hadn't been for a long time, but a slap in the face still remained the worst insult. And coming from a woman . . .

"All right," I said, "we'll see about that later. Go and get the doctor."

Dubois did not arrive until the end of the afternoon, bare-chested, in his *paréo,* carrying his black leather bag. Katherine had come to. We had had a chance to talk. There was nothing the matter with her except a lump on the head and a bad case of nerves. I had given her aspirin and some whiskey. Those were the only two medicines I possessed. More importantly, I had made her talk, I had lent her a very pretty voile shirt which I had bought when I left Paris and which I never wore, and had helped her fix her hair. All this had distracted her, but as soon as she heard a sound outside she stopped talking and stiffened, and a glint of fear reappeared in her eyes.

93

Dubois was with her for half an hour. When he came out he told me, "I've given her a sedative. She'll go to sleep. Would it be too much trouble for you to keep her here for a few days? It would be better if she didn't move around too much. Besides, I'm afraid she's taken a dislike to my *faré* . . ."

He looked tired and old.

"What are we going to do?"

Coming from him, the question surprised me. I told him what Tapoua had said. He shook his head.

"That was fatal. She overreacted."

He sighed. "I thought I was doing the right thing in letting her stay with me. I gave her the illusion of freedom. I was probably wrong. It's very difficult to help people. The simplest actions . . ."

He sighed again, and concluded, "But we can't let things go on this way. It would drive her crazy. We must do something."

I had an idea. "What if I invited everyone for a drink? We haven't been together since Christmas. That makes it almost a year . . ."

"Perhaps," said Dubois. "Whenever you like."

16

IN THE WORLD that we lived in before the great cyclone, many things were good. Other things were not so good. Among the ones that weren't so good you could include leisure time, or vacations. You've read a great deal. You know how little freedom we all had in those days. I was about to say that this was the fault of the rulers of that world. But that wouldn't be fair. Everyone was a party to it, and those who suffered the most were the most insistent on defending the hoax.

It happened in three phases. In the beginning, and for a long time, work was regarded as a curse. It was considered difficult, tedious, and tiring. Only those who had no choice engaged in it. The higher you rose on the social scale, the less you worked; the highest class, the nobility, were forbidden to work, under pain of losing their rank. In reality, work was a vile or ridiculous thing.

Then little by little, everything changed. People forgot that work was a malediction from God. The social structure changed. The nobility disappeared, the lower classes rose. The latter wanted to be independent, responsible, free. To prove their moral worth, to demonstrate that freedom is not license, instead of abandoning the tasks they had once been forced to do, they deified them. They transformed this work which they were no longer forced to do into something sacred. Now the quality of a man was measured by the amount of work he was able to offer, of his own free will. To describe a good man, people started saying, "he's a worker."

Contemptuous at first, the powerful were eventually impressed by this ethic. To maintain their superiority, to show that they were no more cowardly or stupid than the rest, they entered into the game, at first for fun, later with a vengeance. They, too, began proving things to themselves by means of idiotic *tours de force*. At this point everything was ready for the third and final phase. This one was easy to bring about. Man was forgotten at the expense of effort, effort was henceforth regarded as normal, and all attention was focused on its result: things.

People began manufacturing things without limit or reason. They put them everywhere, without really knowing what they were for. That was not important. They were difficult to make, difficult to acquire. When you had enough of them, you were happy.

In order to make more and more things, everyone went to work. From the greatest to the smallest, each contributed his pinch of guile, his pebble of malice. People kept on proclaiming everywhere that work was honor, health, and so on. But at the same time they divided it up so it could be done even faster and more efficiently, without caring for a moment that each man's job, thus amputated, had now lost all interest.

So there we were, caught in our own trap. Work was boring, but if we gave it up, we despised ourselves . . .

Some people will tell you that I'm making it up, that it didn't happen this way, that economic factors were decisive, that races that did not work died out, that technological progress required ever more discoveries, more factories, more products . . .

Let me tell you point-blank that those arguments are nonsense.

All that came afterward. The whole thing started when people began taking work seriously.

Leisure time, vacations, are the proof of this. Let me explain.

Without some sort of escape, we would have gone mad. So we invented a very short period, set aside a long time in advance, during which we could be free with a clean conscience. In fact, it was our duty to be free.

The contrast between this period and the work days was so great, it made such a radical change in our lives, that it made us sick. We thought about it all the time. We made preparations. We waited. As soon as the moment arrived, we changed our personalities overnight. Like crazy people, we threw ourselves into activities as remote as possible from our usual occupations.

City dwellers left for the country. Sailors went to the Alps. Northerners with delicate skin baked in the sun until they were burned to a crisp. Laborers read, professors gardened, responsible persons slept, sedentary persons traveled, bureaucrats went in for sports, tradesmen took up watercolors. Thus we all played at realizing our dreams, at mimicking those whom we were not. It was a strange and ridiculous way of dividing up one's life.

If we had really wanted to be economical, wouldn't it have been better to do all year round, but only a few hours a day, work that suited us better, and to find in it or alongside of it those satisfactions that we went to such great expense to ourselves and to the community to find elsewhere, in the absurd and childish wonderland of vacations? Nowadays, does anyone even think of taking a vacation?

No, believe me, in this case economy was only an excuse.

In the old days, many people used to disappear every year for a month, leaving their family, friends, and problems behind them. They would go far away to a land where they had no responsibilities and turn themselves over to specialists who, in exchange for a large sum of money payable in advance, would devote themselves to making them believe that the world was theirs, free of charge. For one month, life was a dream: laughing faces everywhere, a warm ocean, docile horses, dependable trails, free drinks before dinner. Meanwhile, back home, the bailiff could take away your furniture, the boss could lay you off, your daughter could get pregnant or your son become a revolutionary; it didn't matter because you didn't know about it. You wouldn't know about it until afterward.

Well, in Raevavae, you see, we were all on vacation. We played our little games, we admired the landscape, we wore our costumes, and we carefully avoided thinking about what was waiting for us at home. We carefully avoided asking ourselves any questions, for fear we would find the answers disturbing.

And then, because of Katherine, suddenly, without warning, without our asking a question, an answer came to us. It was the worst possible answer, the one we were least prepared for. The one that called everything into doubt. This answer was force.

The world into which I was born had become, in its last years, a world of old men. It was so complex, so subtle, and also so hypocritical, that to get a foothold took time, a great deal of time. A young man who wanted to go into one of the professions could not hope to complete his training before the age of twenty-five. A professional man could not arrive at a position of real responsibility before the age of forty. A politician of forty-five was a beginner.

A world of old men, then, and a world of hypocrisy. How could there have been any room in this world for force?

I read somewhere that King Artus, when he received young Galahad, then unknown, in his castle for the first time, offered him his own bed, for he was *strong and valiant*.

King Artus knew very well that, being no longer young or strong himself, he must, if he was to continue to reign, and perhaps to survive, honor strength and youth. But he couldn't have liked it. And his successors strove to create a world in which strength and youth were no longer important.

This had some very unfortunate results. Elites the world over became rotten without being replaced. Governments of all kinds became museums of outworn revolutionary ideas. Nations deteriorated for want of conquerors. And individuals lost their heads and started blaming the wind, the snow, bad luck, or death, when in spite of everything they had been told, they encountered a force against which they were powerless.

Oh, I know prfectly well that the old men weren't the only ones that benefited by this system. Women and children lived more peaceful lives. The mad were less often locked up. Serious people could work undisturbed to make the world even more complicated. But it ended badly. That is why, as soon as our population started to increase, I established the Council of Youth to supplement the Council of Elders, and allowed young people to vote as soon as they had left school.

As for us, who were only ordinary people, we believed like everyone else that force is bad. Being well-bred, we felt it was better to buy than to steal. And do you know what the act of buying really means? Properly speaking, it is the conquest of the weak.

In making all these generalizations, I'm not really digressing. For after all, what had happened? In our vacationers' paradise, we had been confronted for the first time by the reality of force.

My party took place two days after the attack on Katherine. She was still at my house, recovered, but unhappy. Once again, as in the days when her face had been burned, she was avoiding people. I didn't know what to do for her. She agreed to join us, although she didn't really want to.

"They'll look at me as if I were a strange animal," she said to me angrily.

Everyone knew what had happened, and they all showed up. Odile Peyrole had brought her two children. The baby slept, but little Daniel cried constantly. I was surprised to see them. It occurred to me later that Pcyrole was more worried than he let on and hadn't wanted to leave any of his family without protection.

I had hesitated about inviting Tekao. I wanted the Europeans to come to a decision together. But after thinking it over, I was afraid we might make a mistake due to lack of information or ignorance of the local customs. After all, Tapoua had already been of service. So I invited Tekao.

After everyone had been served coconut milk and orange juice—we were saving the few bottles of alcohol we had left for very important occasions—I took the floor. I told briefly what had happened, reported Tapoua's comment, and asked for their advice.

Bourdaroux laughed contemptuously. "Attempted rape . . . it's very simple. The only thing to do is catch the boys and give them a punishment they'll remember the rest of their lives. Since you know who they are . . ."

"And suppose," Dubois asked quietly, "that after they've recovered from their punishment, as you call it, they attack one of us in the woods?"

"Well," said Bourdaroux, "we have justice. That's what the police are for."

"See here," said Leguen, with an energy that surprised me, "we can't let them get away with what they did to Mademoiselle Katherine, and not say anything about it. After all, we're not savages."

"No, we're not savages. But they are. I say that, when we found out . . . well, as soon as things changed, we should have decreed a state of siege. Martial law, yes. We still had time to build something rugged, a fort, something. Monsieur Peyrole had guns and ammunition; we had nothing to fear. But now . . ."

I looked at Tekao. He was listening quietly, his face expressionless, neutral.

Bourdaroux's violence made Leguen back down. "A fort," he said mockingly. "And what would we eat? Besides, let's not exaggerate; the boys here are good guys on the whole. Granted, there was an accident, but let's not dramatize it. We shouldn't let it go, I agree. But all we have to do is catch the boys and give them a trial. Am I right, Monsieur Peyrole?"

Peyrole looked numb. At Leguen's question, he uncrossed his legs and knitted his brows. Before he said anything I decided to take a risk in order to help him out. I said, "This meeting is absolutely private. We're all equals here. Monsieur Peyrole is a friend, and we should be addressing him as a friend."

Peyrole threw me a grateful look. "As an official," he said, hesitating, "I . . . But as a private person and the father of a family, it's different. I'm the only one here who has a wife and children. I'm not any happier than you are to see the first signs of disorder. Believe me, I regret what has happened to Mademoiselle Binzer, but we must be careful. How many of us are there? Ten, counting everyone, even the two women and the two children. And the official records show seven hundred and eleven persons. I checked the figure yesterday. Well?"

I made a gesture of assent. "What do you think, Doctor?"

"Well," said Dubois, "I'm of two minds. I think we're confusing two problems. One is the problem of Katherine. I regret what has happened to her as much as anyone. More, perhaps, for it happened under my roof and I'm partly responsible for it. But I think, that is, it seems to me that it is an unfortunate accident, and . . ."

"I agree with you completely," I said without thinking. "What happened to Katherine is not a matter for the police."

Dubois gave me a thoughtful look which made me uncomfortable and went on, ". . . and I think we should treat it as such. Perhaps the best thing would be to go and talk to the boys in question. But nothing official. Now . . . there's another problem, a much more serious one. This is the problem of our, or rather—" he gave a quick smile—"your future. It's curious that we've never talked about it, but that's how it is. Today, because of a chance happening, this problem has been raised. And I don't know how to solve it."

"But," said Bourdaroux with that arrogant manner which I hated and which he always put on to say something stupid, "have we no more protection here? Peyrole speaks to us as a private citizen. Fine. But what does he have to say in his official capacity? Eh?"

"In my official capacity," said Peyrole calmly, "I'm on leave. As a matter of fact, I've been on leave for the past six months.

We—my wife, my children, and I—are in France, and I'm waiting to be assigned to another post. And now I'd like to point out that I have received no salary for twenty-two months, and that a policeman is a member of the military who may under certain circumstances be answerable to the requisitions of the civil authority."

"And what's that supposed to mean?" snarled Bourdaroux.

"It means that I'm the only person here who's doing something. While you're playing war, and Monsieur Beaumont is playing cowboy, and Leguen is playing farmer, and the doctor is playing Indian, I'm continuing to do my job. I make my rounds, I look after the supplies and munitions, I attend the village councils, I do what has to be done. And if you want me to do something else, then you'll have to make other arrangements."

He was very red in the face and spoke with emotion. To prevent Bourdaroux from replying, I turned to Tekao.

"What about you, Professor, what's your opinion?"

Tekao shook his head and laughed. "Please call me Tekao. The way things are now . . . well, my opinion is the same as the doctor's. What happened to Mademoiselle Binzer was an accident, and we must not aggravate the situation. There was a misunderstanding. To strike someone on the head is a great insult here. Even I, who know very well that it is not that serious— if someone slapped me, or punched me, I think I would lose my temper first, and think afterward. Yes, it was a misunderstanding. If you wish, I can go and talk with the boys. I do not know who they are, but Tapoua will tell me. I am sure they are good boys. Perhaps they had drunk a little too much kava or palm wine—" he gave a charming and very knowing smile— "these things happen. As for the future, I personally believe that we have no choice. We here in this room may be the only remaining representatives of civilization. It is our duty to pass on our knowledge, to rebuild civilization. If we do not do this, our children will be savages."

"*Oh, là là!*" said Leguen, laughing softly. "Representatives of civilization—speak for yourself, and for these ladies and gentlemen. I'm only a poor peasant with no education. I barely know how to read. If you're counting on me to rebuild civilization . . ."

Dubois interrupted him with heat. "Tekao is right, and you're mistaken. You *are* a representative of civilization, our civilization. Do you think a peasant is nothing? It took centuries to produce the peasant, you know. And just as you are, you can help us. And Tekao is also right when he says that we should rebuild civilization. It's our only salvation. I'm only afraid that it won't be hard enough. And I wonder . . ."

He smiled and looked down. ". . . no, nothing."

I was rather disconcerted by the turn the conversation was taking. I had completely forgotten the impromptu speech I had made to Tekao a few weeks before. Now that my words were coming back at me, they struck my ear with a bizarre sound. They provided a presumptuous and melodramatic answer to all the questions I had been asking myself for the past two days. They were ridiculous, and yet . . .

"Madame Peyrole, what is your opinion?" I asked.

She was short and brunette. There were dark circles under her eyes, and because she wasn't looking well, her face seemed thinner than it was. It made her look sad and stubborn.

"I agree with my husband, she said. "We should avoid . . . that is . . ."

Suddenly, she summoned her courage: "We can't fight the whole island over a stupid misunderstanding. We've been here for four years now. In that time no one has ever been disrespectful to me. Oh, maybe a word or a gesture now and then, but what do you expect? It's not the ones who talk the most who are the most dangerous. We have children, we need to live in peace. That's my opinion. And if you ask my husband to get mixed up in this business, well, I'll tell him not to do it. Now, if you'll excuse us, we should be getting home . . ."

Everyone got up. Bourdaroux barely shook hands with me. Leguen came up to Katherine.

"You know, Mademoiselle Katherine, they're right; we haven't much choice. But if anyone bothers you, you can always come to me. I'll teach him to respect you, I will."

"Thank you, Leguen," said Katherine curtly.

Peyrole and Dubois parted very amicably, as usual. Everyone performed a complicated series of dance steps so that Katherine and Odile Peyrole would not find themselves face to face and could avoid each other without rudeness. Tekao left last. As I was thanking him for what he had said, he replied with the smile of a healthy man, "I only repeated what you said to me. I owe you my life, you know, Pierre."

I laughed idiotically.

When I found myself alone with Katherine, I said to her with a smile, "I'm afraid we can't regard the evening as a great social success . . ."

She gave a dry little laugh, set the glasses she was collecting down on the table with a crash, and rushed out of the room.

Soon, from behind the mat that served as a partition between our rooms, I heard her stifled sobs.

17

EVEN TODAY I still can't understand why I behaved so stupidly toward Katherine for such a long time. And I'm still amazed at the way things turned out.

You know I don't like to see people suffer, and I can't stand to see anyone cry. When I heard Katherine sobbing, I shouted through the partition, "I'm going to look at the horses, I'll be right outside."

Then I went and had a bite with Tapoua. When I got back two hours later everything was quiet in the bedroom of the cottage. I lay down, sorry that I had no light to read by for a while, as I usually did. I thought for a few minutes about Katherine, about the evening and what might come out of it, and then I fell asleep.

The next day I decided we had to make a fresh start. I woke Katherine and invited her to go horseback riding. I didn't think it was too imprudent, and I wanted to change her attitude.

I'm sure she agreed in a spirit of defiance. But the island

was beautiful, and the horses spirited. She soon forgot her anxiety and gave herself up to enjoyment. When we got back we had lunch, chatting rather gaily.

After lunch there was a lull, and I sensed that she was about to fall back into her fantasies. To keep this from happening, to occupy her, and just for something to do, I said, "Do you know what we should do? I'll cut your hair, and you'll set it in curlers . . ."

"Curlers?" she asked in her funny accent. She had never heard the French word for curlers, and didn't know what it meant.

"It's easy," I told her. "You can make very good ones out of electric wire. I'll go and get some. Get ready, I'll be back."

I ran all the way to the Navy House to bum a little electric wire from Peyrole. He wasn't home. His wife opened the door. I made my request, explaining the purpose. She laughed and offered to lend me some of those pink and blue sausages that women used to put in their hair in France to make it curly. I think she was a little ashamed of her attitude the night before. I had to refuse, in order not to antagonize Katherine. Finally I got my electric wire and a pair of real hairdresser's scissors, which were much easier to handle than the paper shears that I used now and then for myself.

I found Katherine sitting in my armchair and wearing my bathrobe with a towel around her neck.

We had a very good time. It was hard for me, but the result was not bad. To prolong the fun, I imitated the conversation of a hairdresser. She responded in the same spirit, but never took her eyes off her reflection in the mirror. She guided me very skillfully. I had no idea that women knew that much about fixing their own hair.

After the haircut was over she washed her hair and I showed her how to put in the curlers. We made a few false starts, for my memories were vague. Then she sat in the sun with her legs stretched out and her eyes closed, as if under a dryer.

I hesitated. She opened one eye and looked at me without moving her head, and said, "Go take a walk. I'll be all right for an hour."

I went to see Leguen. It had been months since I had visited him. In the interval he had recreated, with the materials available to him in Raevavae, a Breton farm—just as snug, disorganized, dirty, and homelike as a real one. Since it was the hottest part of the day, he was at home. He was sitting on a three-legged stool made out of a log, shelling beans. His native woman was sitting across from him on the ground, helping him. She was a fat woman, no longer young, who had lost an eye, I don't know how. Leguen called her Nana.

When I walked in Leguen stood up with a big smile.

"Well, well. Monsieur Beaumont, what a surprise. Nana, go heat up the coffee, quick. You will have a cup of coffee, won't you, Monsieur Beaumont?"

It was all so perfect that I laughed with delight. Leguen made me sit down, served me the coffee, and with a series of winks and mysterious airs that were altogether wasted on me, placed on the table between us a bottle containing a white liquid.

"This is my brew, Monsieur Beaumont, I made it myself. Try it, and tell me what you think. It's not Calvados, of course, but I planted apple trees on my land, and you'll see. You'll see what I'm talking about . . ."

The brew in question was a white rum, very young and very strong. I tried it and was amazed. Leguen leaned toward me.

"You won't tell Monsieur Peyrole, will you? You see, I have a still. I put it together with Bourdaroux. It works. But you mustn't say anything. I'll give you some, if you like, good stuff, just like this. But don't say anything."

We chatted a moment, politely. Then my host asked shyly, "You wouldn't want to take a look at my farm, would you?"

I smiled. That's why I had come. At once Leguen got up, all excited, and insisted that I put on a straw hat like the ones the natives used to sell to the tourists in Papeete. He put on one just like it, and we went outside.

With his Nana and a few native friends, he had really worked hard. His house was in a rather fertile little valley with a stream running through the middle. Behind the house he had completely cleared the east side of the hill and somehow or other had plowed it. It made a well-defined, almost square field of close to three acres. All around it some badly trimmed stakes had been planted close together, but without forming a continuous enclosure. I didn't understand what they were for. Leguen saw my look.

"It's a local shrub. I've forgotten the name. It's full of thorns and it grows anywhere. I'm trying to make a hedge. That way, later, the cattle will stay out! Officer Peyrole has a few rolls of barbed wire, but we should save those . . ."

He also had a little orchard protected by a corral fence made of peeled logs, a very snug pigeon house with three fat specimens of the green South Sea Islands pigeon, a pig sty in which, Leguen told me proudly, "the filthy little things make me manure," and a tiny wood in which three of those miniature cows which are the specialty of the islands were grazing.

"They aren't very good milk givers, but I have high hopes. By careful breeding, and with a better diet . . . My big problem is parasites. The doctor has given me medicine, but . . . In the meantime, they're cleaning out the underbrush for me. That's all to the good. Next year when it's cleaned out, I'll clear."

"But you're doing all this alone?" I asked, amazed.

Leguen chuckled. "The boys here are a pretty good bunch, you know. As long as you're not too stuck up with them. Then I have my brothers-in-law; they help me. And besides, they don't turn down a drink, believe me!"

He was pensive for a moment. "Deep down, they're people, just like us. The only difference is, they aren't educated.

"In short," I said, "you're happy."

He made a little face. "I wouldn't say that. But I don't complain. As long as you've got your health, you know . . ."

I spent over two hours with him. When I returned to my cottage Katherine was no longer outside. Her chair was still there with a book and my sunglasses. I called her name.

She was standing inside. She was waiting for me.

She had made up her eyes somehow and had put on a very simple skirt of beige gabardine and a blouse I hadn't seen before. Her short, shining hair looked very pretty.

She was waiting, leaning lightly against the central column of the cottage. She must have chosen her place and her position, for the light from the small window fell right on her. But she was tense from head to foot. I smiled, walked in, and took her in my arms.

With her nose against my shirt she said in her rather harsh voice, "You don't find me too repulsive?"

I laughed and kissed her. Afterward she said again, "Do you feel sorry for me?"

I answered, "No, I want you."

And I held her close so she could feel that it was true.

I have never regretted what happened. It happened naturally, without our thinking about it, and it was certainly the most intelligent thing we could have done. In love, one always anticipates too much. One should be free, and not have one's mind made up.

What is the value of a love that is merely a conquest?

Before, you never know. Anything is possible. After, if your head isn't full of nonsense, you always know immediately whether or not it's important.

The next day I went to see Peyrole to ask him to marry us. I also looked for Simon, but I couldn't find him. His wife who, as I told you, was a poor, grey creature, told me that he hardly ever came home any more. In the end it was Léné, his assistant, who performed the ceremony.

Although I have always believed in God, that didn't make me a church person, and I would have been quite content to do without the church's blessing in this matter. But I wanted to take advantage of this opportunity to bring together all the inhabitants of the island in as solemn a celebration as possible. It seemed a good idea to have the church be associated with it, all the more so since Katherine was Protestant.

Preparations for the wedding lasted over a week. Mai insisted that only the people of his village be in charge of the fish. The people of Matotea protested, and to restore peace we had to allow them to furnish the lobsters and other shellfish. More than fifty pigs were slaughtered. Every woman on the island wanted a new dress, and since there had been no more fabric anywhere for a long time many young women, under the guidance of the old, tried making tapa, a fabric obtained by steeping the bark of the mulberry tree and then beating it. Bleached or hand-painted with the juices of certain fruits or certain mineral substances, this tapa, when skillfully draped, can be extremely attractive. This was the first time in quite a while that it had been seen in Raevavae.

All along the path that led from my *faré* to Anatonu, Tapoua and Leguen, with a large team of helpers, planted pairs of small trees. By binding the tops together they turned the pathway into a bridal path. Finally, on the beach they dug an enormous trench in the shape of a rectangle. This was the banquet table. The people sat on one edge with their feet in the trench and placed their food across from them on the other edge.

During this time of preparation I hardly saw Katherine at all. Odile Peyrole had decided that it was not proper for her to continue living in my house and had practically forced her to move into the Navy House. Odile Peyrole was more emotionally involved in this marriage than Katherine herself. She asked me shyly, biting her lips, whether her three-year-old son Daniel could be flower boy. Armed with my consent, she retired to her house and imprisoned Katherine there, and I had no way of knowing what they were doing together.

Peyrole laughed but said nothing. He was very busy himself, for he had taken it upon himself to issue official invitations to all the villages.

On the eve of the wedding hundreds of natives were already camped around Anatonu. When I got up during the night, for in my *faré* I was as excited as a young man of good family about to take the big step, I saw long columns of fire moving along the sides of Mount Hiro. These were more guests, with their torches.

On the morning of the wedding Dubois, Bourdaroux, and Leguen called for me. Leguen gave me a little barrel, very well made, full of rum, and Bourdaroux with great dignity presented me with a weathervane made out of sheet iron in the shape of a cupid, such as were still seen in the old days on certain provincial chateaux. As he handed it to me he said that it would certainly always indicate fair weather on my roof. Dubois smiled but said nothing.

As we were leaving, Tapoua brought me a carved cane inlaid with mother of pearl, probably very old, and very beautiful.

"My friends and I will come with you," he said. And very naturally he took me by the hand and led me outside, where some musicians were waiting.

We walked all the way like this, hand in hand. Around my neck I wore a collar of flowers which his wife had brought me. Like troubadours, the musicians sang of my glory and my qualities as a horseman while accompanying themselves on flutes and drums.

The grounds of the Navy House were black with people. We could hardly get through the crowd. Peyrole came to greet us at the door but would not let the musicians in. He was sweating profusely and smelled slightly of mothballs, for in honor of the occasion he had put on his number one uniform of heavy black cloth. While we were waiting for Katherine he showed us into his office, whose windows were tightly shut, and offered us a *pastis*.

As my best man I had, after much hesitation, chosen Tekao. I was fond of this gay and unassuming boy. Above all, I wanted my marriage to be a ceremony of friendship. When I arrived he was already there in one corner of Peyrole's office, dressed in navy blue with a yellow tie, very elegant. He smiled and had a drink with us.

Then Odile Peyrole came in and motioned to her husband, who went out for a moment to talk to her. He came back and resumed the interrupted conversation, until finally behind the door there were whispers and muted sounds.

Both leaves of the door opened and Katherine appeared, absurdly dressed in a long white dress with a veil and carrying a bouquet of white flowers.

She was very pretty and looked at me uncertainly.

Behind her Odile Peyrole, frizzed and powdered, was lead-

109

ing by the hand her son Daniel and a little native boy with big round eyes, both dressed in white. I walked over and kissed all four of them. Odile Peyrole's chin started to tremble.

"Well," said Peyrole, "if you're ready, we'll proceed with the ceremony."

That man really had something. He took a pair of white gloves out of his pocket, put them on, picked up a piece of paper from his desk, and went straight to the window, which he flung open wide. The noise suddenly entered the room. He motioned to us to come over to where he was. Then, turning to the crowd, he raised his hand and commanded, "Silence."

The noise retreated, to die like a wave on the furthest ring of spectators. Then Peyrole said in a loud voice: "By virtue of my authority as official registrar I shall now, before the population of the island of Raevavae, record the marriage of Monsieur Pierre Beaumont and Mademoiselle Katherine Binzer. If anyone knows of any impediment to this marriage, let him speak . . ."

For ten seconds the silence was total, absolute.

Peyrole then went on, "Good, we will now proceed with the marriage."

After the traditional phrases, he had us, as well as everyone who was present in the office, sign the register, and then he kissed Katherine.

Afterward, when we came out to go to the church, the bell began to ring and the crowd to shout. Tapoua's musicians were transformed into bodyguards. Dubois gave his arm to Katherine, and I gave mine to Odile Peyrole. We moved forward very slowly; everyone wanted to touch us, to shake our hands. At last we arrived and Léné nervously came to welcome us on the steps.

The church was collapsing under the weight of so many flowers. Léné gave a rather good sermon in Tahitian and concluded by wishing us much happiness in French. Then we sang some hymns, and we were married.

As we left, I kissed Odile Peyrole. She said something that I didn't catch. I asked her to repeat it. Hysterical, she almost shouted, "Try to have a girl! We'll marry her to Daniel."

Then she burst into tears and disappeared into the crowd.

I kissed hundreds of men, women, and children. Katherine did the same. Her white dress was stained with sweat. At one point I asked her, "You're not afraid?"

"Of whom?" she answered, pressing a huge middle-aged woman to her breast.

The wedding feast lasted three days. There were many speeches. I spoke first, in Tahitian. I was given an ovation. It seems that my gestures were noble. And of course there were also singing and dancing.

We left about five in the afternoon, after asking Tapoua to see to everything, collect the gifts we had received, and redistribute them if necessary.

Just as we were slipping away, Katherine opened her hand. "Look what Dubois gave me."

It was a reddish-gold chain of very old workmanship, very long and heavy, with a locket.

I smiled and closed her hand over it.

The next day we came back to see our guests. In the evening we danced by the light of the torches. Katherine put on a *paréo* made of tapa and went swimming with the women, while I stayed at the house and talked with the men.

The day after that everyone was tired. Some slept on the beach, others made preparations to return. Only the young people danced. Everyone thanked us for this beautiful party, and we thanked them for everything, too.

It was a very beautiful wedding.

18

UNLIKE MANY PEOPLE, I do not believe that human beings are bad. But I think they are foolish and easily frightened, and many times it has seemed to me that their foolishness and their timidity lead them into evil.

Because we were foolish and because we were afraid, we did not become bad, but we went on vacation again.

After the warning which we had just had, we simply went back to our little occupations. The only difference in my life was that as a married man it was easier for me to entertain and that people came to see me more often. But our circle was not large enough for these get-togethers to make a change in our lives.

However, we had learned something, without really being aware of it, and we were better prepared than we thought. And although once again we were taken by surprise, we weren't at a loss for long.

The incident began in a comical way. One afternoon as I was taking a walk I saw a crowd of excited people milling around on the outskirts of an isolated *faré*. I thought someone must be having a party and I walked over.

As soon as they saw me everything came to a standstill. In fact, several men broke away from the main group and walked toward me. There was something tense and sullen about them that I had never seen in the natives before.

Like Leguen, I had always believed that the natives were people like ourselves. I always treated them just like anyone else. So I kept on walking toward them and forcing myself to smile, and I greeted them ceremoniously in the Tahitian manner.

Natives are sensitive to words and gestures. These forms have the power to arrest them, to fascinate them, to change their minds. The men who were standing in front of me were no exception. I saw them relax, but not completely. I passed through them as they stood motionless, and walked toward the others.

They didn't move either. They didn't look hostile. No, they just stood there, that was all. Behind them was something they were concealing. And behind me were the ones who had come to meet me.

I should have made a joke and gone on my way, I should have let it pass; I didn't do it. Yes, I was afraid; but something wouldn't let me leave. You see, I liked my vacation, I liked my island, and I liked these people. Try to understand me: It seemed to me that to go away would be to show contempt for them, to treat them as Bourdaroux would have done.

I kept on walking. If they hadn't moved aside, I don't know what I would have done.

I saw two or three I knew by sight, none really well. What struck me was that all of them were either old or very young. There wasn't a single adult male or a single female among them.

At the last moment they stepped aside reluctantly, just enough to let me through, and I saw what they were hiding.

At first I didn't understand. And then I almost threw up. There, on a kind of bamboo chair, was a completely naked man, the color of mahogany, in an extraordinarily weakened condition. Someone stammered in my ear, "You know old Maono . . ."

And indeed it was old Maono, the man who had taken me in, and with whom I had made a retreat when I arrived in Raevavae. Since then I had been up to his place once or twice on horseback, to walk around and enjoy the view. But I didn't know he was dead.

I couldn't breathe. The smell was unspeakable. I almost threw up again, and then out of the corner of my eye I caught a movement on my right. I looked. There was a young boy, very savage-looking, with a machete in his hand. This cured me of my nausea, totally.

I leaned over and looked with interest. Maono was revolting. He had nothing over him but a strip of red cloth that encircled his waist and fell between his legs. On his chair, which was actually a litter, he lay hunched up, his arms limp, his head flung back, like a big wizened baby. His whole body was the color of an overripe banana. In a flash I was reminded of the dead of Tahiti, but their bodies had been dessicated. Maono gleamed with grease, his belly was distended, his eye sockets were empty, almost dry by now, and his arms and legs were beginning to lose their flesh. Yes, the smell was abominable.

I straightened up and smiled at everyone in turn.

"What are you doing with old Maono? Taking him for a walk? He was old, he was tired, and now he is dead. Don't you think he has a right to rest?"

From where I was standing I couldn't get a good look at the men who were surrounding me. I was too close to them. I took a few steps with my hands in my pockets and then I turned around. There was a tall, thin man, rather light-skinned, with a face that reminded me of an Arab. I decided to address myself to him, so as not to be talking to the air: "I knew him well, Maono here. He was my friend. I lived with him, in his hut. Yes, I knew him well. If I had known he was dead, I would have come. But nobody told me anything . . ."

I waited for a reply which did not come. The men, embarrassed, shifted from one foot to another, nodding their heads vaguely. I tried again: "This man has been dead for a long time. Aren't you going to bury him?"

I hesitated, but I wanted an answer. I added, "He smells horrible. He should be buried. He is not clean."

The man I was addressing, the thin one with the grey hair, had looked at me once as if he were about to say something, and then stopped. But he was in a better position than I was to see what was going on around me.

All of a sudden he raised his hand with a great deal of authority. I turned around. The young boy with the machete was right next to me and he was holding his weapon in both hands. There was a moment of absolute silence and then abruptly, the tall, thin man sat down on the ground as if nothing had happened, as if he suddenly lost the use of his legs. He picked up two pebbles from the ground and began playing with them.

I sat down opposite him. One by one, the others did the same. I'm sure I heard them heave a sigh. I didn't look behind me again. I waited. At last, the man said: "You ask questions because you do not know. This concerns us, the people of Raevavae. Yes, it smells."

He gave a quick smile, very young, then became serious again.

"It smells, but it is supposed to smell. Before, it was always like this. And this is what must be done. Maono was the son of Tarakeha, who was the son of Tehei, who was the son of Maono, who was the son of Mai, who was the son of Mahaine. You do not know this, and many who should know it have forgotten. But all the fathers of this one here were treated like this when they were dead. Because they were important men. Maono, too, was important."

"But other important men have died. You have buried them

near the church, with prayers, you have put them in the ground . . ."

"Before," said a voice.

"Before what?"

"Before the Death of the Islands," said the man with the pebbles. Coming to life a little, he said: "Mai and Tapoua told us everything. Toukahoukou spoke, too. Now on the sea and on the land, there are no more people living except the people here. There are no more ships, no more airplanes, no more *poupas,* white men . . . There are only the men and women of Raevavae. Before, you came here from far away, and you said: It must be done like this. Now, no one will come again, and in Raevavae, we will do things our way again."

I was truly amazed. I had heard somewhere that at one time the Polynesians, instead of burying their dead, smeared them with oil and carried them around until they were completely dessicated, and then hid them in caves or crevices of the mountains, but I thought this was a custom that the populations had forgotten all about. Actually, it didn't concern me. Not personally. Smoothing the ground in front of me with the palm of my hand, I said: "You are right. The people of Raevavae must do things in their own way. But all the old ways are not good. You know that dead flesh attracts diseases. You would not want old Maono to give a disease to the whole island?"

The man gave a superior, bitter smile. "Old Maono here will never give a disease to a friend. Diseases come with ships, or from the Atuas. The Atuas like this custom, and there are no more ships . . ."

I sighed, and smiled. "What is your name?" I asked.

"Poumi," said the man.

"Well . . ."

I got to my feet as calmly as possible. He did the same. I noticed how distinguished he was. This quality seemed to come from the control, probably very strict, that he had constantly to exercise over himself. I also noticed his eyes, which were very deep-set, very alert, very honest and intense.

"Well, Poumi, my opinion is that you should bury Maono. But you will do as you like. However, if the disease comes, you will know where it comes from. I'll say no more. And I'll be on my way . . ."

They stood aside to let me pass.

I went straight to Dubois. He listened to me in silence, and then said, "I'd heard something about that. It's not very serious. Maono certainly died of old age, and he'll probably dry in the sun, without incident. The only trouble is that it's a beginning. At one time there were human sacrifices here. There were cannibals in Raevavae, as there were on all the islands . . ."

"Oh! But you don't really think . . ."

"Would you have believed it if you had been told that they would expose Maono? Eh? I know Poumi slightly. He's an honest man, a quiet one, a solitary. I'm surprised . . . Well, no, actually I'm not surprised that he's trying to restore the old customs. What surprises me is that he's strong enough to carry out his plan all by himself."

Suddenly he changed his tone. "You ought to talk to Tapoua about it. He doesn't strike me as much of a mystic. And you should certainly ask Peyrole to set up a permanent council with a few serious-minded natives. No doubt we'll have need of one."

He smiled at me again, that slow, rather sad smile of his, and inquired after Katherine. I told him she was fine and asked how he was.

"Oh, all right," he said. "That is . . . no, I'm really fine."

I asked him if he didn't feel a little isolated, so far away from us.

He laughed. "Do you think I should make fortifications, like Bourdaroux? Are you going to build a citadel, as he advises?"

I laughed in turn. "Katherine is fond of you. And we need a doctor. We want you to be here long enough to train a successor, you know."

He looked at me attentively, suddenly serious. Then, in his quiet, gentle way, he came out with: "Raevavae is a paradise. A paradise can't be improved. Don't delude yourself. When people are happy they don't want to do anything, they don't want to change anything. And that's the way it should be."

I was laughing as I left him, but I was touched. Following

his advice, I went to tell Tapoua about Maono. He seemed horrified.

"They are disgusting savages," he said. "They will die of germs and filth, and it will be very just. How can people do such things?"

"Then you think they should be forbidden to do it?"

He hesitated, then shook his head. "Who would forbid them? You, me, Officer Peyrole? Why? Nobody knows about it. And besides, it is disgusting, but who said it was forbidden?"

"I don't know," I said wearily, "but it should be said. Perhaps we could call a meeting of the village councils, for example, and hold a trial . . ."

"A trial?" Tapoua seemed astonished. "Trials are only for *poupas'* business. They say you should not do something, you do not know about it, you do it, they find out, there is a trial, they explain it to you and then they punish you a little, because you have a thick head. That is when you have a trial. But the village councils are only for natives . . ."

"Well, then, don't you try people, too?"

"No. Why should we? If you do something, everybody knows whether it is good or bad. If it is bad, they make fun of you and they forgive you. If it is very, very bad, they kill you. It is very simple. Why have a trial?"

"You're quite right."

I had no answer for that. When an entire population is in agreement on everything, it has no need of judges or executioners. It doesn't even need laws. Its unanimity takes the place of law.

I sighed. Suddenly, I remembered a detail I had forgotten. "Who is Toukahoukou?" I asked Tapoua.

He began to laugh. "He is completely mad, that one. He is not even from Raevavae and he tries to learn the old sayings. He has talked with all the old men, like a real *harepo*. And nowadays, if you see him . . ." Tapoua stifled his laughter behind his hand.". . . . He is a real savage. His new *faré* is over there, on the mountain. He has three wives all for himself. They have made him a red tapa, as if for a king. He puts it on when he is all alone and he walks around his *faré* without bending his knees, like this . . ."

I smiled as I watched Tapoua suddenly imitate the noble bearing of an ambassador or a bishop. I asked him again, "But who is he?"

"You know him well," said Tapoua, still laughing. "He does not believe in Kerito or in anything anymore; he is a wild savage. He goes to the *marae* with some others. He is Simon the catechist. He says . . ."

"What does he say?"

Serious once again, Tapoua gave me a friendly smile. Then, with that rather jaunty but never insolent independence which I liked about him, he turned his back on me and walked off into the woods.

I sat there alone, thinking about Simon the catechist, reverted to savagery, and trying to imagine him as Tapoua had described him, clad in the royal purple, among his wives, him whom I had known as a timid notable, with his church, his store, and his little grey wife . . .

19

THE NEXT MORNING I went alone, on horseback, to the old *marae* where we had rescued Katherine a few weeks before.

I hadn't paid much attention to it at that time, but I had visited it previously and had rather a precise memory of it.

It was nothing more than a kind of burial mound overgrown with grass and shrubbery, falling down at the edges, no higher than a man, about twenty yards long and a dozen yards wide. It was a little like those bramble patches you used to find in the middle of the French countryside marking the site of a house that had long since fallen down.

I knew exactly where it was and I went there without hesitating.

Nevertheless, I almost passed it by without seeing it.

I had a mental image of a large clearing with the ruin looming up in the middle. But I couldn't find this clearing.

Starting from the last landmark I was sure of, a very jagged pink and mauve rock, easy to recognize, I made several forays. Everywhere I met a dense screen of half-dry bushes.

Refusing to give up, I pushed my horse through this thicket, and suddenly I came upon a narrow but rather clear-cut path which led to a kind of forest chamber where the bare ground was tamped down and hardened like an outdoor dance pavilion.

All this was very isolated and very silent. I urged my horse on, rode across the cleared space, and took the path which continued on the other side. Suddenly, behind a screen of vegetation, I saw the *marae*.

It had been repaired, cleaned up, and restored, and instead of the rock pile I remembered, its black stones were held in place by lime and once again formed the solid geometrical platform on which the ancient Kanaka performed their sacrifices.

My horse had pricked up his ears. His nose in the air, his nostrils flared, his eyes a little wild, he pawed the ground. To calm him down, I rode him slowly around the *marae*. There was nothing on it, but as we passed one corner a large black spot suddenly began to buzz and thousands of flies flew off it. It was a patch of blood, as thick and rich as jam.

I rode the rest of the way around the platform, and then returned to the dancing place. On closer inspection I found at the edge of the bare spot a large number of bones which looked as if they had belonged to pigs and goats. Everything smelled very foul.

I left by the path which I had come upon by accident and followed it to the end. I came to a wattle gate, recently made, equipped with a counterweight that made it easy to open, and concealed on the outside by an impenetrable tangle of bushes.

Cautiously I opened the gate and rode back, slowly and meditatively, to Anatonu.

To do the work I had just seen without attracting attention, it had probably been necessary to mobilize in secret at least fifty men.

When I had related my discoveries and reflections to Peyrole, he agreed with me.

"It's even more serious than you think," he said. "Before, I didn't understand, but now it all makes sense. In Vaiuru the day before yesterday two girls disappeared, and I heard about it. Do you know what that means? In this country where everybody does what he wants and nobody says anything, because nobody can hide anything, they were worried right away. They informed me of the disappearance of the girls almost immediately. Oh, they didn't come to lodge a complaint, no. They saw to it that I was informed, that's all. And they waited for me. Vaiuru, that's the territory of your friend Mai, you know. There were lookouts everywhere. I didn't notice them at first, but . . . And wait—that's not the worst. This morning they found a fellow dead in the bush on the east side of Raraterepa. I just got back from there."

He made a face. "He's been there for three or four days. He hasn't dried out, that one . . . At any rate, three wounds, one of which broke his right collarbone and at least three ribs. A knife, perhaps, or else . . ."

"Or else?"

Peyrole seemed tired and troubled. "It's a crazy idea, but it looks like a blow made with a very heavy, or very dull ax. An ax made of stone, actually."

The idea seemed to fascinate and horrify him.

"What do you think happened?"

He shrugged his shoulders. "I don't know. The victim is from Mahanantoa. He must have been wounded in a brawl or an ambush and gone off to die in the jungle, where the vultures found him. Now the shortest route from Vaiuru to Mahanantoa, although not the easiest, is by way of Mount Raraterepa. Of course he could have gone to Vaiuru after the girls, been caught by one of the husbands, gotten into a fight and died. But it doesn't hang together . . . There are the two missing girls, and the village in arms . . ."

"Do you think . . . ?"

"I think," said Peyrole, his large face impassive, "that it's war."

"War?"

"Yes, war between the people of Vaiuru and the people of Mahanantoa. There have always been rivalries between the villages. Until now, it wasn't serious. I could always work it out with the elders. But this time . . . What bothers me is the stone ax. Unless I'm mistaken . . ."

"Well?"

He shook his head and looked solemn but didn't finish. After a moment he said, "I have every reason to believe that it's serious, and that we may be in danger. I don't like the style, the way they get carried away. Perhaps nothing will happen, but . . . perhaps we should . . ."

He seemed at a loss, unhappy. He glanced up and looked at me: "After all, I'm only a policeman, and all this isn't easy. These are heavy responsibilities . . ."

Abruptly he waved his hand as if to get rid of a bothersome idea and went on, "Perhaps we should regroup the Europeans. It's not necessary that we all be together, but it's not good for us to be isolated. The Navy House is open to all of you. If you prefer, you can stay where you are and invite Leguen and the doctor. Bourdaroux is well protected."

"Leguen won't leave his farm. Dubois wants to be alone. And Bourdaroux has been asking for a gun . . ."

Peyrole looked at me again, sighed, and threw up his hands. "I know . . . Well, we'll just have to wait."

He got up. "I'm going to give you a gun, though. Just you. Don't show it to anyone. If something happens, fire in the air. I'll come."

20

ALL THIS HAS never been told. You've seen the portrait of Peyrole: boots on, buttoned tightly into his uniform, knitting his brows and gazing into the distance. No doubt or hesitation about him. And yet there was another side to him. But he was also the way he is shown in his portrait. You can't see both sides of a thing at the same time.

The simplest side, the one that may, in the last analysis, be the more real because it is the one that most often expressed the reality of Peyrole, prevailed.

But don't be taken in by it. We had no plan. We didn't even have an objective.

I returned home with a dismantled rifle under my arm, wrapped inconspicuously in a bundle of cloth. I went to see Leguen, who listened to me seriously and seemed frightened, but did not want to leave his pigs. I saw Dubois, who smiled, nodded his head, and said nothing.

I paid a visit to Bourdaroux. He had turned the former police station into a real miniature fort surrounded by a dense hedge of thorn bushes. He came to meet me at the gate, an enormous affair made of the local oak that opened and closed by means of a counterweight, and advised me not to leave the sanded path that led to his house. And yet the ground on both sides was bare, tamped down like a courtyard. Only when you got right up to the house were there some vegetable beds, which were also surrounded by sanded paths.

Bourdaroux was not expecting me. But he was freshly shaved and wearing linen trousers and a clean shirt. Automatically, he gave his characteristic mocking laugh.

Inside, the former police station was in impeccable order. In the back room a native woman was languidly preparing dinner. She was wearing a cotton dress and her hair was drawn back in a heavy bun. I could not see her clearly in the half light, but there was something unusual about her silhouette. Bourdaroux saw my look and laughed. "You wouldn't have recognized her, eh?"

He turned toward the woman. "Suzanne, come and greet our visitor."

She was young, rather pretty, made up. Frightened and sullen, she walked awkwardly toward me. Bourdaroux had made her a pair of shoes with wooden heels. Her face was vaguely familiar to me. Suddenly I exclaimed, "But it's Hina, Purea's sister."

Bourdaroux's face darkened. "It is Suzanne, and she is my wife."

There was a silence. Bourdaroux made a gesture and the woman left the room, closing the door behind her.

"She never leaves the house," said the man from Bordeaux. "And nobody enters this house without my permission. They are too afraid . . ."

"Of what?"

Giving his unpleasant laugh he got up, went to the window, closed two heavy inside shutters which I hadn't noticed, and opened a loophole in one of them. He stooped down and picked up off the floor a wooden apparatus that looked like a crossbow, attached it to the loophole with two pegs, placed an arrow in the weapon, turned a little crank handle, released a safety catch, and the arrow flew off with a hissing sound. The whole thing had taken only a few seconds.

"Every evening I fix the door and windows like this," Bourdaroux told me with satisfaction.

What could I say? I shrugged my shoulders in silence.

Bourdaroux peered at me with his sharp little eyes. "Do you know that you're the first visitor I've had here in months? Even Officer Peyrole doesn't come here. When he comes, I'll meet him at the gate. A policeman . . . with you, it's different."

He walked toward me with his hands in his pockets, his stomach protruding, his eye wary; he was repellent. He said again, "You're somebody, you are. You're educated. You've traveled. You're a gentleman, that's what you are. And you're married to Mademoiselle Katherine, an educated woman whose cabin was in first class . . . Oh, I know—the Negroes amuse you. You've screwed quite a few girls. But just for the fun of it, nothing more. There's nothing between you and them, am I right? Between these savages and yourself, there's too big a gap . . ."

I sat there in a rattan armchair, fascinated. I said, "What are you planning to do?"

The man relaxed. "Oh, me, nothing. As long as I'm all

alone . . . But someone is sure to turn up, don't worry. Because it's obvious when you stop to think about it: Things are coming to a boil. When I say the Kanakas are savages, nobody listens to me. But they'll see. And then . . ."

His voice changed. His expression became more vague. He was going into his dream. "And then there won't be any choice. We'll take them, and we'll make them work. Those that accept it will be better off. The others will be forced to obey. We'll divide up the villages, we'll make big estates, we'll clear the island for cultivation. We'll turn it into a real paradise. We'll be in charge. Even Peyrole will be forced to obey."

For a moment he savored his idea in silence. Then he went on, "They say we're alone in the world. Personally, I wouldn't mind. But we won't be sure until we've seen for ourselves. Oh, not with a fishing boat, a *pahi,* as they call it. With a real boat, a solid one with a hold full of provisions, bunk beds, and a motor."

"But how would you make one?"

Suddenly he became excited. "How would I make one? Easy. I've figured it out, you know. The hull will be made of wood. We have all the trees we need. It's a question of discipline and manpower. As for the motor, the propeller, and so on, I'd take care of all that myself. I may not be educated, but I know how to work. There are the reserve supplies in the navy warehouse. Besides, the island has everything. There's coal behind Mount Hiro—well, lignite, anyway. Did you know that? I found it all by myself one day, just poking around. The doctor told me there's iron too. So to have mines all we have to do is get miners. And believe me, we'll get them soon, whether they like it or not . . ."

What could I say? He was neither crazy nor stupid. Just inhuman. So locked into his fear that he saw only his own problems, never imagining that others might have theirs, too.

I got up as naturally as possible. "All this is very interesting. We'll have to talk about it again. Meanwhile, I'm glad to find you so well organized . . ."

And I left with my hands in my pockets, being careful not to leave the sanded path . . .

124

I had left my horse at the gate. I rode home slowly, troubled. I didn't know what to do. In those days I was young. Very young, in fact. I didn't know very much. I had a little philosophy; it didn't amount to much, but it worked for me. It could be summed up in two sentences: "Live and let live," and "We're all born to die."

It was neither very heroic nor very brilliant, but at least it didn't tempt me to take myself seriously. I had seen so many people who didn't know how to live. I felt sorry for them, and they amused me. That was my whole philosophy. No, I didn't take myself very seriously.

Today I'm even worse. When I picture myself as I must have looked that day on little Baucis, the reins hanging down, my feet dangling, I have to laugh. I, the originator of the Idea, I, who am hailed and respected, I, the forefather of you all, I, who have never done a thing.

Yes, life is a curious madness.

When I got home, Katherine informed me that she was expecting a child. Your father. And on the evening of the next day, while we were having dinner with the Peyroles, right under Tapoua's nose, I was robbed of all the antiquities I had collected since I had landed in Raevavae.

21

ALTHOUGH HE HAD seemed hesitant when I had told him about my visit to the *marae*, Peyrole had gone into action. Actually, he didn't like making decisions. But like a good soldier, he knew how to carry out a decision once it was made. I liked him for his modesty and his efficiency.

As soon as I had filled him in on our new misadventure the morning after the robbery, he got up, buckled on his gun belt, and said, "Come with me."

The jeep was in front of the door. He jumped in and drove off at once, barely waiting for me to climb in beside him. He seemed extraordinarily preoccupied.

"Today, we'll do our best," he told me, "but this is the last time. I've had enough. If somebody doesn't set up a new system, I'm going to retire. I'm telling you this for yourself as well as for the others. I have a family, too, and I could be living with them like the rest of you, without any responsibilities."

One after the other, he picked up Tekao, Leguen, and two natives whom I didn't know. Between stops he drove furiously, muttering constantly under his breath. I didn't understand everything he was saying. I felt a little guilty and I said nothing. At one point he said, "Isn't it stupid to risk the lives of the only educated people on the island? If something should happen to you and you—" he pointed to Tekao and me with his chin— "what would we do, eh?"

No one said anything. None of us knew what was going to happen. Peyrole's anger intimidated us. In the end, however, I asked, "What are we going to do?"

Suddenly Peyrole relaxed. He leaned against the back of his seat and took his foot off the accelerator. "You've been mobilized," he said calmly, "all five of you. We're going on a police operation. A man was killed a few days ago. I don't want to know who killed him, or why. But two native women have disappeared." He turned toward the natives, who were listening openmouthed. "Two native women of your village. I don't want a war. I'm in charge here. Is that clear?"

He seemed very sure of himself now, almost calm.

"Open that crate you're sitting on," he ordered Leguen. "Take out the guns. Distribute them."

He looked at each of us in turn. "Do you know how to shoot? Do you know how to load? Good, now listen to me . . ."

His plan was simple. He believed that a group of inhabitants was involved in reviving the old customs, and he suspected this group of having committed the two abductions. He believed that the theft of my curios was related to these abductions, and he was convinced that something was going to happen at the old *marae* whose restoration I had reported. So he wanted to station us in ambush around the *marae*. If a ceremony was going on there, we would intervene.

He could have been mistaken, and he realized this. But on the whole his reasoning was sound, and I agreed with it. I had a few objections, but I didn't want to state them in front of the others. I looked at Leguen. He seemed as astonished and respectful as a child.

"I suspect," Peyrole went on calmly, "that the leaders of the operation are Toukahoukou, alias Simon, the former catechist, and this man Poumi whom you saw the other day. And I promise you that they will be arrested and tried. There won't be any *tupapaous* to help them."

Tekao, who was sitting beside me, made a movement. Deliberately I turned toward him. He lowered his eyes.

"I agree on everything," he said, "and I am not afraid of *tupapaous*, but . . . but if people come to the *marae*, what shall we do?"

"We'll arrest them," said Peyrole.

"And what if they resist?"

"We'll fire at them."

Coolly, he accelerated again and drove to the eastern tip of the island along the coastal path. At a certain place the foothills of Mount Hiro ran down to the beach like the fingers of an open hand. Peyrole drove across two of these valleys, then turned up into the third. The car was soon obstructed by vegetation. Peyrole stopped the motor and jumped out.

"The *marae* is there behind that hill. I doubt if anyone will come before nightfall, but I may be wrong . . ."

"The sun is good," murmured Tekao.

"Precisely. I'll take Leguen and these two men with me. We'll go by way of the beach. You, Beaumont, and you, Tekao, will cut through the bush. Go up through there . . ." He pointed to a rock that stood out against the sky. ". . . and down the other side and position yourselves in the woods, within a hundred yards of the *marae*. If you can see it from the spot you choose, good. If not, do the best you can, but try to stay in sight of the roads. Don't move for any reason until I come. That's it. You'll leave twenty minutes after I do. It's eleven fourteen. Be patient. We may have a long wait."

"Suppose they are already there?" asked Tekao in his courteous way.

Peyrole raised his eyebrows. "In that case, we'll see. But remember: Don't make a move until I give the signal. Let's go."

And without looking back he walked off toward the sea, followed by his three men.

Tekao and I looked at each other. We were each carrying a big rifle in the crook of our arm, like hunters. There was a silence during which two green pigeons flew over our heads. Tekao smiled shyly. "It's a little like a war or a revolution, isn't it?"

I nodded.

"The chief is right," went on the schoolteacher. "I agree with him completely. We cannot let the island return to savagery. But . . ."

"But what?"

"Oh, nothing. I am thinking about those poor devils. They are wrong, but it is from ignorance. I would not want to fire at them. I am not sure I would have the courage."

He seemed to regret what he had just said, and added, "You do not hold it against me?"

I gave him the friendliest possible smile. "Not at all. I feel the same way."

Tekao seemed suddenly happy. "Then . . ." But his face immediately darkened again. "No, we really must do something."

We waited exactly twenty minutes. Then we started off through the woods.

If in spite of myself I can't help admiring military heroes, no doubt because of childhood memories, and if now and then I feel some sympathy for the hardened old trooper, I have a horror of armies. I've already told you this; I can't help it. You can call it irrational, but that's the way it is. As a matter of fact, I detest all establishments, whether they are composed of soldiers, priests, lawyers, doctors, or even architects. You've never known any, you can't understand. But if you take a good look at our teachers, you'll see what I mean. Think about what they would be like, what they will be like when they are no longer informed by the Idea. They'll get together to admire each other and to be admired themselves. The less satisfied they are in their profession, the more they'll want to be respected because of their profession. They'll talk about honor, professional ethics, sacrifice. They'll boast about their humility. They'll refuse to let any of their members be criticized. They'll set up laws of their own which they'll claim only they can understand. They'll elevate themselves to an establishment and they'll decide that for this reason they are superior to the rest of the world. I detest all this. And I don't like it very much that certain men feel no compunctions about passing judgment on other men. I myself have passed judgment. I have killed. But I could never bring myself to believe that it was right. I did it when I thought it was expedient. I've never believed that it was just. In any case, the judge is just as responsible for the crime that he punishes as the criminal who has committed it. Don't both of them represent, each in his own way, the same society?

I'm telling you this because I believe it, and so you can imagine my state of mind as I walked in the sun, my gun on my arm, among the *bourraos,* toward the white rock that Peyrole had indicated. Now, that one . . .

Perhaps I resented him a little at that moment, but he was right. Only too right.

We had passed the rock and the crest of the hill, and I advised Tekao to keep a hundred yards to the side of me. Then, as quietly as we could, we walked down the hill toward the *marae.*

I soon came to the path closed off by a gate that I had discovered when I had come there on horseback. I looked to see if there was someone guarding it, but there wasn't. Nothing is more difficult than to get a native to stand guard. Besides, they must have believed themselves to be under the protection of the *tupapaous.*

Because they were there. It was as I was going through the gate that I heard the muted rumbling of their drum. They still didn't dare beat it as hard as they could, but they already had a drum. As I moved forward through the bushes, I heard branches breaking not far from me. I was afraid. It was Tekao. We recognized each other through the trees. It was time; like me, he already had his gun at his hip.

Staying within earshot, but losing sight of each other and then finding each other again through the vegetation, we continued to advance. There was no wind and the ground smelled of warm decay. Every sound rose straight up. That probably explains why they didn't hear us.

On the *marae* some poles had been erected. Tied to one of these with a vine, hung a quarter of human flesh. There's no other way to describe it. It was an arm, long, thin, already dead-looking, that ended in a chunk of thorax edged with blood. You could make out the shape of the shoulder, and then there was a mass of red and blue fibers. The vine with which this piece of flesh was tied to the pole was wound around the wrist like a bracelet. Above it, the hand was open and turned toward us, and I could see its white palm.

Opposite this piece of human debris which was also a gesture, an appeal, about thirty men were sitting. I don't know what they were doing.

I looked at Tekao. Like myself, he was almost ready to attack. Then I remembered Peyrole's instructions. I looked at my watch. It had been almost an hour since he had left us. I motioned to Tekao not to move. He seemed to hesitate, then sat down with his head between his knees. I forced myself to keep my eyes on the white hand that beckoned me down there.

The drums were still beating. It may have been because we were closer now, but I had the impression that the beating was louder. Suddenly, in the space between the seated men and the hand, there appeared a native dressed entirely in red with a staff in his hand. He began to make a speech which I couldn't hear because of the drums. Although I wasn't sure, I thought it must be Simon the catechist.

Then suddenly the men were on their feet and everything was confused. I saw Peyrole's head appear over the top of the *marae*. There was a pause, then several spears were thrown at his head and it disappeared. At the first shot, Tekao and I rushed forward. We ran into those who were running away from Peyrole. We began to fire, almost at random, as if we were hunting rabbits. Sometimes the target fell, sometimes the man kept on running.

I wasn't afraid. Several times natives who were running away passed right next to me. I paid no attention to them. All that counted were those silhouettes that were between the *marae* and me.

And then it was all over. We climbed up the black stone platform. Peyrole and Leguen were already there. Leguen kept firing over our heads at the men running away. As he fired he cursed and his face looked as if he were about to cry.

Peyrole was standing looking down at the man dressed in red, who was rolling on the ground at his feet. I walked over. Peyrole looked up at me. "It's Simon . . . the famous Touka-houkou."

Only the whites of his eyes were visible. He was foaming at the mouth, and there was a thread of blood in his saliva.

The three of us bound him and carried him down to the soft ground, as much to put our minds at rest as to prevent him from smashing his head on the flat rocks.

Then we looked around. There was blood everywhere. The stones were black with it. When we climbed up the *marae* we had rubbed against it and our clothes were covered with blood-stains. In the woods, men were groaning. Nearby were three or four dead bodies.

The two natives Peyrole had brought with him had found one of the two girls who had been abducted, bound hand and foot like an animal, unconscious. They were untying her. And over the whole scene a quarter of a woman's body floated like a bloody banner.

We began by rounding up the wounded. Then, while we were tying them together, Peyrole went after the jeep. We put the girl and the two natives in the jeep. Peyrole took the wheel again. The rest of us stayed behind to keep watch.

We thought it was all over. Suddenly, an arrow whizzed by me and disappeared into the vegetation.

We threw ourselves on the ground. Two more arrows appeared, both from the same place. We fired in that direction at random. Then everything became quiet again.

We waited almost two hours, lying on the sticky rocks in the sun, surrounded by flies. At last Peyrole came back, accompanied by Dubois and a large team of porters. While Dubois attended to the most seriously wounded natives, Peyrole showed me all the objects that had been stolen from me, which were scattered here and there in a curious order, or simply at random; I couldn't tell.

"Is anything missing?"

I made a quick inventory. "I also had a very long bludgeon with a small stone blade embedded in the tip; I don't see it here. As far as I can remember, there's nothing else missing."

Next we formed a procession and returned to Anatonu. The natives were happy. They sang and shouted all the way back. The prisoners, bound together, awaited death. I wondered what we were going to do with them. I knew some of them. They were neither better nor worse than their guardians. Poumi was not among them, or among the dead.

Katherine and Odile Peyrole were waiting for us at the Navy House. Fortunately, Dubois had made us wash our faces and arms when we crossed a stream. In spite of everything, we looked like mad butchers.

Odile Peyrole hid the faces of her children in her skirt. Katherine took my hand and said, "Come home and change your clothes."

I didn't resist. I was exhausted and ashamed. It takes more than one battle to make a soldier.

22

SIMON WAS COMPLETELY mad. Dubois visited him every day in the little prison where he had been locked up, and one morning I went with him.

He crouched in a corner, still dressed in red, but covered

with filth and excrement. He didn't recognize us. Dubois examined him and tried to get him to talk a little, but the man was in a stupor and didn't reply or move a muscle. At one point, in order to examine his eyes, Dubois took hold of his chin and turned his head toward us. He had grown very thin. A vein throbbed slowly at his temple. He allowed himself to be manipulated by the doctor, but when he was released he gradually resumed his original position.

Peyrole informed us that he wasn't eating. Dubois seemed very weary. "He hasn't much longer," he told us.

Turning toward me, he asked, "Did you see those stains around his mouth?"

I nodded.

"Coprophagy," he said, still addressing me. "In two or three days he will have poisoned himself. Of course, we could tie him up and force feed him. But what's the point?"

After that we went with Dubois as he visited the other wounded prisoners. Out of seven, one had died without regaining consciousness and another had torn off his bandages during his first night in prison and had eventually bled to death. The others, who were almost healed, welcomed us with smiles. They had been penned up in a shed and were being guarded by a native in a sailor's uniform. Peyrole shrugged. "I had to give him something to wear, so he'd understand that he'd been mobilized."

It was very warm under the corrugated iron roof. Some women and children were chatting with the wounded and with a few healthy men who were watching us anxiously.

"Those are some people I recognized," Peyrole explained. "I went to their homes and got them, and put them with the others . . ."

"What are you going to do with them?"

Peyrole's face darkened. "We'll have to talk about that."

We talked about it at his house, over a glass of the *pastis* which he now made himself. He was obsessed with a single idea, and he was right. He refused to go on being a policeman unless he could answer to some higher authority. He wanted us to create this authority.

We liked him. We decided to elect, not a government, for

we still didn't completely accept the idea that we were alone, but a municipal council.

There was a big party to which the whole island was invited. The councils of elders had been informed by Peyrole. During the party we explained as clearly as we could what we had in mind. Everyone acclaimed us, and wanted to vote immediately. It was very difficult to get them to accept the submission of candidacies, and an electoral campaign.

On election day the entire adult population voted, even the prisoners. Only Poumi was nowhere to be seen. He was known to be hiding near the top of Hiro. It would have been easy to take him in, but he wasn't doing any harm and Peyrole didn't want to intervene until this higher authority of his was already established.

We had decided that there would be ten municipal councilors. Leguen was elected, as well as Tekao, Mai, and myself. The others were natives belonging to all the villages. Peyrole, who had announced that under no circumstances would he be a candidate, hadn't tried to influence the choice of candidates, but he had seen to it that each community was represented.

Leguen and Tekao had campaigned, at my request. They had gone around to the villages, made speeches, and distributed gifts. They were very proud of being elected. Like me, Dubois had done nothing. He hadn't refused to participate, but neither had he declared himself a candidate. I didn't care whether or not I was elected, and I thought it was the same for him. But his name received very few votes, whereas I was chosen mayor.

I was amazed for myself, and very sorry for him. Dubois was one of those men who withdraw into their shells like snails at the slightest warning and who always shrink from the least distinction or praise, even when sincere and merited. Even so, for some reason I thought he wouldn't have minded being popular.

After the elections I went to see him. He was in the little vegetable garden that Katherine had started; I think he was hoeing the lettuce bed. He was doing this with the same care and clumsiness that he brought to everything except the art of healing. He welcomed me graciously. Apparently glad to have an excuse to abandon a task that bored him, he took me into the house and offered me a coconut with a pink plastic straw. I was amazed that he had any left. He laughed.

"I take very good care of my own, which I've had for a long time. As for the rest, well, I only serve them on very important occasions."

I smiled. As I told you, I was very fond of Dubois.

"I'm here," I said, "to ask your advice. I've been elected mayor, which is ridiculous; I have neither the ability nor the inclination to fill the position. I've accepted it to please Peyrole. But I need you."

Dubois, completely inscrutable, threw up his hands in silence. This meant nothing, or, if you prefer, it had ten contradictory meanings, but it spared him the necessity of speaking.

Finally he asked quietly, "Did you know that Simon died last night? He lasted longer than I thought he would. I'm always surprised . . . I'm always burying my patients a little too soon."

"Poor devil," I said. "It's partly about him that I came to see you. If he hadn't died, what would we have done with him? And what are we going to do with the others?"

Dubois hesitated. "Simon was sick. So you had no choice but to keep him prisoner until he died—or recovered, which was very unlikely. As for the others, they are simply pathetic fools."

"Murderers, too."

"In their case, it's the same thing."

He was obviously interested in everything that went on on the island, but at the same time he didn't trust me. He must have been afraid I'd get him involved in God knows what. I liked him, but I found him a little complicated.

"I believe they're going to be sentenced to six months in chains. They can't be either executed or just let go. Peyrole can't turn himself into a jailer. They're going to be made to wear an iron band around their ankles with a ball and chain, and they'll be free to go around like that. They'll have to work for the community three days a week, but they'll live in their own homes. They'll be ridiculous and unhappy; they'll be punished!"

I had said all this abruptly because the thing displeased me and because I was annoyed with myself for accepting the principle. Dubois looked at me without changing his expression, but with extreme attention.

"I think you're right," he said at last, "the earthly paradise does not exist. But . . ."

He screwed up his eyes—I can see him as I write the words—and leaned toward me: ". . . have you thought about our responsibility in this matter? Or do you agree with Bourdaroux, that we're totally innocent and that the natives are bad because they're natives? Let's see, let's think it over. What happened? Simon was a good catechist. As a catechist, as a Christian, he depended on a world he admired. When this world collapsed, he was desperate. What did we offer him in its place? Nothing. Me, archery; Leguen, vegetables; you, horses. He tried to work things out for himself with what he had left—the Bible, preaching. He believed in it, our old world. The natives didn't listen to him. Peyrole confiscated his bell. It drove him mad. In certain cases, madness is the only way to go on living. Have you thought of that? Have you thought of the people under your administration? What are they going to live for from now on?"

"But," I said, surprised, "I don't think that's our business. You said it yourself, we're administrators. We're going to try to govern the island as well as we can so they'll be happy. That's all."

"Do you really believe in happiness?" asked Dubois contemptuously. "We're only happy in our dreams. What dreams are you going to offer them? No, believe me, it's very simple: You must either let them sink into the past and disappear, or else offer them a new world."

23

VERY SIMPLE: MAKE a new world. I myself had told Tekao, without believing it, that we had to preserve the memory of the past. But Dubois was proposing something of another order of difficulty, and we obeyed him.

We have created something which is not the innocent paradise of Raevavae, and which is also not the world that vanished forever.

I know what I'm talking about when I say that unhappiness in our society is rarer than it's ever been. We have no exploitation, no tensions, a fairly harmonious life. Everyone has enough to eat, lives as he likes, does what he wants. Our councils are not so much governments as courts of appeal, somewhat abstract, but respected. We are living in a golden age . . .

But make no mistake! Nothing is settled. All of you around me think that through our wisdom we have discovered something that will last forever. Nothing of the sort. We aren't any wiser. There are fewer of us, that's all. And we're living on the leftovers of the old world.

We have chosen—wisely, 1 grant you—medicine, education, crafts, freedom. But we have chosen, do you understand? We haven't invented. Tomorrow our population will double, triple, decuple. What do the few inhabitants of Raevavae amount to today in comparison with our total population? With large numbers of people, the problems return. But solving them isn't a job for me, but for you, you and the others. That's when you'll have to start inventing. I'll be gone. You'll have nothing left to help you out of the traps you'll fall into except books, and perhaps this simple story which you have trouble understanding . . .

Yes, it was Dubois who had the Idea. As soon as it began to take shape, he repudiated it. But it was he and he alone who first thought of it.

When I left him that day I went straight to Peyrole. I had to find out the population of the island.

"Seven hundred and forty-eight, including yourself," he said. "In a year, we'll be back to the same population we had before the *tsunami*."

I returned home overwhelmed by our insignificance and smiling in spite of myself at my folly. How can one rebuild a world with seven hundred illiterates?

But I'm afraid I'm going to start boring you. Does it sound as if I took myself seriously? To read me, you'd think I was involved in the drama. I promised myself I'd hold your interest,

I'd laugh along with you at the personage I've been turned into, and instead I'm creating a drab and disagreeable world, a world that is neither more true nor more false than the official legend you already know.

The truth is that I loved Raevavae, I loved Katherine, I loved my house, the sky, the sea, my horses, and the simplicity of Leguen. The truth is that, end of the world or not, I had been enjoying life since I'd arrived on the island, that is, three years, seven months, and four days before the day I was elected mayor.

Well, approximately that, for in fact we had doubts about our calendar. I still have them. Theoretically, today is supposed to be Friday. But it may not be. It may really be Saturday, or Sunday, or even Monday. Don't repeat this. Not many people know about it. It's not serious. But it might upset the ones with weak minds. What happened is simple. Before the *tsunami,* and for a long time after it, nobody in Raevavae was the least bit interested in the time of day or the date. The sun served as our clock. The services held by poor Simon, and then by Léné, set Sunday apart from the rest of the week. Christmas marked a new year, and I think the retirement of the policeman and the appearance of a new one helped people to feel they were growing old. It was a good system.

Peyrole was like everyone else. But because of his radio communications with Papeete, he had had to pay attention to the date. Every morning he crossed off a day on his calendar, a big cardboard one with six months on one side and six months on the other. It worked very well. And if he happened to make a mistake, Papeete had corrected him.

But right after the *tsunami* he forgot to cross off the days for almost three weeks. He was exhausted and worried, and one day was just like another. By the time he tried to make up for his delay, it was too late. Payrole was an honest man, but he was a military man. He didn't like to be caught napping. Dubois had always intimidated him. At that time, I had just arrived. He didn't know me. He straightened it out by himself, as well as he could. And when people asked him what day it was, he gave them an answer, but without really being sure, do you understand? He had made calculations, had tried to find events to go by, and he was sure, yes, he was really sure that if he was off, it was only by a day. He didn't admit this to me until much later, when we were already well into carrying out the Idea. It wasn't serious, it wasn't really important, but it frightened me.

More than anything else, this little fact showed me how naked we were, how vulnerable. What could be more commonplace than a calendar? Before the *tsunami*, millions of ignorant printers turned out billions of them every year, and distributed them everywhere.

They weren't any smarter than we were. But they had no doubts. They had behind them all the astronomers and mathematicians in the world. We were alone. Seven hundred and forty-eight people on a raft. Anything that slipped away from us disappeared into the depths of the sea. How, on the basis of what observations, does one make a calendar? I still don't know. I've never wanted to know. So I was constantly having to choose, to decide what was essential and to forget what wasn't. Yes, we were quite naked.

But that was later, when we had started working toward the realization of the Idea.

Before that, we were unaware of these things. At the time I married Katherine and became mayor, I hardly imagined any of this.

For me, the vacation was a long one. I had a hard time recovering from it. Perhaps I never have. Of course, I've worked, I've disciplined myself, I've made choices and in so doing I've had to pass up things that were very appealing to me. But this discipline and these choices were only artifice, only the dexterity of the craftsman. In my heart of hearts I have always done what I wanted to do. Since I landed on Raevavae, I have merely followed my natural inclinations.

Take Katherine, for example. I've told you how I married her, to my surprise and delight. One minute before, I had no idea it would happen. One minute afterward, it was done, and well done. I've made a great many mistakes, most of them premeditated acts. With Katherine, I wasn't mistaken.

I don't know whether marriage is a good or a bad thing. Before I left France there was a lot of doubt about it, with good reason. It seems to me that it is a good thing if one regards it as a context, and not as an end in itself. But I can't speak for anyone else. For myself, it's been a good thing.

People are in the habit of taking a successful personal experience and making it into a universal law, and in this way good has led to tyranny. In fact, useful laws are rare. If you want to help people, you can only try to do two things: destroy their fear, and allow them to express their generosity. I've talked about fear, now I'll talk about generosity.

As far as marriage goes, I'll tell you about my own experience. Then you can marry or remain a bachelor, that's your business.

It's obvious that we were lucky. A few years earlier, in Europe, it would have been a struggle. She had a bold personality which would not put up with mediocrity. She liked success, or rather, since success is ultimately hollow, she liked *to win*. Under other circumstances, she would have had affairs or would have thrown herself into journalism, the fashionable commercial world. Inevitably, she would have entered into competition with me. Maybe I would have won, maybe I would have lost. In any case, one of us would have been hurt.

In Raevavae nothing of this kind could happen. As you know, it was through Katherine, or rather because of her, that we witnessed the reappearance of force. In the final analysis, it was to protect her from this that I married her. Having gained protection, she did not forget. Now I represented force. It goes without saying that I never beat her or mistreated her. But just as the manufacturers of calendars I was just talking about depended on science, I was in some sense dependent upon force.

Force was my domain. I did the heavy work, I had men carrying out my orders, I insured the safety of our home, and because of all this, people had to listen to me.

As long as we didn't have children, Katherine accepted this rather graciously. Afterward, she managed to work it out. She was coming from a state of fear, and I was giving her peace of mind. Besides, we loved each other. In bed, of course. A woman's body, for me, is like cool water that you dive into in summer, like a ripe fruit to be eaten, like a velvet sky at twilight that you want to caress . . . But I'd known all this for a long time. I also knew that a body without friendship, without trust, isn't very important.

Love? I don't know what it is. I recognize it when I see it, but I can't define it. It's desire. It's tenderness; it's friendship, of course. It's also something else. For me—just for me, mind you—love is a gaiety that keeps you from growing old.

Anyway, this was the way Katherine made me feel until her death. And makes me feel today . . . there was nothing ordinary about her.

Wait. How can I describe her to you? Twenty years we lived together, the palm of my hand can still feel the texture of her skin, I can still see the color of her eyes, I can still hear her voice, with that funny accent that she could never get rid of and that sometimes made her seem out of place; but I don't know how to make you see her.

Wait. She was independent and proud, but proud without being vulgar. She didn't like to be judged, but judged herself severely. She believed in reason and her own rights. She was brave.

Because my body has always functioned well, there's a kind of vitality in me that causes me to enjoy life. No doubt it was because of this that I was able to survive my youth. Today when I'm walking in the fields and I see the grass billowing in the wind, when I feel the earth under my feet, feel its power rise up my legs and into my body, I want to roll on the ground, to lose myself, to drown in that green ocean. Yes, old as I am, I love life.

I don't think Katherine ever felt anything like that. She had a seriousness I lack, a generosity I've never had.

I said I'd tell you about generosity. I'm coming to it. I have to tell this in my own way.

I'm part of life, like an animal. Katherine, on the other hand was a person. She looked at things and people, weighed them, got along *in relation* to them. Not me. I've always been involved in them. I've always been them. Because of this, I had nothing to give them. Katherine, as mistress of herself, could have ruled her little kingdom to suit herself. If it hadn't been for generosity.

Generosity is my own word, you see. No doubt there are other words that describe what I have in mind. But my education has been hit or miss. And besides, to a certain extent each of us has his own language.

Generosity and fear . . . I said that it was fear, caused usually, if not always, by stupidity, or ignorance, if you prefer, that made people bad. No one is bad by nature. To protect themselves from fear, people develop a second nature that is bad. But if this were all there was the human race would have disappeared long ago, long before the *tsunami,* long before the world became the world.

At the same time, often in the same beings, there is also generosity. Generosity is the opposite of fear. It's the feeling that pushes you to forget yourself, to give, to help, to admire, to paint in order to make something as beautiful as the beauty that you see, to sing like an angel, to write . . . Some people call it soul, others talk about idealism, mysticism, communion . . . I call it generosity. It's a silly word, but simple. And I think it's appropriate.

Well, Katherine had generosity. She had something I don't know how to describe. Kindness, yes, and attention. But also something better than that—true judgment, no illusions, and a lot of indulgence. When she was with people she looked at them, she talked to them, it didn't matter what she said; what mattered was that they felt that she saw them, that she was listening to them, that she could hear them. This is important: to look at people and make them feel that you see them, that they are something more to you than a vague outline, barely substantial enough to reflect your own fantasies. In her, this ability was natural. She was a person in her own right, but one who cared about other people. It was she, you know, who discovered—I might almost say who *invented*—Toutepo. Katherine was defined by her relationships. You can't imagine. Herself and things,

142

herself and plants, herself and animals, too. Herself and the world. Wait, I think I can say: herself and creation.

She was neither pious nor saintly. Before the *tsunami* she had traveled, made friends, had love affairs, had led a worldly life. Wherever she had gone she had sought out the important people, had tried to charm them. She wanted to succeed, you see, and she played the game according to whatever rules were being followed. Her father had had a huge manufacturing business in Auckland; she had been born and raised among people who thought only of success and who were not very poetic.

When Mai fished her out of the sea, and when she discovered our little world, she looked down on us. She told me so. In her eyes we were nothing but a bunch of middle-class French expatriates and island tourists, refugees from life. She looked down on us. A little. Because she was afraid. Afraid, first, of not measuring up, not rising as high as she wanted to, afraid, next, when she found herself among us, with our insignificant little lives, of staying with us and becoming like us. Afraid, finally, of being isolated, hurt, killed.

She looked down on me more than the others. Because from her point of view, I had more assets and did nothing with them. Also, because I was, as they say, her only prospect. Her only possible choice was to accept or reject me. And she so obviously needed me that she was afraid I would take her out of pity. She gave in only when she had reached the limit of her strength.

It was not until afterward that she loved me. I can't help it, that's the way it is; women love me and I love them. She loved me, I loved her, and perhaps because of this, perhaps because of the island, she became the person I've been describing and the person she had probably always been without knowing it. The soul of generosity . . .

We went through some difficult times together, believe me. We doubted, we trembled. But always before difficulties and dangers, never before fantasies.

She was not particularly talented, but I can still hear her singing in her true little voice, precisely when it was appropriate, songs of her country which I did not completely understand. She was more charming than pretty, but so neat, so clean, so free of complacency that it made her beautiful. She wasn't very intelligent, but she listened, looked, forgot herself, and understood everything.

I wanted to tell you about her. She was your grandmother. It is to her that we owe the world in which we live. For if I had force, which she had no wish to take away from me, she, on the other hand, was queen of all those weaknesses which are stronger than force.

She made me what I am. It's because of her that you exist, and that now, as an old man, I can look at girls through your eyes, thus preparing myself, when the time comes, to conquer death by living through you.

Queen Katherine . . .

24

I'M GETTING EMOTIONAL, I who have always detested displays of emotion. One of the great regrets of my life is that my father didn't know my wife. My father, out of stupidity, did me as much harm as one can do to a man: he robbed me of my childhood. For years I had nothing behind me but a gaping abyss. Because of him, solely because of his will, I had to have children of my own in order to discover childhood. I had to grow old in order to forget that nameless fear known to orphans, a fear which other children do not know. And yet I regret that my father did not know Katherine. Perhaps she would have taught him, as she did me, the simplicity of tenderness.

At any rate, to get back to my story, there was nothing simple about the problem that Dubois had dropped in my lap. How were we to make a world with seven hundred illiterates? It's funny, isn't it? Well, it didn't amuse me.

In my heart, I agreed with Dubois. I've never been a revolutionary. I believe that people in general are fairly virtuous—

and very stupid. I think that in history it has been the eternal parade of groups that has often brought about their misery, never their happiness. I am sure that revolutions are just as crude, contemptible, and useless as wars.

In spite of this, I agreed with Dubois. A government—and wasn't I the government in a sense?—must do more than govern. I was all the more convinced of this because I don't believe in happiness.

Don't misunderstand me: I don't believe in what other people call happiness. Comfort is useful but uninteresting. It's not happiness. Happiness is something rare, fleeting, and, all things considered, abnormal. What is normal is calamity, or at least worry. That's the way it is, it's our destiny and our nature . . . We shouldn't say to live and to die, but to live in order to die. I don't know who put us into the world, or why he did it, but we are here to suffer and to die, and comfort is of no use against this.

At best it can spare us the most elementary miseries and equalize the chances of unhappiness. But it doesn't destroy unhappiness, any more than it creates happiness. If, therefore, it was necessary to do something more than govern, if I had also to offer the people a reason for living, I saw only two paths: the sinister standard raised over the *marae* of Haratai, or the future.

Until the *tsunami*, Raevavae had lived a parenthetical existence. Progress reached the island slowly, through twenty filters, like those Paris originals which didn't find a buyer during the season and which, after appearing on one bargain table after another, turned up three years later in some remote province labeled "latest fashion"; but this didn't matter in the least. Those novelties that we hadn't invented, we were free to choose, to accept or reject. Our future was easy.

It seemed all the more logical to keep going in this direction since if we did not, everything that humanity had discovered over the centuries with so much difficulty and on which we had lived until now without thinking about it, like parasites, would probably be lost forever.

Once Dubois' remark had been uttered, all those arguments

which had undoubtedly haunted my sleep for two years without my knowing it, lined up in front of me.

We were, perhaps, the only surviving members of the human race. About forty of us knew how to read. Of that number, only three or four were capable of understanding most of the books. Could we remain at this level? Should we transmit our knowledge at all costs before we died, or were we going to let humanity set out again, naked, toward the discovery of the wheel?

To ask the question in these terms was already to have answered it. It was not, however, to have solved the problem. I mentioned our knowledge, but what did we know? All of us, more or less, were like the manufacturers of calendars: We were living on the knowledge of others. I didn't know anything. Dubois was a good doctor, Peyrole must have had some technical skills, Bourdaroux was a good craftsman, Leguen was a traditional small farmer, and Tekao knew how to teach. Was this enough to reconstruct a world overflowing with intelligence, science, people, wealth?

And even if it were possible, was it wise to recreate the world in the exact image of what it had been? Was it right, on this carefree island, to open the Pandora's box of civilization?

I could think of nothing else. When I became aware of this I felt ridiculous or crazy, according to my mood. But it was a fixed idea.

In the end I confided in Katherine. She was expecting Louis, your father, within a week or so. She was very large, but she carried the child well. Dubois was watching over her fondly, and Odile Peyrole was embroidering a layette. I can still see her. It was in the afternoon, after the heat of the day. She was sitting very straight in her rattan chair, sewing with tiny gestures. I don't know what she was making, some sort of chemise for the baby. Every now and then she looked up and broke the thread off with her teeth, and it looked as if she were kissing the cloth.

I had slept badly the night before. All day I had forced myself to do a thousand unimportant things, but had been unable to take my mind off what I was beginning to think of as a mania.

I told Katherine everything in as light a tone as possible, for as I told you, I felt ridiculous, but without leaving anything out.

She listened in silence. When I had finished and was expecting her to laugh or shrug her shoulders, she looked up at me with her green eyes.

"Of course we must do it," she said. "For the baby, for you, for me. It's the only thing to do."

I had been talking on my feet, pacing up and down. I sat down abruptly. "You think so?"

"Yes, of course. Let me see . . ."

She laid down her work and began counting on her fingers. "You seem to have three problems. First, should you begin now? Next, where should you begin? Finally, how will you succeed with so few people to help you? Am I right?"

"More or less, yes."

"Good. To the first question, I would say yes. To the second, I would say, education. And to the third, well, you simply have to increase the population—no, not the way you're thinking, you beast. Do you know what Dr. Dubois told me? They have no hygiene here. The babies eat anything, there are no sterilized bottles, nothing. Well, infant mortality is three times greater than in Europe or America. Can you imagine? The mortality rate must be reduced. After that, you will have more people to educate. In the meantime, you can try to improve the education of the adults."

"But who will teach them? And what will they be taught?"

"Oh, I don't know. You'll have to look in the books. Anyway, reading, writing, arithmetic, and . . . and the rest, later."

And behold, it was done. You'll say that all I needed was a little encouragement, and it's true. But it came, clear and precise.

I went to work. I talked to Peyrole, who said neither yes nor no. Peyrole's problem was simpler. It was called Poumi. The man was still hiding out in the mountains. Everyone knew more or less where he was. But no one except Peyrole cared. Poumi had the reputation of being an honorable man. He was believed to be a little mad, but why bother the mad? Our municipal council had discussed it and had decided to wait. Peyrole had given in without arguing. But to have at liberty what he called—with good reason, indeed—a criminal, worried and even infuriated him more than he said. He had posted a network of spies around Hiro and kept himself informed of everything. He, too, was waiting. But unlike us, he was waiting for a new incident. Under the circumstances, my project didn't interest him. Before making contact with the good Tekao, who was my most important resource, I wanted to clarify my ideas.

And then your father was born. Everything went smoothly. It was Dubois who delivered the child, but at least ten old women had volunteered, and all during the labor our garden was full of neighbors, friends of Tapoua's and former mistresses of mine, who chatted gaily as they waited and who afterward all wanted to see my son and to kiss the *vahiné Katéléné*.

All this cost me time. As soon as Katherine had recovered, I went and shut myself up for several weeks in what I called the library, which was a shed made of corrugated iron and very hot.

I had put away the books and catalogued them, so I knew what our resources were. Primarily, I wanted to find out how far they went and what areas were absolutely closed to us, either for lack of books or because none of us was capable of understanding the books we did have.

I've forgotten the details of my investigation. I remember only one ridiculous thing: On oriental philosophy, we had only one enormous tome, a very learned thesis, crammed with references to books which we did not possess, and completely incomprehensible.

When I realized that the oriental philosophers were denied us, perhaps forever, I was literally in despair. Personally, I had never had any contact with philosophy except through literature, maxims, reflections, and private diaries. Specialized works bore me.

More than once I came close to abandoning the whole project. I didn't talk about it, I didn't complain about it, I never complained to anyone, but I would become depressed and lose interest. Each time Katherine put me back on the path.

I was paralyzed by the choice of material to be taught. In the end I admitted that I would have to take into account the personal inclinations of the students. Some would be more literary, others more scientific. So I didn't have to worry, at least in the first stage, about setting up an encyclopedic program. It would be enough to give each one a good basic foundation, and to train their minds in reasoning as well as in observation.

Later, those who wished would continue in the fields of their choice. We'd see about that when the time came.

It was with these ideas in mind that I went to see Tekao. He listened to me carefully, but his response was reserved. It took several conversations before I understood the cause of this reserve. Tekao was a schoolteacher, reliable but limited. He knew, admired, and respected only the established curriculum. But the one he was using, which was still the curriculum of French elementary and secondary schools, seemed to me complicated and unsuitable. Also, Tekao had the newcomer's attitude toward teaching. Everything about the curriculum seemed admirable to him. The idea that one might no longer talk about the Battle of Rocroi, that one might even go so far as to neglect Racine, seemed to him a sacrilege. He said that he wanted, as the government memoranda had put it, to "form minds." He dreamed only of cramming them with wonderful and useless information.

I had a lot of trouble breaking down his preconceptions, and I never completely convinced him. Later, I caught him more than once, very quietly but insistently trying to reinstate the old programs I had taken away from him. In fact, this is the reason why today no one is allowed to teach more than five years of his life. But that's another matter.

Despite these reservations, Tekao was my man. He was fond of me and I was offering him glory. He threw himself enthusiastically into studying the practical procedures of the operation. From the point of view of equipment, we had only twenty-five seats in the little school in Anatonu. If, as I hoped, we were to invite adults to take classes, this was totally inadequate.

By chance, we had plenty of ink, pencils, and paper, because a substantial delivery had been made by hydroplane a month before the *tsunami,* and the school had been unused for almost a year due to the indisposition of the teacher. To be on the safe side, though, we decided to make maximum use of the blackboard and the slates. The only thing we lacked was chalk. I mentioned this to Bourdaroux who looked bored, but quickly solved the problem by burning some dead coral and then casting the lime thus obtained. This local chalk was not absolutely white, but it was usable.

The problem of teachers was more difficult to solve. Tekao was ready for anything. But I did not want to exhaust him or his enthusiasm. Furthermore, I wanted to save him for the more difficult classes, for it was my ambition to have the more gifted students go on to advanced work.

It all happened naturally, and I put a lot of effort into it. Sometimes, though, I had to smile; I myself had been a terrible student.

So I advised Tekao to look for two assistants among the natives, and suggested that he talk to Léné, Simon's successor.

Léné felt that his duties did not permit him to take on other activities, but Simon's widow volunteered shyly. Like her husband, this little grey woman had been educated by the Baptist missionaries. In spite of her retiring nature, she was not stupid. Above all, she wanted to make herself useful. A firm believer, she had been heartbroken by Simon's erratic behavior, and his death had been a relief. Humiliated and frightened, she wanted to make amends. She turned out to be efficient and pleasant. Her name was Noémie.

Since we were expecting many students, Tekao remembered one of his former disciples, a very intelligent boy who lived in Matotea and regretted that he could not move to Tahiti as he had hoped to do during his school years. When Tekao offered him a job as an assistant, he at first refused, claiming that he wouldn't be up to it, that it took too much time, that people would make fun of him. When we assured him that teachers came right after the municipal council in importance, he finally agreed to help us out, provided he was fed and lodged.

This boy, whose name I've forgotten, didn't last. He was soon replaced by another assistant who was less intelligent but devoted. During the few weeks that he lent us his services, he was useful, however, for he drew our attention to the problem of salaries.

It's a very complex question. We've almost solved it today, and perhaps you won't understand why it's important. But it will come up again, you can be sure of that. At that time, anyway, it really had me worried.

In the old days, you see, the matter was simple: Everything was handled by means of money. Although at first it was a fairly rare medium of exchange, when people ceased producing for themselves, money became the salary for their work. Finally, it was the reward for success—in other words, a way of measuring the courage, intelligence, and cleverness of those who had it.

All this you know, and the books of the old world explain it much better than I could. But they are right and wrong at the same time. They describe a situation that existed often in order to criticize it, but they don't see the roots of the problem, which I discovered in Raevavae.

In reality, money is an abstraction which permits a kind of tyranny. Because it is universal, colorless, and ultimately completely useless, if you consider it in itself and not as a symbol, it makes it possible to declare all work equal. To carry rocks, to grow flowers, or to govern a great society is all one. The only difference is that more men are capable of carrying rocks, and that therefore their services, being less unusual, will receive less pay. Aside from that, everything is alike. Whether one likes it or not, whether one feels like it or not, one does something that is measured in terms of money.

In Raevavae, this has never been entirely true. Even before the *tsunami,* money was not very important here. It was not a part of everyday life, and served only to satisfy an occasional desire for luxuries.

We Europeans were the only ones who really used it, and

there were few enough of us so that our offers were always interesting. To work for us now and then was an easy way for the natives to assure themselves of having toys and amusements, nothing more.

Once Simon's shop was empty, we saw this clearly: Our money was losing its power. Our means of coercion were becoming worthless. If you wanted a maid, you had to sleep with her; if you wanted men to work for you, you had to interest them, and treat them as friends.

We were a little surprised, a little amused. It didn't bother us very much. We lived almost the same life as the natives, and no one except Bourdaroux—and even Bourdaroux despised the hypocritical tyranny of money—wanted to force anything on anyone.

It worked very well, and there were no incidents, until we hired that boy from Matotea. He didn't want to work at the school. Teaching bored him. Yet he had the intelligence to make a suitable assistant, if he applied himself. In the old world, given an adequate salary, he would have kept his job, looking down on his work but deriving satisfaction from his pay. In our world, the boredom was too great.

It worried me very much. How, indeed, could we expect to progress if we were unable, for lack of incentives, to get the people who seemed best qualified to fill the jobs we were planning to create?

The answer seems obvious. It wasn't to me. Everyone should do what he likes. Individual tastes differ enough so that for every job, there'll be at least one person who likes it. A job that nobody wants is always artificial and useless.

When every man buries his own garbage, there's no more need for a garbageman . . .

We know this now. But in order for us to know it, the world had to collapse. What blinded our predecessors, I think, were both the Bible and the French Revolution. One said, You will earn your bread by the sweat of your brow. The other proclaimed: Equality! You know very well that bread must not be earned but harvested, and that equality is the worst injustice.

Before I finish with all this, I'd like to remind you of one detail. Before the *tsunami,* in every country in the world, certain men performed the duties of policemen, guards, executioners. We have no police, because a man who is accused of a crime and who does not turn himself over to the tribunal is excluded from our community, that is, from his race. We no longer have guards or executioners, and the accuser whose accusation has been proved is responsible for executing the sentence himself, because I wanted to do away with stupid jobs by reducing the number of trials.

It's too easy, all things considered, to kill through the intermediary of an executioner. And the offense must be very great and the offender without excuses before the offended party will agree, after the required period of reflection, to take the ax in his own hands . . .

25

THE MUNICIPAL COUNCIL, or rather the council, as it was immediately called, was elected for three years and normally met the first Monday of every month at the Navy House.

There were ten of us: Tekao, Leguen, Mai and Purea from Vaiuru, Roua and Tepaou from Matotea, Maraou from Rairua, Tara from Mahanantoa, Tehei from Anatonu, and myself.

The first meeting was amusing. The natives were happy, but intimidated. We had a real table and real chairs, we were all by ourselves in a closed room. It wasn't like anything they had ever known before. They looked at each other, felt the old green cloth that covered the table, fingered the sheets of white paper placed in front of them, and laughed discreetly behind their hands.

In our preoccupation with the electoral campaign and the elections, we had thought of everything but this: What is a municipal council for and how does it function? What had seemed obvious to us the day before suddenly became very complicated around this old green table. I had no idea how to proceed. I was familiar with the problems and the solutions, but faced with these ostensibly equal men who had all been invested by the people with the same responsibility, I was intimidated myself. I didn't want to speak. I didn't feel I had the right to put myself forward. Furthermore, I had no desire to do so. Since the *tsunami,* I had taken the initiative in many situations. It had seemed natural. People had come to me, or it had just happened, as they say. I had responded as an individual to an appeal, to a given situation. Why had they come to me? Why had I taken the responsibility of acting? I had never asked myself these questions.

Like everyone else, I like to succeed and compliments don't bother me, but I don't think I'm vain. I recognize my mistakes rather easily, and when I think about it, I don't trust myself. I know I'm superficial and lazy, and I'm not really sure I'm intelligent. Even today, although success and flattery should have reassured me by now, a day never passes that I don't catch myself making a mistake. I pay less attention to it than I used to, for in spite of everything I know my own worth, but I take note of it.

No, I'm not vain. However, I'm forced to acknowledge that since my arrival on the island, I automatically started acting like a leader. I didn't give orders—I've never liked to do that—but I said what should be done, and people did it.

This is all the more curious because I spent the first thirty years of my life running away from decisions, and because even after the *tsunami* it took me years to admit clearly and consciously that my will could have an influence on the destinies of other people.

I'm going to tell you something that you must not repeat. After thinking it over, I find I have unconsciously behaved in Raevavae the way the little feudal lords acted toward their fiefs. If I am to be honest, I must admit, much as it embarrasses and offends me, that for no reasonable reason, except for the fact that I belonged to a more favored social milieu, I have always believed myself to be a little superior to my companions. It's a bit outrageous, but that's the way it is. In specific cases I always recognized in other people a thousand little superiorities of which I was not jealous. But in my heart of hearts, and in spite of the contradictory evidence that ought to have been provided me by my ignorance, my amateurishness, and my superficiality, I felt myself to be different, and yes, superior.

After thinking it over, I believe I actually was a little more disinterested, a little more capable of accepting, as a last resort, the necessity of sacrificing my own interests, a little more capable of negotiating a compromise between two opposing parties, and perhaps a slightly better judge of good and evil.

But in reality there was only one reason for this: something you can call snobbishness, if you like. And it was because of this, I'm sure of it, that people liked me, and that from the very first days, Peyrole himself depended on me.

Now that I was elected a member of the municipal council, invested by others and with others with an authority which until now I had exercised naturally and without sharing it with anyone, I was, yes, intimidated. For a moment I must have believed myself to be like the others. And like them I waited, fingering the sheets of white paper in front of me. Suddenly I looked up. Tekao was looking at me and laughing quietly and without malice. With his eyes narrowed, he made a signal that I didn't understand, then without any transition he raised his arms to ask for permission to speak.

We gave it to him with relief. He spoke only about five minutes, without any rhetorical effects, as if he were talking to his students. He explained to the council very clearly what its powers were and how it could exercise them. Then he went on to its structure, explained what the mayor and deputy mayors did, and voting. He concluded by suggesting that I be appointed president of the council.

A hand vote was taken at once, and I was elected unanimously. This decision restored my equanimity. I sat down at the center of the table, under the benevolent and colorful gaze of a president of the French Republic who had returned to ashes three years before. I thanked them at length, and then I proposed that we discuss the organization of the meetings.

The oldest of the councilors was Tehei, the youngest Tara.

Nevertheless I suggested that Tara and Tekao be deputy mayors. At this time Tara could not have been older than twenty-three or twenty-four, but unlike the other natives, he could read and write rather well. He was very dark-skinned, solid without being fat, laughed often, and his otherwise ordinary face always had an attentive and intelligent expression. He was a former student of Tekao, who had favored his candidacy. I didn't know him particularly well, but he made a good impression on me. Like Tekao and me, he was elected unanimously, but amid much laughter, for the natives were amused at the idea of entrusting responsibilities to such a young man. He avenged himself cleverly by giving his speech of thanks and acceptance in French. Half the councilors didn't understand it. This restored order. In all this I missed Peyrole and his common sense. I understood that he had refused to come forward as a candidate in the elections because he wanted to keep the civilian and military powers separate, but I thought it regrettable, and perhaps dangerous, that he couldn't participate in our work. I suggested that he be appointed secretary general of the council, which didn't make much sense, but was agreed to without discussion after I had explained that he would attend meetings but would not be able to vote.

Once it had been organized, the council discussed what it was going to do. Tekao had enumerated our powers, but in an abstract, rather professional form which pleased the ear without reaching the mind.

There were, as I said, ten of us: Tekao and Leguen; Mai and Purea, both from Vaiuru; Roua and Tepaou from Matotea; Maraou from Rairua; Tara from Mahanantoa; and Tehei from Anatonu.

Tekao had Tara's confidence, I had Mai's, which meant I also had Purea's, Leguen was related to Maraou by marriage, and Tehei, who lived close to the Navy House, got along well with Peyrole. Only the men from Matotea were less familiar to us. But except for Tepaou, who was a clown, the men assembled there had intuition, experience, and a certain ascendancy over their fellow citizens.

They were capable of governing. The only problem was that they didn't know it. Until then, Peyrole had run the island fairly, in accordance with the laws of the French Republic. He could just as well have gone on doing so. If he had wanted an authority superior to his own, it was in order to solve certain serious problems for which, in his modesty, he didn't believe himself capable of bearing the full responsibility. But events comparable to the adventure at the *marae* didn't happen every day. What were we going to do while we were waiting for another one to occur?

During the four or five meetings that followed, we began by concerning ourselves with minor litigations that had formerly been left in the hands of the elders. Although they gave us a taste of power and taught us the mechanics of democracy, they brought us very little satisfaction. These petty legal cases involved so many people, families, and villages, and everybody lied so well, that for some ridiculous matter we were forced to rip open the entire social fabric of the island, which did not take place without pain or protest. For the sake of an incident involving a lost or stolen pig, it would have taken little to bring on a real war, provoked and led by factions in rivalry with our council. Without the cheerful common sense of Leguen and the authority of Peyrole, we would have been in trouble.

I confess that I had nothing to do with this fortunate outcome. I, too, was serving my apprenticeship. Having always lived and acted alone, I was helpless in the presence of the structure I had helped to build. Having believed it to be necessary, I assumed it to be adequate and counted on it to function harmoniously, which was nonsense. Structures have never served any purpose but to allow men to act.

In any case, we were getting nowhere, when Tekao saved us. Bent on progress, he proposed that we set up a five-year plan for the development of the territory. This idea was much too abstract, and met with no response. But it enabled me to step in. I supported it as strongly as I could, and suggested that we start by developing education.

This proposal interested the members because they weren't

expecting it. In Raevavae the people thought well of Tekao and respected the school, and occasionally parents asserted their authority in a mild way to get their children to attend classes. But nobody thought that anything important or amusing could come of it. Leguen was the first to react. Personally, he considered that he was too old to "learn," as he put it, but he told us some goods news: His housekeeper was expecting a baby. He hoped that when this child would be old enough to go to school, it could be taught everything that its father had not been able to learn. Tara supported him, with the prudence and flexibility that he displayed in those days in his dealings with us. Without hurting anyone's feelings, he succeeded in making the natives understand that education is a good thing. Was it not thanks to education that he, an inexperienced young man, had been called upon to sit down with the wisest inhabitants of the island?

This remark was greeted benevolently and slowly made the rounds of the table. Everyone examined it with surprise. It raised a problem, it seemed against nature, but it corresponded to something which was true and which no one had paid any attention to until now.

I took advantage of the opportunity to say that education wasn't just for children, and that in my opinion the school should be opened to adults, so that henceforth each one could add knowledge to his experience.

I don't think this pleased Tara, but he said nothing. The others, however, were enthusiastic. To crown everything, Tekao got up and delivered a highly emotional impromptu speech on knowledge, mother of the arts and industries. It was not original, but he believed what he was saying. He was applauded.

Only one person there had not responded. This was Mai. He was laughing and chattering with those abrupt movements and rather simian facial expressions which I knew so well. He protested that nobody needed to go to school. As far as children were concerned, he had no opinion. Some liked it, others did not. If you asked him, he had not noticed that it did them much good or much harm. They learned to count, that was always useful. But with adults, it was completely different. Until now they had lived without going to school, and they had not died of it. The real school was the sea, the mountains, the woods, and the real teachers were the waves, the fish, the animals, the trees. In saying this, he did not want to offend anyone and he thanked Tekao for his efforts, but if they asked him, he had never heard anything so stupid . . .

He also believed what he was saying and was sufficiently moved to be moving. But surprisingly enough, we seemed to have won their confidence. Anyway, what we were proposing was not very important. Besides, it might be fun.

When it was put to the vote, after Mai had been applauded, the council decided to organize a system of education for everyone by a vote of eight to two. Purea had reluctantly decided that he was obliged to support Mai.

I was very fond of Mai. Since our voyage to Tahiti, I had often gone fishing with him in the sea or in the lagoon. He had an independent and lively spirit and a real authority. In Vaiuru he ran everything without even seeming to be aware of it. Besides, he was funny. As we were leaving the council room I tried to convince him, but he shook his head and gave me a toothy grin. "You are free and I am free, no? You say yes, I say no, but we do not fight . . . So what does it matter?"

He seemed to be thinking something over, then shook his head. "These meetings, these councils, all this is very good and very honorable. But I am only a fisherman, you see. I live like my father and the father of my father. I am a savage—yes, I am. I just lost my last steel harpoon. Now they are all made of bone. And they work! That is Mai: a savage. The fish, the sea, the *pahis*—that I understand. Here there is much talk but what happens? Ha? No, I think I will not come again. I will send my little brother. He speaks well. And the honor will remain in the family. His name is Taiepo."

He fell silent. I thought he was angry, humiliated that he had not been able to convince the others of his point of view. Perhaps this was true, for the moment. But the truth was that the council meetings bored him. He had taken advantage of the opportunity to resign, feeling that a bad reason was better than no reason at all. He never did anything to interfere with our activities. Every time we needed him he helped us—affable, quick, clear-minded. I liked Mai very much. There aren't any more men of his kind today. Illiterates, when they are intelligent, have an originality and a freedom which I admire. I've done all I could to see that there would be no more illiterates, but in succeeding I have lost something.

The little brother, Taiepo, was a sleepy youth who could not be counted on. One day he would wait to hear Mai's opinion before making a decision, the next day he would make up his own mind and then when he returned home the whole village would force him to change it.

To launch our project, we decided to organize a big party to which the whole population would be invited. While the women cooked, the men, in one great burst of energy, built three large huts each capable of holding forty seated people and a meeting hall large enough to contain two hundred.

This took less than three weeks and was done with enthusiasm. During this time there were over five hundred people in Anatonu, the adjacent part of the shore was emptied of its fish, and all the pigs in the village were killed. Every evening people danced on the beach, and on Sunday after church there were games.

Everybody was very happy.

As for me, I had asked Bourdaroux if he would be kind enough to make us some blackboards, desks, and benches, and had suggested that he get the natives to help him. He agreed without making problems. Bourdaroux was proud of his skill, and as long as he was allowed to do things his own way, he was rather agreeable.

In no time he built a carpentry shop near his fortress and went to work. I went to see him after a few days because I was worried about the way he treated the natives.

Things never happen the way you think they will. Furthermore, they're not the way people say they are. People say I *made* the New World. As I was reading this over just now I got the impression, on the contrary, that I spent my time strolling around, enjoying a privileged status of which I was barely aware. Neither my impression nor the legends are completely true or false. If I hadn't been there, the world would be different. And although I didn't do very much, I was always worrying about everything, as much as I was capable of worrying. Governing is like steering a boat or riding a horse—it doesn't take much physical energy, except in case of a storm or accident, but it does require attention. For years, that was my whole job: paying attention.

Getting back to Bourdaroux, whereas I was prepared for the worst, everything was going beautifully. As always when a new activity was getting started on the island, a large number of volunteers had shown up. Bourdaroux had briskly dismissed the curious and the clumsy, and had kept with him only six men whose skill and diligence he had appraised. Now he was reigning over them, imperious and despotic, but competent and fair in the work. They seemed fascinated by him. When I arrived, he was explaining to two of his assistants how to cut into boards with a saw made of sheet iron an enormous tree trunk which was resting on a tripod taller than they were, while the other apprentices were squaring some smaller trees with adzes.

I don't like the idea of division of labor as it was practiced in the Old World in factories. What was gained in productivity was immediately lost in irritation, pressure, and boredom. Man is not made primarily to produce. Those who made the decisions in the factories were different from and unknown to those who carried them out. Their superiority was nowhere apparent.

On the other hand, where you have men carrying out a project together with their own hands, the superiority of certain ones is obvious. This obviousness allows, more easily than in other situations, the formation of undisputed hierarchies. Within these hierarchies there arises a complicity based on a love of work well done, and on admiration. Here, more than anywhere else, the boss is the one who does the best work. Bourdaroux deserved the admiration that his men had for him.

I got the idea of making him responsible for a kind of school for craftsmen. Besides woodwork, he knew how to work with steel, and was a competent mason.

He and his men worked for four whole months. When

everything was ready the members of the council, after noisily inspecting rooms and furniture whose purpose they only dimly understood, but whose solidity and workmanship they admired, went into all the villages and all the houses to announce the opening of the new school.

26

It was a spectacular success. The first day, a hundred and eighty-three students showed up. The next day, there were twice that number.

I must tell you that the opening of classes was really something. I hadn't been involved in it, and most of the councilors were too close to the population, too curious to see the new thing function to think about it. It was Tara who dreamed up the whole thing, with the assistance of Tekao.

Tekao was really a strange character. He served the community with intelligence, perseverence, and generosity. Every time I needed his help, he gave it to me without hesitating. He was as different from the natives of Raevavae as a Parisian of the Belle Epoque could have been from the poorest shepherd of Limoges, but he was of the same blood. He was like them and not like them at the same time. Similar enough to understand them; different enough to be able to explain them. To me, he was a sensitive and dependable friend, perhaps a little too discreet, a little too deferential, but one with whom I felt at home and whom on certain points I was inclined to believe before anyone else. But, from time to time he had a surprise in store for me. Sometimes he was more Raevavaean than the real natives of Raevavae.

One of those times was the opening of the school. He must have been excited. Besides, Tara put him up to it. I had gone to see how things were coming along, without suspecting anything. During the night the ground around the new buildings had been cleared and white sand had been scattered over such a large area that it looked as if the school had been built in the middle of a vast and blinding beach. To break up this expanse of white, shrubs had been planted in clumps, and in front of the buildings there were two very colorful decorative flowerbeds of the kind that used to embellish railway stations in the old days, one representing a clock whose hands pointed to eight o'clock, and the other a Gallic cock. The only thing that made it different from an Old World railway station was that the traditional begonias and pansies had been replaced by colored stones and pebbles.

Everywhere there were strange tricolored flags whose stiff folds and dull rattling sounds amazed me until I saw that they were made of tapa.

The crowd, for there really was a little crowd of people, including children, adults, and old men, was gathered in front of the school facing a platform surrounded by musicians. All this had that modest, natural, and touching quality that can be found in all small communities.

On the platform a native whom I did not recognize at first because he was wearing a white European-style suit, was making a speech. As I came closer I saw that it was Tara. His white trousers were impeccably creased, his jacket fell rather well, and a blue tie had been knotted at the collar of his shirt. His rather ample waist, for although the man was young, he was massive, was decorated with a wide tricolored sash. He was perspiring freely and he had that fixed, slightly pop-eyed expression that I've noticed so often in natives when they are making a speech and are completely absorbed by the inner spectacle of the passions that inflame them and the words they are about to pronounce, and forget their audience.

He was speaking with enthusiasm in Tahitian, and making appropriate gestures, and the spectators, entranced, greeted the end of each period with a nod of the head. What he was saying was not very original, but he obviously believed it. For him, the school represented power, authority, wealth, civilization. Because Raevavae was making a special effort on behalf of its school, because many of its inhabitants were coming to register at the school without distinction of age or sex, Raevavae was going to become, was already, the center of the world. Some day, through the school and through this hard-working population, Raevavae would grow, would spread, would cover the whole earth. The hour of Raevavae had come. The old customs were dead. Power was here for the taking. They must take it, for the honor of Raevavae.

Suddenly Tara started speaking in French, and his voice became affected, for he was concentrating on pronouncing all the words distinctly.

"Fellow citizens of Raevavae," he said, "a great future is in store for you. As I look at your faces, my brothers, I ask myself which of you will be the teachers of tomorrow, the scientists, the administrators. I do not know the answer, for I am not a prophet. But I know, just as truly as Mount Hiro is there, just as surely as the sea is there, just as certainly as the sun is there, that they are among you. Long live the school, long live science, long live the Republic!"

Although fifty years have passed since this speech was given, I think I have reported it accurately. This is partly because the subject was important to me. I cared about the school. But the main reason I remember it is that as he reached the climax, Tara lifted his arms in a dramatic and passionate gesture, and all of a sudden both sleeves of his jacket ripped open to the armpits.

There was a moment of stupor in which the orator stood paralyzed with his arms in the air, and then everyone applauded and laughed. It was a good speech and it ended with a good joke. Who could ask for more?

Tara almost lost his temper. I saw his face harden. He looked at the crowd in front of him. Then suddenly he burst out laughing, took off his jacket and trousers, tore them up, and threw the pieces into the air. He stood there in his shirt, with his blue tie and his black legs, laughing. Suddenly he raised his hand.

"It is an example," he said. "If we are going to dress like respectable people, we need something besides tapa. This suit

164

was made of tapa. Tapa represents the old ways. We must learn to make cotton and wool. We must study hard. It is up to you, my friends, to make real suits, well-made suits in which one can raise one's arms."

He laughed again and walked away calmly in his shirt, surrounded by a little group of admirers which had been following him around for some time.

At the door of the school, Tekao, now master of the proceedings, was jubilant.

When I came home I told Katherine, "The seeds are sown. There's nothing more to do but wait for the harvest. In six months they'll all know how to read. In a year, we can screen the students, and in two or three years, we'll begin to have interesting results. It will be slow, of course, but just think . . ."

I said it was going to be slow, but I didn't believe it. Already I could see real promotions, people who were useful, intelligent, transformed. I was happy. I believed that we had won, forever. The only thing that worried me a little was Tara. I liked his energy and his youth. I was glad to see him adopting ideas that were dear to me. But he was going too fast. He hadn't consulted the council before speaking. His white suit may have been a symbol of progress, or a way of calling attention to himself, of raising himself above the others. I promised myself I would keep an eye on him. But that was my only worry.

While I was talking Katherine was taking care of your father. She was giving him a bath or nursing him, I don't remember. We had named him Louis because I thought it was a good French name. Since the disappearance of my country, I was becoming patriotic.

Katherine finished what she was doing, took the baby in her arms, and asked, "Will they have the patience to wait? They're easily discouraged . . ."

I had just seen them. I was full of contentment and brotherhood. I laughed. "They're fighting to get in. Some will give up, no doubt, but how many? Five or ten percent? So what? What counts is the ones who remain . . ."

A month after the opening of the school, there remained

exactly ten percent of the original number. Thirty-six regular students.

With a few differences, Tekao had simply got his old class back. He was upset and cheerful at the same time.

"We went too fast," he said. "It was too good . . ."

I, on the other hand, was very discouraged. And annoyed. I felt ridiculous, helpless. My hopes had been disappointed. Above all my feelings were hurt, do you understand?

I felt Tekao and Noémie had gone about it wrong. The second assistant, that boy from Matotea whom we had promised glory, had gone back home laughing contemptuously. In the new unused classrooms, the old women of Anatonu gathered in the afternoons to gossip in the shade. It was a total disaster.

Listening to no one, not even Katherine, I decided to ride all around the island, alone, to win back my people. Everywhere I went people listened to me politely and when I became insistent, they smiled. Finally, they burst out laughing. School was no fun. You had to sit there and do nothing but listen, listen, listen. It was long and hard, too. A man told me that in two days they had learned only four letters, he had forgotten which ones. But he had seen real books. In books, there were as many letters as fish in the sea. So how many days would it take to learn them all? And besides, after all, what was the use of it?

If I had forced the issue, things would have turned out badly. I wasn't crazy enough to persist openly. But I was upset. In politics, one should never become upset. If something doesn't work, you have to try to find out why and eliminate the principal obstacles. A failure should always be a lesson. It should never hurt you personally, profoundly, even if you believed with all your heart in what you were proposing. Remember that.

I didn't know it yet. So I wanted to win immediately, without waiting for things to cool down. That was it—I was no longer thinking about my project, I had almost forgotten it, I wanted victory. This was childish and dangerous.

I looked everywhere, in all directions, like a madman. I found an idea. You'll see what it was.

Since the natives don't want to improve themselves, I

thought, the least they can do is multiply. One can't, or perhaps one can't, make a world with seven hundred and fifty people. But with fifteen hundred? With two thousand? I just told you I was crazy.

So I went to see Dubois, and asked him what should be done. He gave me a precise answer. The only workable procedure was to lower infantile mortality by taking appropriate measures. He gave me a lecture on child care and provided me with a list of things that should be done for newborn babies. But throughout our conversation I felt that he was adopting a reserved, neutral attitude toward me, and was confining himself to the role of the expert who is consulted and who replies.

I wasn't at home with all this business of boiled water and sterilized compresses. I felt he was making a fool of me.

Since my nerves were already raw, this threw me into a rage. I looked at him.

"You don't like me," I said.

Dubois smiled. "But of course, I like you very much."

"But you don't approve of me . . ."

He shrugged slightly. "I didn't say that."

"Well, you're not against hygiene, are you?"

He looked at me with that blank expression that made you feel like an idiot. "Don't get excited," he said. "Don't be disagreeable. What I think of you is not important. I'm just one man. But . . . I don't dislike you. And I'm not against hygiene. Certainly, too many babies die . . . but how long have we been in Raevavae, I mean we Europeans? A hundred, a hundred and twenty years? And what have we brought? Peace, measles, and whooping cough. These two diseases have killed more people than the wars did. Rather negative, when you add it up. And aside from that? This island is a little society. It's found an equilibrium. Don't force it too much, even for its own good."

"But see here," I said, angry, "it was you who wanted to offer it a new world."

He looked inscrutable. "Yes, I did say that it was necessary. I didn't say that it should be done. In surgery there are often cases of this kind. An operation is necessary, but to perform it would be an act of barbarism. Sometimes it's better to let the patient die . . . As time passes, it gets harder for me to intervene. I even wonder if I wouldn't do better simply to keep silent."

He wasn't really responding to my questions, or my anxiety. I suppose he was doing it deliberately. Dubois had a way of carrying on a conversation that was all his own. He was very conscious of privacy, his own as well as other people's. Furthermore, his life had not been an easy one. Perhaps this explains why his ideas about the simplest things so often had a slant that was abstract, general, almost philosophical.

I don't have a bad character. That's how it is, it's a matter of temperament. Things and people interest me so much that I forget myself easily. I mean, I forget the attitudes, the preconceived ideas that I may have had before the fact. That day, the simple act of talking with Dubois calmed me a little. I got a new idea.

"I'd like your help," I said suddenly. "I'd like you to train one or two nurses. Haven't you ever come across anyone in the population . . . ?"

Dubois' expression changed immediately. To interest him, all you had to do was guess what was on his mind.

"One or two nurses, one of whom could become a doctor, if necessary? It's an idea that could solve . . . yes, it's an idea. I should have thought of it myself. I must have thought of it myself. Because I know someone, but . . ."

"Tell me . . ."

"Katherine, your wife."

I didn't like the idea. I talked about Louis, about the other children who would come. Dubois looked at me silently. Finally I said, "I'll speak to her about it. It's not up to me to decide."

Then I left, taking my notes.

As soon as I got home I reported our conversation to Katherine. I ended by saying, "Of course, there's no question of your doing it."

"Why not?"

When she felt strongly about something Katherine didn't show it, but her accent became more pronounced. I noticed this, and it added to my state of nervous irritation.

"Why not? Because it's impossible, that's why. You have your hands full with the baby, the house, everything . . . And besides, Dubois is nice, but . . . Anyway, you're afraid of the natives. How could you take care of them?"

"I'm not afraid of the natives any more," said Katherine in a metallic voice. "I haven't been afraid of them since we were married. You know that very well. As for the other problems, I can work them out. Odile will take Louis. There's nothing to do here. Hina is better at running the house than I am. All I have to do is put flowers in vases . . ."

I was angry. She took my hand and smiled. "Sit down. Why are men such babies? You're not jealous of Dubois, are you?"

I looked at her blankly. "Of course not. That's ridiculous."

She gave a little laugh. "With a haircut and a new suit, he'd be . . . But if you're not jealous of him, is it me you're jealous of? Do you want to be the only important person in the family?"

I shrugged. She laughed again. "This is serious, you know. I'm being silly, but it's your fault, too. You want to change Raevavae. Don't I have the right to help you? I think I'd make a good nurse. I've had a very good education. I'm capable of learning difficult things when I want to. And I want to do this work."

"But it's ridiculous. The men will never let you take care of them."

"Then I'll take care of the women and children. I'll teach classes in child care . . ."

She was making gentle fun of me, but I knew her. She was serious. I gave up. "Nothing is easy," I said, discouraged.

She smiled. "No, but I want to help you. I want to be useful. Besides . . ."

She came over to me. ". . . I'm a good wife, aren't I? I cook you French food, I make love, I give you a beautiful baby, I entertain your friends . . ."

"Yes," I said, "you're a good wife."

"Then let me feel useful. I have the right."

That was always her last word. When she felt she had the right to demand something, she didn't give up. She often confused right and honor. I was no longer really sure that I was right, I only knew I wasn't happy. The very next day she went to see Dubois.

Dubois was a strange man. The respect I had for him was based partly on the difference in our ages, but that wasn't all. He intrigued me. I got to know him very well, by piecing together fragments that he revealed. I'm the only person who reconstructed the story of his life. Until now I haven't talked about it to anyone. People say he was a hero. Toutepo says he was the first saint of our New World. It's not necessarily untrue. But you'll see what goes into the makings of a saint.

Dubois was the only son of a little Protestant doctor from Deux-Sèvres. Obedient and disobedient at the same time, he became a doctor himself, but in the navy. He served in the first world war, then in Indochina, then in Algeria. Soldier and doctor. Killer and healer. As a child, he had wanted to be both a country doctor and a sea captain.

I don't know why he never married.

For a long time he led the comfortable and Bohemian life of an unmarried officer and then suddenly, at the end of the Algerian war, he resigned his commission for no apparent reason.

The truth was that his life was already over. Something had happened in Indochina which you might say he never survived.

It's a simple story, almost commonplace. The navy had sent in a number of platoons which were operating in the rice paddies and on the beaches, at the mouths of rivers. These troops were very isolated, living off the land like natives, and employing native guides.

One day, Dubois joined one of these groups. Out of curiosity, he told me. He wanted to see the war from somewhere besides Hanoi or the deck of a ship. The platoon in question had some sick and wounded men. Dubois volunteered to take care of them. His assignment was supposed to last forty-eight hours. But a Viet offensive developed and the platoon took a severe beating and lost all contact with the outside world. Dubois stayed with the group for three weeks.

It's a commonplace story, but a revolting one. I don't enjoy remembering it any more than Dubois enjoyed telling it to me. I didn't question him directly, but I encouraged him to talk. I was expecting something from him, I don't know what. I was patient. In the course of a lifetime, if we're lucky—there are people who live to be a hundred without discovering anything— we learn from other people two or three things that are really important, two or three things that are such that after learning them, we are no longer the same. But these things we keep to ourselves. Dubois had kept his story to himself for half a lifetime. At any rate, he and his platoon wandered for three weeks in the rice paddies, enduring ambushes, mosquitoes, leeches, mud, and heat. The men rested in the daytime and marched at night. The leader of the platoon was killed; they had to leave him unburied. The enemy was very close, but elusive. They fired at each other blindly, through clusters of reeds.

One night a sailor who was marching at the back of the column was captured. Dubois' companions didn't notice it at first. Then they heard screams. It was the youngest. They were torturing him, hoping his screams would draw the French into an ambush. But the sailors were well seasoned, and under the leadership of an officer who knew the Viets. They had the courage to run away.

But the enemy followed them. And the boy was still screaming. It wasn't until almost dawn that he gave a last cry, then was silent. When the sun rose his comrades found his body, which had been carefully displayed in a place where they couldn't fail to see it. They held out for a few more days, until the Legion came to relieve them. They even asked to participate in the operation that followed.

I told you that there were some natives with them who served as scouts. Among those was a certain Bo, whom everyone liked because he was always gay, always in good spirits.

The clean-up operation was a success. In this large district there were barely a hundred Viets. They were almost all killed. The army took several prisoners. And Bo got his prisoner, too.

With a few compatriots, he took him into the woods. Dubois, who was wandering around, for the battle was over, happened upon them. They had stripped the Viet, and tied him to a tree, and with their knives they were very carefully flaying him alive.

The man was moaning softly, in a flutelike voice.

Dubois was a soldier and a doctor. He knew what could be extracted from the human body in terms of horror. He wasn't even very surprised, for he knew that such things existed.

But he saw the eyes of the condemned man. Thirty years later, he could still see them as he described them to me: They were, he told me, wide open, still very much alive, and extraordinarily lucid. The man had gone beyond despair, exhaustion, pain. He was watching his tormentors, following them, understanding them, becoming them. Then suddenly his attention shifted and it was himself that he contemplated, through this unbearable horror which he knew that he would soon no longer be able to endure.

Dubois waited for the end. Until the end, he suffered the gaze of this man looking at his fellow men. He knew that there was nothing to be done. Anyway, it was not in his nature to act.

But he was scarred for life.

He waited a few more years, then sent in his resignation without giving any reason. He had vague intentions of setting up a practice in La Rochelle or Paris, but he didn't even return to France. Almost by accident—but there are accidents that make perfect sense—he went to Israel, then on to India, and slowly made his way to Tahiti. Somehow he landed on Raevavae, and liked it. Nothing mattered anymore.

He was a good man, but without force, brought up according to the ideas of another century. He was temperamentally made to live in a secure country, with boundaries, a currency, a victorious army, and a religion. Even as an atheist, even as an anarchist, he would have enjoyed this religion, this army. Since he did not have them, he enjoyed nothing. He drifted.

And then, in the eyes of a dying man, he thought he deciphered the message that would give a meaning to his life. He thought he read there that the world was falling apart, finished, done for.

A man of a different temperament would have smashed Bo's head in, or if he hadn't been able to do that, would have decided that the war he was taking part in was rotten, or even that all Orientals were savages. Dubois simply accepted the end of the world.

At the same time, and perhaps because of his Protestant upbringing—you never really know a man who's that private—he retained a kind of hope, based on human nature. If man was capable of the worst, he reasoned, he was also capable of the best. The rottenness of the world did not damn the creation. If he had been Catholic, Dubois might have entered a monastery. Alone with himself, he settled in Raevavae and led the life of a monk.

He believed that anything was possible on the level of the individual. One day he told me that he would willingly have become someone else. I didn't understand what he meant. In fact, he was actually trying to become someone else. This refined and comfort-loving old bachelor wanted to turn himself into a doctor at the service of the community. But there weren't many sick people in Raevavae. To fill up his spare time, and because in spite of everything, one doesn't change, he was constantly thinking about things, looking for causes, tracking down explanations.

Not that this was of much help to him. Solitary reflection, when it's really solitary, when it lacks the support of faith or of some creative work, always ends by lapsing into banality.

Dubois realized this. To keep from leading a completely empty existence, he had invented a list of duties. His life was regulated by a program that allowed him no freedom. Everything in it was prearranged, measured. There was an hour for walking and an hour for painting, a day for the laundry and a day for gardening, a month for fishing and a month for hunting. It was rather stupid, but I understand it. Dubois wanted not to belong to himself. He was managing his own personality on behalf of someone else, who was also him, and this duality was his drama.

All this explains why it took a long time and was difficult

173

for him and Katherine to agree on a working arrangement and a time schedule, but that once it had been arrived at, everything worked perfectly.

27

WITH ME, IT was different. I was fixated on this question of infant mortality, because I thought it would be easy to regulate, and because I wanted to believe it was important.

In fact, it wasn't that vital, and it caused a lot of trouble.

Every year the seven hundred and forty inhabitants of Raevavae gave birth to between thirty and forty children. Two percent of these, that is, less than one individual, died before reaching the age of one year.

In Europe the percentage was only six per thousand. My ambition was to arrive at the same result. But to save this annual child, I found that I had to attack the entire population of Raevavae.

For after all, what happened? Men and women, thrown together on a little lost island, knew each other from infancy like people who live in the same village, played without constraint in a landscape made for love. As children, they made the gestures of love to imitate the adults, and one fine day they found to their delight that they no longer had to imitate and could operate on their own. They kept on playing but they also had children.

These children were born anywhere, alone in the bush, or in the village, surrounded by a large audience. As soon as they were born they were washed in the sea or in a stream, wrapped in dirty rags, and fed whatever was there. If they survived the first year, they began to walk, talk, and swim, and took their independence. They grew cheerfully, became strong, imitated the gestures of love, made love, and had children of their own. It was a whole civilization.

Based on what Dubois had taught me, I was now determined that mothers be examined at least every three months during pregnancy, that delivery take place in the presence of the doctor, and if possible in a clinic, and that the newborn child receive the proper treatment and nourishment.

It wasn't too much to ask. But Polynesian women, although not shy, feel that letting anyone see their pudenda is the most disgraceful act of indecency in the world; and the local midwives, who were also the wisest and most experienced women in the villages, had their own ideas about what treatment should be given to women in childbirth; and coconut milk and raw fish were, all things considered, easier to find and cleaner than milk from scrawny cows that was squeezed into an old tin can with dirty hands; but above all, in order for children to be supervised, there has to be a family.

It was obvious. If it hadn't become a personal issue with me, I would have realized it immediately. But at the time I believed that with power, you can do anything. I think that being elected mayor had made me crazy. I had tried to force the school on them, and they had refused. I was having my revenge. It had become a fixed idea. You can't imagine how much trouble I made for myself. I never laughed anymore.

The natives found me bizarre, but they continued to treat me with courtesy and good will. When I started telling them about my plans they listened pleasantly, because they thought I was crazy. Then they went about their business without comment.

Obviously, I should have given up. Instead, I went and got from the stock of Simon the catechist, which had been confiscated by the administration, a case full of hideous but brightly colored plastic flowers, and I promised two of these immortal flowers to every pregnant woman who would go and be examined by Dubois.

At last, a young girl escorted by three fat old women decided to risk the examination. In fact, she didn't know what she was exposing herself to.

When Dubois had explained it to her she changed color, ran out of the house, and began screaming, while the fat old women hurled insults at the doctor.

The story went all around the island. People were offended,

in spite of my explanations. For two months, until it was forgotten, the sick stopped coming to Dubois, who never complained to me, however.

In a subtle way, something had gotten out of balance in Raevavae through my doing. The natives' liberalism, and perhaps their indifference, prevented it from becoming serious, but Peyrole, who kept track of everything that went on on the island, insisted on telling me, with unpleasant coldness, his opinion of my effort.

By a strange swing of the pendulum, Bourdaroux came to see me the next day to congratulate me. This man, who scorned progress when it allowed other people to interfere in his life, suddenly declared himself a modernist, since the natives were on the side of tradition.

His visit and his advances were just as disagreeable to me as Peyrole's coldness. I was alone. Katherine said nothing. Leguen looked at me sadly without daring to approach, and Mai, Tapoua, and all those who called themselves my friends changed the subject skillfully whenever I tried to talk about the matter.

I won't say that I was unhappy, that would be too strong a word. But I felt extremely uncomfortable. I was young. I loved the people, and at the same time I looked down on them a little. I thought I knew what was good for them, and their resistance astonished me.

Today I still look down on them, just as I look down on myself. As far as I can see, this is the only way to feel. But I also respect them. Crazy or not, they're free. They still have the right to refuse, even stupidly. Anyway, they're more ignorant and fearful than animals.

While I was meditating on their horror of hygiene, Tekao came to bring me some good news. Obsessed by my fantasies and anxieties, I had forgotten about the school. Well, it now had about sixty regular students. The inhabitants of Anatonu, who were closer, had started the movement. Then the other villages, not wanting the work they had put into constructing the buildings to be wasted, began to compel their children to attend classes.

176

Meanwhile, Noémie had launched a little publicity campaign of her own in a style quite different from mine. A poor *vahiné* without a man and without beauty, every afternoon she went from house to house and read the Bible. The natives were very much impressed by these readings, and listened to them with admiration. Noémie took advantage of the opportunity to offer each family a copy bound in black paper which she took from the supply at the mission, explaining how nice it would be if a member of the family could read it aloud.

This stratagem was beginning to bear fruit. People were trickling back to school one by one, not to learn to read, but to learn to read the Bible, which was different.

Thus I discovered that I could be both right and wrong at the same time. The school was filling up, Bourdaroux still had his apprentices, and one morning Katherine informed me that Dubois, who had been training her on a regular basis since the day he had accepted the idea, had recruited two young students, one of whom, according to my wife, was very intelligent.

I was happy and humiliated at the same time. What I had wanted was under way, even if, as I estimated, it would take a hundred years at the present rate to teach the whole island to read. But it was being done without me, almost against me. For years my father had told me I was stupid. Perhaps he was right.

This sudden modesty brought me back to myself. I believe, perhaps mistakenly, that grace, that is, the ability to do things easily and to get along with people, is bestowed by maternal love. Motherless children like me must learn everything themselves, by feeling their way. I've been lazy, no doubt, but I've had so many things on my mind. I was perpetually having to examine myself, clarify my thoughts, reassemble the pieces of myself. In the old days, this hadn't been hard for me. My hatred for my father, which had kept me alive until the age of twenty, was a simple emotion and, all things considered, convenient. Women had occupied me without absorbing me. True, I had applied myself to learning equitation, but that had never been anything but a pleasure.

But for six months I had forgotten myself. I had lived only

for what I was doing. Suddenly I gave it all up and went back to my wife, my forgotten records, my horses, Tapoua, and nature. It was at this time that my daughter Anne was conceived.

I took long walks around the island, went fishing with Mai, who welcomed me with a laugh, and discovered my son, to whom I had paid no attention until then.

Soon I was cured. I was able to see myself clearly and I laughed with all my heart.

I organized a big boar hunt, and we had a feast on the beach which coincided with the birth of Leguen's daughter, a little skinned cat, very brown, but with her father's eyes, whom he insisted on naming Pierrette, after me.

Once again I had plenty of friends, and the island, happy to find itself in harmony again, settled back into a peaceful existence. After three years, I was reelected mayor unanimously.

Secretly, however, and without really admitting it to myself, I continued to keep my eyes open, obstinately searching for some way to get my companions moving.

28

My CONCERN WAS real, tangible. It rested not so much on a more or less prophetic vision of the future, as very solidly on a profound part of myself that wanted to do something, anything, and was sustained and encouraged by my natural curiosity.

But once again it was not on me that the solution depended. When I think back on my life I am always amazed to see how seldom I created circumstances and how often I took advantage of existing ones.

I should also say that what was put into operation before my eyes was very subtle as well as fortuitous.

One Sunday morning while Katherine was at church with your father and I was lazing about the house, an old man leaped over my hedge like a wild boar and rushed up to me, panting.

He was so out of breath and excited that at first I couldn't understand a word he was saying. I tried to calm him down, but whenever I succeeded in doing this for a few seconds, as soon as I began to question him he immediately went back to stammering and rolling his eyes. I finally made out that he was from Vaiuru, and that Mai was his nephew.

That morning at dawn he had set off by himself in a canoe instead of going to church. He should have gone, of course, but he had started very early, and was sure he would be back in time. Well, that's what he said, but maybe he didn't feel like going to church. He was old, and the walk tired him. Anyway, he had no intention of offending God. He only wanted to catch a few crayfish in the lagoon and take a look at some coconut palms that had been planted on various small islands of the outer reef.

So he had fished a little at dawn, then, taking his time, he had visited three of those small islands, the ones known as Mano, Maha, and Vaiamanu Motus. He had intended to go east as far as the big motu, the one that had the largest plantation, but in the meantime the sun had become very strong. So he had stopped on Vaiamanu to eat a bite and rest. He had taken a nap in the shade, then had decided to be on his way. It was at this precise moment that he had seen, right across the water, on the beach of Araoo Motu, a fleet of canoes lined up side by side on the sand.

They were big canoes—he made a sweeping gesture—big enough for forty men at least, with prows such as had never been seen in Raevavae, bows like this, sides like that, in short, strange canoes.

The old man had watched for quite a while without seeing anyone, but he had counted the canoes. There were, he told me, holding up his fingers, seven—no, eight. That was something, no?

When he had finished counting, he had returned to his boat and paddled very quietly west, being very careful to remain in the shadow of the small islands he passed. When he arrived opposite Yaiuru, he had landed and then had run all the way across the island without stopping or talking to anyone, to tell me.

Now that I knew, I would go to the church right away, talk to Officer Peyrole, talk to the men, ring the bell, do all these things, wouldn't I?

As a reaction to his excitement, no doubt, I sat there like marble. The news he was bringing me was so extraordinary that I scarcely believed it. The natives are observant and intelligent, but their world is peopled with phantoms and invisible things which they have nevertheless seen. My informant was old and I wasn't sure who he was. He could have been dreaming, he could have been mad, or he could simply have mistaken his desires for realities.

Calmly I dressed, took little Anne, who had just been born, to Tapoua's mother-in-law, who was very fat and had ulcers on her legs and never went anywhere, came back, wrote a note to Katherine, and saddled Baucis.

The little old man followed me everywhere, grumbling and trying to make me hurry, but I didn't feel like it. When I was finally ready I mounted Baucis and turned to him. "Show me the way."

He looked at me, dumbfounded and unhappy. I understood slightly. All the time he was running to get me he must have told himself what important news he was carrying, he must have imagined a big meeting, noise, excitement, a little glory of some kind. Instead he was trotting beside my little mare, holding a leather strap to steady himself, and I wasn't even talking to him. He got back at me by incessantly muttering pessimistic predictions and harsh evaluations of the intelligence of *poupas*.

It took us a little under two hours to cross the island. The old man had left his boat under a clump of mangroves. Before I got into the boat, I looked at the chain of motus located about two miles in front of me. I saw nothing but a thick dark-green bar lying on a white line. Not a boat, not a puff of smoke, not a movement. The rays of the sun fell straight down through a grey mist, the sea was like molten tin, and the reflection was blinding.

I jumped into the canoe. My guide pushed it into the water and then climbed in himself and sat down behind me. It was a very small skiff designed for one person, and my weight caused the sides to sink almost level with the sea. There was only one paddle. There was nothing to do but sit back and relax.

Almost immediately we headed due east, and soon I recognized Motu Araoo on my right. I turned to my guide, who pulled in his head, hunched his shoulders, and made a toothless grimace, like a turtle.

"The big rock," he said.

I understood that he was referring to Motu Nuipapahiti, located immediately to the east of Araoo. It was an enormous mass of limestone, jagged as a sponge, where the sea birds came to lay their eggs in great numbers. From its summit one had a view of all the surrounding landscape.

I gave a nod of agreement, and the little canoe turned thirty degrees and pointed its nose toward its new objective.

The man paddled quickly, but gracefully. His idea was a good one. I began to think that he was neither crazy nor too old, and turned around again to get a better look at him.

As soon as he saw my look he guessed that I was now convinced and gave a big, silent smile, full of triumph and malice.

I smiled back and returned to examining the motus that were coming into view. If the man was right, I may have been wrong to come alone without informing anyone. Between two islands, on this smooth grey water, we floated in a universe without consistency or color, where the sun was drawing off a thick mist. I thought that if the boat overturned and we fell into the sea there would be no sound, no ripple. The water would divide, we would disappear, and a moment afterward there would be no trace of us anywhere.

At last we landed on the northern face of Nuipapahiti. While my guide was tying up his boat, I climbed up as if on a ladder, by placing my hands and feet in cavities full of droppings and feathers, until I reached the summit.

Fortunately it wasn't the nesting season, and only a few birds rose in front of me, crying.

When I had reached the crest I lay down and waited, flat on my face on the burning rock, as much to catch my breath as to give my companion time to join me. Then, slowly, I looked up.

Lying above the narrow arm of sea that flashed below me, mottled with ripples, was Motu Araoo. And drawn up on the sand, just as the old man had said, were the canoes. In front of them two men were swimming between the breakers, and many others were lying here and there on the edge of a grove of palm trees, as if they had been flung there. They looked dead or exhausted. The distance and the shadows cast on the ground by the trees made it impossible to count them. I was sorry I hadn't brought my binoculars. The fact was that I hadn't taken this thing seriously.

I lay there motionless for a moment, trying to accumulate as many details as possible. The strangers looked to me taller, thinner, but just as dark-skinned as the people of Raevavae. Nowhere did I see modern weapons or make out the flash of metal. It seemed to me that some of them had bows, lances, and clubs lying next to them, but I couldn't have sworn to it.

I was amazed. Suddenly, everything we thought we had figured out about the world was becoming false. Without taking my eyes off our invaders, I leaned toward the old man. "Where are they from?"

He raised himself up a little and his dry hand cut off my field of vision. "Not from here, not from there," he answered promptly, indicating first the direction of Tahiti, then that of the Gambiers. "Perhaps from there . . ."—he pointed to the west, where the Cook Archipelago was—". . . or way down there, from the Great Island."

Just then a few men emerged from the trees carrying coconuts. The ones who were lying down got up lazily and joined them. In contrast to this movement, I noticed that guards had been posted in various places.

I lay there for another moment watching, then I slid over the rock covered with guano. "Come on," I said to my guide, "we're going back."

Our return trip was without incident. As soon as we reached the island, to save time I made the old man get behind me on Baucis, much to her indignation.

We went directly to the Navy House. The hour for lunch had long since passed. The natives were sprawled in the shade of their huts, talking softly and laughing from time to time. Peyrole was taking a siesta. I asked his wife to go and get him.

He appeared bare-chested, barefoot, his eyes swollen, his hair disheveled, with a sour expression. Odile Peyrole put the coffee on to heat.

I made my report almost in one breath. Then we went over every detail, one by one, like peasants. This annoyed and pleased me at the same time. These repetitions were as childish as they were soothing. At last Peyrole pulled himself together. "Who are these men?" he said. "Where do they come from? What do they want? These are the questions. And they will give us the answers. But we must interrogate them."

He rose heavily and left without waiting for my response. As he went through the door, he sighed, "I'll go and get dressed."

We waited in silence; a fly buzzed in the shade. It is at moments like this that peace can truly be savored. Odile Peyrole silently refilled our coffee cups, gliding around in some strange sandals that she had made herself. My old guide sat hunched in his chair, immobile. Only his eyes moved, to follow the flight of the fly, or to pass from one idea to another. I was hungry. I asked for a piece of bread.

"What, you haven't had lunch?" Odile demanded, remorseful.

She ran and got some cold meat and fruit which I ate slowly, resting my elbows on an oilcloth tablecloth which had once been flowered, but which had become completely white in the middle and was beginning to peel. The old man had silently refused to join me. Odile was standing opposite me pressing on the table with her fingertips.

"After all," she said, "just because these men are there it's not necessarily bad. At least it proves that we're not alone . . ."

I nodded silently. She was about to add something when from the back of the house a child began to cry.

"Excuse me," she said.

Almost immediately Peyrole reappeared. He had put on a regulation uniform, probably the last one he had left, was wearing his kepi, and had fastened his revolver to his belt. He was carrying a pair of binoculars and a package.

"We'll take the jeep as far as Vaiuru. Mai and his relatives will come with us in the canoe. Run and tell Leguen and Tapoua. I'll pick you up in a few minutes. I'm putting a few guns in the car, just in case . . ."

He met us at Leguen's house. The jeep was loaded with cases of weapons. We sat on top of them.

"Show your strength so you won't have to use it," said Peyrole, as if excusing himself.

In Vaiuru everything was still asleep. The dusty white alleyways between the huts were empty. Mai wasn't home. We finally found him in his little house on the hill, in bed with an adolescent girl who could have been his daughter. He saw our looks and smiled, very proud of himself.

Peyrole scowled and explained to him the reasons for our visit. Mai understood at once.

"You want many men, yes, and many boats? With guns, yes?"

"Yes," said Peyrole, "but we're not going to make war. Those people there may be like you and me. They may have been driven here by the wind . . ."

"With eight *pahis* . . .?" Mai laughed. "That would be a funny wind. And besides, those are war *pahis,* not fishing *pahis.*"

Peyrole shook his head like an honest peasant. "We're not going to make war. We're going to see them, to talk to them. After that, we'll decide."

"Yes," said Mai, "we'll decide to kill them."

Peyrole raised his hand, but did not reply.

It took a while to prepare for the expedition. They went and got some fishermen from Matotea and Rairua, which slowed things down even more. While we were waiting almost everyone on the island, drawn by the rumor, poured into Vaiuru. We had to prevent them from shouting, making fires, showing themselves too much. We were visible from Motu Araoo.

By the time everything was finally ready, dusk was falling. Peyrole decided to post watches on Nuipapahiti, send home all the people who were standing around doing nothing, and postpone the expedition until the next day.

184

The people we had chased away went into the bush on the outskirts of the village, and all night long the air was thick with their incessant talking.

We slept on the beach. At dawn, when a pale grey light was barely showing in the east and the sea was still almost black, we embarked. There were close to a hundred and fifty men in twenty canoes. I had sent word to Katherine, so she wouldn't be worried, and to Dubois, asking him to join us. Bourdaroux, who had been informed by I don't know who, arrived in Vaiuru an hour before our departure, furious because we hadn't sent for him. Peyrole handed him a gun, with firm instructions not to use it. There was nothing else he could do, for Leguen, Tapoua, Mai, Purea, Tara, and Roua, as well as myself, were already armed.

Working swiftly but silently, the paddlers took us away. I was sitting in the front of one canoe with my gun between my knees. I was cold, and I wondered what was going to happen. At one point I turned around and looked at my companions. They were all grinning broadly and almost trembling with excitement. They were going hunting, to a party—in a word, to war.

When we arrived alongside Motu Araoo, our fleet divided into three parts. One group went back north to wait alongside Nuipapahiti. The next group glided south, in the shadow of Vaiamanu. The third group, my group, hove to for a moment, facing the beach, then slowly made for the small island.

Peyrole, who obviously believed in timed movements, had asked me not to land before a certain hour. I had quite a time getting my men to obey me. Since we weren't talking out loud, so as not to raise the alarm, I had to express myself in gestures. I made some that were so vigorous, in my efforts to keep the canoes lined up together, that I almost fell in the water. In the end, I pointed my gun at an oarsman who was in too much of a hurry. If he hadn't obeyed me, I would have fired.

At times like that you don't think about firing, you don't believe you're going to fire. All you want to do is solve a problem quickly. It's stupid.

When I finally gave my men the go-ahead, they jumped out and with a single movement carried their heavy boats onto dry land. Many were armed with lances, bows, or clubs. All were laughing. I motioned to Leguen, who was with me, and we led the party into the woods.

The palm trees weren't very dense, but under their leaves the thick bourrao bushes made walking difficult. In spite of our efforts, we made a great deal of noise.

Nevertheless, we heard the others arrive. We caught a glimpse of them from approximately the middle of the island. They must have seen us at the same moment. Everything became quiet. We didn't move. Neither did they. This lasted two or three minutes. A very long time.

And then we again heard the sound of twigs snapping. The others were drawing back. In the same movement, my men were carried forward. I had to run to remain at the head. I had decided to do everything I could to prevent a battle breaking out through our fault. If the others made the first move, though, I wouldn't have minded.

Suddenly we smelled salt air through the trees, and then we saw the sea. We had crossed the island.

Our visitors were gathered near their canoes. Out to sea, among the breakers, part of our fleet was cruising. To the right, Peyrole was arriving with his group, walking along the shoreline. To the left, another group led by Mai were already in position and were chattering in very loud voices, with that dangerous intoxication I had seen before.

When we left the woods, I stopped my men. Peyrole saw me and stopped his.

In the middle of the semicircle we formed facing the sea, the strangers were waiting for us with weapons in their hands. But they were pretending to talk among themselves and not to see us. This, too, I had seen before.

I remember that I sighed. I felt heavy, incredibly tired. It only lasted for a moment. Overwhelming things become light as soon as they are done. I threw my gun to a native standing next to me.

"Don't fire. Wait for me here."

Then, empty-handed, I walked forward. Peyrole did the

same. We walked toward each other, as if we were going to fight.

The spot we were heading for was the one where the largest number of strangers were gathered.

We covered about fifty yards this way, while nobody moved or even seemed to see us. Then Peyrole stopped, and I did the same.

He raised his hand. "Does one of you speak French?"

Heavily, slowly, as if they had been awakened from sleep, the intruders looked at him. After a moment, Peyrole repeated his question in Tahitian.

There was a movement, like a little ripple, among the strangers, but no reply. So then I questioned them in English. All the heads turned toward me, and a tall native with close-cropped hair and filed-down teeth said in English, smiling arrogantly, "Yes, sir, I do."

He was about to add something when his neighbor stepped in front of him as if to conceal him from our eyes. I called Peyrole. Together we walked toward the men. When we were three yards from them I sat down, as I always did when I wanted to talk seriously with natives, and Peyrole did the same. After a moment's hesitation, a dozen strangers squatted down opposite us.

I spoke English very badly. I still do. I know it only from the movies and from conversations in bars. Katherine often addressed me in that language, for pleasure and to teach it to me, but out of laziness I would answer her in French. Yes, I understand it rather well, but I speak it badly. I needed help. Dubois had come with Peyrole's group. He was waiting with his men. I called him. Then, to balance things, I motioned to Mai to join us. He came forward immediately, in a jovial mood, leaping about in that way of his. He kept his gun pressed to his heart.

This worried me for a moment, but nothing happened.

For a moment we simply looked at each other in silence. Our visitors were handsome men, almost black-skinned, taller than the people of Raevavae, slimmer, but just as muscular. Some of them wore fragments of European clothing. Most of

187

them had on only loincloths of raffia. All were heavily armed with native weapons. Not one, as far as I could see, had a gun or a pistol.

"Who is the leader here?" I asked in English.

They looked at each other for a split second, and then one of them raised his finger discreetly. I was familiar with those silent, almost instantaneous conversations in which, in moments of danger, the natives excel. I wasn't taken in. The one who had called attention to himself had done so at someone else's command and was of no importance. However, I addressed myself to him.

I told him that he and his companions were welcome to Raevavae, which was a French territory, and that Peyrole, who represented the military authority, and myself, in the name of the civilian government, were happy to greet them.

But we were surprised to see that, contrary to good custom and good manners, they had landed secretly on a motu that did not belong to them, without bothering to make their presence known to the inhabitants of the village directly across from them on the shore of our island.

We were sure that only pressing reasons had led them to act with so little consideration, and we would be very happy to learn what those reasons were.

I made an effort to speak slowly and as eloquently as possible, with gestures. All natives are sensitive to gestures.

The men facing me understood me. Although at first they did not move a muscle, gradually they began to nod their heads every time I came to the end of a sentence. Some of them even made a few exclamations. When I had finished, they conferred together rapidly. Then one of them, who was neither the one who had first spoken to me nor the one who had pretended to be the leader, answered me in rather good English.

They came from one of the Fiji islands whose name I have forgotten. Or is it because they didn't mention it by name? We could have found out later, but . . . In any case, on this island, a few years before, there had been a great misfortune—a great cyclone, with very bad green waves, which had destroyed a large part of their island. The Europeans and their servants had been killed by the waves, by the waves alone. The only ones who survived were those wise men who, in order to follow the old customs, had long ago moved away and built their villages in the mountains. For these men the fear had been great, but they had not suffered. After the cyclone some of them had gone down to the shore and had found the houses full of dead people and good things. Some had tried to take advantage of this, but they had died, too. So the truly wise men had decided to leave the island. They had built big canoes and had escaped over the sea, with their families.

They had headed toward a neighboring island which they knew well, but this island also belonged to the dead. Then they had gone to the Tonga islands, then as far as Samoa, without finding anything satisfactory. Finally they had landed on an island north of the Cook Archipelago, where they had found fresh water, game, and fish in large quantities. There was no sign that the curse had fallen here. So they had stayed. But the island was small. After several months of rest, the bravest men had put to sea again in search of a large piece of undamaged land. They meant to sail westward, but the wind had carried them off course, and they had been hungry and thirsty. Several canoes manned by gallant men had been lost or had sunk. The survivors had landed on this motu at the point of death. They had eaten and slept. They had no intention of doing any harm.

I wouldn't swear that I've given you an exact account of their voyage. They were talking about places located thousands of miles from Raevavae, and these places, which they didn't always know themselves for sure, sometimes had different names on English and French maps.

But that's not very important. They came from the Fiji Islands. And the main thing was not so much their point of departure as the fact that they were here. Besides, what they were saying was less important to me than what they were really thinking. Mai didn't understand English, or even French. But when the spokesman for our visitors had finished, he leaned toward me with his eyes sparkling.

189

"That man is a big liar," he said. "All these men are robbers. They are looking for women and land."

Without really knowing why, I was inclined to agree with him. The catastrophe to which they alluded was our own, but why, on this island which I did not know, had it spared the virtuous people and destroyed the wicked?

In Raevavae, only someone with a mind like Simon the catechist's could have believed such things to be possible. But it didn't really matter whether they were right or wrong. What counted, what we had to reckon with, was not so much their motives as their plans. These men in front of us were ready for war. Whom had they chosen as their enemies? What did they really want?

I leaned toward Peyrole. "What do you think?"

Peyrole made a face. "No question of letting them land. We'll give them food, but . . ."

Dubois, who was listening, sitting crosslegged holding his ankles, put in, "They're exhausted. Some of them have skin diseases that I'd like to examine. If you want my opinion, I'd say they need two weeks' rest, fresh vegetables, fruit, meat . . ."

"All right, but only two weeks . . ."

I got up and gave another speech. We understood, we sympathized. We, too, had suffered from the same storm. But the island we lived on was too small for us to receive so many strangers properly. Tubuai was only a few days north of here. It was a beautiful island, fertile, and as far as we knew, uninhabited since the disaster. We thought it would be perfectly suitable for our visitors and their families. We were ready to help them settle there. At Tubuai they would find fresh water, good farmland, plenty of fish. They would do well there. In the meantime, if our friends wished to rest, they could stay here on Moto Araoo, and we would bring them provisions to spare them any effort. We would be happy to be able to help them this way for at least another week.

When I had finished speaking the strangers thanked us formally but without warmth, and then without paying any further attention to us, clustered together and began talking among themselves in a dialect we did not understand. Those who accidently let their eyes fall on us did so lightly, with disdain. Beside me, Mai muttered something under his breath and spat on the ground. I grabbed his arm. Peyrole, without taking his eyes off the strangers, signaled to Dubois, Mai, and myself to approach.

"We may as well leave. On the way I'll post guards on Nuipapahiti, the way we did last night. Mai, you'll put guards on Vaiamanu. That way, they'll be surrounded, and . . ."

"What?" said Mai. "We do not kill them?"

In spite of my real concern, I couldn't help smiling. "Maybe they're really lost. It could have happened to you . . ."

"Yes," said Mai quietly, "but not with a hundred friends. These people will come and kill us in the night. We should kill them now, while we are here . . ."

"No," I said. "Only if they attack us. If they stay in peace, they will leave in peace."

Shrugging his shoulders, Mai collected his men and walked toward the sea. He wasn't happy. Neither were his friends. Their group made a point of walking right by the strangers, and laughing loudly as they passed. We were ready for anything, but nothing happened. When Mai's group had gotten in their boats and disappeared toward the west, Peyrole withdrew to the east, and I started back through the woods toward Raevavae. My companions were both furious and frightened. They hung around me and claimed that we were being followed. They swore we would never reach the canoes alive if I didn't fire there, and there . . .

I saw nothing, heard nothing. I finally got irritated and walked off without them. They followed me at once. We got to the boats without difficulty, but as soon as we had put out to sea some enemy scouts appeared at the edge of the wood. Each one was holding a spear.

"See?" said the natives.

I shrugged. I must have felt noble. Or maybe I was just tired. In any case, they annoyed me. That infuriating quality they had of reacting as a unit, with one accord, without thinking for themselves . . .

29

WHEN WE GOT back to Raevavae the entire population was waiting for us, squawking like birds. By chance, I was among the first to land. I took the opportunity to make a speech on the laws of hospitality. Speeches relax the nerves and warm the blood. Well, it wasn't quite that. I knew that my men didn't share my point of view. To restrain them, if not convince them, all I had was words. I was desperately determined to do anything I could to preserve the lives of this handful of human beings the sea had just washed up and who were as precious to me as the single grain of wheat found at the bottom of a pocket by the castaways of the Mysterious Island.

I also saw them as the seed that might one day repopulate the earth.

It's strange: At the time I loved Raevavae, its people, its customs, its landscape, more than anything. This little island was a paradise designed to my scale. I loved its broken-down, wrinkled old men who did nothing but laugh quietly and sit on their haunches, smoking the native tobacco; I loved its naked children, curious and lively as fish, its young people, its girls, always elegant, never dressed, its peaceable and fun-loving adults; I loved its landscape, the air, the water, the earth under my feet that belonged to me, its dawns and its twilights, its sun and its clouds, its delicate mists and its warm tropical rains that fell straight down . . . I loved this simple life, these easy relationships, these healthy people who were fond of me.

Yes, I loved all this. And at the same time, I couldn't forget the empty space that surrounded us.

After living with crowds and laws, I enjoyed the small number of people and the courtesy that characterizes relationships where there is a necessary solidarity and an exact understanding of others. But I was hoping to repopulate the earth. A solitary paradise is incomplete.

I didn't want these disdainful strangers the sea had tossed us to be killed.

I made a beautiful speech. My performance was hailed, but I convinced no one. Nevertheless, since the natives were still in the habit of trusting us in emergencies rather than their compatriots, they ended by accepting the idea of a possible co-existence.

Meanwhile, Peyrole had arrived with the others. I no longer felt responsible and left the gathering for a moment to send a message to Katherine.

When this had been taken care of, I walked back toward Peyrole. He was in the middle of a group of people, struggling against the same obstacles I had encountered ten minutes before. I drew him aside.

"All the members of the council are here. Why don't we call a meeting?"

Peyrole didn't have an expressive face. With him attention and dissatisfaction looked almost the same. He threw me a curious look which I didn't understand until much later, and which at the time surprised and even intimidated me. Then he nodded. "Excellent idea . . . it's the best possible cover."

Peyrole had discerned the seriousness of the situation more clearly than I had. He saw the meeting of the council as a way of releasing himself from responsibility. This irritated me. Today I think he was right, and that I was wrong not to understand.

We met in Mai's little *faré* on the rock. Yes, all the councilors were there.

For the benefit of those who had not taken part in our expedition, I described it. Mai interrupted me several times with sarcastic remarks. I pretended not to notice. Then I asked each member his opinion.

Without exception, the natives regretted that we had not taken advantage of the surprise effect and killed the strangers. Courteously but clearly they indicated that they thought we were stupid. If they weren't rebelling against our way of handling it, they said, it was only out of politeness and friendship. Tara, Tekao's former pupil, who was the youngest and the most natural, was particularly explicit. "Since you did not kill them when you had the chance," he told us in substance, "we must think of another way. All we have to do is poison the food you have promised to send them. This way we will be rid of them without danger . . ."

At that time Tara was a little like a young dog. Without being handsome or really eloquent, he was attractive because of his strength and vitality. At council meetings he contributed life and gaiety. But arguing with him wasn't easy. He had a tendency to oversimplify, to reduce every problem to a choice between two equally abstract solutions. He was so good at discovering these abstractions, at making them real, at developing them before your eyes, that it was often difficult to destroy them in order to arrive at a search for a real solution.

That day, however, he was closer to the majority than I was. So I began by agreeing with him. Then I added, "If these men all eat together and die together, all will be well. But if one of them eats before the others, it will turn out badly. We will be bad people. And the others will be able to insult us and to demand compensation . . ."

There was a silence. I concluded, "You decide. If you say kill, we will kill. But there will be deaths in Raevavae. If you say peace, we will take them food today and every day until they leave. If they don't want to leave, or if they try to land here—well, we'll see about that when the time comes."

Peyrole cleared his throat. "They have no guns. But there are more than a hundred of them. They won't let themselves be killed without putting up a fight. If we had fired before, how many of you would be dead now?"

Three mornings in a row we took live pigs, vegetables, and fruit to Motu Araoo and left them on the sand. The Fijians didn't come to collect the things until we were in our boats again.

We were escorted by an eager fleet, ready for anything. However, our guards noticed nothing unusual. The strangers ate, slept, swam, fished a little. At night they lit many small fires, perhaps to protect themselves. There were no indications that they intended to leave their motu, either to return to sea or to land on our island.

On the third day I went home.

Many of the natives had done the same without waiting for me. Boredom set in. Peyrole had trouble keeping his guards. Without Mai's help, he would have been just about the only one keeping watch.

I wasn't as blasé as the natives, but the matter no longer concerned me directly. Besides, I believed the Fijians to be peaceful.

Katherine asked me many questions about them. The fact that they spoke English made her feel close to them. She wanted to see them. To avoid incidents, we had prohibited women from going to Moto Araoo. I couldn't make an exception for Katherine. To soften her disappointment, I made fun of her a little: "I thought you weren't sentimental," I said.

Katherine was a mixture of good manners and primitiveness, if not ferocity. One day Odile Peyrole said something to her that she didn't like. For all her sweet manner, Odile had a sharp tongue, and she looked down on anything that wasn't just the way it had been in Rabastens. At the time Katherine hadn't said anything. I had called for her at the Navy House. The two women kissed goodbye, like friends. On the way home we didn't talk. At the time I was a happy husband, that is to say, rather indifferent. I sensed that something was wrong without giving it too much thought. When we got to our *faré*. I asked what had happened.

Katherine stopped in her tracks. She turned and looked at me like a she-wolf. That was it—the look of a wild beast. Then she let loose.

She called the whole French contingent a bunch of nasty, vicious lower middle-class snobs. She picked up a basket of fruit that happened to be on the table and threw it against the wall. She screamed insults in English, and carried on like a London slut.

But these outbursts were exceptional. She had been well brought up and controlled herself well. She was always playing a part. With men she played gaiety, with women respectability, with me seduction. There was no duplicity; she simply knew how to combine her upbringing with her natural temperament.

I rather liked this artificial side of her, which was emphasized by her foreign accent.

That day she answered me, with a meaningful look, "I'm very sentimental, but your cruel nature oppresses me."

It sounds ridiculous when you tell it, but I liked this sort of thing. We had fun together.

On the sixth night after the discovery of the Fijians there was no moon. Someone came to my house and woke me up around two o'clock.

"They have landed near Anatonu. Officer Peyrole says to go to the Navy House, and to be careful."

We ran through the night, Katherine carrying your father and me supporting Tapoua's wife, who was very fat, with little Anne in my other arm. When we reached the Navy House, Odile Peyrole was waiting for us. She was outwardly calm, but seemed consumed with anxiety. "My husband was here five minutes ago. He has just left. They're trying to surround them. My husband said for you to stay here and take command of the operation. Here is the key to the armory. You have to put mattresses in front of the windows . . ."

Suddenly she sat down with a desperate look. "My God, they have guns."

"Guns? Who gave them guns?"

"No one knows. But they're certainly not alone. Some people from here are with them, showing them the way. Think of it—they came directly to Anatonu . . . My husband thinks Poumi has something to do with it. My God, I hope nothing happens . . ."

I turned her over to Katherine. Together they took care of the children, who were crying, and Odile pulled herself together enough to make coffee.

I went out and walked around the house. There were a lot of people from Anatonu standing around silently in the night. I knew all of them. Without hesitating I asked them to come in, and placed two men with guns at each window, as well as three or four sentries in the garden.

From the direction of the church, that is, rather far away, a few shots were heard.

I was concentrating on trying to figure out what would happen. I wasn't afraid. Over and over, I kept asking myself where the attackers had gotten guns, and how we had let them leave their motu.

Suddenly, from the side of the house that rested against the hill I heard a scream, then a shot. I went out on the doorstep. The air smelled of sugar and incense. In the dawn light about thirty men were silhouetted against the sky, on a level with the roof. I couldn't tell who they were.

At the same moment, from all the windows at once, my men began to fire. The others replied. For five minutes things were very hot. My men fired without aiming, but calmly and deliberately. I think they were playing at being soldiers. The women were moaning. Katherine and Odile had taken all the children into the kitchen and were pressing their faces against their breasts. I was going from room to room watching the shooting. Once again, I had nothing to do but be present. Suddenly, there were two or three shots very close to the house, almost against the north wall, then I heard the sound of running and everything became quiet. Almost immediately Peyrole arrived, revolver in hand. He was very hot, in spite of the chilliness of the morning, but he wore his old faded kepi and his shoulder belt, which had left a sweaty mark across his chest.

"They tricked us, but it was badly planned," he threw at me as he passed. "We got them almost as soon as they landed. Those men up there"—he pointed to the green sky—"slipped through our fingers. We killed quite a few of them. Leguen . . ."

"Where are his wife and family?"

"They're fine. We picked them up on the way. Leguen is on the beach trying to keep them from killing the prisoners."

"How many are there?"

"Forty or fifty. I haven't counted. The rest are dead or hiding now. We'll catch them later. Those bastards from Mahanantoa helped them. If it weren't for Tara . . ."

To finish up this war of one morning, however, took us seven more days.

Those of the bandits, the rebels, the invaders, I don't know what to call them, who had managed to escape had naturally taken refuge on the slopes of Mount Hiro. We armed the villagers and surrounded the mountain, and for seven days and seven nights we searched among the bushes, rocks, and caves.

After a couple of days, by interrogating the prisoners, we found out exactly what had happened. The Fijians really were lost sailors looking for land where they could settle with their families. After wandering for three years they believed, like us, that they were alone in the world.

Discovering us had astonished them. Because we were numerous, well-armed, and polite, they had decided to accept our suggestions honestly, rest for a few days, and then go and look at Tubuai. But two days before the invasion, while a man from Mahanantoa was on guard on Nuipapahiti, Poumi had landed among them.

Poumi had been living alone on Hiro for a year, but he hadn't lost all contact with his village. Without going so far as to welcome him back into the community, his relatives visited him, brought him food and news, and gave him the affection, contempt, respect, and fear that was accorded in those days to the mad.

Natives don't take well to complete solitude, except at sea. They need to hear the heartbeat of the village. Poumi was something of an exception to the rule. He had always built his *farés* in secluded places. His personal reflections prevented him from being dominated by daily existence. But his family, his children, a minimum of social life kept him in the group. When he was truly alone, his mind began to wander. Sincerely, following his own logic, he adopted the mad ideas invented by Simon in his weakness and cowardice. He lived with spirits and gods, waiting for them to give him an opportunity to establish their law.

When he was informed, shortly after we were, of the landing of the Fijians, and learned that these men also believed that the *tsunami* was caused by the abandonment of the old customs, he thought his hour had come. He went to see them, talked with them, in spite of the difference in their language, thanks to that curious faculty the natives of the archipelagos have always had for understanding each other beyond words, communicated his passion to them, awakened their dreams.

In practical terms, he promised them the death of the Europeans, and of Léné and Tekao, the restoration of the old customs, and a share of the island.

Nobody could roam the seas for three years, after enduring the punishment of God, without becoming slightly mad. The Fijians had been easy to convince. They hadn't attacked us at once because it was almost dawn, and had spent the day letting their excitement mount. When they got in their boats the following night they were ready for anything. Poumi was waiting for them on the shore, together with about thirty men from Mahanantoa, several of whom were armed with old guns.

We killed Poumi against our will because he refused to surrender, on the fourth day. The men from Mahanantoa gave themselves up at once. But the Fijians, who expected no quarter, kept fighting until we forced them, one by one, into corners where they couldn't escape.

30

I TOLD YOU that before the arrival of the Fijians I was obsessed with finding a way to wake up the island. And I implied that if they hadn't come, I wouldn't have succeeded.

It's quite true. If this has never occurred to anyone, it's primarily because, in this drama which can be played back like a game of chess, everything happened very slowly and very subtly. You had to be as closely involved in it as I was to be able to say at what point things really got started. It's also because the legend of our people has it that we did everything with our own resources. Finally, it's because for a long time I only played the role of a silent and rather stupid onlooker.

To excuse ourselves, of course, we can argue that it's hard to see something you're too close to, and claim that pressing daily preoccupations prevented us from seeing things in perspective.

We'd been thrown off balance by learning that we were not alone in the world, then we'd been afraid and had felt hatred. When the flush of victory was over we tried to take stock, reasonably. It wasn't easy.

During the week of fighting we took our prisoners to Anatonu, where Peyrole had them guarded by men he could trust. He had instructed these men under threat of the severest punishments not to let them escape, and to see that the crowd of women and children that surrounded the shed that was being used as a jail didn't molest them. Almost all the prisoners were wounded, and Dubois, who had moved to quarters nearby in order to attend to them, had taken charge of the post. For this reason, no doubt, there were no incidents.

But once the military operations were over, the men who had fought with us returned to Anatonu and joined the group in front of the jail. As the victors, they demanded a celebration and the prisoners. The women did nothing to calm them down. Immediately there were incidents involving the guards, who threatened to desert. Dubois, who didn't want to leave the prisoners, sent us a message saying that he didn't know what would happen when night came.

Peyrole and I were at the Navy House, where Odile had had my wife and children staying with her all week. We looked at each other anxiously. Fundamentally we were in agreement, without even having discussed it: The prisoners should not be executed. I'm sure that for Peyrole it was a question of honor; no delinquent left in his custody was going to be lynched. As for myself, I was guided by my habitual logic; I didn't want to lose a precious human resource.

Under the circumstances, we had a real problem on our hands. We didn't want any more deaths, but we were incapable of guarding these men under our protection indefinitely. Dubois' message only added to our uneasiness. If the crowd became more insistent, the guards would desert us. We couldn't ask them to resist the unanimous will of their people. Wisely, Peyrole had disarmed our native troops, and we might be able to prevent the guards from leaving with their guns. We would then have absolute superiority in terms of weapons. But could we face the possibility of firing on the crowd?

I believe Peyrole could have forced himself to do it out of duty, although it would have broken his heart. I couldn't have done it.

The worst of it was that we had no solution to offer. Gloomily we hashed over the situation in Peyrole's office, one window of which looked onto the jail and the throng of natives. The windows had been closed because of the noise. I remember that it was very hot. Now and then the voices would get louder, and we would glance outside. The spectacle was always the same. While most of the natives grouped around the small fires would continue to converse, sitting on their heels, a few individuals who were never the same would walk over to the walls of the jail and begin shouting, either to summon the invisible guards, or to insult the prisoners.

This would last a few minutes, sometimes a quarter of an hour, and then the demonstrators would get tired and go back to their places.

We noticed that as the morning advanced these incidents became more frequent and the crowd seemed more interested in them.

"Let's call a meeting of the council," I said.

Peyrole shrugged. "A lot of good that'll do . . . I already know what they'll decide!"

Forgetting our worries for a moment, I looked at him, interested. "Whatever they decide, they'll be responsible. We'll be off the hook."

Peyrole threw me a black look. Then, with his eyes on the floor, he said sullenly, "It's not a question of responsibility. It's a question of what's right!"

"I know," I said.

My anxiety returned, but at the same time I was happy. For a moment I weighed the pros and cons, then I asked, "How many are there in the jail?"

"Who, the prisoners? Eighty-three. Sixty-four Fijians and nineteen from Mahanantoa."

"As for the ones from Mahanantoa . . ." I hesitated. The idea I had just had wasn't clear in my mind. I went on slowly, "In the council, Tara is the representative of Mahanantoa. Couldn't we make an agreement with him? The men from his village are obviously guilty, but they are friends and relatives of his. It seems to me that he won't want them to die. After all, the real culprit is Poumi. But Poumi is dead. We might offer to let Tara take back his people and, in exchange, ask that the Fijians be allowed to live . . ."

Peyrole thought it over. "I don't quite understand your idea. In the case of the men from Mahanantoa, you may be right. But as for the others . . . Besides, Tara isn't the only one concerned. The other villages will want a voice . . . What will your friend Mai say?"

"I know," I said, disappointed, "but what else can you suggest?"

Just then there was a loud uproar outside. We went and looked out the window. At last I said, "Come on! Let's do something. We don't have much time. Call a meeting of the council for two o'clock. In the meantime we must alert Tekao and Leguen so they will support us. And I'd like to say a word to Tara before the meeting."

Peyrole shrugged again. "That's up to you. I'll take care of the schoolteacher and Leguen. But Tara is shrewd."

"So am I," I said. "The whole problem is getting hold of him."

"When we came back this morning he told me he was going home to sleep. He must be saving himself for tonight."

"All the more reason!"

I don't know why, but the part of the island around Mahanantoa was the area I was least familiar with. It was a sort of cape of grey sand with a few scrawny trees and masses of bramble bushes, and it was very hot when there was no sea breeze to stir the clouds of spangled dust. I went there on horseback, and by the time I reached the first *farés,* the sun was directly overhead.

The village looked bleak, almost deserted, and the few people I saw all disappeared very quickly from my sight. Tara's *faré* was brand new, and although I had never seen it before, there was something familiar about it. I soon saw why: Although built with palm tree trunks and banana leaves, it was as exact a replica as possible of the Navy House, down to the last detail. The builders had even included the shed that had once been used as a radio station.

This resemblance, with all that it suggested, would have put me on my guard if there had been any need for it.

But before I had set foot on the ground Tara, followed by several men, rushed out of his house and ran toward me laughing, bursting with health and friendliness. Before taking my horse by the reins, he grabbed my knee and squeezed it in an amazingly eloquent gesture, deferential and affectionate at the same time.

"At last you have come!" said Tara. "I had this house built *farani* style, to please you. But you didn't come. Ah, how happy I am that you are here. You are my guest. And you will see how Tara treats his friends!"

This spontaneity and trust touched me. To us Europeans Tara, when we stopped to think about him, was a source of astonishment and worry. Psychologically, he wasn't like the other natives. He thought of everything, saw to everything, and amazingly enough, was capable of planning ahead and persisting. In the council, because unlike the rest of his fellow citizens he had plans and was concerned about carrying them out, his influence was preponderant. Above all, he had faith in his destiny. He was one of the very few people on the island who knew how to read fluently. This superiority impressed him and his natural ambition compelled him to outdo himself constantly. This combination of qualities made him unpredictable and often gave us suspicions that turned out to be quite unfounded, for he was open to the opinions of others, as long as they were expressed in the right way.

But let me repeat that these reservations didn't occur to us unless we stopped to think about his importance. Tara had such gaiety, such naturalness, and such an innocent seriousness that no one was capable of resisting his charm. So I gave in, and let him show me into his house.

The interior reflected the man, at once calculated and natural. In the middle was a long table whose legs, like those of the two benches on either side of it, were made of logs driven into the ground. When I arrived it was covered with vegetables, fruit, fishhooks, javelins, arrows, tools—all the things natives are always carrying around with them, but already some women were hurrying to clear it off. To the right, against the gable, was a stone fireplace, obviously unused, that was a pretty good imitation of the one Leguen had built. To the left, a very low door must have led to the kitchen and the women's quarters. Taking up all the rest of that wall was an enormous native-style bed with bedposts of carved teak, a framework of stretched rope, and a mattress of ferns covered with the skins of goats and cows. Nailed to the carved bedposts were seashells, the jawbones of sharks, the beaks of birds. As it was, the whole thing was more like the throne of a barbarian chief than the bed of the man whose support I needed to help the island progress.

Putting his arm around my shoulders, Tara led me toward this dais-like affair. "Come," he said, "let us sit here. We will have a drink and a song while the women make something to eat. Why did you not tell me you were coming?"

For a man who had been running around all night in the mountains and the jungle, he was amazingly fresh and rested. I sat down beside him on the bed with my legs folded under me, and Tara's friends squatted on the dirt floor in front of us. No sooner were we seated than a fat woman brought us some palm wine and fish marinated in lemon.

I didn't resist. With the natives in those days it was impossible to broach a serious matter without first going through long preliminaries that had nothing to do with the case. Besides, I knew Tara pretty well. Although he seemed completely absorbed in his duties as a host and his delight in entertaining me, he had certainly guessed that there must be a serious reason behind my visit. Perhaps he already knew what that reason was. After the rites of hospitality had been observed he would give me an opportunity to express myself without being rude.

But I was in a hurry. In less than two hours the council would meet in Anatonu. We had to allow at least an hour to get there. I was trying to figure out a way to speed things up, and it distracted me from thinking clearly. I smiled and drank my palm wine, but I wasn't really listening. Also, my position, half lying on these animal skins facing these squatting men who were watching my every move, was uncomfortable. Beside me, Tara was bubbling over.

"We will have a party, a big party!" he said. "You will see. This is my village. It is a good village, you know. Of course, there was Poumi, but that man . . ."

"There are others, too," I said automatically.

Tara said nothing for a moment and looked at me, then went on, "Yes, there are others . . . But above all, there are my friends. And with them, you will see, we will dance . . ."

I didn't want to lose the opportunity. I broke in, "I came to tell you that the council is meeting in a little while to talk about the others."

"Ah," said Tara.

Suddenly he turned toward his men and motioned to them. Without hurrying, they got up, nodded to me, and left the house. They sat down outside, where we heard them laugh. Then Tara got up from his bed, took my hand, and led me to the table, which had now been cleared. He sat down opposite me, crossed his arms, and leaned on them.

"Those men are certainly guilty," he said calmly, "but they are brothers. They have wives and children. That village is sad. And besides, Poumi is dead . . ."

"Yes," I said, "but there are other villages. And there are also the Fijians."

I was prepared for a long, complicated negotiation in the native manner. Tara smiled candidly.

"In the old days we would have eaten the Fijians. Today, no. But we can kill them perhaps, no?"

I seized upon an idea I had had while talking to Peyrole.

"They can be useful," I replied. "There is work to be done—hard physical work—which we don't want to do. We could have them do it. They won't be able to refuse. If the island is going to progress . . ."

"What about the others?"

"The ones from Mahanantoa?"

"Yes."

"You take care of them," I said simply. "We'll turn them over to you, and you'll punish them as you see fit. After all, it's a village matter."

I had spoken these last words as casually as I could. Tara looked at me in silence.

"You are right," he said at last. "But do you think the other councilors, those savages, Mai and the rest of them, will agree with you?"

I looked down. "Leguen, Tekao, you, me—that makes four. Maraou is a friend of Leguen's. And Officer Peyrole can talk to Tehei. That will make six. A majority . . ."

"And will they listen to you about the Fijians?"

"It's you who will make the suggestion. Besides, if you take back these people, it will only be justice."

"Ah!" Tara grinned like a child, showing all his white teeth. "That is different. In the old days, we would have eaten them. But for the sake of progress, I will try."

So in ten minutes the matter was settled. I drank a little more of the palm wine and ate a few mouthfuls of grilled pork so as not to be impolite, and started back to Anatonu, urging Tara not to be late.

On the way I brooded on my astonishment. As always when I wasn't with Tara my suspicions started up again. I had believed him to be too aggressive. I was discovering him to be too flexible. What did it mean? Had I been tricked, or too well supported? I wasn't any happier with the style of the discussion than I was with its conclusion. They were too different from native custom. Suddenly I laughed. To do what I wanted to do— my ideas still weren't very precise, but I felt very keenly the need for *action* of some kind—I needed new men, men who were both adapted to the land and independent of it. Tara had just shown himself to be such a man, and it worried me!

In spite of this ironic observation, I continued to be uneasy about such a high degree of adaptability. Did it conceal a secret ambition, or was it merely the mark of a vacillating mind, an impressionable nature? If Tara had been European, I would have thought no more about it. But as a native, he worried me.

Riding my horse in the midday heat, I found this idea unpleasant. Was I a racist without knowing it? Although you know what the word means, it has no reality for you. Racism is inconceivable among us for the good reason that we are a few thousand people with the whole world to ourselves, happy to be living together, very aware that we all belong to the human race because this race almost died out. For this reason we regard our physical and psychological differences as interesting curiosities rather than as disagreeable characteristics. This hasn't always been the case, and no doubt in my own way, I was a racist. I told you that because of the accident of my birth I believed myself to be a cut above the others. This caused me to classify these others into various categories, the most despised being those most different from myself. My equals were middle-class people who had lost their social status, penniless aristocrats, well-educated adventurers. Lower down on the scale, but still very close, were the French peasants and craftsmen. A little lower down, but not much, were those I called the barbarians: Arabs, blacks, the natives of Raevavae. Much further down were tradespeople, civil servants, lower middle-class people panting with the desire to be different, but remaining themselves. As for real middle-class people and civilized foreigners, I had no opinion. I found them either ridiculous or like myself, and consequently I liked them.

That was my racism. I was aware of it without thinking about it.

When I arrived, just in time for the meeting, I decided not to trust myself, and not to allow my opinions to be guided by feelings of this kind. The meeting was almost a pure formality. Tara, who had come by sea with a crew of paddlers, had arrived ahead of me. He had already spoken with most of the members. After we had opened the session he asked for the floor and set forth the case of the Fijians skillfully and in reasonable terms. It was almost as if the meeting were taking place at his request. I looked at Peyrole sitting in his chair as secretary general behind Tekao. He saw my look and lowered his eyes. I also looked at the native members of the council. They were listening seriously. When Tara was finished, Mai, who contrary to custom was present, got up. He rolled his eyes, showed his teeth, made a few expressive and mysterious gestures, smiled, sat down again, and said simply, "Since we still have not killed all these men, there is nothing to do but let them live, especially if they are useful. In Vaiuru they can build a fine wooden pier for big ships . . ."

In front of Vaiuru, up to a hundred yards from the shore, the ocean floor is never more than three fathoms deep, and none of us knew when a "big ship" would dock at Raevavae again. Nevertheless the council agreed to Mai's proposal. It also decided that the Fijians would construct a road that would be a direct route linking Matotea, Vaiuru, and Anatonu, and that after that they would build a big reservoir at the foot of Hiro to supply us with water for the dry season. Next, it tried to entrust the job of guarding the prisoners to Peyrole, who declined the offer. Then Tara politely offered to take charge of this, with the cooperation of the people.

He explained that a prison would be too much trouble to guard, and that the simplest method would be to place the conquered men under the supervision of the men and women of Raevavae. They would not be allowed to go near the shore or the villages without a reason, to possess arms, or to refuse to do the work that would be assigned to them. The citizens could be on the alert to make sure these rules were respected. In every other way, the Fijians would be free. I found the idea fair and ingenious. The members of the council were flattered and accepted the proposal.

After the meeting I took Tara aside to thank him. He smiled unselfconsciously. "You like the idea? I am glad. It is true that these men will be useful. If you need horses, you do not kill them, do you?"

I laughed and he left to go to the jail to pick up the men from Mahanantoa, whom Peyrole was releasing. As for myself, I was very much relieved and was getting ready to return to

Katherine, my children, and my *faré*, when Tekao, who must have been watching me, walked over.

"What do you think of all this?" he asked.

I smiled. "It's fine, isn't it? That Tara, he's the man of the future . . ."

Tekao didn't return my smile. He stroked the ground with the tip of his bare foot. "You don't think that all these lives that have been placed in his hands . . ."

I shrugged my shoulders. "He saved those lives, that's the main thing. Without him, what could we have done? Besides, what pleases me about this business is that he didn't hesitate. I thought I was going to have to fight, but I was understood from the moment I opened my mouth. Tara immediately grasped the political and human value of generosity . . . No, I'm really happy about it."

Tekao looked at me sideways, his face impassive. "It's quite contrary to the native mentality . . ."

"I know," I said, and for a moment my uneasiness returned. Then I remembered what I thought I had discovered on the way back to Anatonu, and I laughed. "You mustn't say that, my friend. Here we are all equal, citizens of the world . . ."

"Oh," said Tekao with a funny smile, "I'm not much of a racist. And if you think it's all right . . ."

"Yes, I do."

And as I went home, for the last time in my life I put myself in a vacation mood, not realizing that everything had just begun.

31

No, I HAD no idea what a difference the Fijians were going to make. It was enough to have saved their lives. In the days that followed I was perfectly aware that their fate was not an enviable one, but I believed that everything would work itself out in time. I knew that after the villagers from Mahanantoa who had gone with Poumi had been brought home by Tara, they had been beaten and insulted for two days, then had been returned to their families and exonerated forever, according to native custom. Expecting that the same thing would happen in the case of the Fijians, I decided to forget them, avoided them when I saw them at a distance, and had no trouble returning to my usual life as if they hadn't existed. Yes, that was it—they raised a problem that I didn't know how to solve . . .

I was happy. I had just had my thirty-eighth birthday. We had been in Raevavae for eight years now. I had hardly noticed. I liked my life. I had everything I needed, and what I had just done was both generous and clever. I felt as if I had been born fully grown in Raevavae.

At this time your father was four years old. He was a strapping blond boy who lived with the children of Anatonu and didn't take to the discipline imposed by his mother. Even at that age, he dreamed of having the run of the island, going to sea with the fishermen, eating raw fish, and dancing alongside the adults.

We had a hard time getting him to speak French. He understood us, but he always answered us in Tahitian. He hated the European clothes that Katherine still made for him sometimes, his blond hair, our way of living and eating—everything that set him apart from his comrades. But he adored his sister Anne, who was born two years after he was. When he was in the house he obeyed her. When he was outdoors he must have thought about her constantly, for he was always bringing her shells, flowers, feathers, smooth stones, pieces of driftwood.

He scorned the Peyrole children, who were older than he, but who led a totally European life under the eye of their mother. To the children of Leguen, who were younger, he paid very little attention.

And yet they were charming youngsters. The little girl, with her pale skin and light clear eyes, promised to be beautiful. Her brothers, who had their mother's stocky build, somehow managed to be ruddy and darkskinned at the same time. Actually, they were the color of mahogany. Always together, always dirty, they spent their time on their father's farm, surrounded by animals. I knew them well, as I did all the people on the island. I had the time. In spite of myself, I lived the life of a native because it suited me: plenty of leisure time, few regular occupations, and now and then some aborbing job that was always too brief to become tedious.

Katherine, on the other hand, led a life full of obligations. I saw her seldom. She was very well organized and knew how to make people work, either as a favor to her, or by convincing them that they would enjoy doing a certain job. Toward her own children she was a responsible but reserved mother. She would have preferred them to be like herself, but she knew that this was impossible. Although she never complained about it, it must have bothered her. It gave her efforts as an educator a kind ot emptiness which her sense of duty prevented her from admitting. Outside of this, which was certainly important, I think she was happy. She was thirty-six and in good health. In some ways, she had become more beautiful, had taken on new assurance and vitality. I alone could see her losing that sheen of youth that had surrounded her like a pearl when I met her, and this invisible erosion made her even dearer to me because it showed me she was fragile. Her first concern was for the hospital. In it she had found a reason for living which suited her nature better than any other: she was useful there because of what she did, not because of who she was. They often sent for her at night. In the evenings she came home late, always tired, always full of her work. To the natives Dubois was still the master, but the women entrusted themselves to her willingly, and her perpetual seriousness was beginning to amaze the men. If we happened to be walking together, people would stop her to ask her advice. She approached her examinations and diagnoses with extreme care and caution. Afterward, she would agonize over them in silence.

I was pleased to see her so passionate about her work, although this passion sometimes annoyed me. I accepted the fact that it was her destiny, but this didn't keep me from regretting that it wasn't her destiny simply to be my wife and the mother of my children. When she talked about her work I listened politely, but sometimes I made fun of her a little, and I was always putting off paying her a visit at the hospital which she expected. Such were my little acts of revenge, as mild as was my irritation. If our lives were separate, our respect and fondness for each other hadn't changed.

The island was also giving me cause for satisfaction. Tara had waged such an effective campaign, with a lot of explanation and a few threats, that there was now a permanent clinic for infants and a monthly visiting day for pregnant women. What two years ago had seemed ridiculous and shocking, everyone now accepted. If by chance a pregnant woman forgot her monthly checkup, her neighbors would scold her.

The same thing was happening at the school. Tara had suggested that there be a solemn distribution of prizes once a month, instead of once a year, and had dreamed up an impressive ritual for this occasion. As president of the council, I was the master of ceremonies. Seated on a red platform with six steps leading up to it, I waited for the prize pupils to come forward when their names were called. I would shake their hands, congratulate them, and present them with their prizes, which were usually a table and chair from Bourdaroux's workshop, now elevated to the role of a symbol of civilization. Then the list of honor students was turned over to Léné so that on the following Sunday, before his sermon, he could ask the Lord's blessing to fall on their heads.

All this pomp and ceremony pleased people so much that it awakened a real spirit of emulation among the students, who were supported and encouraged by their villages, their relatives, and their friends.

Tekao, who was getting a little stouter, was profiting from this success. In addition to Noémie, who was running the girls' school, he now had five assistants to whom he had turned over the job of teaching the elementary classes. For himself he had reserved the novelty of the year, which we called the Baccalaureate Class.

You expend so much energy inventing new things that it's tempting to save effort by using old terms, even if these terms no longer correspond to anything. In the Baccalaureate Class that first year there were five girls and three boys selected from the best students. They all wore *paréos* of red tapa and took themselves quite seriously. But they worked with fervor, and we brooded over them like eggs of a very rare species. Each of us, I think, was haunted by the fear that he might disappear before he had trained a successor.

Even Bourdaroux, who pretended to despise our efforts, must have had this feeling. He was giving a rigorous training to twenty coworkers and apprentices who were fascinated by his skill, and he was covering everything: building, carpentry, metal work, and masonry. He had been raised in a very small village where he had seen old men working according to techniques that were a thousand years old, and he remembered them. Whatever he lacked, his ingenuity in handling raw materials supplied. In spite of his disdain for books, every now and then he would come and consult a technical work at the library. He had built a lime kiln, started a stone quarry, and set up a forge. In his off-hours he was teaching his wife how to spin goat hair, and boasted that he would wear the first new suit on the island.

Leguen, who was more modest, regarded us with envy. He pretended that he couldn't do anything. And yet his place, which was now fenced in by hedges, divided into fields and meadows, and boasted a stable, a pigpen, and a pigeon coop, was becoming a real farm. Because of him we never went without the hard but fragrant bread which he mixed and baked himself and brought us every Saturday in big, round loaves, his pleasant, birdlike face wreathed in smiles.

His small but well-cared-for cows gave enough milk for him to make cheese. His pigs, raised on whey and copra, which gave their meat a flavor all its own, were twice as fat as the half-wild pigs of the natives. And finally, his fruits—apples, pears, avocados, and mangoes—were at our disposal all year round.

The natives thought he went to a lot of trouble for not much result, and it's true that in his determination to blindly copy the ways of his Breton village he sometimes got himself involved in hard and unnecessary work. But they liked him because he was gay and obliging, and knew how to make rum. In spite of themselves they got ideas from him which they half carried out or abandoned after one season, but which imperceptibly altered the appearance of the island.

One day when I was going with him to get lime from Bourdaroux's kiln in an unlikely looking cart drawn by two little yellow horses, I pointed out that all the houses we were passing were surrounded by hedges and almost everyone had a little garden.

"It's your influence," I said without thinking about it. "It was you who introduced hedges and gardens here. Before you, there weren't any."

He looked at me, and then seeing that I wasn't joking, said timidly, "Then I'm a teacher, too, in a way?"

I think it meant a lot to him.

Among these people whom I loved, in this land that was beginning to move, however gradually, watching my dreams slowly coming to life, I should have been happy. I was merely satisfied. No, I'm not rewriting history to suit myself like the others; I remember. I was satisfied, but a nameless uneasiness kept me alert. I sensed that the appointed time was approaching. On certain mornings in the middle of summer the air has a touch of mist which suddenly, in the height of the season's glory, reminds you that autumn will come, and then winter . . . It's delightful and painful at the same time.

These Fijians, whom I didn't want to see or hear about but who in spite of everything sometimes passed in front of my eyes as indistinct but all too recognizable silhouettes, were my mist.

I held out for about four months, and then one morning without saying anything to anyone and without even being sure myself why I was doing it, I decided to pay them a visit.

32

ACTUALLY, I DIDN'T even decide that. I just told myself that I was going to go hunting alone, and I chose an itinerary which led me, by the end of the afternoon, to the silvery, dense, and aromatic bushland that separated Mahanantoa from the rest of the island.

It was here that Tara was keeping the Fijians.

At first I found nothing to indicate their presence. A road had recently been laid out between Anatonu and Mahanantoa, and some parts of it had been crudely paved. According to the rumors that had reached me the camp of the Fijians was near this road, but I didn't know exactly where. I looked for a big clearing, huts, something resembling a village. I found nothing but some paths which disappeared after a few yards among those spiny, metallic bushes that I didn't like.

Slowly, sitting straight up in the stirrups, I rode almost as far as Mahanantoa, then when the first houses came into view, I turned back and continued my search. Finally I chose at random a path that seemed a little less narrow than the others.

For several hundred yards I saw nothing. The grey sand absorbed the sound of my horse's steps and the silence was disturbed only by the squeaking of my saddle and the scraping of the branches against my legs. Then, in the distance, I heard the sea, and almost immediately I came upon the camp.

At first I didn't see it. I stopped because the landscape I had just discovered on emerging from this metallic bushland was strange. Picture a shallow, pear-shaped basin, whose narrow end touched the sea, which you could see shining in the distance, and whose bottom consisted entirely of what I at first took to be a very green and very flat meadow. In the midst of this expanse rose an almost round hill whose diameter did not exceed fifty yards. It was covered with an enormous accumulation of dried branches which almost totally concealed the ground and which in some places rose as high as two yards, in an incredible disorder.

In spite of the immobility of the landscape under the sun, in spite of the freshness of the stiff vegetation, the whole scene had an air of mystery and—yes—of madness. I was sitting there trying to discern the cause of my uneasiness when my horse stretched his neck and snorted. At once I began to understand. What I had taken to be a meadow was a swamp. Taking a better look, I could see bubbles appearing and bursting endlessly on its surface. There was also the smell, and the mosquitoes.

In Raevavae, we all knew the deadly south mangrove jungle with its exaggerated greens and its apparent fertility. Even the natives avoided it. My first thought was that its memory and its legend had warned me in spite of myself. But this didn't explain everything. There was also that tangle of branches and dried leaves whose meaning I couldn't guess.

With the reins flapping and my hands on the pommel, I was standing up in the stirrups, looking around with a mechanical curiosity and about to continue my search, when something flashed among the branches for an instant and I distinguished the shape of a man.

I called out immediately. I can still hear my voice, flat and incongruous. At first nothing moved. Then, slowly, the man reappeared and straightened up with his arms dangling at his sides. He was an old man.

"How do you get through here?" I shouted.

He looked at me as if abstracted, then bent down and disappeared. I waited. Everything was motionless again. Then I rode down into the basin to the edge of the green algae, where my horse paced back and forth in a rich compost, and decided to ride around the swamp. It was bigger than I had thought. I had never seen it before, and no one had ever mentioned it to me. I was beginning to think that there was no way across when suddenly from the direction of solid ground I heard voices, the foliage moved, and a group of men appeared. I stopped my horse.

It was the Fijians returning to their camp for the night. They were being guarded by about fifteen natives armed with clubs. They had been divided into teams of eight to ten men and were carrying some palm tree trunks.

From where I was hidden in a clump of bourao, they could not see me. The silence was broken only by the brittle laughter of the armed men. I tried to stay out of sight. When they had reached a certain place, the group stopped. A guard pointed to a spot on the ground with his club, and immediately a team of porters began raising their tree trunk vertically on that spot, as if they intended to plant it there. When the trunk was upright, there were some maneuvers which I didn't understand, and then the men released their burden, which fell into the swamp. I expected to hear a splash, and then see the log disappear. Nothing of the kind occurred. The upper end of the trunk had fallen precisely on a solid spot, either a rock or a piling, planted in the midst of this quivering verdure. As soon as the first tree was in place a second team carrying another trunk walked out on it and, in the same way, threw its burden toward another solid spot. Another followed that one, then still another, and another. From this spot, five tree trunks were enough to get to the island that I was trying vainly to reach.

All this had happened swiftly and easily, as if the same men had already repeated the same gestures dozens of times. As soon as the last three had been put in place, all the porters walked onto this strange bridge that zigzagged along at the same level as the ground that surrounded it. Since the sun was about to set, their silhouettes stood out against the sky, and I had no trouble counting them. There were thirty-nine.

When the last man had reached solid ground, three of the guards followed them, but when they had reached the next to the last trunk, stopped and bent down. Just then my horse snorted, and I came out from behind my bush.

For a fleeting, almost imperceptible moment, the scene froze, and I felt the eyes of all the actors on me. Then the Fijians resumed their march and began to disappear behind the piles of dry branches I had noticed in the beginning. Their guards, straightening up, came over and surrounded my horse, smiling and greeting me. I returned their smiles and their greetings.

Two of them were vaguely familiar to me, but most of them belonged to that group of young men, not really settled yet, who turned aside shyly when they met me on the paths, and who never showed up at gatherings.

I didn't want to question them. It was already serious enough that I hadn't known about all this, but to admit my ignorance . . .

"All through work?" I asked.

They laughed. "Yes, we take away the bridge, and we go home. In Mahanantoa there is dancing tonight, you know. We have dancing every night now. And for the ones who are 'on' that day, it's a real party, with food and everything, you know."

"I know," I said. "And the ones who are 'on' for the day today, are you?"

They laughed. "Of course. It is not easy. There are some who want to be 'on' every day. Even men from Matotea, Anatonu, all over . . ."

"From Vaiuru?"

They looked away. "From Vaiuru, no . . . But," they added, laughing again, "that does not matter, because only the ones from Mahanantoa have the right."

"Yes, of course . . ."

Then pointing with my chin to the swamp and the piles of branches, I said, because this I could easily not know, "And what is it like over there?"

They laughed loudly. "We do not know. We went there the first time to watch them while they were sawing up the trees, but no one has gone back there since. What is the use? The first time it was good, because we had to be sure they were not hiding big logs that they could have used to escape, but now . . .?"

"Of course," I said again.

They stood there calmly, showing no embarrassment, perhaps completely innocent.

"And they never escape?"

There was a quiet, toneless laugh. Finally one of the ones I knew answered, "In the beginning, a few. But they cannot go far, you know. It is not like the motu."

"Of course. And in the morning, do they all come out and work?"

"If they wish to. But if they do not wish to, they do not eat. It is clever, no?"

"Very clever, yes."

I shuddered deep inside myself, without showing it, but I was awake. Calmly I dismounted and handed my bridle to a man at random. "I'm going to take a little walk over there," I said, heading toward the palm tree trunks, which were still in position.

There was a very slight rustle. Perhaps they weren't so innocent after all. Perhaps, too, they were afraid of Tara. Three of them appeared on my path. They took my hand, my arm.

"You cannot go there. You are alone. It is almost dark. They are all together. You will not see anything. You cannot go there."

"It is still light," I replied, putting my arms around them in a friendly way so they would let go of me. "It won't take me long. I just want to look around. Besides, you are here. You'll wait for me for a little while . . ."

And I went on. The palm tree trunks were solid but greasy. Even so, it wasn't very difficult.

Halfway across the swamp I stopped and said to myself, "They'll kill you. It will serve you right."

I couldn't see any movement on the little island. On the other side of the swamp, just in front of the bridge, the villagers were crowded around my horse, watching me. Dusk was falling. There were stars out already. I thought, "This is idiotic."

I had forgotten Katherine, your father, Anne, the island, and that barely emerging feeling that was to become the Idea. I started walking again, holding my arms out a little, being careful not to fall.

When I reached solid ground, I hesitated. I couldn't see anything except that extraordinary jumble of branches and dry leaves. Behind me I could feel the villagers watching me. I didn't know what to do, and I was afraid. I had left my bow on my horse, and the only thing I had to defend myself with was a knife in my pocket.

Nevertheless, in the green twilight that had now fallen, I made out a path and started up it. It turned right almost immediately. As soon as I was out of sight of the villagers, I stopped. I was sure that I was being spied on. For a minute or two I stood still. I could hear nothing but the lazy slap of the sea and once or twice some indistinct words spoken in the distance by Tara's men.

Finally, forcing myself to sound natural, I said in a loud voice, in English, "Anybody here?"

I wasn't even sure of my accent.

At first nothing happened. I repeated my question.

Then a man appeared right in front of me. I smiled at him in the semidarkness, and made sure he could see my empty hands. I asked him in English where his camp was.

"Here," he replied without moving.

"I see," I said, "but where are your *farés?*"

"Here," he repeated.

Both of us, me with my false naturalness, he with his reserve, were very tense. I could probably still get away. Anything could happen.

"Listen," I said, "I want to talk to you. I was on the motu the first day. It was because of me that they gave you food. And it was because of me that you were not killed when you were taken prisoner after the battle."

I was making an effort to speak correctly. My biggest fear was not being understood. But suddenly another man appeared beside the first. I thought then that they weren't going to kill me. If they were, they would have done it from behind.

"I want to talk to all of you," I repeated.

And since they still said nothing, I added, indicating our surroundings, "I did not know about . . . this."

One of them then made a vague, constricted gesture which might have indicated a direction. I started walking again, following the path. They came with me. When I stumbled they took my arm with a reserve that could have been either respect or repugnance. As we walked several men appeared, buried to the shoulders in the branches that were everywhere. They watched us without moving or trying to follow us, and disappeared silently after we passed.

After a while we reached the middle of the island, where an irregular clearing had been made. It was filled with sitting or squatting men crowded tightly together. Since a narrow moon had risen, I sensed their presence more than I saw them. There was no fire or light of any kind. No one was talking. When I had reached the middle of the group, I stopped. There was nothing but the distant sound of the waves and these pale shadows that were so difficult to decipher.

I cleared my throat. Remember, I could see very little. I

couldn't make out the details of the scene. But it was no longer fear—at least not only that—that gripped me. It was the silence, the immobility, the emptiness . . .

Almost shouting, I asked, "Is there no light here?"

No one answered.

"No fire?"

The man who had accompanied me answered politely, "It is forbidden."

Just before he said it, I had understood. At once I leaned over and pulled some branches toward me and got out the little fire-making kit that I always had with me. Now that we have sulphur, we have matches again. In those days we used a flint, a piece of steel, and a kind of tinder that was made by heating damp tapa until it was completely dry. When the first spark appeared there was a movement in the crowd and almost immediately someone leaned toward me holding out a thin flame.

"It is easier and faster with two sticks," they said.

"Yes."

So I set fire to my branches, which did not catch for a moment, and then suddenly burst into flames and began to crackle. I drew back at once.

"This fire is mine. I lighted it. Clear the area around it, or it will spread to the whole island . . ."

They obeyed me silently, slowly. When the ground had been cleared around the fire, which I continued to feed, they waited with their bodies turned toward me, some sitting, others standing, and now I could see them by the light of the flames.

They were no longer the men with the big *pahis* whom I had seen on the motu. They weren't even the defeated warriors whom we had taken prisoner in the chase on Mount Hiro. All of them were extremely thin; their skin had a greyish color that had become whitish under the eyes; many of them had open sores or purulent scabs; and several bore the marks of recent wounds on the arms, the back, and even on the face. All of them had empty eyes, and not one was looking at me.

"Make the fire bigger," I said suddenly, with fury. "Make a fire so big it will be seen everywhere. It will be my fire."

Without hesitating, as if they had forgotten everything but

obedience, they began throwing branches on the fire, and soon the flames rose several yards, throwing cinders at the sky.

There are certain kinds of stupidity I cannot tolerate. I didn't give a damn what happened. All I cared about was to prove to these men that I was in no way responsible for their fate, which was not true. But at that moment and all that night I was completely sincere.

I sat down on the ground, all alone in the firelight in the middle of their circle, and in my poor English I said, "Tell me about your life."

There was a long silence, and I had to ask the first questions. Then, slowly, drawing strength from each other, they told me everything, and as they came back to life, they became furious. The afflictions they had borne in silence became all the more horrible to them as they heard each other describing them.

At that point I was in great danger. But at the same time that they hated me, they needed me so they could go on talking, so I would go on listening. When everything was said, the night was almost over and they were drained. By then things had changed.

But there at the beginning I was in great danger of my life.

Ever since we thought we had saved their lives, they had been the possessions of Tara. Tara had total control over them, did whatever he pleased with them, along with all the men of his village, and no one objected, not even the ones who, under Poumi's influence, had at one point made common cause with the Fijians. It was Tara who had thought of penning them up on this island, it was he who decided what work they would do, who directed them at the construction sites, who judged the quality of what they had done, who punished or rewarded them. They did not have the right to talk to anyone. Even children could throw stones at them and they were not allowed to defend themselves under threat of punishment. If they lit fires they risked being shot with arrows. They couldn't go near the sea. Finally, for food, they had the lizards they could catch in the bush on their way home, the insects on the island, a few fruits and roots. All of them were dressed in rags. They were foul, whereas natives are always so clean. To sleep in, they had made holes in the piles of branches that surrounded us. They were too exhausted to build *farés*. Finally, they had no women. Not one. While they were saying all this in flat, neutral voices punctuated by sudden exclamations, my eyes were glued to the ground in front of me, where a lizard skin to which a small piece of flesh still adhered was being eaten by worms. It was moving as if it were alive, with its little feet splayed out and its blackened head thrown back.

Many had tried to escape. Some had drowned in the swamp. Others had been shot to death with arrows. Some who had looked for ways to escape and found it impossible had simply committed suicide.

Of the sixty-four survivors of our war, twenty-three were dead. Another very old man had permission not to leave the island. Still another, whose foot had been crushed and whose leg was swollen with infection, was waiting for the end.

Sometimes they all shouted at once, sometimes they listened while one of them described their misery. And depending on whether their hatred was temporarily dulling their pain or whether they were grieving over their afflictions, they would lean toward me or fall back into the shadows. I don't think I'm lying or deceiving myself when I say that at those moments I accepted as natural the idea of my death.

They hadn't said anything for a long time when there came shouts from the bank of the living. They were calling me. Once again there was silence around me. I noticed that some men on either side of me were leaning forward as if ready for anything, no matter how desperate, because my presence had aroused them. I got up and shouted back. I was forced to speak Tahitian. I tried to translate what I was saying into English immediately. It was very difficult. And there in the firelight were those ghastly bodies, those human skeletons with their unseeing eyes.

I walked down to the swamp and over to the bridge. There on the opposite shore, illumined by torches, I recognized Tara, surrounded by his followers. I told him that I had lighted the fire myself, that I was talking to these men, that I did not want to be disturbed. And then I had the last tree trunk pulled up onto the island like a drawbridge, and I went back and sat by the fire. Tara called me a few more times in the night, but I didn't pay attention. The men had started talking again.

Later, as the night was ending, I had to decide how to leave the island. I could barricade myself in and wait with the Fijians. I doubted that Tara would dare to attack me, and I was sure that after twenty-four hours Peyrole would comb the island to find me.

But then what would happen? No one likes to lose face.

I could also cross the swamp, get back on my horse, and go for help. There would be confusion, a lot of time would probably be lost in discussion. What would the Fijians do in the meantime? And what would happen to them in my absence?

Finally, I made up my mind. I looked at the lethargic shadows that surrounded me, crowded together around the coals.

"Who speaks for the rest here?"

Several voices answered at once, "Loualala, Loualala."

"And who is Loualala?"

A man got up; I could hardly see him.

"Will you come with me to get help for these men? Will you . . .?"

I felt like begging him, and at the same time I sensed the absolute necessity of appearing calm and assured. He hesitated for quite a while, shifting from one foot to the other. Then he replied, "Yes, I will come."

We waited for the first light of day before crossing over to solid ground. Tara was there. He ran over to me, took my hand to steady me, and said, smiling, "I was worried about you."

I looked at him. His smile disappeared, then returned, truly friendly.

I didn't really understand Tara. That was because I had overestimated him. Because he was successful I believed him to be complicated, full of plans, tricks, stratagems, a manipulator. He wasn't like that at all. He was a strong boy of average intelligence, but extremely diligent, and not particularly human. By this I mean that when he had chosen a goal he picked the best path, that is, the shortest one, taking into consideration the obstacles he couldn't overcome, and then followed it with no thought of hurting anyone, without even imagining that a good idea could do any harm.

I found this out much later. That morning I had just seen a spectacle of pain and evil such as I had forgotten since I landed at Raevavae. I wasn't in a mood to understand. However, I knew instinctively that Tara's smile was sincere. Since this discovery was useful to me, I paid attention to it. I smiled back.

"I knew I had nothing to fear as long as you were there," I said.

Then without giving him a chance to speak I added, indicating the Fijian who was huddled against me, "This man is coming with me. There is a bad disease among these people. It would not be good for you to catch it, or these men from Mahanantoa. I am taking this man to the doctor. As for the others, stay away from them. They will not work today. Don't talk to them. Don't go to see them. Leave them alone. Tomorrow, we'll see."

"What about you?" said Tara.

"I didn't know about it, and I'll see the doctor at once. But it's serious . . ."

"What kind of disease is it?" he asked me then, in French.

"Fatal," I answered in the same language.

While we were talking, the villagers had edged away from us. When I asked for my horse they brought it to me but they threw me the bridle and no one held the stirrup for me. I got into the saddle unaided and turned to Loualala. "Come on," I said in English.

Then we plunged into the rough bushland, while they stood watching us in silence.

33

THE MAN WHO was trotting alongside me was exhausted, and he was afraid. He didn't even know where we were going. Only out of desperation had he decided to overcome his mistrust and

225

come with me. He didn't want to be separated from me, who perhaps represented a hope, and he didn't complain. But his perspiration had a sour smell, and as soon as we were out of the bush and had entered the woods I had to stop to let him catch his breath.

While I waited for him to rest, I looked at him. In this country where only old age robs the bodies of their beauty, he seemed old. His thin shoulders and scrawny neck had a fragile, wasted quality. His skin, as I said, was pale, covered with filth, scurf, and scabs. Nevertheless, he still had a kind of dignity. While my horse munched some leaves he remained standing in spite of his fatigue, his head held high, looking slowly and calmly around him.

"You will have to learn French, Loualala," I said suddenly.

He looked at me without smiling and made no reply. I didn't know whether he had understood me. I wanted to reassure him, to explain what I intended to do, but I couldn't. My only plan was to find Peyrole and Dubois, to get back to Anatonu, to get away from Tara. How could I explain that to him?

Because the hospital was almost halfway to Anatonu, that is where we slowly headed. On the way we crossed a stream. To the left of the road was a little shaded pool surrounded by ferns. I stopped to drink, then sat down for a moment with my back against a tree. My companion took a drink, looked at me, hesitated, then moved downstream a few steps and washed his whole body very slowly and carefully. I waited until he had finished, and then we started off again, even more slowly.

We arrived at the hospital around nine o'clock in the morning. It had taken us three hours to cover a road which would only have taken me one if I had been alone.

I hadn't seen the hospital since Katherine had started working there, and it had never been very familiar to me. I knew from my wife that it had been enlarged and that Dubois now had a laboratory there, but I was surprised by what I saw.

It was a long stone building with a thick roof of leaves that came down very low like a thatched roof. The facade had six square windows with grillwork lattices and two open doors. At both ends the walls stopped a yard from the ground and the roof was supported by stout wooden pillars. The bays thus formed were enclosed with the same grillwork as the windows. The grounds had been cleared, hoed, leveled, and sanded, but in this open area two groups of trees had been left. Further back, all around, the forest formed a thick and shining curtain. When we arrived a young native girl dressed in white was sitting on a stone block next to one of the doors rolling what looked like strips of cloth. She was talking and laughing with someone inside whom we couldn't see.

I stood on the edge of the woods for a moment looking at this scene, then I urged my horse and Loualala followed me.

When she saw us the woman stopped working and got up and walked toward us, looking surprised.

"Where is the doctor?" I asked.

She pointed to the right end of the building. But I had had to raise my voice so she could hear me from where she was, and before I had reached the place she had indicated, Dubois appeared, barechested and wearing a *paréo*.

He recognized me, smiled, saw my companion, stopped smiling. He took my horse's bridle and handed it to a girl who had come out another door. Then he stooped over a little and showed us inside.

This room enclosed by grillwork was both his office and his laboratory. Opposite the door, against the wall, was a big sink of black stone whose counter was covered with bottles. The wall on the left had a door leading to the interior of the hospital. The right wall was taken up by a chest with about thirty drawers. In the middle of the room a very heavy table, crude but well-polished, and a huge wooden armchair were the only furniture. The room was cooled by breezes and the light that came through the grillwork cast golden, diamond-shaped patches on the ground.

I have forgotten many of the details, but I remember the peace and the calm. Chairs were brought in, then a sort of breakfast. Dubois invited us to have something to eat. My companion was standing silently staring into space. We showed him to a seat and served him some food. After the first few mouthfuls he revived a little and began to eat slowly, in that calm, slightly disdainful way that is a mark of good breeding.

I told Dubois about my night. As I recalled it, I was again overcome with rage and indignation. To keep from losing control I merely presented the facts without adding comments or judgments. I was very brief and to the point but I think I covered everything.

Dubois sat across from us, turned slightly sideways with his legs crossed, swinging one foot as he listened. He never stopped smiling that rather vacant smile that I thought made him look Chinese, and while I spoke his eyes were fixed on Loualala with total attention.

When I had finished he asked Loualala whether he was still hungry, or would like to rest, then he turned to me.

"The hospital is practically empty today. The wisest thing, if you're not too tired, would be if all three of us went to see Peyrole."

As usual, Peyrole listened carefully. When I had finished he sighed, "Well, it doesn't surprise me . . ."

There was a long silence. Dubois looked out the window at the sea.

"You suspected nothing?" I asked Peyrole.

He made a grimace. "Nothing, that's saying too much. I didn't think they were having a picnic. But nobody complained and besides, it was convenient."

"Yes, I know," I said. "I found it convenient myself, and . . ."

Dubois stirred. "Don't you think these reflections could be postponed until later? You said there was a wounded man . . ."

"Yes. And they're all hungry and dirty."

"The problem," said Peyrole slowly, "is Tara."

"Tara and the rest of them . . ." I was furious again. ". . . they all seemed to enjoy playing slave drivers. Who would have thought . . ."

Dubois laughed softly.

"I have a dozen boys . . ." Peyrole was talking slowly, as if to himself. ". . . I have a dozen boys who will do just about anything I tell them to. I think they'll do it. If we could keep Tara in Mahanantoa, we could go and get your Fijians. But what will we do with them afterward?"

"It seems that the men from Vaiuru didn't agree with Tara," I said.

Peyrole waved the idea aside. "All the more reason not to get them involved. We must try to save these fellows, but not at the risk of war. No, no one from Vaiuru."

"Tara is too clever to let himself get stuck in Mahanantoa," I said.

"True."

There was another silence. Loualala looked at us, trying to understand without showing his anxiety.

"We'll have to take them to the hospital," I said at last. "And Tara will have to agree. That way we'll gain a few days, and while they're there we'll think of something."

"Yes," said Peyrole, and went to round up his men.

After that everything went smoothly. Several things operated in our favor. Time had passed, and the natives are no more persevering in hate than in love; I had announced that the prisoners were sick, and the people of Raevavae were afraid of disease, which until the arrival of Dubois had almost always meant death; finally, we Europeans were so ashamed of our past indifference that our decision was irrevocable, and that must have been clear.

Tara gave in very gracefully. He pretended to believe what we said—his men did believe it—and this way he was clever enough not to lose any of his rights. We were taking the sick men to the hospital to avoid contagion and to restore strength to his human cattle. We were doing the right thing, without breaking any conventions. When the men were cured they would go back to work . . .

I can still see our miserable procession on the way back to the hospital. The men recruited by Peyrole surrounded the Fijians, who seemed more like prisoners than ever. Loualala walked at the head of their column, despite his extreme fatigue, for it was his second trip. He was the only one in the group who was clean. In addition, he displayed an aloofness and dignity that were remarkable. Behind him his companions, carrying the sickest, leaning on each other, looking around anxiously all the time, seemed to belong to another species.

Peyrole and I followed this herd very slowly, chatting with Tara, whose presence showed the natives who had come to watch the scene that the prisoners still belonged to him. More precisely, Peyrole said nothing and I made conversation with Tara. I didn't feel like it, and he wasn't pleased. But nevertheless we chatted pleasantly.

Dubois was waiting for us at the hospital. When we got there, for the first time I saw my wife actually performing her functions. Dressed in white, with great calm—I alone could guess what strong emotions it concealed—she welcomed our prisoners with a short speech in English. This speech had an immediate and surprising effect: As soon as they had heard it the Fijians relaxed. It was as if at last they had come home.

Katherine assigned them beds, had them bathed, given haircuts, and bandaged. The aides bustled quietly around her, anxious to do well. Dubois, confined to purely medical duties, accepted his role.

By the end of the day the wounded man had been operated on, all the men had eaten, each had his assigned place. I was very tired. I had taken Tara back to Mahanantoa, talked with many of the natives to explain what had happened, helped Peyrole round up provisions. I had been up all night. Now I stood there uselessly leaning against a wall, watching my wife give orders.

She noticed me and came over. "Go home and sleep. You're exhausted."

"What about you?"

"I'll spend the night here."

Suddenly she touched my arm. "Thank you, Pierre," she said.

I smiled wearily. My only excuse was that all of us together, out of laziness, had chosen to be blind. But this didn't satisfy me. It seemed to me that on the contrary, my responsibility in the thing was greater than anyone else's. And I was concerned about the future.

34

RAEVAVAE WAS A paradise, that is, a place without sin. The sin of societies is mistrust. Because on the whole we had always tried to behave well, and because we had never made any serious mistakes, the natives had confidence in us.

The day after the liberation of the Fijians I called a meeting of the council. For the first time, Peyrole did not agree with me. With his blunt nature and his military ways, he should have been a believer in quick solutions; in fact, he preferred for things to be negotiated subtly through discreet and carefully calculated pressure, peasant style. I, on the other hand, didn't care for such games. Anyway, in the present case I didn't think that was the method to be used.

I had a very narrow margin within which to maneuver. I wanted to free the Fijians once and for all. I wanted to place them under the protection of the council. But I had to arrive at this result without making use of Mai, and without antagonizing Tara.

It was impossible. I brought it off with vague statements and by appealing to each of the members as friends. They gave me the consent I requested, but without conviction, and the meeting ended in an atmosphere of uneasiness.

I was aware of this, but didn't dwell on it. In those days I made my moves one at a time, a day at a time, without a precise plan. I had in mind only a vague sense of the direction to be followed. But I was unfamiliar with either the landmarks or the terrain, and to tell the truth I had no idea that these were even important.

Now that time has put the improvisations of a vanished present in perspective, we explain everything in terms of the Idea. We talk only of the Idea. We judge what is good or bad only in relation to the Idea. But have you noticed that the Idea has never been defined? We say "the Idea," and that's enough. Everyone understands.

It's true that it is the Idea that sets us apart from the few groups of human beings whom we have encountered. It's correct that it is to the Idea that we owe our cohesion and our vitality.

We call it "the Idea," and it's as good a word as any.

But is it really an idea? I wonder.

You see, only islands are immutable. The world never stands still. And there is no such thing as a society without a plan. It doesn't much matter what it is: to defend oneself against others, to get rich, to go to heaven, to honor the gods . . . men have imagination.

For a long time, Raevavae lived without a plan. For the sake of comfort, and out of habit, we made use of the last benefits of routine: the religion of Léné, the French colonial government, natural morality, the riches of the earth.

But comfort is nothing. Only certain poets like the unfortunate Poumi, and a madman, myself, had guessed this truth. To fill the empty space we had all tried to invent a future based on our past, since we were not content with the present, like the common people. Poumi chose savagery. I believed in education.

But remember, I wasn't aware of this at first. In the beginning I had made up some nonsense to save Tekao. Later I took this nonsense seriously, but without foreseeing its consequences. I was looking for a successor, I wanted the good of all, I needed something to occupy myself and the people. I acted under the pressure of events, instinctively, without seeing anything in advance. Besides, at this time no one was talking about the Idea, no one knew it existed.

That came much later, when things really began to change, and it became necessary to justify these changes and place them in some context. The complications brought on by our migration, by the growth of the population, by our success, in short, required that our action be founded on a simple principle, and no longer simply on the lessons inherited from the past. It was then and only then that the myth of the Idea was born.

In the end, the Idea is perhaps embodied in that remark of Dubois' that I told you about: "Either let them sink into the past and disappear, or offer them a new world." Perhaps it is also the decision I made in the name of the whole population of Raevavae not to be satisfied with a simple and happy life, but to recover for ourselves the whole past of the human race, so we could lay the foundations of a more amicable society.

But with one slight difference: I never made this decision. It was events that made it for me.

Dubois wanted the Fijians to spend two full weeks in the hospital. Cleanliness, adequate nourishment, and a little care were enough to restore most of them to health in a few days. But in spite of the consent I had forced from the council, we didn't know what to do with them. The hospital was their best refuge.

At first they were very suspicious, silent, and apathetic, and simply submitted to the good treatment that Dubois prescribed for them. Little by little, however, the peace and plenty began to have their effect. And then there was Katherine. The fact that she spoke English to them like an Englishwoman was certainly a decisive factor. But it wasn't everything. I think they recognized her as one of those creatures whom they had so long obeyed, from whom they had at a certain point separated themselves with contempt, perhaps with hatred, but who were symbolic of a normal and, on the whole, happy past. I said a moment ago that in her presence they relaxed as if they had suddenly come home. This was true, but it wasn't all. It was true that all of them, even the oldest, saw her as a mother capable of protecting them in an incomprehensible and hostile world. And yet Katherine didn't seek popularity and she wasn't familiar with them. She treated them coolly and fairly, she gave orders, but she never explained.

At least twice a day I stopped by the hospital. The rest of the time, without admitting it to myself, I hung around it like a dog who can't make up his mind to abandon a scent. I was trying to find a solution. No doubt I wanted to be sure that the prisoners didn't escape, but also I was interested in my wife.

She was playing two roles there that I had never seen before. First she was a head doctor surrounded by assistants, respected, obeyed without discussion, admired. This classic situation didn't surprise me much. I had often imagined it, and one of the reasons why I had always put off my visit to the hospital was precisely that I found all this a little artificial, a little false. I grant that it was a bad reason. When I saw her I had to admit it: Katherine was my wife, but she was also a real doctor, capable of making decisions, dressing wounds, and taking care of people, a doctor whose expertise everyone recognized but me. If through Dubois she had acquired all the little mannerisms of doctors, it wasn't because she wanted to look like them, but because she wanted to act like them, because she wanted to be as efficient as they were. All this was interesting and instructive, no more. But what fascinated me was another side of Katherine that I saw. Since our marriage, she had ceased to be afraid of the natives. She listened to them willingly, helped them, and knew how to get them to obey her. Her work as a doctor had merely made more natural and automatic an attitude which may have been difficult in the beginning. But, and this is what I'm driving at, when she talked to the natives in French or in Tahitian, she instinctively adopted the tone she saw me use toward them. With the people of Raevavae she made jokes, and was not afraid of a vulgar word or an off-color allusion. I had always found this natural; it had never occurred to me that one could use any other language with them.

But when she spoke English to the Fijians she went beyond me, beyond the rest of us, beyond our democratic, French-speaking, down-to-earth, and fundamentally rather human little world back to a society and a way of thinking that I had never known, and in which I had no place. Without ever raising her voice or smiling, she behaved with an extreme courtesy which did not rule out firmness, quite the contrary. It was as if her simplest remarks were loaded with implications, and as if her politeness were that of the executioner. I'm convinced that she wasn't aware of it, for she gave of herself unstintingly for her people, and showed them the kind of attention that one doesn't think of unless one is profoundly anxious to please. But that's how it was; that's the way we spoke to the natives. We treated them like beloved but incompetent children to whom everything had to be taught, and whose smallest blunder deserved, for their own good, to be severely corrected.

The Fijians were sensitive to this tone, and obeyed her. They did better than this; they anticipated her requests. After a couple of weeks, as soon as their physical condition was back to normal, without her having to ask it of them, they began looking for a piece of land near the hospital where they could settle, and after requesting tools, began to clear it themselves.

When I saw them, I asked my wife what they were intending to do there.

"Oh! Build a house, I suppose. They don't want to be too far away from the hospital, but they want a place of their own. That's normal. Besides, they have to make room for the sick . . ."

We had never talked about it. I felt guilty. For once I, the one who held the power in our marriage, had been beaten on my own ground through no fault but my own. I didn't think it would be useful, or even possible, to justify myself. Katherine didn't want to overpower me. Perhaps she looked down on me and forgave me at the same time. So the two of us devoted ourselves to righting the wrong without even mentioning it.

One must be forearmed against errors, but accept the possibility that one will make them. I have often made mistakes, and almost always I have been the first to notice, so that I had time to correct them before being criticized. The only thing that really hurt me was Katherine's silence. She often gave me advice before I made a decision. But once the blunder had been made, she would drop the subject. Silence. I, who was always in control, would work like a dog to win back her respect.

In the case of the Fijians I felt this more strongly than ever afterward. Besides, that wasn't just a mistake, but an act of cowardice.

I bustled about, helping with supplies, doing busy work; I continued to distribute prizes to deserving students, seated on my purple throne; I greeted the old women and smiled at the young ones. But underneath, I was enraged. All I could think about was finding an honorable solution to this disgraceful episode. I had to do it.

But suddenly the island gave way under my feet. I felt as if Raevavae had turned into a swamp where before you could take a step you had to feel your way and make sure you were on solid ground. Places and people still had the same laughing look; a mangrove swamp looks like the loveliest meadow, yet anyone who ventured into it would disappear without a sound or a trace.

Peyrole was awaiting my orders, tense and alert. Leguen suspected nothing. First indignant and then reassured, he had gone back to his work with a clear conscience. I hadn't heard anything about Bourdaroux. But I expected nothing from him.

That left Tekao and the natives.

Tekao smiled at me but said nothing, his big eyes full of fondness and pity. If things had become critical he would have chosen our side without hesitation, but there was nothing he could do to prevent a crisis.

The truth was that I had taken on the whole island alone.

Laws, votes, agreements are meaningless if they are won by surprise or fraud. The council had agreed to the freeing of the Fijians. But it had given its consent only to avoid opposing me. The decision it had made seemed to it stupid and dangerous. In the eyes of the council, the decision did not exist. It bound no one. In fact, because of its solemn quality it may have obliged people to take a position against us. I knew all this, I sensed it. I had to start all over again, honestly, without trying to force people. I had to convince the ones on whom the solution depended, that is, the people of Raevavae. And to do this I had to get out of this swamp, I had to find something solid I could depend on.

I could only think of one solution: Mai. Peyrole was right about the risks we ran if he were to get involved. Such a step might provoke a war between Vaiuru and Mahanantoa that would spread to the whole island.

But I had great respect for Mai. And after thinking it over carefully, I decided that there was nothing else to do. The slavery of the Fijians was a canker. If we were going to return to savagery, if we weren't strong enough to overcome this crisis, we might as well get it over with once and for all than slip into it gradually.

35

I FOUND MAI alone in his *faré* on the cliff, looking at the sea and scratching the calves of his legs. As always, he gave me a friendly welcome.

"I think some whales are swimming around the reefs. I have not seen them, but sit here with me. We will watch for a while. If we see them, we can have a good hunt. It is fun, you know, and besides it makes much meat, much oil . . ."

I sat down beside him and for a few minutes we talked about whales, fishing, and the weather. Finally I pulled myself together and said, "I came to talk about the prisoners . . ."

He laughed, and I realized that he had known why I was there all along.

"Oh, them," he replied, "we should have killed them the first day, as I advised. Think of everything they have done. And now they are worrying you . . ."

"They aren't the ones who are worrying me."

"Oh, it is the same thing. It is because of them that you are worried. If we had killed them the first day, or else when we caught them . . ."

"But we did not kill them."

"That is true. And now I understand. It is also too bad that we burned their *pahis*. We could have sent them away, and we would be left in peace."

"Mai," I said quietly, "you are my friend and I am worried. They are here, we have to protect them. Almost half of them died in a few months. I do not want this to happen again. I want to protect these men. But how?"

"Oh," said Mai, "these men are bad men. They came where they should not come, they did what they should not do, and now they suffer for it. It is not your fault, or ours."

"Do you want Tara to take them back, and finish killing them?"

He gave me a penetrating look. "Tara is nothing. That man . . ."

I immediately backtracked a little. "That man is good for the school, for the hospital, for the council. Therefore, he is good for the island."

Mai smiled and threw up his brown hands. "If you say so . . ."

There was a silence. Finally I went on hesitantly, "Mai . . . do you think we could just leave them alone somewhere where they will not bother anyone?"

"Why not?"

"Do you think," I said hopefully, "that nothing will happen?"

Suddenly Mai looked at me, his face impassioned. "Listen, *tané*. These men are a bother to everyone. Whether they live or die, it does not matter. We do not care about them. But you want them to live. So why you do not say so? After the war we wanted to kill them. You told us not to do it. Now their lives belong to you, to you and nobody else. Why did you give them to Tara? And why did you take them back? You say Tara this and Tara that . . . but who is Tara? A man who knows the words in books, a man who pretends to be a *poupa,* a man who does not wait until he is old to rule. It was he who mistreated your prisoners and let some foolish people mistreat them. It was a game. A cruel game, but only a game. Now it is over. We are not savages here. We must forgive the foolish people. But Tara is different. Wait, I will tell you something. Before, when everything was good, Tara would not have existed. But you put him in the council, you listened to him, you made him an important man. So you say to him, Tara, that is enough! And if he does not obey, you kill him. But those men with the big *pahis,* it does not matter whether they live or die; we gave them to you."

What an idiot I had been! But I laughed and went on with the conversation, long enough so that Mai would forget the lesson he had just taught me.

Then I went back to the hospital and asked to see Loualala. The two of us sat under a tree a little apart from the others, who observed us curiously but did not dare approach, and decided the fate of the Fijians. I assured him that they were free, and that if they so desired they could even build new *pahis* and leave the island. I also reminded him that he and his men had enemies in Raevavae from whom they had to protect themselves. Finally, I told him that we would help them with their new quarters, as long as they were not in the way of the other inhabitants of the island, that we would not tolerate any acts of vengeance or fighting, and that from now on they had to be self-supporting.

Loualala listened to me with that rather disdainful manner I was getting used to and replied, "We only want peace. Many men died at sea, many men died here. Now we want peace. We will not leave this island. Not now. We shall do as you have said."

I spent the days that followed helping them in every way I could. We gave them some tools from Peyrole's supplies, Leguen contributed some seeds and some animals. They built a very large collective *faré* in the style of their country, with a roof that was much steeper, much higher, and much thicker than the ones in Raevavae. On the day they moved in they ceremoniously invited Katherine, Dubois, Leguen, Peyrole, and myself to share their meal, which consisted solely of fish and wild fruit, as if they wanted to show us that they were capable of living without our help.

Then, after instructing them never to travel around the island alone, at least during an initial period, we left them to themselves, and they slipped out of sight. They cultivated the land around their *faré*, made themselves tools and utensils out of wood quite similar to the ones our natives had started making again, and carved some tall, decorative poles covered with solemn faces such as I had never seen. They didn't move around much, and only rarely would I run into them in groups of three or four in the woods, for they never used the roads.

At first the population observed them from a distance. I had announced, and Peyrole had repeated, that they were to be left in peace. Their life was so uneventful that eventually the observers got bored. Sometimes in the night you could hear them singing. Léné had offered them the services of his ministry, but they had politely declined. Katherine had no reason to go and see them. Even Dubois visited them rarely now that all the sick had recovered. Day by day, with imperturbable calm, they buried themselves deeper in a deliberate solitude, and took possession of an invisible island within our island which nobody set foot on.

I was very alert, as you can imagine. But nothing happened, and my concern could have been interpreted as mistrust. So I limited myself to walking by the big *faré* as often as possible, greeting the Fijians I ran into, exchanging a few words, and asking Loualala, when I had an opportunity, whether he needed anything.

Since his response was always negative and since my presence did not seem to be welcome, I went less and less often, without stopping altogether, and above all without ceasing to be on guard.

A month after the Fijians had moved into their own *faré* I bumped into Tara coming back from a fishing party. He was very friendly toward me and didn't mention my protégés. And no one brought up the subject at the meeting of the council that followed this encounter.

Peace had returned.

36

ONCE AGAIN I was showing my extraordinary naïveté. Peace is like happiness: It hovers around you without your seeing it, perches for a moment, and flies away as soon as you move . . . This has never kept me from pursuing it. But believe me when I say that anyone who thought only of peace wouldn't accomplish much. It's strange—I hate violence, confrontations, wars, revolutions. I believe all these things are wasteful, crude, and stupid. But I can't help thinking that they are here to stay, inherent to life and human nature, and I have always tried to take them into account, although my objective has always been peace.

I'm telling you this today. When one has ceased to act, one

becomes very philosophical. At the time I am telling you about I had neither philosophy nor perspective, in spite of the lectures I have given you. I was very active and very foolish.

Not completely, though. This business of the Fijians, I tell you, is the turning point of my story and of our history. Imagine: Against the whole island, or at least in spite of it, I had chosen to act, I had imposed my will, and not only had I not brought on a catastrophe, but things seemed to be arranging themselves in accordance with my wishes! I have never been ambitious, as you know. I have never connived. Not out of modesty, but out of indifference. Under normal circumstances, I would never have become mayor. I had arrived at this position, I realize today, by a kind of consensus that had nothing to do with either my abilities or my intentions. In fact, I had been elected the way one assumes a hereditary responsibility. And like a little prince who had received a good education, I hadn't tried to take advantage of my position or abuse it. I hadn't so much governed as organized, or, if you will, administered. And then suddenly, when it was time for the Fijians to move into the big *faré*, I had made use of my authority. I had said, It will be thus because I say so.

And I had been obeyed.

For several months I savored this with amazement. On my island, not a leaf stirred against me. Bourdaroux worked silently. The school expanded at a reasonable rate. Tara surrounded me with attentions. For my own pleasure, I resumed my archaeological studies, and for the pleasure of the island, we began making plans for the museum of Raevavae.

One evening as we were having dinner, after the children were asleep, Katherine said, "Did you know that the Fijians have wives?"

I sat up in my seat. "Since when? And where did they come from?"

I was annoyed that in spite of my vigilance I hadn't been the first to know.

"Oh! you know," replied Katherine, "it's easy here. Men and women communicate with each other even if they're miles apart. On the one hand you have all these men without women, on the other, all the girls who haven't found husbands . . . Did you know that since the *tsunami* there are a lot more women than men here?"

"Yes," I said. Peyrole had pointed this out to me. "But how many of these women are there? And where do they come from?"

"Seven or eight, I think, but the number is increasing all the time. Two more arrived yesterday, probably during the night. Yes, this morning there were seven or eight. I know this because Aya, a little girl you don't know who has worked at the hospital for two months now, is one of them. It must have been going on for some time, secretly. The men finally persuaded them to move in. When one of them set the example, the others followed. Aya is from Matotea. I don't know where the others are from. I can ask . . ."

"I wish you would. I'm interested . . ."

Then to hide my concern I asked with a smile, "Are they pretty, at least?"

Katherine shook her head. "Not particularly, no. The pretty ones stayed home. These girls are more the type you don't notice. No doubt that's why they took the plunge!"

"Poor things," I said, meaning the Fijians.

The next day I went to tell Peyrole the news.

"Oh-oh," he said, wincing. "I half expected something of the sort. The only thing they have to fight over here is women. That's natural, since they don't own anything . . . Well, we'll have to keep an eye on them."

"Is that all?"

"As far as I can see. Those Fijians . . . things were much quieter before they came!"

"Well, there's no law saying that things have to turn out badly. I'll know by tonight which villages these girls are from. I doubt if any are from Mahanantoa. Perhaps nothing will happen. In that case, we'll just have one more village in Raevavae, that's all."

"That's all," repeated Peyrole throwing me a sideways look.

He hitched up his pants, wiped the sweat off his forehead with his arm, and smiled. "After all, it's your business. I'm going to take a drive along the coast and see what the people think about it. Incidentally . . ." He looked at me oddly, and seemed embarrassed. "We have roads, but we're practically out of gas. I have barely two hundred liters left. I take care of the jeep as well as I can, but she'll give out one of these days. Already the tires . . . And besides, I'm putting on weight . . ."

I let him go on, not understanding what he was driving at. It was true that he was putting on weight, and suddenly I was amazed to see that his hair was greyer at the temples, his face more lined and heavier than I had realized. Without my being aware of it, he had aged.

"Do you think it would be ridiculous if I asked Bourdaroux to make me a little cart? And maybe you could find me a horse? It's highly irregular, I know, but it would be convenient. Of course, I could do as you do and ride the horse, but I don't know how. Besides, I think it would be more convenient. In a cart you can carry guns, supplies, even prisoners . . . not to mention that the children, on Sunday . . ."

"Of course," I said, "I should have thought of it myself. Go talk to Bourdaroux at once. I'll give you one of my horses."

And I left, laughing to myself at the image of Peyrole riding in a cart.

In spite of the women the Fijians didn't make a move, and neither did the island. Around the hospital and the big *faré*, there continued to be a kind of spider's web of plans, desires, looks, pretended nonchalance, and sudden tensions, but to see it you had to know where to look. The truth was that we were all on guard, but no one would have admitted it. The Fijians were on the lookout for women, and the women mistrusted the men of their villages, who posted discreet sentries. Dubois, fearing that the hospital would get a bad reputation, patrolled the area without seeming to. Peyrole had his spies, too. And I moved through all this trying to look as if I saw nothing.

During the day the calm was undisturbed. But at night everything came to life. From the woods there came the sound of footsteps, rustlings such as no animal has ever made, sometimes a sudden commotion that sounded like the beginning of a fight but was only someone running away. All these men whose paths were constantly crossing thought only of war. But each time the fight would come to nothing just as it began, perhaps because I was feared a little, perhaps primarily because the time wasn't ripe.

One morning when I ran into Loualala I advised him to avoid these abortive hostilities.

"Then we are not free after all?" he asked, throwing back his head.

"Yes, you are," I said, "but that's how it is. You're doing rather well, you have women now. Don't ask for too much too fast . . . After all, it was you who chose to come to Raevavae."

He looked at me for a moment, almost said something, and then walked away with that cool and dignified air which amused and exasperated me at the same time.

I seem to remember, though, that after this warning there were fewer nocturnal outings and that the tension decreased a little.

For a while the Fijians seemed to be interested only in their work. First they enlarged their fields by taking over some of the surrounding forest land. Next, around the vast clearing that now surrounded the big *faré*, they carefully constructed a palisade over six feet high which might have been designed to protect the crops from wandering animals, but which would also have prevented possible attack.

It was not without concern that I watched this defense go up, and I increased my visits. If I could, I wanted to prevent the foreigners from shutting themselves up completely in a world that was totally independent of Raevavae.

During one of these visits Loualala asked me without smiling, but with a glint of irony in his eye, whether the council would like to attend a celebration that his friends were preparing.

"The first crops are coming in," he said, "and now we can repay your hospitality. I will ask the doctor, too . . ."

My relationship with Loualala was polite but cool. Not once since the day I had taken him and his men to the hospital had

I succeeded in establishing a real contact with him. I was gambling on his honesty, without really being sure that he was honest. So far he had never proved me to be wrong, but he had never had an opportunity to. All at once I got the feeling that there was something sinister in his invitation. I threw him a look which he understood.

"We will all eat the same food," he said calmly, "and there is nothing to prevent you from coming armed. You know that although we have been able to make spears and bows with our tools, we have neither guns nor revolvers . . ."

I assured him that I feared nothing, and promised that I would pass on his invitation which I, personally, accepted. Then, for something to say, I asked him pleasantly what kind of a celebration it was.

The expression on his face became even colder and more distant. "A celebration of our country, which can't be described," he said brusquely.

Then, as usual, he left without saying goodbye.

37

THERE WAS A long discussion when the council met days later. The invitation was for the following Sunday. We had four days to reply. Before the meeting I had talked to Peyrole, Leguen, and Tekao. Leguen thought the idea was natural and agreeable. Peyrole and Tekao were more cautious.

"You know, Pierre," Tekao told me, "there are many ways of killing people. I'm not talking about *atuas*, or anything like that. I'm thinking about plants, poisons . . . How can we be sure that these people haven't trained themselves to tolerate poisons that will kill us? I don't want to sound like the movies"—this was one of his favorite sayings, I think he thought it was elegant and rakish—"but I've heard of specific cases . . . even in Tahiti. Imagine what would happen if we all disappeared."

"I don't believe they have evil intentions," I said. "It seems to me . . . it's a vague impression, but it seems to me that they do have some ulterior motive for this invitation, but that it's not our death. I wonder whether they don't want to impress us, or humiliate us a little, in their own way. They've been working constantly, they're very well-organized, very secretive. They are certainly preparing a surprise, but what is it? Personally, I trust Loualala. How can we refuse his invitation?"

"Yes," said Peyrole slowly, "I'm tempted to agree with you. They must want to make an impression on us. Actually, with their mania for speaking English and their way of not looking at you, they're snobs. But anything could happen. It's hard to imagine Tara in there. And Tekao has a point, too. With the council gone, they could take over the island. And then . . ."

"Yes," I said, "but I don't believe that will happen. I've decided to go, alone if necessary. Will you come with me?"

"Yes," they all said in unison. Tekao smiled, and Peyrole raised his eyebrows and grimaced.

I asked them not to reveal their decision to the council until I asked them for it. They agreed again, and separately we went to take our places around the green tablecloth which Odile Peyrole had mended several times and which was beginning to turn brown.

I explained the situation and said that in my opinion we had to accept the Fijians' invitation. Then I asked that each member in turn give his opinion.

While they were listening the natives had looked at each other in alarm. As soon as I had finished Mai jumped to his feet.

"You are crazy! Those people want to kill you, and us, and the whole island. It is as plain as Mount Hiro! It is normal, too, and we cannot blame them for it. After the way certain people treated them . . ." Here he threw a cutting look at Tara, then went on, "We would do the same, if we were in their place. But only a crazy man would go there, and . . ."

I raised my hand. I did not want to give him time to say he would not go, because with him what was said was said.

"They have women now. Besides, I know them better than you do. These men are not like us, but they are honest. For several months they have been living in peace, and they want to thank us."

"Yes, they have women," said the man from Matoteo, "women they have stolen from us."

"Don't complain," said Tekao, "they took the ugliest ones off your hands. And an ugly woman in a village is like a disease . . ."

Everyone laughed, and I was able to go on calmly presenting my case. While I spoke, I observed my companions. As always, most of them were listening with their mouths open or were scratching themselves absentmindedly and staring into space. Mai was making faces. Only Tara sat completely still, his eyes fastened on the tablecloth in front of him. Finally I asked him what he thought. He sat up slowly, as if he had just woken up, sighed, and said, "I am not afraid of those men. They have invited the council. If you decide to go, I will go with you."

"Afraid? Afraid?" Mai was choking. "Who is afraid of them? Not me, anyhow. But I am not crazy. And they will think we are crazy to go and throw ourselves on their mercy like that. Afraid of being taken for a fool, yes, but afraid of them? Bah!"

I smiled. "If I go, will you come with me?"

"Naturally I will. You are not the whole council. Although this council . . . Before, I sent you my little brother, that was enough. I do not know why I came to listen to you again. But I will go with you, of course."

Since Mai had spoken, all the others agreed to go.

So we arranged to meet the following Sunday at the hospital and go together to the big *faré* a little before nightfall, as Loualala had asked.

I was the first to arrive. I remember very clearly that for the occasion I had put on my last Paris shirt and a pair of pants whose seat had been mended but which in those days, when if we weren't wearing a sarong, we were dressed in rags, still made a good impression. Dubois was waiting for me. He was wearing one of his indestructible uniforms without the gold braid or insignia, and welcomed me with a vague smile. We were soon joined by Peyrole and Leguen, who had come together. They, too, had gone to some pains over their appearance. We started to laugh, but the arrival of the other members of the council prevented our commenting on these efforts at elegance. The natives, on the other hand, looked exactly as they always did. Only Mai was carrying a very beautiful carved cane similar to the one Tapoua had given me as a wedding present, which had been stolen. Tekao had put on his only blue suit; it was badly creased and too tight, like those wedding clothes that you get out later to wear to a funeral.

I had completely forgotten about those suits that used to be so common in the country in France. When you got married or went into business you bought a good black suit, you put it on thirty times in your life for big family reunions, and you were buried in it. How much of what I am telling you must escape you! But I can't explain everything. It would take too long, and it probably wouldn't be of much use.

Wait; let me give you an example. You've seen the equestrian statue that was made of me a few years ago. I find the idea ridiculous. You don't display the effigies of men in public life while they're still living. But that's not the problem. I hate that statue. I find it absurd, grotesque, a caricature. I think I've even said so in public.

And yet I'm very fond of the sculptor, a boy named Menaou. He's one of the top students in our baccalaureate class. I've followed his progress and encouraged him, and I don't think he's devoid of talent. But I find his statue, my statue, ridiculous.

And do you know why? Simply because I've seen real equestrian statues, that is, statues representing riders mounted on real horses. So I'm in a position to compare. The artist has portrayed me triumphantly straddling a sort of goat. How am I supposed to like that? And how am I supposed to communicate my disapproval to people who, until a few years ago, had seen only the horses of Raevavae, which actually do look a bit like goats?

But let's get back to our story. So we made our way in a group toward the big *faré*. We walked in threes and fours, making small talk as if this visit were quite natural. I told you that the big *faré* was located in the middle of a vast clearing which was itself surrounded by a palisade. This palisade was unbroken, except for an opening about three yards wide which served as a gate and which had never been closed off in any way, as far as we knew.

Loualala and two other Fijians were waiting for us by this gate. All three were wearing new loincloths made of raffia, had colored their hair with lime, and had had their faces painted in black, white, and blue. They welcomed us very courteously and shook hands with all their guests in turn.

Then Loualala told us in faltering Tahitian that if we liked, before dinner and the dancing he would show us around the grounds. We accepted and we had already taken a few steps with him toward the center of the clearing, around which several small buildings had been built, when we heard a dull rumbling sound behind us. Using all their combined strength, five Fijians were pushing shut an enormous gate made of raw logs mounted on wooden wheels. In an instant the passage through which we had entered was completely blocked. We all started involuntarily. That idiot from Tepaou almost let out a scream, but Roua, his crony from Matotea, kicked him just in time. We looked at each other. Loualala observed us in silence. Mai and Tara laughed in unison. We did the same. Then Loualala said to me in English, in his cold way, "There is no point leaving the gate open for everyone. You are our very honored guests."

I thanked him and added that whatever he did would be fine, for I was sure that he meant well by us. To tell the truth, I was shaking in my boots.

Next, we were given a tour. After a few minutes the native members of the council stopped looking, and began talking and laughing among themselves. At first I attributed this to their lack of seriousness, and I was irritated. In fact, they were humiliated and wanted to retaliate. Everything that Loualala showed us was perfect. Leguen was amazed.

"Did you see this?" he would ask me over and over. "Did you see this corn? This sugar cane? This manioc? Did you see the way they cultivated this ground? Did you see the fish preserve, the water supply, the irrigation? Did you see the way they piped in the spring?"

249

Everything was neat, clean, and well-organized, like a well-kept barracks. There was no question that the Fijians possessed agricultural skills that were superior to those of the people of Raevavae. With his contemptuous politeness Loualala showed us everything, emphasized the details, and without belaboring the point, forced us to recognize an obvious superiority. But for some reason, whereas my admiration should have grown, it was more and more undermined by an uneasiness that I couldn't quite pin down. Mai helped me. When in an attempt to recover my poise and also to overcome an indifference on his part which was becoming insolence, I pointed out the little irrigation canals lined with wood, he shrugged his shoulders disdainfully and muttered, "That is nothing! These people have done all this to annoy us."

Suddenly getting the point, I took a better look at Loualala, whose arrogance now seemed obvious. I cut short his explanations and started talking about how the islanders managed to live just as well with less effort, implying with perfect courtesy that the cleverest ones weren't always the most industrious. At this Loualala smiled briefly and calmly conducted us to the open space in front of the big *faré*, where he showed us to some seats that had been prepared in advance, and we were served drinks.

In the meantime, night had fallen. The Fijians lit some torches that were attached to long stakes that had been driven in the ground all around us. I was sitting next to Peyrole. He leaned toward me.

"You can say what you like, they may not be geniuses, but they're amazingly well-organized, I'll say that for them! And hard workers, too."

I nodded in agreement and was about to reply when suddenly out of the night ten almost naked men with their bodies covered with paint, their hair stiff with lime, carrying spears and carved shields, rushed toward us screaming. At our feet three of their compatriots beat out a rhythm that was strange to us on a hollow log and a very crude lyre.

The dance lasted twenty minutes, and was full of a force and brutality to which we were not accustomed. There was no doubt that it was a war dance, and at least three times the warriors rushed toward us with their spears raised, stopping only when they were almost touching us. Once again they had become very handsome men, with the grace of animals, and in the glow of the torches their eyes and teeth sparkled.

My companions, unimpressed, continued to chatter without watching the spectacle, seemingly totally engrossed in a thousand funny stories which they told each other while giggling like women.

Finally, at a signal from Loualala, I think, the dancers withdrew and we were shown into the big *faré*, where dinner was awaiting us.

The meal was long, and was made up of dishes which were unfamiliar to us, very carefully prepared and very correctly served. Loualala made a show of tasting all the dishes before he served us. Then he passed what was left to the Fijians, who were sitting in three rows facing us. At no point did I see any sign of women.

The scene was illuminated by oil lamps and candles made of crude wax. The framework of the big *faré* and all the columns that supported it were carved with those stern faces I mentioned. In spite of their deliberate show of indifference, my companions secretly watched the flickering light bring these faces to life, and I don't think they appreciated them very much. The Fijians didn't talk. Our conversation consisted of an occasional compliment on the cuisine. The silence was broken only by the sound of chewing and, here and there, by the stifled laughter of the men from Raevavae, when they thought of it. It was a very long evening. After dinner I gave a speech in Tahitian which was politely received. Then we got up and left.

The gate of the enclosure was opened for us, and as soon as we had left it was closed behind us again.

It was pitch dark outside. Behind the palisade we heard noises, sensed a presence. Stumbling, we made our way to the hospital, where Dubois asked us all to come in, instructing us to keep our voices down.

We sat down. I looked at Peyrole. He looked dignified but

seemed very upset. Tekao kept his eyes lowered. Leguen yawned and looked at me sadly. The others were ashen with anger. Only Dubois was smiling. He chuckled to himself.

"We've been given a lesson," he said at last. "These good people have given us back good for evil, and I must say they know what they're doing! As a doctor, I wish all the villages on this island were as clean as their *faré!*"

Mai spat on the ground, looking as if he wanted to bite someone. Leguen made a vague gesture.

"It's true they're clever. With their drainage ditches and their knowledge of cultivation, they've taught me something I didn't know. But all the same, they're not much fun."

At this point the natives all began talking at once and Dubois had to ask them again not to disturb the patients. Then Tara said, "We can do better than those people. Anyhow, we beat them at war."

The way they looked at him, I thought he would have done better to have kept his mouth shut. But Maraou, who was habitually a peaceful man, said, "Yes, we beat them, and we will beat them again. Those people invited us there to insult us. They do not understand good manners. We know that insults mean war. Those men are not civilized. It is true that they are clean. But we can be as clean as they are, if we choose."

"They have suffered," said Dubois.

Mai stiffened. "Why did they come to kill us?"

I was tired and disappointed. I raised my hand. "The fault lies with the wind, with the sea . . . and with Poumi. These men are the way they are. It is true that they have given us a lesson. But we deserved it. Don't forget that half of them died *after* the war. How do you expect them to love us? The important thing is for time to pass, and for us, as wise men, to forget. Eventually they will do the same. Now I'm going to bed . . ."

We parted in silence. Although I shook hands with Tara, I managed not to look at him.

As he took me back to Anatonu in his little service cart, Peyrole said, "This will end badly."

I replied, "Not at all. Soon they will have children. That will solve everything. In ten years, it will all be forgotten."

38

I WAS RIGHT. That is, I should have been right. I was logical and disinterested. I saw things clearly. But not all things.

In the days that followed Peyrole was constantly trotting around in his poor peasant's cart and then collapsing anywhere, at his house, at my house, at the hospital, like a sack, morose, silent, his elbows on his thighs, his shoulders sagging, his brow knotted. Once he said to me, "I'm too old for this . . ."

I made fun of him, advised him to start a school for policemen, to choose a successor. He nodded.

"You laugh at me, but you're just as worried as I am. What were you doing yesterday morning in the bushes behind the big *faré*, eh?"

"Well, your nervousness is catching . . ."

"Yes, of course, that's a good excuse. Now, as far as finding someone to take my place, I'd like to. Or even an assistant. I've thought of it. Often. Only . . . look here, can you see a native in my place?"

I smiled, surprised. I almost said Yes. And then I thought it over. In all honesty, I couldn't see anyone taking Peyrole's place. I tried to dodge the question.

"Right now, no. But in two years, in five years . . . someone will turn up. No one is irreplaceable, Peyrole. Not you or me. Some day we'll step aside, and . . ."

Peyrole shook his head. "I don't think so. I've thought about it, you know! It's just that . . . well, I must be getting old. But I'd like to retire. Tend to my own business and let other people tend to theirs. Sometimes I say to myself . . . My children could have been brought up differently, you know. I let their mother have her way because it pleased her and because I wanted to be free for my work, but now—now I'd like to retire. Only it's not time yet. You have your ideas, and you're probably right, I don't want to argue with you. But what's to become of us? A strange species, a strange race, I'm sure there's never been anything like it: everyone in his own little house, living his own little life, everyone educated, no money, no rich people . . . I'm not against it, mind you. In my business, you see things . . . In short, I hope you succeed. And then there'll be no need for police. Or a mayor either, for that matter. It's hard for me to imagine, but if you think it over, that's what you want, isn't it?"

Suddenly he smiled that slightly bitter smile of his. "In any case, I have news for you. In spite of them—" and he nodded his head in the direction of the big *faré*—"in spite of them, I went over all my books this morning. Including the Fijians, there are now exactly one thousand and two persons on the island. The last two were born yesterday in the hospital, and the day before yesterday in the bush, between Matotea and Rairua. Both boys."

"But that's wonderful news," I said, as much because I was really pleased as because it changed the disturbing quality the conversation was taking on. "We'll have a big party. Everyone will be invited, even the Fijians!"

The party took place, and the Fijians did not appear. The whole island knew they had been invited and felt the insult. After having scorned these strangers so totally, they were amazed to be scorned by them in turn.

Bourdaroux, who had left his fort for the occasion, told everyone in a loud voice what all of them were thinking. Bad luck always pleased him, because it fulfilled his predictions. And telling the natives, whom he looked down on, that someone else felt contempt for them must have delighted him, too. I had to step in.

Tekao was a big help. In those days parties went on for several days. As soon as it became obvious that the Fijians weren't coming, we went ahead and suggested that these days would demonstrate the greatness of Raevavae. Everything we had achieved, learned, or discovered, we displayed. I've forgotten the details of all this, but I remember a competition of builders in which one team, to save time, completely demolished an almost new *faré* and built another house exactly like it in its place. There were also a flower-garden contest, history and geography quizzes, an arithmetic tournament, athletic events . . . And almost always the winners felt the need to go and take a stroll afterward between the hospital and the big *faré*, laughing very loudly and explaining how and why they were better.

It could have turned out badly, but in fact it was very useful. Inside of two months there were more changes in Raevavae than in the ten years that had passed since the *tsunami*. The people were seized with a frenzy for perfection. Almost all the houses were rebuilt. Each village chose to be redesigned according to its own individual plan, which now allowed room for real streets. Peyrole and Léné were called upon to marry an incalculable number of couples, and the use of the bed, the table, and the chair, until then regarded as a permissible but inconvenient affectation, was established forever. When Leguen informed me of the amount of land that was being cultivated, I had to intervene before the island turned into a desert.

When these two months were over many people got bored, and many things went back to what they had been before. But certain things were irreversible. In the villages the young boys and girls who came out of our school did not replace the elders, but they were listened to as equals. The landscape had changed. Here and there food-storage centers were being set up. And above all everyone, even the most indifferent, now believed that progress was underway in Raevavae. All this to show the Fijians that we had contempt for their contempt.

I don't remember exactly how long this lasted. I'd have to do some research, make some cross-checks. But there's not much point. Anyway, it's simple: Louis was born four years after the *tsunami*, and Anne was two months old when the Fijians arrived. They are three years apart. So the period I'm talking about is located approximately in the middle of our ninth year on the island. Nine years! I didn't notice them go by, and when I think back on them they seem so light, so uneventful! And yet they were the best years of my life: my youth, my wife, my children, a land I loved under my feet, my good friends around me, and nothing to do but plan successful parties . . .

We waited five or six months, every day less attentive, more forgetful, more trusting.

In my own way, which is erratic, I worked hard. Oh, I still took walks, of course, I talked to the people, I played mayor, but

I also read. In all seriousness, I began to realize that I had set something in motion which would go beyond me. I was trying to figure out how far it would go.

It was around this time, I remember, that I started to draft a proposed constitution. I didn't get beyond the first article. It went something like this:

Happiness does not exist, but every man is free to pursue it. Anyone who opposes this pursuit will be punished by death . . .

It's stupid, but the question of happiness really preoccupied me in those days. I must admit that I didn't feel comfortable. I wasn't on familiar ground. Nothing I read really answered my questions. The most intelligent writers only sent me back to my personal problems, not one gave me even the beginning of an answer. They were much more intelligent than I; I respected them because they were writers, and because they wrote well. However, the only way I could get out of my impasse was to repudiate them, or at least to refute them, and then to take their places, pen in hand. No, I didn't feel comfortable.

Even so, I succeeded in arriving at three things that seemed to me fairly reasonable. I've never told them to anyone. Not even Katherine. To do so would seem to me at the same time so self-important and so pitiful . . . I'll tell them to you.

My first observation was that there is no such thing as a perfect government, or a perfect society. It's pointless, therefore, to expend a lot of effort trying to invent an infallible system. The needs and desires of human beings govern their actions. A system of government is good when it is adapted to a given situation. If the situation changes, the system must change. That's all there is to it.

Next I observed, as I have already said, that work is the root of all evil. I realize, of course, that we lived in an agreeable climate. But even so, our isolation could have been cruel. In fact, it had merely demonstrated to us how few and how easy to find are the things essential to life. A few hours' work a week by a few people who are so inclined is all you need to provide them. Finally, the third point I considered important was that societies are only as vital as the people that compose them, and that therefore the personal progress of individuals is essential.

To sum up, three clichés: perfection is not of this world; money is not the key to happiness; and it is citizens who make nations . . .

Even when I was learning the catechism for my first communion, I didn't find these ideas very original. I'm sorry not to have found anything better. And I'm sorry that at the time I didn't make note of a fourth point, which may be the most important: you always have to allow for human stupidity.

One evening Katherine and I were having dinner alone. Little insects buzzed around the coconut-oil lamp, then flew into the flame and disappeared with a tiny frying sound, just as the May flies used to fly against the light on the porch of my grandmother Gerzat's home in Berry. The children were asleep. Everything was peaceful. Katherine was tired and was eating slowly; I was waiting for her, sitting sideways and smoking my pipe. Suddenly she said, "Do you know what Tara wants to do to the Fijians?"

I shook my head.

"He wants to prohibit their children from going to school."

I shrugged. "They don't have children yet. And Tara doesn't have the right to decide that. That's up to the council. The council would never . . ."

"Did you know about it?" asked Katherine.

I shook my head again. "What difference does it make?"

I was relaxed, and a little sleepy. My wife put down her fork and sat up in her chair. "The Fijians trust us, Dubois and me. But they don't come to the hospital. I go and see them. They have fourteen women with them. Eleven are pregnant. One is about to give birth any day now. She's a girl from Matotea. She heard about Tara. Some people from her village came and shouted to her over the palisade. I saw her this morning. She wanted to have an abortion because of it. That's what difference it makes."

It was serious, but I didn't feel like spoiling my pipe. I snorted. "She's very stupid. Tara has no power of his own."

"Except the power to kill people and put them in concentration camps."

Suddenly we faced each other. I looked at her and sighed.

"Let's not argue about it. You're right. But you know that that was my fault. I admit it, I admitted it . . ."

"And the Fijians had to suffer for it."

"Well, what do you want, anyway?" Now I was awake, indignant.

"Pierre," said Katherine slowly, "I know you're honestly doing everything you can. But still . . . aren't you easier on yourself than you used to be? A few years ago, when you first got interested in all this, you always wanted to succeed. Now you still do your best, but if you fail, you say, 'I made a mistake,' and you think about something else. You're right; you're not getting anything out of it personally. You're really honest. And besides, as you say, *errare humanum est*. You let Tara kill the Fijians. You saved the ones that were left. Your mind is at rest . . ."

"What do you know about it?" I asked angrily.

"Nothing, but I know you."

I had gotten up, and was pacing up and down the room. I was angry and upset. I said, "You're really lucky, you know. You're an important doctor. You take care of the sick. That's fine. And to take care of the sick all you have to do is be intelligent and work hard and do what it says in books. Me, I'm just a poor, dumb mayor who has to make it up as he goes along. I don't even have books to guide me. I . . ."

Suddenly I looked at Katherine. There was a silence, and then we both burst out laughing. Our lives had become separate, but our regard and affection had remained the same as in the beginning.

"Well," said Katherine, putting her head on one side, "are you going to do something for these Fijians?"

"Yes," I said, "yes, yes, yes. But at least wait until the children are born."

"No. Even if no child is ever born you must do it, and you know it."

"Yes. You're right. I'll do it."

Katherine looked at me for a moment, smiling, then she got up, too.

"Listen," she said, "it's a long time since you've seen Dubois. I think he'd like it if you paid him a visit. Why don't we go there right now? It's early. He's sure to be home. We could take the horses. How long is it since we've taken a ride together?"

I laughed again. "What are you trying to tell me?"

"You'll see."

It was April. The rainy season, which was a little late that year, had just ended. The night was very clear, and there was a slender moon. In the woods, on the path, the air was still warm, and the flowering trees were fragrant. Our horses walked side by side, their narrow shoes slapping against the stones in unison. I took Katherine's hand.

"You're right, it's a long time since we rode this way. It's my fault. I should have suggested it."

I could feel her smiling in the darkness. "It's my fault, too. But it's not easy to be a good wife and a good doctor at the same time. A doctor isn't a mayor, but even so . . ."

"Which would you rather be," I asked to tease her, "a good doctor or a good wife?"

I felt her stiffen almost imperceptibly. "Must I choose?"

"Just for fun . . ."

"For fun? Then I think I would still choose to be a good wife. But . . . I don't know whether I could still be a good wife if I didn't go to the hospital."

"Who says you're a good wife?"

"You . . . oh! to hell with you. If you're not satisfied, why don't you divorce me?"

She pulled her hand away, spurred her horse, and galloped ahead of me. I caught up with her immediately. We were joking. But it wasn't easy, you see. She hadn't been happy in Raevavae until she was doing something on her own. Until she had become independent, in other words—but it was I who guaranteed her independence.

Dubois certainly wasn't expecting us. Katherine would have told me so. Yet the way he was lying in his hammock with one foot on the ground, holding a coconut with a plastic straw stuck in it, lost in the twilight a few feet from his house exactly the way I had always found him at this hour, he somehow seemed to be waiting for us.

From behind his *faré* came the sound of a stream that made a waterfall there. There wasn't a breath of wind. The silence was broken only by the stream, the creaking of the hammock, and sometimes from below, in the distance, the voice of a native, strangely resonant, saying something I couldn't understand.

I felt more than friendship for Dubois. I would have liked to have had him for a father. But for reasons that you know, I have no talent for being a son, only a natural inclination. In France in my youth I allowed this inclination to express itself several times by seeking the acquaintance of men older than myself. It always turned out badly. I would admire them before I knew them. By the time they became convinced of the genuineness of this unexpected respect and were ready to grant me their friendship, I already knew them too well and had catalogued their faults. Yes, it always turned out badly.

In the case of Dubois it was almost the same, with the difference that I wasn't as young, and it would have been impossible to lose touch with him.

So there were times when I would visit him every day, tell him my problems, and listen to his advice and his memories. Then a word or gesture of his would alienate me and without any excuse or apology I would disappear for months at a time. But he was honest and kind, and didn't try to win me back any more than he held it against me. Besides, the island was small, and eventually our paths would always cross again.

That evening I was in good spirits. First there was a very lazy exchange of news, interspersed with silence. It was as if each of us was trying out his voice and also listening to the voices of the others so he wouldn't be out of tune when the orchestra began to play.

Then Katherine, who when she was with Dubois always acted like a student in front of her teacher, said, "At dinner, Monsieur, I talked to Pierre about Tara and the Fijians."

Dubois must have smiled. I couldn't see his face, but I knew him well. He said, "Ah!"

There was another lazy silence. Dubois had a certain talent for making people talk without saying anything himself. I was waiting for Katherine to get the conversation going again and give me a chance to speak. I was startled when he sat up in the darkness, put his feet on the ground, with his hands resting on the hammock on either side of his body, and said quietly, "It's a worrisome business. It upset me. Of course, it won't come to anything, since you've been informed. But this Tara—I don't like him. This is the second time he has taken you by surprise. How long have you been mayor?"

The question caught me off guard. "Four years, going on five."

"Yes . . ."

". . . And how long will you continue to be?"

"I have no idea. As long as I am elected, I suppose."

"Yes . . ."

Dubois thought this over for a moment, then went on, as if forcing himself, "Don't you think it's a little paternalistic? I mean, this lack of competition, this absence of opposition?"

I raised my eyebrows. "Perhaps. Yes, it probably is."

"I think so too. You're . . . you're established, you and your colleagues on the council. Even Tara. That one . . . I . . . well, I've decided to represent the opposition. In the next election, I'm going to be a candidate in Mahanantoa. I'll run against Tara. If I'm elected, I'll keep an eye on all of you. I'll keep you on your toes. You can depend on it."

For a moment I sat speechless, stupefied. "That's fine," I said at last. "It's your right. But why? I'd be glad to give you my seat. Run in Anatonu. I'll campaign for you. I don't care about staying on the council . . ."

"Oh, but you must!" said Dubois. "You're made for it. Besides, you don't understand. I don't want to replace you, I want to watch you. And I want to show the people that Tara can be beaten. At least, maybe."

"He won't appreciate your idea," I said.

"Precisely. Anyway, one should always follow one's instincts. Don't you agree?"

"Yes, of course . . ." Suddenly I asked him, "Doctor, how old are you?"

He chuckled. "Seventy-one. And believe me, your wife is now just as good a doctor as I am. She's the one who'll be training successors . . ."

I was totally flabbergasted. I tried to keep the conversation going, to get an explanation, to understand the reasons for this incredible decision. But Dubois wasn't inclined. All he would do was laugh, rather derisively.

Sensing that my anger was mounting, not against the decision itself, but against his hedging, he finally did offer a sort of explanation.

"Call it a lesson, if you like," he said. "It's true that I don't like Tara. But . . . I want to help you in my own way. You're succeeding too well. Man is various, everchanging. I want to give your people a lesson in opposition . . ."

I couldn't make any sense out of it.

39

THE ELECTIONS WERE four months away, and theoretically the electoral campaign was only supposed to last one month. But as soon as Dubois' plans were known, tongues began to wag. The natives had been interested in the creation of the council, and generally speaking, they enjoyed voting. But it must be admitted —Dubois was right about this—that the elections had never been much disputed. In fact, we on the council chose our fellow members, and when we were in agreement we asked the people to ratify our choice.

This time things were going to be different. There was an innovation here which the natives didn't understand very well. This was exactly what I was afraid of, knowing only too well their love of novelty.

I agreed with Peyrole, who felt that the council should be called together and informed as soon as possible. We called the meeting for a Wednesday. I remember, because Wednesday was consulting day for pregnant women, and Katherine left for the hospital much earlier than usual.

But that morning, just as I was about to leave for the Navy House, Loualala came to my house to see me. With him were two old men and four young men carrying heavy sticks. This, and the fact that he had never visited me before, in spite of my invitations, made me think that something serious was up. I asked all my visitors to come in, but the ones carrying sticks refused, and took up positions around the *faré* as lookouts. Loualala and his two companions, however, accepted my invitation, and sat with dignity sipping the orange juice I offered them.

Quite a long time passed during which we made polite conversation about nothing. The hour of my meeting was approaching, and I was very conscious of the minutes that were being wasted. To occupy my mind I looked at Loualala, whose solemn and dignified face showed great control. I was careful not to let the conversation die and at the same time not to give it too much fuel, so that there would be short pauses propitious for bringing up serious subjects.

At last Loualala said, "Madame Beaumont and you have always been very correct with us. So it is to you that my people have chosen to address themselves, through me."

I bowed. The ceremonious side of the Fijians—which seemed especially important to them now since, being of British origin, it enabled them to feel different from the natives who were nevertheless very close to them—this side of the Fijians had always charmed me. Loualala acknowledged my bow with a flutter of the eyelids and went on in a soft voice, almost under his breath, "My people wish to learn French so that they may have every opportunity among the citizens of this land. I have been entrusted to ask you whether this is possible, and on what terms."

It was the last thing I expected, and I was delighted. I replied that the school was open to all, and that Tekao himself, although he spoke very poor English, would welcome the Fijians and would be responsible for them. Still speaking very slowly, Loualala then pointed out that all the men could not attend class at the same time, and that they would have to set up two shifts, so that the animals and the fields would never be left untended. I thought to myself that this way the big *faré* would always be guarded, but I didn't care. I even liked the idea, for they say that deserted places attract bad people. So I assured Loualala that we would schedule two groups of classes, and thanked him for giving us this proof that, in spite of many unfortunate accidents, he and his friends finally intended to participate fully in the life of the island. He smiled briefly with great contempt, and then became serious again and said, as if it were all the explanation that was needed, "Soon there will be children to raise. They will not speak Tahitian, but French and English . . ."

I realized then that Tara was the involuntary cause of my delight. I was convinced of it after Loualala had me go over the assurances I had just given him point by point, and concluded in a tone that was almost light, "Then it is understood that there will be no discrimination?"

"No discrimination," I assured him.

Then we had to have another pointless conversation in order to pass from serious subjects to neutral matters propitious for departure.

When I got to the Navy House Odile Peyrole showed me to the meeting room, whose door was closed, motioning with her hand to hurry.

I didn't need this encouragement. The meeting must have been going on for at least a quarter of an hour. When I walked into the room no one was talking. Mai had a superior smile on his face, Tara looked dignified. Peyrole seemed annoyed. I greeted everyone quickly and sat down.

"Well," I said, "you don't look very jolly!"

Nobody said anything.

"Who was speaking?" I asked Peyrole.

"Tara."

"Well, Tara, if you will excuse my lateness and tell me what you were saying . . ."

Then there was a real silence, one that consisted not just

of the absence of words, but of the total cessation of all sounds, even the almost inaudible sounds that muscles and skin make when they move.

"Well!" I said again.

Tara looked at me, took a deep breath, and suddenly stood up. I looked at him calmly—perhaps, in spite of myself, a bit ironically. I motioned to him to go ahead.

He gave a very classical speech in a very elaborate, traditional style, to the effect that since no one could accuse him of ever falling short in his duties as a municipal councilor, it was inconceivable to imagine that a competitor could come and steal his votes in Mahanantoa. He harbored no ill will toward Dubois, who was a very wise *poupa,* but was old and had been advised by bad men. He was counting on me, on us, to make our friend listen to reason, and declared himself ready, for the sake of friendship, to build him a new *faré,* to present him with a good canoe, or even to send one of his own nieces, who was as young as she was pretty, to be his servant.

I was very careful not to interrupt him. As I listened to him I saw that he was sincere, in his own sly way, and that the native councilors appreciated his style as well as the generosity of his offers.

I could have let him go on. The council would have applauded him and gone on to the business of the day. But that would have proved Dubois right. Besides, there were the Fijians. Besides . . . besides, I wasn't struggling with myself and with others to make a few people happy. I raised my hand.

"It's not that simple, Tara," I said.

It took me a few seconds to find my rhythm. I, too, knew how to give speeches in the traditional style. But I used these techniques to be more convincing, whereas Tara, as I realized later, resorted to them in order to control his temper.

When I had finished, the council was disturbed. Tara was openly furious. His face pale, his voice constricted, he accused me of showing partiality to a *poupa.* Never, since I had landed in Raevavae, had anyone said this to me. I cut him short. "No, Tara, it's the law, it's not me."

Standing there haughtily, with a wild look in his eye, Tara

gave a bitter laugh. "Nobody has ever mentioned this law here. Two times already we have had elections, and nobody has ever said that *poupas* could be candidates in any village they wanted. You just invented this law, and that . . ."

"Here, here," said Peyrole suddenly, "let's not get carried away."

He was holding an old and rather dirty pamphlet, which he handed to Tara. "Do you know how to read? Well, read this, and you'll see."

Then while Tara pored intently over the pamphlet, moving his lips, he turned to us. "It's the manual of the secretary of the mayor's office. It tells all about elections."

There was a silence, then Tara looked at me. He seemed lost. I don't like to hurt people. Besides, it's embarrassing. I didn't dare smile, but I said in as friendly a tone as possible, "Would you read us the passage? I've had experience with elections in France in the old days, but I wish you'd refresh my memory on the exact terms . . ."

Tara hesitated, then began to read in French very well, which flattered his pride. This is what I was counting on. Then, cautiously, I engaged him in a technical discussion in which I got Tekao and Peyrole to participate too.

After giving in on a few details, I let him sum up.

"It's the law," he said nobly.

Everyone was relieved. But I was sure this didn't mean that anything was settled. Also, I decided not to talk about the Fijians' visit, as I had originally intended to do.

As soon as I got home that evening I asked Katherine why Dubois was so anxious to run against Tara. She shook her head.

"I don't always understand Dubois. In spite of his gentleness, he's not a man whom women understand. But in this case I think I do. He's old and alone; he feels like a failure. You're always saying that you love the people and the island. Dubois never says so, but he loves them more than you do. It's true that you know them better than he does, but that's another reason. He *invented* them. They are the setting of his life. He found peace among them. They are exactly the kind of people he needs:

vague and distant enough not to bother him, but natural and warm enough so that he still feels alive. He loves them. That's how it is. Perhaps he's afraid of all these changes that are starting to happen. He was very distressed by what happened to the Fijians. He loves them, too, although he never talks to them. He must think it's his duty to protect them."

"But he won't succeed. He hasn't got what it takes . . ."

Katherine reflected for a moment. "He has strange ideas sometimes. I don't know whether the idea of success is that important to him. He believes that what matters is the gesture, the attitude. In the final analysis, perhaps he'll be fighting not so much for them as for himself . . ."

"Yes," I said, discouraged, "he's going to throw himself into politics for his own salvation. But he'll make a fool of himself, no doubt about it. And he's not young any more! And then there's Tara . . ."

"Do you think he's dangerous?"

I shrugged. "I don't know. He wants to be perfect and is going to a lot of trouble to get there. But this effort feeds his pride. The harder he tries to be just, good, and civilized, the less tolerant he is of criticism. He is strong, brutal, ruthless, and always has the best intentions . . ."

Katherine suddenly grabbed my hand. "Will you watch him? And will you watch Dubois?"

I nodded. "Yes. But it would have been simpler if Dubois didn't run . . ."

40

PERHAPS TO IMPROVE his chances, and also, no doubt, because he was unaware of the laws, Dubois decided to begin his campaign before the others and also to campaign all over the island instead of limiting himself to the territory of Mahanantoa, as he should have done.

I could have pointed this out to him. But I was ashamed

for him and I felt sorry for him. Suddenly he was no longer the devoted doctor, a wise eccentric, but a poor old man who flew to pieces at the slightest contact with other people. I avoided him as much as I could. But he was really pushing himself, and in spite of my efforts I was always running into one of his meetings in my rambles in the woods.

A group of natives had become his followers. I knew one of them very well, a toothless old fisherman, a friend of Mai's who laughed at democracy and the Fijians, but who found the game amusing and used every trick he had to win. With slight variations, the others must have had more or less the same sentiments.

They had built a kind of portable platform on which, when they had arrived at their destination, they would perch Dubois in one of the big rattan armchairs that habitually decorated his *faré*. For the campaign Dubois had given up his *paréo*, his archery, and his painting. Now he only appeared in an old white uniform which was too big for him but very clean, and on which he had been clever enough to sew back or to leave the gold braid and insignia he had worn as a navy doctor.

In order to attract bystanders his followers played music, sang, and danced while he sat motionless and indifferent, a tall blurred silhouette tense with fatigue, his hair blowing in the wind. Gradually a crowd would gather. Some people would bring him gifts: necklaces of flowers, fruit, even animals. All these things would be piled on the platform as if at the feet of an idol, and he would pay no attention to them, whereas after each offering the shouts of his people would grow louder.

At last, when he felt that the time had come, he would get up slowly, holding out his arms for silence, and his face would change. Suddenly, he would become eloquent.

In my opinion he was much too direct, much too natural for his audience, by whom he wanted to be understood, and who took his deliberate simplicity for innocence, but he believed in every word he uttered, and this was unmistakable. After laughing at first, his listeners would go away silent, vaguely uneasy and troubled.

Dubois also showed an adaptability and shrewdness I would

not have thought him capable of. In the beginning, his whole argument was based on the Fijians. He wanted to demonstrate that these people were our equals and that what had happened to them could happen to us tomorrow, if we weren't careful.

These ideas seemed ridiculous to the people of the island, who felt that the Fijians, those rotten bastards, were very lucky not to have been killed, and had only themselves to blame if they had to put up with a little unpleasantness.

Dubois realized this, and he very quickly changed his theme. Abandoning all allusions to the foreigners, he focused on the few mistakes made by the council in an attempt to show that no one was infallible, that it was necessary to be vigilant, and that only the people could know what was good for the people.

These arguments struck me as demagogic and unfair. But since in a sense they were directed against me, I was a poor judge. On the other hand, I was aware of the sincerity with which they were presented, a sincerity which made the enterprise of my old friend seem all the more illusory.

Each time I stumbled on one of these meetings I would listen for a moment in spite of myself, and then, ill at ease, I would slip away without being seen, sure to be angry and upset for the rest of the day.

What shocked me most about the thing was what, in spite of everything, fascinated the people and prevented Dubois' attempt from being as ludicrous as I had at first thought, namely, the innocent severity with which he denounced the important men of the island, and, first of all, myself.

I don't say that he was wrong. Indeed, I have always been ready to hear his advice. I would have listened to him, I think, if he had really wanted to talk to me. But why, for what absurd and unfortunate reason, did he come to exhibit himself this way, to address himself to people who weren't ready to understand him, to call everything into question and to risk everything, even my friendship and my respect, which however were his without question?

He was so stubbornly determined to win that he had made —and the time it must have taken proves that his decision had been made well before our conversation—a whole series of signs out of dried and braided banana leaves, on which he had prettily painted flowers and written, "Vote for Liberty," or "Vote for the Doctor," I don't remember anymore.

These signs, which were fastened to trees in the woods, didn't fail to attract attention. I wasn't opposed to this new practice; although these somewhat private notices may have humiliated the illiterate, who were still numerous at this time, they also introduced writing into daily life and thus indirectly were good publicity for the school.

In fact, I was angry when I noticed, after a few days, that they had disappeared. I accused Tara's men of taking them without trying to prove it, to avoid additional tension, and this little incident, as you will see, had a very unfortunate influence on my judgment. Much later, months after everything was over, I found three of these signs hanging on the walls of mountain *farés* as decorations.

I could have cleared up this matter at once. I ran into Tara by chance. At least it seemed unplanned. I had gone by myself to fish for fresh-water shrimp in a stream that flowed right through the jungle at the eastern end of Raevavae. It was a place that the people avoided, for since it was close to the *marae* where Simon had tried to glorify his madness, it was believed to be haunted by the *tupapaou*.

I liked this place. Situated at the bottom of a little valley that was very hot and fertile because it was protected from the sea breezes, there was a kind of tunnel of branches and vines beneath which a fresh, clear stream sparkled in the dappled shade as it ran over the rocks that grazed its surface here and there.

I had come on horseback, but I had left my horse tied up on the bank and had taken off my clothes and waded into the stream. Completely naked, I was walking slowly upstream toward the source, with a net made of coarse fibers in my hand. I was fishing the way the natives did, that is, slowly and without making any noise I was driving my prey toward the headwaters simply by my presence. I would zigzag from one bank to the other in water that came halfway up my calves, until I came to one of those basins that form naturally at the feet of the little waterfalls, no higher than a step, that dotted my stream. Then I would stop and quickly build a little dam by piling up stones, branches, and moss. After that, I would simply walk into the basin thus formed and pick up the frightened shrimp with my hand.

For someone like me, who spent my childhood in a country where rain is a common and almost daily occurrence, the climate of Raevavae, however pleasant, is foreign. And since my arrival on the island I had always been sensitive to the smell of mist, the fragrance of damp earth, the musical sound of running water. I loved this spot, I loved this solitary fishing. I was totally engrossed in my own pleasure. I was like a child in the old days, playing all alone in the country when there wasn't any school.

Suddenly I heard a shout and the sound of twigs snapping. Tara was standing on the bank smiling at me.

"Hey!" he said, "how's the fishing?"

I stood up and smiled back at him, showing him my net.

"How's the hunting?"

He made a face. "I'm looking for wild pigs. They're around here. But they're clever . . ."

"Maybe they got my scent. I didn't know you were here. Usually there's no one here . . ."

He shrugged, laughed, and walked into the stream, leaving his bow and javelin on the shore.

"It doesn't matter. Hunting, fishing . . . I will help you."

Side by side we walked together to the next falls, and fished together. My net was almost full; I now had more shrimp than I wanted. We looked at each other and laughed, happy. All around us was peace. Even the light that filtered through the branches was gentle. Tara looked first upstream and then downstream, and smiled at me sweetly.

"Hunting is like fishing," he said. "You do not always catch something, but it is always good. You are alone, at peace, you can think . . ."

He trailed off as if he had forgotten me, then smiled again

and put his hand lightly on my shoulder. "I am glad I found you here."

"So am I."

And it was true. I told you that in spite of myself, I was susceptible to Tara's charm. Yes, charm. He was a beautiful animal, gay and loyal. Intelligent, too. And even today I am sure that he had a kind of affection for me. According to the ways of Raevavae, I could have been his father. At the time he had become a member of the council, I had paid particular attention to him. Responding to his youth and his open mind, I had made an effort to tell him about our intentions and explain the rules of the game. I had encouraged him to speak up often, to accept responsibilities. Actually, I realize now that I am trying to explain all this to you that for several years I acted as if I had found in him a possible successor.

This helps me to understand many things: the collapse of still unformulated plans, unknown to anyone, even myself; a profound, visceral disappointment . . .

The Fijians had spoiled everything between us. But there was still something left because that morning, in that jungle stream, I felt as if I had found an old friend.

With his hands Tara caught me some fish that looked like trout which the natives scorned in spite of their fine flavor, because they were small and had many bones. Then before we returned, he to his hunting implements and me to my horse, we sat down for a moment on a flat rock in the middle of the stream.

Somehow or other Dubois' name came up. I didn't change the subject. On the contrary, I wanted to take advantage of the serenity, the pleasure we were feeling in being together.

"He's old," I said. "He's a good man, a fair man, but he's old. He won't hurt you. He won't be elected. You'll beat him. So let him be. Even if what he says annoys you a little. It's not important. And he's old."

Tara laughed briefly. "He does not worry me. Everyone laughs at him. He is only hurting himself. But he is not fair. He does not like me. He says that I am bad for the island. Why? You see, that man . . . he is bored. He is crazy, and he is bored.

He is a *poupa* and a good doctor, but he is a crazy man. He has no wife, no children, nothing. When nobody is sick, he has nothing to do. So he says that everyone is unhappy, so he can feel important, and because he is bored. It does not bother me, but . . ."

"But what?"

"Well, it is not serious. Of course he will not be elected. But he talks, and people listen. It is not good. Afterward people talk about the council . . . On this island, people talk too much. What we need is more work and less talk. We need to be serious. Everyone should work. I mean, my wife, my children, my *faré*, everyone. It is like school—it should be compulsory. For everyone—the young, the old, the boys, the girls . . ."

"And the Fijians?" I couldn't resist saying it.

He looked at me, his brow knotted in thought. "The Fijians are not important. Those men are good for nothing except stealing women. I know that you were angry at me because of them. Perhaps I did wrong. Some died, that is true. But after all . . . if they had obeyed us, it would have been different. Perhaps I made a mistake. You could have told me so, instead of getting angry. You did not say anything to me, but you were angry. The Fijians are not very important, but they are like everyone—lazy and undisciplined. You want school? Well, I say school for everyone. For the Fijians and for the others. But it should be compulsory. With punishments if you do not work. School means progress. Those people must progress . . ."

"But," I said quietly, "you can't compel them. You have to convince them, not force them. Even a horse . . ."

He burst out laughing. "To convince, you have to use the stick and the reward, you know. To convince with words . . ."

Suddenly he turned toward me, his eyes shining. "Listen, let us do it together. You will tell them what to do and I will see that they do it. I, Tara, understand you. I, Tara, will help you. The others are idiots or *poupas*. You are a *poupa*, but you are not like a *poupa*. You will speak and I will obey. Eh? Eh?"

I smiled and shook my head. "Thank you, but it's not possible. The people are free. Even if they make mistakes, like us.

More so than us. Listen—what do I do? Do you think I give orders because I am the mayor? I only obey, I obey them. I tell them to do what they already want to do. Sometimes I try to change their desires, but it's difficult. I don't feel I have the right to do more . . ."

"That is because you are not from here. You are more intelligent than we are, and it is natural. But you always say, Rome was not built in a day. You cannot have everything. If you were from here . . . but you are a *poupa*. Some day . . . some day, you will want to rest. You can give me your place. I am from here. And I am the best one on the council. So . . ."

I shook my head and smiled. "Not if you go on thinking the way you think today . . ."

We didn't say any more about it. We knew that we were both serious, but everything was peaceful around us. We got up, we walked back downstream together, and I left him to collect his weapons with a friendly wave. Then I went back to my horse and put on my clothes.

It was then that I remembered Dubois' campaign posters. It was too late.

After that I never had a serious conversation in a place I hadn't picked myself.

41

IT WAS ALSO around this time, a month or two before the date set aside for the elections, that Katherine made an important discovery.

Actually, she made it without realizing it. One evening she brought home an adolescent boy from Matotea whom I didn't know. He was a thin, shy boy who hardly said a word and his name was Toutepo. Yes, *our* Toutepo.

I can't remember how he had turned up at the hospital. Perhaps to get medical treatment. More likely because, come to think of it, it was the only haven of peace on this island which thought of itself as peaceful. At the hospital people took care of you. They didn't order you around or make fun of you. Dubois and Katherine were there to help, attentive, serene, reassuring.

When he first arrived, I noticed nothing about the boy except his beauty. The natives are dark-skinned and rather stocky. What gives them their charm is their health and, in the case of the women, their youth. Toutepo was neither dark nor stocky. His arms and legs were long but solid, his shoulders very broad, his hips narrow. Under his golden-brown skin you could see the muscles working slowly and freely, with an animal grace. His hair was black, his nose small, and his enormous almond-shaped eyes, whose whites were slightly bluish, seemed to reach all the way to his delicate temples under heavy, half-closed lids. His feet were ugly, like those of all the natives, but his long, narrow hands seemed made less for work than for the curious and mannered gestures with which he accompanied his remarks.

Perhaps because there was something feminine about him and because for a long time I had regarded all young and beautiful women as potential prey, I at first found him very unpleasant.

Katherine realized this. She explained that the boy wanted to learn to read and that if I were willing, she would like him to live with us for a while. During the day he would go to school. In the evening he would do odd jobs for us. In exchange we would provide him with room and board.

Katherine was a serious-minded woman. I found it hard to understand why she wanted to saddle us with this silent and too-beautiful boy, when the natives always worked out cases of this kind very well among themselves; but I trusted her and I thought that some day she would tell me her reason for this unusual step. Before agreeing, however, I asked where her protégé came from.

He was a child of the *tsunami*. The storm had brought him into the world and had killed his parents. Some neighbors had taken him in, which was a common occurrence on the island. But it seemed that he had never completely adjusted to them, or to anyone, for that matter.

"He came with the others to help Dubois," said Katherine after she had sent him to have supper with Tapoua. "He's fascinated by his speeches. I wish you could see his face when he hears him talk about justice, happiness, and so forth . . . But I don't like to see him get mixed up in this business. I've talked to Dubois about it, and he agrees with me. He . . . he has something that I couldn't define, but . . . it's true that he's beautiful. It was because of his beauty that I noticed him. After all, I'm a woman, aren't I? But you'll see; when you get to know him, you forget about his beauty. And he has no idea that he's beautiful. I don't know how to explain it—the other boys make fun of him because he's very slow, and because he's always thinking. You get the feeling that for him, everything is a problem—eating, drinking, walking, sleeping. Before he does something, anything, he thinks about it, and then decides. It's not surprising that people make fun of him. In Matotea they call him an idiot. He believes it. You'll see—he has no vanity whatsoever. He's a strange boy; it's almost as if he has no existence in his own eyes. We spend our lives looking at ourselves: me, me, me. The natives less than us; and Toutepo, a thousand times less than the natives. They call him an idiot. I don't know. Dubois thinks he's not completely normal. But he's not sure of his diagnosis. Toutepo is someone who is transparent, but very hard to understand. Yes."

She paused for a moment, as if to catch her breath. Her eyes were shining. She was very pretty, and looked younger than ever. In a flash I remembered what for me is the definition of love: Love is something that keeps you from growing old. For that instant I was a little jealous, but I immediately thought about something else. Otherwise I would have had to be jealous of all the patients, all the attendants and nurses, and even Dubois.

"He's very appealing," Katherine went on. "I wouldn't want anything to happen to him, surrounded by all these madmen. Neither would I want him to vegetate inside this personality of an idiot that people are making for him. He's completely different from the others. In certain ways he's a child. In other ways he's more adult than we are. I don't know—I'm sorry if

I'm boring you—but he touches me as if he were my own child. Louis is my son, but I don't really understand him. He never needs me. He rejects us, you and me. Oh, he's a good son, and he loves us, but look at him—he wishes he were a native. He finds us abnormal. It's quite true, I assure you. If it weren't for Anne, I wonder whether he wouldn't have chosen other parents, like all his friends. Soon he'll begin to run after girls . . . No, he doesn't need us. Toutepo needs us."

I thought to myself that it was really she who needed him. This idea didn't correspond to what I knew about my wife. I wasn't jealous anymore—I was really only jealous for a second; I was worried. My life in Raevavae was all I could hope for. But Katherine was more reserved than she seemed—was she as happy as she said she was? I smiled amicably.

"Since he's a child of the *tsunami,* we must help him. I'll take him to Tekao tomorrow."

That's what I did. The boy was totally tongue-tied and didn't look at me once. Tekao and I exchanged smiles, and he assured me that he would keep an eye on my protégé, and turned him over to Noémie.

I had a very poor impression of him. I reported the incident to Katherine, and then dropped the subject. But I didn't lose sight of Toutepo.

I admit that at first I found nothing remarkable about him except his beauty and his stupidity. Whereas the natives catch on quickly and adapt themselves to everything, he required a thousand explanations—which he didn't ask for—and exhibited a clumsiness so enormous that it seemed deliberate. Tapoua, to whom I had turned him over, was amazed.

"If I tell him to split logs, he breaks the handle of the ax; if I send him to get water, he gets lost; if I tell him to hoe the garden, he cuts off half his toe . . . I tell you, that boy is made to sleep."

Since the boy said nothing and looked submissive, I thought he was sneaky. I thought he was pretending to be stupid to discourage us from giving him work. I took him with me, determined to have a clean conscience about him.

I took my time, for I didn't want my report to Katherine to be open to the slightest objection.

We began with the horses. I explained to him everything about them: how they ate, how they slept, what their dispositions were like, what they were afraid of, what they liked, the right way to approach them, how to stroke them, what parts of their bodies were particularly sensitive, what they did when a fly stung them, when they were too hot, when they were afraid . . .

When I had finished, I asked my pupil to repeat his lesson. He smiled and gave me quite a full account of what I had just explained to him. Then I taught him to clean the stalls, to change the litter, and to brush down the animals. I watched while he took care of Baucis, who was now old and very placid. Each time he made a mistake or got in a position where he was in danger of getting kicked, I pointed it out. We spent a whole afternoon doing a job that usually took me twenty minutes.

The next day after the siesta, without saying anything to me, Toutepo went off in the direction of the stables. I waited for a moment and when he didn't come back, I went after him. Philemon and Baucis, their coats shining, were snorting in their stalls with fresh bedding up to their bellies. Toutepo was now taking care of a two-year-old foal, a rather stubborn one whom I had named Ardent, and whom I had barely started to train. He had taken him out of his stall and tied him to a post and he was emptying out the manure, while talking to him softly in Tahitian. I was barefoot. I took up a position in a dark corner of the shed and waited.

When the dung was cleaned out, Toutepo went and got a big armful of crisp, dry litter. When the horse saw this walking haystack coming toward him, he reared, wild-eyed. But my apprentice sensed the movement and stopped, lowered his arms, showed his face, and laughed. Then, still talking the whole time, he lined the stall and went to get the brush. Fifteen minutes later, everything was in order.

I came out of hiding, examined the floor of the stalls under the litter, the horses' feet, flanks, and legs. Everything was impeccable.

"Very good," I said.

The boy, who was looking at me silently, barely smiled. He agreed with me, and found it natural that I was satisfied.

"But if you can work this well," I asked him, "why have you made nothing but mistakes until now?"

He looked at me in his serious way. "You explained it well," he said.

I didn't give in immediately. After all I was the boss, Katherine's husband. People often tried to flatter me, to take advantage of me. So I showed Toutepo how to split wood, where to get water, how to hoe a vegetable bed. He listened to me, watched what I did, and sometimes asked me to repeat myself. But once he had understood, I didn't have to tell him again.

I never caught him shirking, nor did he ever try to take advantage of me, or even just to please me. I had to admit it: He wasn't like everyone else. For him personal experience or instinct didn't count. If unfamiliar food had been set before him, he could have starved to death before he would even have thought of tasting it. He knew only what he had been taught. Fundamentally, he was quite clumsy. But his conscientiousness and patience enabled him to arrive eventually at a kind of perfection in which he took no pride. He was himself—childish, pure, at once dependent and free, unskilled at doing ordinary things, yet capable of coming out with the most incredible remarks. He was neither stupid nor crazy. He was a little bizarre, and very touching.

After a few weeks, when I was sure of my position, I said to Katherine, laughing, "I believe we have under our roof the only intellectual in Raevavae."

42

DUBOIS WAS REALLY amusing the natives. Aside from our protégé, who went to drink in his words whenever the horses and his schoolwork permitted him to get away, nobody in Raevavae took him seriously any more.

Gradually he was losing people's respect. In Mahanantoa he

had been the hope of certain persons who, once it was obvious he was not going to win, pretended to go on helping him but ridiculed him more than anyone else.

In the beginning, sitting on his platform, he had been a kind of Gulliver in Lilliput. Now he was turning into a sideshow freak.

He was certainly aware of the decline in his prestige, but he said nothing. He had undertaken this campaign against his personal inclinations, knowing that he didn't have what it took to win. Just because it was making him unhappy was not sufficient reason for him to call it off. Anyway, was he unhappy? Dubois always observed himself as if he were a stranger.

I was tempted to go and see him and advise him to withdraw. I didn't do it. He wouldn't have listened to me. And I didn't say anything to Katherine, because she felt the same way I did and was also suffering for him. More than I was.

And then there was that sordid incident that distracted my attention.

One day Peyrole came to my *faré* and asked me if I wanted to go hunting. Right then and there. How could I refuse?

We walked for a while, carrying our bows under our arms. It was morning and still cool, but it was going to be a hot day. Peyrole seemed very preoccupied. I waited to see what was on his mind, annoyed at being disturbed and silently cursing the mounting heat. Finally Peyrole stopped on a barren ridge where the sun was beating down, but where nobody could come near us without being seen. At first he fidgeted, kicking the stones like a child. Then suddenly he said, "Bourdaroux is negotiating with the Fijians . . ."

He waited for the news to sink in, then went on, "Three nights ago he went to the big *faré*. Well, I don't know whether he went to the big *faré*, but he got inside the palisade. Someone was waiting for him at the gate. Yesterday he took some crossbows there. He also has that gun that we didn't get back from him after the battle, when Poumi died. At the time we thought it had fallen into a ravine during the fighting. Maybe Bourdaroux found it, I don't know. But I'm sure he has it."

"Was it Loualala who met him?"

Peyrole hesitated. "N . . . no. Not at the gate, anyway. We don't know the Fijians very well, so I'm not sure of anything. Apparently there's a man named Nakoro who always opens the gate. But I repeat, we don't know them well, and it always happens at night. Anyway, once inside, Bourdaroux could be meeting with anyone."

"Anyone," I repeated. Then suddenly I asked, "But what does he want?"

"To govern, of course!"

I shrugged. "A lot he cares! He's never shown any interest in being elected. And he despises the natives too much to want to rule them!"

Peyrole shook his head. "You don't know him. I do. He's afraid, he's consumed with envy, he thinks he's smarter than the rest of us because he knows how to make a pickax. It's true that he hates the natives. But the Fijians don't like them either. I think he means to use them now and cheat them later. Besides, the campaign of our friend Dubois is stirring people up a little. Bourdaroux is a peasant; he's narrow-minded and grasping. He wants everything for himself, and he despises anyone who doesn't think the way he does . . ." He laughed quietly. "He must think we're a little senile."

I didn't laugh with him. "I don't think Loualala would make a deal with him," I said. "He's a man who . . . No, I don't think he'd do it."

"I'm inclined to agree with you there. But we don't know them. They're very isolated, very uncommunicative. And then, after all, it may be that Loualala . . ."

". . . doesn't know about it. That's true. What shall we do?"

"That's what I'm asking you," said Peyrole stiffly.

"A show of force . . ."

"Oh," said Peyrole, "we still have the advantage. We can blockade them inside their wall for however long we need to. As for Bourdaroux, I'll take care of him. Even with his fortress. When I think that it was a police station . . . don't worry, no waiter is going to teach me my job. I have tear gas, smoke bombs, everything I need."

"Would you arrest him?"

"That's another question . . ."

There was a silence. We looked at each other. We understood each other.

"Well," I said at last, "we'll have to find a gimmick, and fast. In the meantime, we mustn't talk to anyone. Especially the natives."

Peyrole shrugged. "How do you think I know about it?"

The whole thing was so desperately stupid. "Well, anyway," I said firmly, "keep quiet. Don't confirm anything. And be ready for anything. I'll see you tonight. In the meantime . . ."

Without further explanation, I left Peyrole and walked away with a firm step, straight ahead. I must have looked as if I was in a hurry. I was only in a hurry to leave my companion, whose discouragement was adding to my own.

For a while I walked at random. Then I calmed down and my ideas became clearer.

To avoid an explosion, two problems had to be solved: the problem of Bourdaroux, and the problem of the Fijians. The second one wasn't real to me, I hardly believed it existed, although I was paying the closest possible attention to it. I couldn't connect this betrayal, this conspiracy with the contemptuous dignity of Loualala. I didn't understand. There was something unusual, something incomplete about it that kept me from coming to a decision.

But in the case of Bourdaroux I didn't have to think it over. Bourdaroux was French, do you know what I mean? And this made his attitude seem all the more disgraceful. This wasn't prejudice. But we had so many things in common, in spite of ourselves, in spite of all our differences, simply because, like our parents, we had spent our childhood in the same country, speaking the same language, enjoying the same holidays, learning the same words, going to the same schools, rooting for the same teams, listening to the same conversations about the same wars. This man was Cain. I wanted to kill him, not because of the danger he represented to the island, but because he insulted me and hurt me as a person.

I started walking toward his house automatically, seething with rage.

I should have calmed down on the way. My rages don't usually last. But this one, because it was ineffectual, refused to subside. Bourdaroux was a traitor. I would not, I could not regard him as an ordinary citizen guilty of a crime. It was impossible for me to denounce his behavior to the natives and punish him in front of them. I was wrong, but he was my brother, my family, my blood. It's ridiculous and dishonorable, I know. But I'm telling what happened, not rearranging the facts.

And even at that moment, as I was walking toward his house under the midday sun, I knew it was dishonorable. That was why I couldn't calm my anger. This traitor who was forcing me to betray the island . . .

I'm glad I'm the last European.

As I was passing behind my own *faré,* I ran into Tapoua. He appeared in the trees ten yards away, and stopped and looked at me. Just close enough to be seen without intruding. I called him over. "Go and put away my bow," I said. "I'm going to see *tané* Bourdaroux. If I'm not home by five o'clock, go and tell Peyrole. Hurry."

Tapoua didn't know everything, perhaps, but he knew something.

"I will do as you ask," he replied with a certain solemnity. "*Tané* Bourdaroux, after five o'clock . . ."

He almost added something, but shook his head and left, while I plunged down the shady path.

43

THE PATH WOUND through the woods and ran for several hundred yards beside a stream edged with ferns. I walked quickly, enjoying, as I did every time I took this path, the coolness that rose from the water and the quality of the place, which was peaceful and mysterious at the same time. I even stopped to drink at a falls, and I can still feel the cold water on my chin and its iron taste in my mouth.

That's the way I am: No worry has ever kept my body from feeling good, and in fact it was this feeling of well-being that calmed me down.

Before you got to the former police station, you passed the workshops. They looked pretty quiet. The three men who were puttering around inside gave me uneasy looks. I asked them where Bourdaroux was. One of them pointed silently to the painted iron roof that was all you could see above the high hedge.

I thanked him and walked to the gate of the enclosure. I was about to push it open when I remembered the instructions I had been given at the time of my previous visit. Bourdaroux was both a skilled craftsman and a madman. I decided it was wiser to call him.

At first nothing moved and I felt ridiculous standing there alone in this remote and peaceful spot, forcing my voice and hoping it wasn't trembling. But I persevered, and suddenly the shutters of one of the windows opened part way.

"What do you want?" came the voice of Bourdaroux, whom I couldn't see.

"To talk to you."

"What about?"

I sighed. "Look, Bourdaroux, I'm not in the habit of being received like this. Do you always make people stand outside your gate like beggars?"

"I have nothing against you," he growled.

"Then let me in . . ."

For a moment everything was suspended, then the shutters closed again, I heard some heavy objects being moved, and soon Bourdaroux appeared. Walking quickly, with his head hanging and that projecting lower lip that made him look a little like Peyrole, he came toward me over the sanded path, disappeared from sight for a moment behind the gate, then reappeared as he opened it. "Come in," he said, "and don't leave the path."

All the windows were shuttered, and the house was almost cool. When my eyes had become accustomed to the dim light I saw a pile of boards by the door and in the middle of the room a table on which a little earthen casserole was steaming. Only one place had been set, only one chair had been moved. Bourdaroux was about to have lunch alone, like a king.

We looked at each other over the cooling stew. Then from the kitchen there came a slight·clink of dishes. Without taking his eyes off me, Bourdaroux shouted, "Suzanne! Go and see if everything is all right outside." Then automatically he added, "And don't leave the path."

The woman walked by us barefoot with her eyes lowered, and we stood there until after the door had closed behind her.

Then Bourdaroux went and got me a chair from against the wall.

"Well, what can I offer you?"

I said idiotically, "Don't let me interrupt your lunch."

He hesitated. "If you insist . . . It's a *daube de boeuf*. Suzanne does it rather well. I showed her how. Of course, it's not . . . that is . . ."

He now seemed anxious for me to accept his invitation. I nodded my consent because I thought it would facilitate our conversation, and also because I could see the confusion in the eyes of this man whom I didn't like and whom I believed to be dangerous.

He immediately went and got me a plate, some new and very well-made wooden utensils, an earthen cup, and a white napkin made of tapa. Then he stood behind me and served me the *daube* and also, with apologies, some palm wine. When he was sure that I had everything I needed, he sat down and served himself.

Katherine and I never ate anything but broiled meat or native dishes. The *daube* tasted delicious. I said so to my host, who beamed. "This is the way we always had it at my mother's house. The whole secret is in the searing. Of course, it's only palm wine, but he"—he jerked his chin in the direction of Leguen's farm—"has planted grapes, and he says that in two years we'll have wine."

Feeling very clever, I said, "So we're not doing so badly here, after all."

Immediately Bourdaroux's face darkened and he squinted at me. "Not so badly, perhaps, but . . ."

Suddenly he had lost interest in the meal. In a hurry to have it over with, he quickly emptied his plate, didn't offer me a second helping, and barely waited until I had finished eating to clear the table.

Then he sat down again, crossed his arms on the dark and shiny wood, and looked at me silently with his big eyes.

I ran my hand gently over the surface of the table and said, "Bourdaroux, we've been here for over ten years. We've done rather well. Because on the essential things, we've always agreed . . ."

"Why are you telling me this?"

"Because it seems that this is about to change. Wait, let me finish. I know about your conversations with the Fijians. They constitute a serious offense. Very serious. You haven't a chance of succeeding. By surprise, you might have had. Now it's too late. At the first suspicious move, we will strike. You will kill a few of us, but not all. And the survivors will destroy you. Starting with me, if I'm there . . ."

The man laughed like a horse. "*Oh là là!* What have we here? Threats of death! And why? Because I happened to talk to three nobodies who made up some nonsense. Well, let me tell you something; I agree with you, I haven't changed my mind. After all, you wouldn't want to make war on a fellow countryman . . ."

He disgusted me. "You have given arms to the Fijians," I said curtly. "You even stole a gun from Peyrole. Yes, stole; if you found it, you had only to return it. Unless you were preparing for war . . ."

"Well, excuse me," said Bourdaroux, "but I have my rights, too. Why are you all in the council except me?"

"Dubois . . ."

"Precisely. You can't deny it; he's not in it, but he wants to be. Good for him. But I'm watching him; he won't succeed. It's well-planned, your machine. Well, for me to get up there and make a fool of myself . . . And besides, meetings and speeches— no, thank you. But I have the right, even I have the right to defend myself, don't I? And what else am I doing? I'm a white like you, aren't I? Well?"

None of it made sense. "No one has threatened you. I don't see whom you have to defend yourself against. So you're not on the council; so what? You weren't a deputy in France, were you? Being white, as you say, doesn't give you any special right. In any case, not the right to do what you have in mind. And anyway, what are you doing? Think about it: The Fijians hate you as much as they hate everyone else on the island. They'll use you, and then they'll kill you."

"I'm taking my precautions," said Bourdaroux. "Anyway, I don't even know what you're talking about."

I tried another tack. "Why are you against us?"

He shook his head stubbornly. "I have my rights, and no one respects them."

"Bourdaroux," I said quietly, "that's not true. We've always informed you, always consulted you. We respect you as much as anyone else. You are indispensable here, you perform an extremely valuable service. The council is nothing. Anyway, you don't want to run for it. I don't understand."

Bourdaroux made a violent gesture, opened his mouth to say something, but changed his mind. After a few moments he said without looking at me, "I think you'd better leave now."

Before I got up, I asked, "And what about the Fijians?"

"I'll think it over. But now you must go."

After I got up, I asked him for Peyrole's gun. I thought he was going to jump on me.

"I don't have it," he said finally. "You're mistaken."

I looked at him. "You're well-protected here. But your territory is not very large. Three or four armed guards would be enough to prevent you from leaving. Of course, we'd have to tell the natives that we have a disagreement with you, but . . . With a little patience, I could come and get the gun myself."

Bourdaroux looked more astonished than angry. "You'd do that? In front of the natives? With their help?"

"No," I said, "because you're going to give me the gun."

We looked at each other, then he backed down. The gun was under his bed, wrapped in a rag.

I took it, wiped off the grease, and looked Bourdaroux in the eye. "You will never talk to the Fijians again, is that clear? You will do nothing. And you will obey. If not . . ."

Then without waiting for an answer I walked out with the weapon under my arm. I had won.

44

I WALKED HOME quickly. My success was giving me energy. My depression was turning into contempt. All alone, I had won. And all alone, I would see it through. But before I went to see Loualala, I had to put that gun somewhere.

At the *faré* there was no one but my son having his lunch. He didn't feel at home unless we were away. I didn't hold it against him. I understood him.

I would like to have been for him the father I hadn't had myself, but he didn't approve of me. Well, he had his reasons.

I loved Katherine, I swear I did; I still love her. And she was at least fond of me. It's true. And yet I sometimes suspect that we got married for another reason. It seems to me that perhaps without knowing it, or without wanting to admit it to ourselves, we did it to preserve the race. Reasons of state, if you will. A royal wedding. I'm not sure about this. There were a lot of other factors operating, too. But then it would be a suspicious accident. For we did preserve the race. And this, I know now, was a mistake.

Your father suffered as a child because of his blond hair, his blue eyes, his pale skin. He was never happy. You're happy, because you're a halfbreed. But I couldn't do much for him but love him and make sure he was left free to solve the enigma of his birth as best he could. I was patient. I hoped that some day we would come together. It happened late. After you were born. And then he died. And Katherine died . . .

Never mind. That day he slipped away, and I didn't try to

detain him. I remember, because I really wanted to tell him how clever and strong I had just been. I dismantled the gun and hid it, and then I saddled one of the horses and went and knocked on the palisade of the big *faré,* and asked to speak to Loualala.

A Fijian whom I didn't recognize took my message and left me waiting alone in front of the enormous gate. I waited for a good quarter of an hour. Then I heard voices, the tree trunks moved, and Loualala appeared.

His face was as expressionless as ever. But I watched him with such intensity that I thought I distinguished a trace of surprise under this blank surface. I took this to be a good omen. I had a theory which I hoped would prove correct. I greeted Loualala, dismounted, and left my horse with one of the gate-keepers. Then I asked the man whom I regarded as the chief of the Fijians to take a walk with me. Just the two of us.

The men at the gate lost their composure. They started whispering excitedly among themselves. One of them ran off toward the big *faré.* Loualala registered no emotion.

"If you wish," he said.

We started walking side by side, very slowly. I didn't know how to begin. I was afraid my theory might be wrong. Loualala waited politely for me to speak. Suddenly I started talking. I told him everything.

He wasn't expecting it. He looked up at me and waited until I had finished. Then he said, "Wait for me; I'll be back."

I waited almost an hour. At one point there was shouting behind the palisade. I didn't even look through the gap. If I wasn't mistaken, it didn't concern me. And if I was mistaken . . . At last Loualala came back. He was carrying five small cross-bows. Bourdaroux was a very skillful craftsman. They were dangerous weapons in spite of their size. Loualala handed them to me.

"It is better that you keep these. The incident is closed. There will never be another one like it."

We looked at each other. His face almost came to life for a moment as he added, "Thank you for your confidence."

I shook his hand warmly. I never found out exactly what had happened. Even their women said nothing. There were no dead bodies, no groans. But I did hear shouting and I took away those crossbows.

It was then that I decided I would like to see Loualala on the council. Of course I didn't say anything to him. We parted without further communication. The palisade was closed behind me. I got back on my horse and rode home. When I got there I realized how tired I was. I decided to rest for a few minutes. I lay down and slept like the dead until five o'clock. Nerves, no doubt.

When I woke up I had to act fast. I took a shower anyway. Then I put the gun and the crossbows in a bag and headed for the Navy House.

Peyrole was waiting for me in his office. "I was about to go and look for you," he said. "Tapoua came by a quarter of an hour ago. I was ready . . ."

He pointed out the window to about twenty men sleeping in the shade. I smiled. "Unnecessary."

I opened my bag. Peyrole took out the crossbows one by one like poisonous insects. Then he took out the gun and re-assembled it, slamming the breech closed. Cautiously, he placed it on his desk beside the other weapons. Finally he said, "Perfect."

We looked at each other, apparently unconcerned, but pleased. This went on for a while. Then Peyrole said, "Come and have a *pastis*."

In the kitchen, in front of the pitcher of cold water, he questioned me. Quietly, I told him the facts. I concluded, "Bourdaroux has lost face. He won't make another move. As for the Fijians, I get the impression that the ones who wanted to make trouble can't do it now. It's all over. And I'd like to see Loualala on the council."

Peyrole made a face. "If it's as you say . . ." Something was bothering him. Finally he grumbled, "If everyone starts taking the law into his own hands now . . . After all, they have to realize that there's a law here."

I laughed. "Well, I'm not unhappy about the way it turned

out. Now we'll have to tear down the palisade and put an end to this ghetto. It's too much of a temptation for all the weak minds on the island."

Peyrole shook his head. I insisted I was right. The *pastis* was cool, we had just won, we could take our time. We were two wise men comparing our experiences. We knew how to govern men.

Just then Tapoua burst in without knocking. "Come quick," he said, "the doctor is dead. There is a big fight."

It was in Mahanantoa, where Dubois had decided to have a rally for the first time.

The jeep was out of gas. Peyrole wanted to take his cart. I suggested that we ride my horses. We stood there dazed and helpless.

In the end we ran all the way, carrying our guns in our hands. It took us almost two hours to get there. On the way we met some men who came along. Peyrole's twenty volunteers were already with us. We must have looked like madmen, because the natives around us said nothing. Two or three times Peyrole, who was very red in the face and dripping with sweat, almost fell down. When we arrived the village was empty. There was no one in sight, either in the streets or in the doorways of the *farés*. There was only the sun setting over the grey sand, and in the middle of the little crooked square, beside his broken platform, Dubois was lying on his side, as if asleep. Beside him Toutepo was kneeling, weeping silently.

I knelt down beside him.

Dubois was dead. I didn't have to touch him to know that. The heavy spear, almost a stake, was still in the wound. It had passed between two ribs on the left side and must have pierced the heart. A little blood had oozed out, staining his shirt and disappearing into the sand.

Yes, I saw at once that he was dead. His face had been rejuvenated; that is a sign you can depend on. He looked as if he were sleeping peacefully, with a faintly ironic curl to his lip.

I touched his still warm hand, then I looked at Peyrole. "We can't leave him like this."

Peyrole shook his head in agreement. I got up and gently tried to withdraw the spear from the wound, but it had a barbed tip. I pulled a little harder. The body moved. Behind us the natives were watching. I looked at Peyrole, then I put my foot on Dubois' chest right next to the wound and pulled on the spear with all my strength. I felt the ribs separate, the flesh tear. The shirt tore, too. I saw the wound when the steel tip came out, then the water and the black clot.

It must have happened very fast. I handed the spear to Peyrole, then I laid Dubois flat on his back.

Peyrole was looking at the spear. I looked at it, too. It was a short, thick weapon made of ironwood, with a heavy, rather well-made tip of a very cruel design.

Peyrole turned to the natives. "Who does this belong to?"

"Tara," answered Toutepo, pointing to a band of mother of pearl of remarkable workmanship on the weapon.

It was the name we had been expecting to hear for two hours and which no one had yet spoken.

With what was left of the platform we made a litter. We laid Dubois on it. Then four men lifted it to their shoulders.

Night had fallen. Torches were lit. We walked with the litter bearers. Toutepo never left my side. The others followed behind. Sometimes one of Dubois' arms slipped and started to hang down. We would stop and lift it up and place it beside the body. The march was difficult. The litter bearers had to be relieved frequently.

At one point as we walked under the litter I asked Peyrole, "Shouldn't we have left someone back there?"

He growled, "No need. Tomorrow, the investigation. They won't go far. Since everyone knows . . ."

Yes, everyone knew.

In the crowd that was gathering around us and beginning to weep, in the native manner, I took a man by the arm at random.

"Run to the hospital and get the *vahiné* Katéléné. Take her to the doctor's *faré.* Go with her, do you hear? Don't let her go alone. Do you understand?"

The man nodded and slipped away. I didn't know who he

was. Peyrole said, "Don't worry. All these people are friends."

Then he added, "I just can't understand it."

Stupidly I answered, "Anger. Pride."

45

By THE TIME we reached Dubois' house with the litter, there were at least a hundred of us. Almost all the natives were carrying torches which cast huge leaping shadows and bathed everything in an angry, copper-colored light, the light of a slaughterhouse.

While they carried the body inside, I stood under the porch roof looking around, trying to recognize this place that I knew so well. But nothing was the same, although nothing had changed. The night sky was like soot. In the garden, the natives were trampling on the vegetables. The empty hammock was hanging motionless. In the few moments of silence that came now and then, only the stream could still be heard.

It was then that I first realized that Dubois was dead. I think I turned toward the darkness, but I didn't have time to be moved. Just then Peyrole came out of the *faré,* and at the same moment the first mourners began to weep.

For the natives, all the events of life were occasions for ceremonies, and they had a kind of instinctive genius for organizing them. "Organizing" is a bad word, though. They would get together and experience the same emotions at the same moment. Tradition would give them style.

That night they experienced the death of Dubois. They were together, they wept, they sang, they said we had lost a grandfather. In their grief, which was superficial but real, they felt exhilarated and consoled by their sheer numbers. All night long from all the *farés* on the island they came, whole families together, to take part in this great communal ritual of sorrow.

Katherine, the two Peyroles, Leguen, and I were also together beside the body of our friend, which had now been bathed and dressed in his best uniform, but unlike the natives, each of us was alone. And the circle of mourners in the center of which we found ourselves only added to our misery. Odile Peyrole wept openly. Katherine, her face drawn, was trying to control herself, and the effort gave her a hard look. The other two men and I were as impassive as masks.

We were suffering. We loved Dubois, we respected him, we needed him. But there was something else. For us, the shipwrecked, the survivors, this was our first death. It confused and upset us. This dead body, on this island where up to now we had lived as if immortal, was a monstrous novelty. This first death was the death of us all. We weren't ready for it.

Toward daybreak the weeping subsided around the *faré*. The nurses from the hospital, who were sitting in front of the door, had fallen asleep on each other's shoulders, looking like children in their white tapa tunics. Now and then Leguen would snore and wake himself up. The others had vacant expressions on their faces, which were stamped with fatigue.

I rose quietly and walked outside, stepping over the bodies on the floor. In the yard everyone was asleep. Only a dozen old women and matrons, crouching at the foot of a tree, had managed to stay awake and stubbornly continued to utter, every ten seconds or so, a soft rhythmic cry that no one heard.

All around us were the woods with their trees washed by the dew, their ferns, their mosses, their birds just beginning to wake up, and beyond the shadows, on the horizon through the leaves, the calm sea whose glassy surface was being illumined by a pink sun.

I stood there for a long time in the midst of these bodies lying every which way, in this place where it seemed as if a battle had been waged, this place full of bitterness and solitude, watching the beginning of another day.

Then the sea turned blue, the sun touched the edge of the mountain, and suddenly it was morning. A few men stirred, a woman sat up and yawned and rubbed her shoulders. An old man got up and walked quietly into the woods.

Almost immediately, as if he had gone to get them, some men appeared. Bourdaroux was at their head. They were carrying on poles a very heavy burden beneath which they were trembling.

At first I didn't realize what it was. I was too busy glaring at the disagreeable face of Bourdaroux, who hadn't come to sit up with us.

Around us people were waking up. Some men ran to help the porters. The weeping started up again. Bourdaroux was leaning on a cane. He walked heavily with his head lowered. When he was right in front of me he stopped and looked at me with eyes that had dark circles under them, eyes full of questions. Behind him the porters set down their burden.

It was an enormous coffin whose rounded lid had been carved out of a solid piece of wood and decorated with inlaid work, a large cross surrounded by geometric designs. It was beautiful, and had the elegance and refinement of the old world. I looked at Bourdaroux, who immediately dropped his eyes.

"I'll have plenty of time to make another one before I need it," he said sullenly.

Then he turned his back on me and walked away, leaning on his cane, without looking at me or explaining or coming inside the house. Alone in his fortress, he must have spent hundreds of hours making himself this coffin fit for a prelate or a prince. His gift touched me, as did his rudeness. In both I saw the proof of his friendship—and his solitude.

We put Dubois in Bourdaroux's coffin and screwed down the ornate lid, after Léné had given the body a last blessing. Then, very quickly and naturally, we had a beautiful funeral. Sixteen men representing all the villages carried Dubois to the cemetery. Léné walked in front of the procession with the best singers from the church. Katherine and I followed with Odile Peyrole. Peyrole, in uniform, led a detachment of four men wearing *paréos* but carrying rifles, who were to give military honors at the cemetery. Finally, behind us, around us, everywhere, the crowd flowed like a river, adapting itself to the terrain, spreading out in the open places and pressing together when the road narrowed.

We covered about three kilometers in this way, stopping

frequently to change pallbearers. The sun was very hot. In the distance someone was ringing the church bell. The lamentations of the crowd, subdued by fatigue, sounded like running water.

The cemetery was a very small one facing the sea, with only three palm trees for shade. The ground was covered with white shells, and the light was blinding.

All who could manage to do so slipped in among the graves. Léné said a prayer, and then the coffin was lowered into the ground while Peyrole's men fired their guns overhead, and an emotional young boy who had been coached by Tekao played the first few bars of taps on an old bugle but broke off heart-breakingly.

After that the people brought masses and masses of flowers. There were so many flowers that they filled the grave and the gravediggers were barely able to cover them with sand. As the flowers withered in the days that followed, the people had to keep shoveling in more sand to fill the hollow that kept forming in the shape of a bed.

Yes, we loved Dubois. We wanted to preserve his memory forever. We built for him that pyramid of white stone facing the sea which you know, and which the natives immediately named "The Memory of Dubois." But who really remembers him today?

The day after the funeral we had a meeting of the council and called for an investigation. This was natural. In Raevavae there were never any crimes. Oh, once in a great while there would be a murder. Everyone would know who had done it, and it was usually only a duel. But in the case of Dubois' death two days had passed and no one was saying anything.

To Peyrole and myself the matter was clear cut. But the crime was so great, the offense so brutal, that we wanted everything to be proved and the murderer to be accused in front of the whole island.

We started by having the murder weapon identified. It did belong to Tara. Next we established that neither Tara nor certain other men from Mahanantoa had attended the funeral, or had even returned to their homes.

Finally, we tried to find witnesses who could tell us exactly what had happened.

But nobody seemed to know anything. Something had happened that had resulted in Dubois' death. But what? We couldn't get any details.

First we tried asking Dubois' supporters, the people who were with him when it happened, but curiously enough, they were nowhere to be found. Some were out at sea on fishing boats, others were hunting far from their homes. We thought they were afraid of being held somehow responsible for his death, which they were, because without their mocking support, Dubois would not have been able to carry on such an extensive campaign. We went to a lot of trouble to find them and reassure them. We were disappointed. They were interested only in exonerating themselves. They hadn't seen anything clearly. A big fight had started with the people from Mahanantoa, a fight in which Dubois had died. But they had been so busy protecting him that they had not seen who had dealt the fatal blow. Why didn't we ask Toutepo, who hadn't taken part in the fight and must have seen everything?

Toutepo wasn't quite like other people. The night following the crime, before Katherine returned for the wake, she had taken the boy to the hospital and given him a sedative. Then she had taken charge of his life. By this I mean that if no one had looked after him at this time, he would have let himself die. In spite of her own grief and the extra work she had because of Dubois' absence, she fed and took care of him. He followed her everywhere silently, running after her if she disappeared from sight, peaceful and abstracted as soon as he was near her again. When I asked her whether I could question him, she warned me that I would get very little out of him. He trembled and answered haltingly, but he tried to help us. It was long and cruel. Katherine stayed with him the whole time. I was with Peyrole. We wanted to do our duty, but never had we felt our efforts so futile. After all, the crime had been so clearly signed! From shreds of information we managed to get from Toutepo we finally pieced together a story that seemed to make sense.

You will remember that the boy passionately admired Dubois. When he found out that Dubois planned to speak in Mahanantoa, Tara's stronghold, he could not resist. After struggling with his conscience, he left my horses and ran all the way to the rally.

It took place on the square where we found the body. The platform had been set up, and a group of natives who were not from the village were standing around it singing and playing musical instruments. Without saying anything to Dubois, they had all brought clubs with them so they could defend themselves in case a fight broke out. At least that's what they said. But everyone expected a fight because that day most of Dubois' supporters came from Vaiuru and Matotea, where there was some dissatisfaction over the way the fate of Poumi had been decided. Did they want revenge? Did they really want to defend Dubois? In any case, many of them had come.

As for the people of Mahanantoa, after at first holding back, they eventually joined the group around the platform. Dubois began to speak. Toutepo told us that he found him noble and fair. My impression was that it was a rally much like the others and that things could have ended on a light note, as usual, if it hadn't been for this tension, and above all, if it hadn't been for Tara.

For Tara arrived fresh from a hunting expedition, fully armed and accompanied by his men, who were carrying two dead pigs.

This struck us as very crude. Tara must have known that Dubois was going to come. So why did he have to choose that day to hunt?

At first Tara pretended to be surprised. Then he stopped in front of the platform, surrounded by his party. He began making fun of Dubois in French, not in Tahitian, but I got the feeling that it was good-natured fun. It was to be expected, for that matter. He was on his own turf, young, strong, and he had made a good kill. He was probably enjoying himself. Dubois answered him in the same tone, in Tahitian. Every so often he displayed a gift for repartee. Besides, the presence of an audience is stimulating. I know about that.

In short, at first everything went calmly enough. But Dubois thought he was defending a just cause and Tara, although he didn't believe he was guilty of any wrongdoing, had a reputation to uphold. Suddenly he became irritated. He began to insult Dubois, then he challenged him. To bows and arrows, spears, knives; to a fight. Dubois just laughed at him. So to show the difference between a real man and an old man, Tara began shooting arrows into the air, hurling his spear into the trunks of palm trees, and beating his chest. In short, he acted like an idiot, or a man who is very angry.

Nevertheless, he managed to control himself. But around the platform everyone was tense. Fearing an attack, Dubois' supporters had taken out their clubs. Immediately the men of Mahanantoa had gone to get theirs. It almost turned into a general brawl. This may have been what calmed Tara down.

It was then that Bourdaroux stepped in. I hadn't known he was there. He hadn't said anything to me when he brought the coffin, and I hadn't thought to ask him. How could I have imagined that after our conversation that noon, when I had left him shaking with rage and fear, he had gone all the way to Mahanantoa? And how could I have guessed that this man, who despised his fellow human beings, would go to the trouble of attending an election rally and mingling with the natives? And yet Toutepo was clear on this point: Bourdaroux was there, and he had tried to interrupt the meeting by appealing to both Tara and Dubois.

He was right. No one had listened to him. People weren't accustomed to seeing him so far away from his workshop. They didn't like him. And their passions were too inflamed. Tara was in his element. Dubois must have thought that he was winning. They started matching wits again, the tone became sharper, and once again Tara lost his temper.

At a certain point he called Dubois impotent, adding that an impotent man has no right to rule. Katherine's name was mentioned.

For me, this was never of any importance. The natives, like peasants, like all people whose work is solitary, like to observe and make comments. I knew they told stories about all of us. It didn't bother me. If I tell you that that day Katherine was mentioned, don't think I felt any resentment or anger when I found this out. I mention it only because it helped me to understand Toutepo's behavior and the sequence of events that followed.

Remember, Katherine discovered Toutepo, brought him home, and asked me to take charge of him. In a sense, Toutepo was the child of Katherine and Dubois.

That day, he lost his head because of them. Forgetting his innocence and his shyness, he jumped onto the platform next to Dubois and faced Tara. Much later, he told me that he had seen clearly what it was his duty to do. He was indignant and unhappy, you understand, but above all, he saw his duty. That's the way he was.

In the silence that fell after he had done this, for the whole island regarded him as a clumsy boy who never said anything, he shouted to Tara that he should be ashamed to talk that way. That the value of a man is judged by his actions, and that the actions of Dubois were good, whereas those of Tara were bad. He blamed him for his debauchery, his brutality, his anger, his pride, for exploiting his villagers, and, possibly remembering conversations I had had with Katherine, he concluded by saying that if the Fijians revolted some day, we would know who to blame.

Tara let out a yell. For this, and for what I have just told you, I had ten witnesses. This yell touched off everything. The battle was on. The men from Mahanantoa were ashamed for Tara. Dubois' men knew that the words that had just been spoken were intolerable. There was no possible outcome but violence.

Things quickly became chaotic. There were perhaps two hundred people fighting. The platform was shaking and threatened to collapse. There was nothing but shouting and dust. No one could see anything but his immediate adversary.

Suddenly a spear, Tara's spear, was hurled at Toutepo, who was standing stockstill looking at the mêlée. Dubois saw it and stepped in front of the child.

Who had taken aim, who had thrown the weapon? No one

knew. They had only seen it fly through the air and hit Dubois. But the spear was Tara's.

Toutepo held himself responsible for the murder. The natives weren't opposed to this point of view. But Peyrole, Leguen, and I did not agree. The weapon betrayed the murderer, and the story was logical. The fact that no one had seen the hand that threw it was not very important. Because he was almost out of his head with grief, we listened to Toutepo but did not bother to ask him questions. He hadn't told us that Tara was the killer, but it wasn't necessary. We knew everything we needed to know.

Next, to be absolutely certain, although my mind was already made up, I went to question Bourdaroux. He received me in a bizarre manner in front of his gate, and refused to let me inside. He glared at me, and I saw to my astonishment that he had been drinking. I thought that he was still angry at me for confiscating the stolen gun, that he hadn't recovered from his humiliation. So I forced myself to be conciliatory without acting apologetic. Nevertheless I was obliged to ask him some questions about his presence in Mahanantoa that afternoon. He started to answer me reluctantly. Then, suddenly, he exploded.

"If you think I'm guilty, why don't you shoot me, since you're the boss? If you don't, why don't you leave me the hell alone with your niggers and your council. Do you think you're going to bring back Dubois? Eh? Eh?"

He was shouting like a madman. I thought he was angry that he had been unable to prevent this death and ashamed that he had conspired to betray us a few hours before. Personally, I felt sorry for him. But he also disgusted me. I told him coldly that nobody was accusing him of anything, and that I was only interested in Tara's role. He confirmed, with an ill grace, that Tara was in a violent rage. After that he refused to say another word and without even saying goodbye, closed the gate in my face.

I didn't ask him for more. Now convinced that I knew who the culprit was, I reported my conversation to Peyrole. A week later, after the council had declared him guilty and after Léné had pronounced the malediction of God on his head, we arrested Tara, who was turned over to us by one of his own men.

Here I must pause for a moment. I'm not trying to excuse myself, but I have a right to explain myself fully. I acted honorably. In spite of the weight of my first suspicions, I looked for evidence, witnesses. I found them, and on the whole they agreed. There was nothing about the case that was calculated to arouse one's suspicions. Even Tara's character suited this murder. I was young, of course, and profoundly upset by Dubois' death, but I repeat that I did my job honestly. So did Peyrole; so did Leguen. It is important to realize this if you are to understand what happened next.

Tara was brave. When we arrested him, he stated that he had always respected Dubois, and that he hadn't intended to kill him. After that he refused to answer our questions. We thought his statement was a confession. Didn't we know that our friend had died because he had shielded Toutepo with his body?

We convinced the council, pronounced the sentence, and carried out the punishment. Tara was shot, the first man to be executed in the New World.

He was innocent, of course. You've guessed this, you who are reading these words, you to whom I have just presented the pieces of the case in cold, rational terms, devoid of that spark of life which sometimes makes things so difficult to see clearly.

Yes, Tara was innocent. When I learned the truth I trembled for nights and days, because I had had him killed unjustly.

Today, with the detachment of old age, I do not blame myself so much for the execution as I do for the error. Tara made a good criminal. If he had not committed this crime, he had committed others. He was responsible for the despair and death of some thirty Fijians. He had within him a blind force that could only have led to catastrophe. Even if at the time he was sentenced to die he had not yet deserved his punishment, everyone on the island, natives and Europeans alike, agreed that he was dangerous, a troublemaker.

The murder of Dubois called for vengeance. What better victim could we offer him? Yes, the death of Tara was good for the island, and I do not repudiate it.

302

What I do not forgive myself for, what I will never forgive myself for, is being wrong, not having guessed, not having acted with my eyes open.

A mistake is never an excuse. But for someone who has agreed to be responsible for other people, for someone who is obeyed and honored, it is the worst, the most degrading fault of all.

46

IF IT HADN'T been for Toutepo I would never have learned the truth, and I would not be exactly what I am. I was, as I have told you, at peace with myself, my mind was at rest on the matter. In my eyes justice had been done and justice purified everything.

And because two men whom I had admired were dead, because after the punishment had been carried out I could merge the victim with the murderer in my grief, I was more anxious than ever to put an end, once and for all, to this thorn in our sides, the Fijians.

I thought about it all the time.

My first job was to convince Loualala. I pointed out to him that if his people remained in their ghetto, they would never blend in with the other inhabitants of the island, that they would always be a threat, a temptation, and a target, and that for this reason anything could happen at any moment.

I also explained that since we were now alone in the world, we should join forces instead of opposing each other. Finally, I told him about the feeling that became the Idea, and promised him that every one of his men was necessary to its realization.

To conclude, I gave him a choice: Either the Fijians, fortified by my support and protection, must blend into the population or, shut up inside their palisade, they would eventually die out, cut off by the hatred of the island.

We were sitting alone on the edge of a woods facing the

sea, on the hill that overlooks Matotea, near that big rock where I had taken shelter during the *tsunami* on the day I arrived.

While he listened to me Loualala looked at the sea and absentmindedly braided three ribbons made of banana leaves. His face was sad and dignified. Since I was speaking English and the poverty of my vocabulary made it difficult for me to express abstract ideas, I wasn't sure he understood me.

When I had finished, he sat looking at the sea for a moment. Then, as if he were waking up, he looked down at the little braid he was holding in his hands, tossed it away, and turned to me.

"There are many differences between us and these people," he said quietly. "Language, food, customs, houses, boats . . . and much blood has been shed. What you are offering us, in either case, is death. Either we disappear, or we become something we are not, since you do not give us the right to observe the customs that make us ourselves, the sons and grandsons of our fathers. One death or another, is it worth the trouble of choosing?"

"I don't want any more deaths," I said, but I understood what he meant. "I want your life. And your peace."

I can still see his smile, very calm, very intelligent. "It is the same thing. But I trust you. I know now that you are honest, and that you want what is right. What you say will be done. Some men from my country have wives from here. All these women are pregnant. The children must be at home here. For them, we shall do as you wish. We shall die."

"You will teach them to carve coconut trees, to cultivate the earth as you have at the big *faré*, and to dance the dances of your people," I said, to console him.

"Very well," he replied, lifting his chin. "Raevavae will be their land, Raevavae will teach them . . . We are learning your language, we shall learn their customs."

Fortunately, some of his men were less pure than he. When they had been relocated in the villages of their wives, after the big *faré* had been burned and the palisade torn down, they forgot to be Fijians and became human beings. To make themselves a place in the community, they displayed their talents as sailors and farmers. Although they changed their names and began to speak our languages, they also brought to the island their manual skills, a certain style, a very lively sense of competition, and perhaps most important of all, a slightly different point of view which destroyed forever the lazy unanimity of Raevavae.

Loualala ordered and directed the dispersion of his people. Then, when he had seen that the households were set up and on the way to being accepted, the bachelors had melted into the population, and the old men were resigned, he disappeared. One day he borrowed a small *pahi* and went off to sea by himself, to fish. He was never heard of again. Did he try to rejoin those of his people whom he had left thousands of miles away? Did he get lost? Did his boat go down? The sea was very calm, and he hadn't taken any supplies. But I'm getting ahead of myself.

After I had convinced Loualala, I had to persuade Raevavae. We had postponed the elections because of the funeral and the execution. I took advantage of this delay to lay siege to the council, one member at a time. I wanted the Fijians to disappear as such, I wanted them to die, perhaps, but only so that they could live. I was clever, insistent, convincing.

I had a hard time bringing it off. Everywhere I turned I encountered not ill will, and certainly not any open opposition, but once again, a total indifference. They didn't oppose me—they didn't listen to me.

Again, Mai was the most candid. "If you had let us have our way," he said with an ironic smile, "it would have been over with a long time ago, and there would not have been any more deaths, since deaths frighten you so much. We would have killed the worst ones on the spot, the others would have surrendered, we would have beaten them a little, and then we would have forgotten about the whole thing. We are not savages! Otherwise, you are right . . ."

Out of boredom or politeness, the others finally decided to let me have my way.

However, when I proposed to them that we unanimously support the candidacy of a Fijian to replace Tara, they almost rebelled. But as I say, the matter did not really concern them. If it made me happy . . .

Loualala stepped aside and presented me with one of his compatriots named Vaiuli, assuring me that he would be the best man for the job. He was a middle-aged man, rather slow and dull-witted, but polite and eager to do well.

He was elected unenthusiastically in Mahanantoa, where the villagers felt he had been forced on them—which was true—to humiliate them and to punish them for the murder of Dubois—which was not true. After that they got used to him, although they never regarded him as an important person, but rather as a convenient intermediary, and he was reelected regularly until the big embarkation. He made a diligent but negligible councilor who was treated in a rather offhand manner but whom, when all was said and done, it was impossible not to respect.

If it hadn't been for the Fijians, Raevavae would have remained forever peaceful, confident, happy. At best it would have produced a few enlightened amateurs. Never would it have achieved that degree of tension which is the prerequisite for greatness.

The new citizens, however well-assimilated they had become, had a position to earn, a reputation to defend. Although superficially they were now like us—provided with new names, dressed in our tapa, eating our food—they nevertheless remained different, and they knew that the smallest detail would be enough to reveal the fraud to which we were all lending ourselves.

So in order not to appear vulnerable, as well as for their own personal satisfaction, they wanted to be the foremost citizens of Raevavae.

Since they no longer had any traditions to fall back on, they listened to us and imitated us more than the other natives. They were the first to build stone *farés* in the style of the hospital and the Navy House. They were the first natives who tried, like Leguen, to practice a deliberate selection with their livestock. Their women were cleaner and more alert. Their children were ambitious students.

Not all of them were successful. Diligence isn't always enough. But because of this tension which they created for themselves, they brought a note of dissonance to the carefree harmony of the island, they stimulated competition, they aroused a desire for professionalism. Yes, they were my leaven.

All the diplomacy I employed to reach this stage absorbed my attention more completely than I can say. Told quickly this way it sounds simple. In reality it took me much planning, speechmaking, and conniving. This explains why, in the months that followed Dubois' death, I didn't do anything else, I didn't pay attention to anything else.

Not even Toutepo.

And yet Toutepo was the tragedy of the island. He had taken upon himself the disappearance of Dubois and perhaps of Tara as well. Because he was alive, each of them was dead. After the first few days, which he spent at the hospital being nursed by Katherine, he was sick for a long time without my noticing it. Gently but stubbornly he announced that he didn't need to be taken care of anymore and that he could resume his normal activities.

In spite of my wife's remonstrances, he came back to our *faré* and forced himself to go to school every morning without fail, and also to take care of my horses every afternoon.

Katherine talked to me about him several times, but I didn't really listen to her. His despair seemed exaggerated to me and frankly, unbalanced. Anyway, to me he was just a too-beautiful boy who was doomed from birth to unhappiness. The fate of the Fijians seemed much more important to me, and callously, with a shrug of the shoulders, I put him out of my mind.

But one afternoon, probably around the time my scheming was having results so that I was less preoccupied with it, I ran into him at the door of the stables and all at once I saw him.

He was so thin, so frail, so helpless that he frightened me. Right then and there I forbade him to take care of the horses, ordered him to rest, and went to report my discovery to Katherine, who also shrugged her shoulders.

I didn't do anything else at the time. But several times, to my amazement, I found myself thinking about him. I observed him. Since he had nothing else to do now, he was with us constantly, except when he was in school. He would sit down in a shady spot against a wall and remain there, not moving or speaking, unless Katherine called him to come and have something to eat.

His almost animal beauty had lost its perfection and was being replaced by a distinction that was rare in one so young. His face was changing. Once innocent and submissive, his gaze now burned with a haggard intensity.

I was sorry for him and afraid for him. I talked to Katherine about him again. After all, she was our doctor now. She raised her eyebrows and pursed her lips.

"I've tried everything, I've considered everything. His recovery is up to him . . ." She hesitated, about to go, then turned to me with dignity. ". . . Perhaps I'm mistaken. Perhaps there's something I can't see."

I took her arm affectionately. She softened, then shook her head, pulling herself together. "It's terrible," she said with a little laugh, "to be like God, not to have anyone to turn to for advice."

Then she gently disengaged her arm and left. I don't think she ever brought up this subject again, either with me or with anyone else. But because I loved her and because I couldn't do anything to help her, I watched her slowly, day by day, bury herself in the solitary world of unshared responsibilities, watched her cut herself off from everything that wasn't her job, holding herself accountable for every wasted minute, every weakness, every mistake, becoming more and more strained, more and more pressured as her fragility increased and the idea of her death became more plausible, her gestures cut short by fatigue, her communication curtailed, devoting herself wholly to what had become for her the essential, the prisoner of a world where soon neither her children nor I could be with her.

She died at the age of forty-nine, of exhaustion. She never said a word to me. She had forgotten how to talk about herself. Singlehanded, she had trained five doctors and two surgeons. As you know, she wrote a compendium in which she recorded all the prescriptions for making drugs with the means at our disposal. For this purpose alone she studied chemistry and botany. She instructed more than a dozen pharmacists and I don't know how many nurses.

She always refused to rest. One day she returned to the house about ten o'clock in the morning and went back to bed. I'm sure she knew that her end was near. At four o'clock she was dead. I was informed about noon, and went to be with her. She lay there not moving, quiet and peaceful. In a very low voice she talked about unimportant things, smiling slowly to herself. She seemed happy to have the three of us with her. Her face was relaxed. She looked rejuvenated. We wanted to hope. But at four o'clock, without a gesture, she ceased to live. I think she was happy to know that she was dying, to know that she would be able to rest at last. A will of iron.

But all this happened much later, after the big voyage. Toutepo, on the other hand, recovered. One day he sent me a message by Tapoua that he wanted to live alone for a while, and that he was going to build himself a shack in the woods in an isolated spot between our *faré* and the school. I didn't object, and I gave your father the job of taking him food every day. Your father, like his mother, had a serious nature and a tendency toward self-sacrifice. He performed his duty faithfully. I didn't interfere, and now and then I contrived to run into the person I mockingly described as the hermit, for mockery is an effective way of avoiding questions.

Toutepo was making slow progress at school, but Tekao and Noémie were pleased with him. He learned with difficulty, but he never forgot what he knew. He didn't try to learn about what didn't interest him, but that didn't matter, for we had long since established a policy we still follow, of letting students choose their own course of study, since we were more interested in awakening vocations than in organizing competitions.

Above all, Toutepo loved the Bible. He had really begun to read the day Noémie, to reward his efforts, had given him a copy bound in black with red edges. In no time he had learned passages by heart and kept adding new ones all the time. From then on he saw the world only through its pages. If I walked by his shack in the afternoon, I was sure to find him alone, reading it.

Toward me he had a strange attitude—not of fear, he was never afraid of anything or anyone—but of reserve, and almost of waiting.

I am neither shy nor oversensitive, but I've never been completely at ease with Toutepo. Even today, at my age and after everything that has happened, I can't manage to be altogether natural. When I seem to be, that's when I'm controlling myself best. The minute I start to relax, I become sarcastic, I make fun of our holy man, I have an urge to bully him. I don't know why I'm like this, but I am.

In any case, when I came upon this child half lying against his shack, I had trouble looking him in the eye. Can you imagine? This scrawny adolescent who looked at me and seemed to be sizing me up, judging me . . . One day I walked over and said to him, "Well?"

He looked up at me, his head on one side. He was leaning against the palm-tree wall, his body barely covered by an old *paréo*, his knees spread apart, his feet turned sideways exposing the light soles. He was smiling mysteriously in that restrained way of his.

I know, I have known many natives. I know that they are like children—they love secrets and rituals. But Toutepo's smile wasn't that kind. He knew something which I couldn't guess, which worried me, and which made him smile.

I repeated, more roughly, "Well?"

With a wave of his long hand, he indicated that I should sit down. I think I looked around before I obeyed him. For a moment he looked at me with his woman's eyes, trying to find the right words. Then he said, "You are strong. You do not understand why I look at you, and that makes you angry. Before, there was something that I, too, did not understand. Only one thing, and I felt as if I could no longer understand anything. I am not like you. I became sick. Fortunately, God helped me. So I would get well. He spoke to me. Here . . ."

With his mauve palm, he caressed the black Bible with the red edges. I didn't understand him. I said, without anger, for I didn't want to be ridiculous, "What are you talking about?"

"The death of Dubois," he answered calmly. "You said, It is Tara who killed him, Tara must die. I thought you knew. Everyone in Raevavae knows. Why not you? I thought you said it because Tara was bad and because Bourdaroux is a *farani*. Everyone thinks this. But you are a great *tané*, the *tané* of the *vahiné* Kateléné. I did not like to see you lie. I did not understand you. If you had asked me, I would have told you. I saw what happened. But you never asked me the right question. How could I know whether you wanted to hear the truth? I did not understand anything then. But God healed me, and I understood. You were mistaken. That was the will of God. He did not let you say the words that would have enlightened you. You had to be mistaken so Tara would perish, for God has said . . ."

He picked up his Bible, which opened by itself to a dog-eared page which I will quote, for later I asked him for the reference. It is from the Second Book of Kings, during the reign of Manasseh. It says, ". . . And the Lord spake by his servants the prophets, saying . . . And I will forsake the remnant of mine inheritance, and deliver them into the hand of their enemies; and they shall become a prey and a spoil to all their enemies; Because they have done that which was evil in my sight, and have provoked me to anger . . ."

Toutepo read me this very slowly, but without hesitating, for he knew the passage by heart. When he had finished, he looked up at me and smiled openly, happily.

"Tara was the inheritance of the Lord, like all men. But Tara was cruel. He held the prisoners in slavery, and let them die. He was afraid of Dubois, whom God loved. He displeased God. Bourdaroux wanted to kill Toutepo, but Bourdaroux is crazy, and Toutepo is nothing. Two instruments of God. Tara was not crazy, and Dubois died so that by putting Tara to death, you would do the will of God."

This logical exercise amazed me. Without looking at Toutepo, I repeated, "So Tara didn't kill anyone? And Bourdaroux was aiming at you and killed Dubois? Is that what happened?"

"It is as I have said," replied Toutepo firmly. "And it is right that it happened that way. Whatever happens is right. I was sad for you, for Dubois, and even for Tara. He was good too, sometimes. He was a very strong man. He could have lived to be very old. But God did not wish it. We are in his hand, as this island is in the sea."

"Are you sure?" I asked.

He looked at me with his beautiful, trusting eyes. "Yes."

He had nothing to add. But I had to know. "And everyone knew what you've just told me?"

"Yes."

"And no one said anything to me?"

"Why should they? Tara was troublesome, you know, and Bourdaroux is a *farani*. Of your blood. People thought you did the right thing."

"What about you?"

"God spoke to me," he said sternly.

In a daze, I got up and left with a feeble wave of farewell.

47

WHAT I'VE JUST told you I've never said to anyone. Toutepo has remained silent, too. And no one has ever referred to it in my presence. That's how it is. After I am dead and Toutepo is dead, you'll be the only one to know.

This incident, you see, is one of the keys to my life. Some people would have gotten over it, others would have shared it with someone else. Not me. I've carried it alone, inside myself, over the years, do you understand? And it has eaten away at me, transformed me, changed me. Oh, it isn't that I thought about it all the time, except at first. But even after I thought it had been forgotten, it was there, serving as my touchstone, and observing me.

My first impulse was to tell Peyrole everything, to call a meeting of the council, to rehabilitate Tara, to bring Bourdaroux to trial—in short, to undo what I had done. Shame held me back. I would have gone through with it if shame hadn't given me time to think it over. By speaking, I would call into question the authority of the council, which had sanctioned what I had done. I wouldn't bring back the dead. And I would kill Bourdaroux.

And strangely enough, Bourdaroux was the most useful man on the island. And I firmly believe that Tara was born for royalty or for the gallows. I have never feared competitors. Remember, I have never courted the people. But Tara would not have been a good king.

I kept quiet for the good of the island. These words I have just spoken—how long I deliberated before I could say them to myself with a clear conscience. Even now, before I wrote them, I turned them in every direction like precious gems on a piece of velvet to make sure I could find no fault in them, no imperfection. For the good of the island, and for no other reason, I accepted insomnia, and I left to others the sleep of the just.

By acting in this way, I wasn't seeking to avoid punishment. What wrong had I done? And who would have reproached me? For the first time in my life, I deserved the role that fate had assigned me. I ceased to be a rather well-meaning amateur and became, if you will, a professional. I knew something the others didn't know, I knew that we had all been deceived, and I carried on my own shoulders a calamity we had all created. I discovered my own strength, which gave me an incomparable feeling of confidence and a touch of contempt. It also taught me mistrust. I was an outlaw, perhaps, but not an outcast. In the first place, I had made a mistake. Next, they say that a murderer, after his first crime, tends to repeat himself, for once he has broken certain taboos, he is morally ready to continue. I had no desire to repeat myself. A combination of confidence and mistrust is the indispensable foundation of every great undertaking.

During the period of uncertainty which preceded what I can also describe as my cure, I avoided everyone except my wife and children. But the sight of your father was almost unbearable to me. I knew that if he ever found out, I would lose him forever.

313

I couldn't forgive him for forcing me to pretend twice: for everyone else, and for him.

Katherine was just starting down that narrow path which became narrower with every passing day until it became the tightrope on which she finally walked out to meet her death. She was already separating herself a little from us. I don't know how much she guessed. She communicated her affection for me in little ways. Perhaps she had guessed that I was suffering without knowing the cause. Although with women, you never know—they're so realistic . . .

That left my little daughter, Anne, who was my life. And Toutepo, who said nothing.

When I had recovered, I went to see Bourdaroux. I hadn't had any contact with him since my last visit before Tara's death, that is, for almost a year. Yes, for a year he had stayed there, wondering what I knew, laughing at my stupidity one day, fearing my clairvoyance the next. From reports I knew that he kept to himself, that he never left his house except to go to his workshop, and that he talked to no one.

But no one had told me how much he had changed. My first surprise was to discover that he had pulled up his hedge and taken down his gate, and that in front of his house there was now just an ordinary yard partially overgrown with grass and weeds; the famous sanded path had disappeared. As for the man himself, he had become flabby and pale. The yellow eyes that peered out of the puffy, discolored skin that surrounded them were slow and vague. He had almost stopped talking altogether, and answered me in monosyllables. He didn't seem so much aged as castrated.

He must have seen me coming, because as soon as I knocked on his door he opened it as if he had been standing behind it waiting for me. Without a word he motioned me in and showed me to a chair. Without hesitating he went to a cupboard and got out two glasses and a jug of rum. Since I declined to join him, he poured himself a glass standing up and drank it down in one swallow, then sat down heavily in the other chair, facing me, his face expressionless.

314

At first, as I have just said, I was struck by how much he had changed physically. But as the silence became more prolonged, I looked around the room and noticed an air of abandonment and neglect. The floor and furniture were covered with dust. The door that led to the back of the house was open and I could see the deserted kitchen, filled with pots and garbage.

Bourdaroux saw my look and gave a little shrug, but said nothing. It was then that I decided not to talk about Dubois. What was the point?

Without introduction, as coldly as possible, I told him in a few words why I had come: I wanted him to drop all other business and round up all the help he could in order to construct a large ship, preferably a steamship, capable of safely transporting about fifty of us to New Zealand or Australia. He listened to me in his new manner, without interrupting, or looking at me, or even seeming to understand. I remember noticing this. Was he going crazy, getting stupid? However, when I was finished he gave a sigh and said, "It will be done."

Then, making an effort, he sat up a little and looked at me—only for a moment—and added, "I knew this would come up sometime. I've already considered the problem. I've made a preliminary plan. It's possible, but . . ." There was a long pause. ". . . but it will take much work, much effort, much manpower. Right now, I . . . if I can do it, I'll do it. But I'll need people to help me. And I'll have to be able to give orders . . ."

"I'll take care of everything," I said. "You'll have all the men you need. You'll direct them, as equals. I'll see to that."

"I know," said Bourdaroux.

At the time I had nothing more to say to him. But he was so submissive, so hopeless, that it bothered me to leave him like this.

"Since you've already made sketches," I said brusquely, "let me see them."

He went to the cupboard from which he had taken the rum and pulled out a big roll of unbleached tapa. Before he unrolled it he went into the kitchen and got a rag with which he carefully wiped the table. Then from the same cupboard he took a small box of stones which he put on the floor beside him. Finally, he spread out his plans, weighting the pages with stones as he laid them out.

He moved slowly but surely and with concentration, as if he were repeating for the hundredth time gestures that had become sacred. So I could see better I walked around the table and looked over his shoulder.

They were much more than sketches. On the fibrous and uneven tapa he had managed to draw, with great care, in full detail, the complete diagram of a ship, including hull, superstructure, sleeping accommodations, and machinery.

I looked for a moment, full of admiration, and then I said, "Can you make this?"

"Yes."

"It won't hold fifty people," I said, straightening up.

"No, fifteen at the most. But it's a matter of proportion . . ."

I was hardly listening. I was looking at this detailed, finished diagram. Suddenly these neat lines, this careful work had brought home to me the precariousness of our state, the uncertainty of our lives. We were lucky, no doubt, for with the means at our disposal, we had managed to retain some links with the past. But what links? Dressed in our strange cast-off clothing, we were pursuing dreams in which no competition was to be feared, dreams for whose realization all memories, all scraps of knowledge were jewels. In our paradise, without realizing it, we had become respectable bums.

All this became clear to me from the line of the hull, the drawing of the engine room, the deck, the stairways, the cabins. The more I studied the details, the more impatient I was to build this boat and be gone. I said, "It has to work. Rethink the whole thing. Estimate your needs in manpower and materials. Try to calculate how long it will take you to build it. And bring me everything as soon as possible, at my house."

"At your house?"

His surprise woke me up. I lifted my head and looked back at him. "Yes," I said.

He wasn't clever. He didn't know anything about people. His intelligence functioned only when he was alone, confronting a given problem. I wish I could have seen him in his old job as steward. As he saw me to the door, he stammered out some kind of thanks. I was ready for him, stiff with hatred. I told him very coldly, "I need you. That's all."

And I walked away without turning around.

48

No ONE KNOWS about this visit, although there's no particular reason for this. At the time neither Bourdaroux nor I would have wanted to bring it up. Later we decided independently that it was pointless to reveal something that had accidentally become a secret.

It's good for you to know about it, though, if only to prove to you once again how unreliable the history of historians is.

The idea of building a boat had occurred to me some time before Toutepo told me about the death of Dubois. In those days, I was probably bored. Perhaps because I didn't know what everyone else knew, I had lost touch with the island, I had lost my sense of its future. I had the feeling that everything was coming to a standstill around me. It's possible that because of this, I was looking for a big project to carry out.

Or perhaps it was just that the time had come. When Dubois died, we had been alone in the world for almost ten years. During this period not much had happened, and yet many things had changed.

When I landed in Raevavae, I had found a happy and irresponsible population, living and thinking in common, like those schools of tiny fish who can change direction in a flash without breaking formation, as if the same impulse simultaneously moved all the fins, determined the direction of all the tails. Ten years later these reflex movements still existed, but they were rarer, slower. Education, by separating the children from their parents, by competing with tradition, had started to break up the pattern and to emphasize individuals.

At the time of my arrival all the natives were fishermen,

farmers, and hunters at the same time. Gradually, at first for the fun of it, to imitate Leguen or Bourdaroux, they had become specialized. We now had a few peasants, a few masons, a few builders, carpenters, and metalworkers. We also had nurses, interns, two junior chemists, six assistant teachers, weavers, basketmakers, a tanner, and I forget the rest. All this was, as it were, my workmanship. I was proud of it and worried about it at the same time. I was afraid that what I had done might be ridiculously inadequate. I was afraid that my structure was too fragile, too artificial, and in danger of falling apart. I was sometimes afraid that I was writing on sand and that a breeze could come along and erase it all, reducing things to what they had been before me. Above all I remembered what Dubois had said: You can't change a paradise. And also, I was tired; islands may be self-sufficient, but they are also limited. Everything on them is the same, and on a small scale. What can you expect of a kingdom that you can walk across in one morning?

All this entered into it. In the beginning I thought of it as a big project capable of changing every aspect of our lives. At first I visualized a migration in canoes, the way it was done a long time ago, and the way the Fijians had come to us. Then I decided that that would be inadequate, that it would only have value as an adventure. I wanted to invent something better, something that would both arouse our passion and test our solidity. I abandoned the idea of canoes, and decided to make a real boat with an engine.

The grand scale of this project was my guarantee of its value. In order to succeed, we would have to work hard, persevere, bring together all our knowledge, all our strength, all our resources. This boat, if we succeeded in building it, would be the masterpiece by which we would be assured of our progress. And if we did not succeed, it would remain a goal, a hope, a lesson.

Just then the information that Toutepo gave me came along and upset all my plans. Without Bourdaroux, my project was doomed from the start. But how could I ask Dubois' murderer for help? I hesitated for a long time, believe me. In the end I think my decision was made the day I knew I wasn't going to denounce Bourdaroux. But it took me a while before I admitted this to myself. And then all of a sudden one morning everything became clear. Because knowing what I knew I was remaining silent, Bourdaroux belonged to me. I could, without any compunctions, make use of him for the good of all. He couldn't refuse. His cooperation would be his secret punishment. As soon as I realized this I made my visit without speaking to anyone, last of all the members of the council. Having involved them in Tara's execution, I wanted to keep them out of my plans for a while, so they would be free to reject them when the time came.

Actually, I didn't have to wait very long. Bourdaroux paid me a first visit at the end of a week, and another in the days that followed. He had worked well, and we found a tone that made it bearable to be together. I gave myself a week to think it over, and then I launched the project. Or rather—correction!—I almost launched it. This is very important.

Many of my mistakes, which must seem incomprehensible to you, can in the last analysis be attributed to my education, and to my having lived in the Old World. When I thought about this boat I realized that if I were ambitious enough, extravagant enough in my aims, we would find ourselves engaged almost in spite of ourselves in a great collective undertaking which would carry us beyond ourselves. But I had conceived of this great work in the most traditional possible manner. I had found an engineer, Bourdaroux, and had asked him for a plan, an inventory, a schedule. I had carefully gone over and discussed everything, then, convinced that I possessed a complete, perfect plan, I was about to put it on the market and recruit workers whom I would have paid—in praise and honors, no doubt, but whom I would also have given salaries for jobs determined by me.

Fortunately, I had trouble at the beginning. I started by explaining my intentions to Peyrole. He listened to me in his way—grumpy, but attentive. Then he began to raise objections. He didn't like Bourdaroux and he was afraid that the man's technical abilities, by elevating him to the rank of foreman, might provide him with the prestige he needed so badly and drive him to some rash act. He didn't believe the natives were capable of such a sustained effort. He was afraid of accidents, setbacks. Finally, he was resigned to his fate and satisfied with his lazy life, his petty authority. He was afraid of adventure and couldn't imagine that we could discover a place more suitable than Raevavae.

He irritated me. Although younger than myself, he was infinitely more cautious and set in his ways—in short, older. As he pointed out to me, policemen usually retire at an early age. Without ill will he had thought it over and realized that under normal circumstances, he would for four years now have been puttering in his garden in Rabastens and supplementing his pension with an easy job in some government department. He was conscientious, loyal, and proud of his responsibilities, and he didn't neglect his duties, which he knew would come to an end only when he died. But lately he was performing his functions with a new calm and detachment. Gradually he had lost the spirit of the professional and had become a volunteer. Although he privately considered himself retired, he generously continued to offer the community the advantages of his experience. If he had almost ceased to appear in uniform, it was not so much because his clothes were wearing out as because he had finally discovered that the *paréo* was more comfortable. In the cart that took him everywhere he always had a fishing pole, and behind the Navy House he had planted a flourishing vegetable garden. Finally, the *pastis* that he made himself out of rum and certain aromatic plants which he had selected after much experimentation, was a source of pride to him.

I hadn't reached that point. I cut short his comments and went to look for a more sympathetic listener.

I thought I had found him in Tekao. He had also grown much stouter but he was as charming as ever and still interested in hearing about my projects. He listened attentively and immediately expressed his enthusiastic approval. I thought I had won him over, and unrolled my plans and started discussing the details. Engrossed in my subject, I didn't look at him. Suddenly I noticed his silence and glanced up. His expression was embarrassed, almost guilty. When I looked at him questioningly he shook his head and smiled uncomfortably. Then he laughed that boyish, friendly laugh of his and said timidly, "The people of this island are born sailors."

"Well?"

"Well . . ." For a moment he stood there balancing himself on his fat legs, then he made up his mind. "Wouldn't it be better to ask their advice instead of bringing them this finished plan and telling them to get to work? Bourdaroux is clever, of course, but he's not a sailor. Besides . . ."

"Yes?"

"Oh, I don't know—the people don't like him very much, you see. I'm sure you're right. A ship is useful, and building it would mean that everyone would have to lend a hand. But you don't like forced labor any more than I do . . ."

He was embarrassed and uncomfortable. Because I was annoyed I didn't help him out and waited silently for him to go on.

". . . To work like that for something you don't understand is a little like slavery, isn't it?"

"But then what are we to do? Make a *pahi?*"

He shook his head slowly. "No, not a *pahi.* A steamboat. Like this one. Maybe even this one. But it should be . . . I think it should be . . . how can I say it? A ship that the people would design themselves, don't you see?"

"A ship that the people would design themselves," I repeated, beginning to get the point and suddenly very interested.

"Yes. You want progress, don't you? For the people of Raevavae, right? Then you should try. I don't know, it may be crazy. But I think you should try. All the men on the island have seen big ships, before the *tsunami.* They know how they were made. And then there are our graduates; we mustn't forget them. They can work. There are books in the library. Yes, I think we ought to try . . ."

"You mean, that we should propose the idea and that they should decide on the design, the tonnage, the method of construction, and so forth?"

Tekao's eyes were shining. He nodded. "Yes. With our help, of course. But only our help—not our control. They'll be proud.

And besides, they'll know that they're capable of building something besides a *pahi!*"

"I'll think about it," I said, gathering up my plans.

The idea was crazy and naive, but there was something about it that appealed to me. The more I thought about it, the more it seemed to me that this was what I had really wanted all along without knowing it myself. I thought of Dubois. I was sure that he would have liked this fantastic project. If it succeeded, it would be a true masterpiece, a touchstone, an awakening, a real revolution.

It also pleased me to think that if we approached the problem from this direction, Bourdaroux would not be the master craftsman of our wonder, but only a humble technician, and I had no doubts about his accepting this role.

Yes, it was all fascinating. I gave myself two days to think it over, because a decision of this kind should not be made in a hurry. Then when I had made up my mind, I took a whole week to plan my strategy. On this, too, I consulted Tekao.

Finally, when everything was clear in my mind, I talked to Peyrole again. To my surprise, he was more interested this time. Far from raising new objections, he simply said, "If the people agree to it, why shouldn't I?"

49

ALTHOUGH FOR SEVERAL weeks I have done nothing but write to you, I am not a writer. I admire writers, but the idea of imitating them doesn't tempt me. For me writing means talking, and talking means telling a story or explaining something. I'm using writing as a means to an end, and I expect it to serve me. As an activity in itself, it neither interests nor worries me, and when it ceases to serve me, I will forget it.

I'm unlike a writer, I think, in that for me writing doesn't exist. I'm also unlike a writer in that I'm not interested in using writing to create beauty. That's not my business. Besides, according to what I have read, beauty depends not so much on the way a thing is said as on the quality of what is said, and on a certain necessary relationship between style and substance. For me, nothing is really beautiful which is not true, and which does not help people to live.

So I don't care about the style in which I'm writing you, as long as I can communicate to you exactly what I think. I use words in my own way, and if sometimes it sounds too much as if I'm talking, I can't help it.

All this to tell you that nevertheless I shall not use the only expression that fits. It's a cliché which I don't like but for which I can find no equivalent. I won't tell you that we built the ship the way they built cathedrals in the Middle Ages. And yet, that's exactly what happened.

And it took almost as long.

It started as a conspiracy, of which Tekao and I were the only members.

Quietly, inconspicuously, we began planting a desire for travel. Tekao gave more courses in geography. I asked one of the Fijians who spoke rather well to give a sort of lecture in which he presented his native land with all the poetry that exiles can put into such descriptions. Leguen told us about his Morbihan, without any encouragement, for in those days he was beginning to get a little soft in the head from drinking too much, and at his farm he ran a kind of club for drunks who loved to tell stories. Odile Peyrole gave courses in French cooking, and even Katherine, carried away by the current of exoticism, suggested that we build a tennis court.

You'll say that such an agreement of interests, even though brought about indirectly, could not pass unnoticed, and that many people must have gotten wind of our conspiracy. Nothing of the sort happened, thanks to the arts of leisure.

I've already told you that I fear and despise personal ambition, salaried work, everything that leads people with their own consent into domination and servitude. It's obvious, though, that certain individuals don't realize themselves fully without it. To deny it to them would be cruel, and besides, all societies, even the most frugal ones, need some workers. As soon as I spotted one of these individuals, I would direct him toward some strenuous activity which, though temporary, could give him pride and calm his fever. But for the others, whom I did not want to abandon to idleness for fear they would either go to sleep or become drudges, too, I had invented the arts of leisure.

Remembering my early childhood in Berry with its country fairs, I began by organizing games in all the villages: sack races, shinnying up greased poles, hitting targets, etc. Next, I arranged matches between the villages to bring together the winners in each field, and gave prizes to the champions, who very quickly acquired considerable prestige.

I took advantage of the interest in these games to introduce team sports. At one point there were seventeen football teams. It took all my patience to communicate to everyone how important it was to respect the rules of the game. In the beginning the competitors were so eager to win that they all cheated. In their eyes victory proved the superiority of the individual as a whole, including his cunning. I succeeded, not without difficulty, in making them listen to reason. When this was accomplished, I organized dancing contests, singing contests, poetry contests. Here, too, I had to explain that the poets must under no circumstances borrow stanzas from the traditional songs or plagiarize Victor Hugo.

We also had contests for the best painting on wood, palm leaves, and rock. We honored champions in building houses, gave grand prizes for fishing, held finals for the most skillful *tapa* beater, the best hunter, the best cook. We had competitions in everything. The extraordinary thing was that everyone turned out to be a champion in something, everyone could do something better or faster than the rest.

All this kept me busy, but it excited and amused the people. The seeds of exoticism and nostalgia we planted were mixed in with the rest and weren't noticed.

They sprouted, though. The oldest inhabitants remembered the Tahiti of their youth, the big ships that used to dock in Matotea, the seaplane that had brought me, and reminisced about all these things. The youngest caught the fever, and made up stories of their own. A dozen of them met secretly and planned to build a *pahi* and set off, trusting to fate. But the world that surrounded us was too cold and forbidding for them. They didn't carry out their plan.

All this frenzy would eventually have died down if we hadn't fed it from another direction. I made a long report to the council on the growth of our population and the risks of famine that we would be facing before long. Peyrole, who knew what was stored in his warehouses, confirmed this picture. A few weeks later Tekao gave the same audience a lecture on meteorology and concluded by saying that if another cyclone, this time brought on by natural causes, was not probable, neither was it impossible, and that if one should occur, the human race, which had taken refuge in Raevavae, might die out altogether.

These rather intellectual arguments were suited to sober minds. The council members listened to them and weighed them silently, then adopted them and circulated them to the rest of the population, where they helped to reinforce and focus the vague aspirations we had aroused.

This went on for a year. Then one day Mai, who was the best navigator on the island, who had taken me to Tahiti, and who was now an old man, came to see me and asked me whether we couldn't build a boat and set out in search of a larger piece of land.

I knew him well enough to be sure that he wouldn't have taken such a step unless the whole population shared his feeling. So you can imagine how happy I was.

Concealing my emotion, I pretended to be amazed, at a loss. A boat? Why? What kind of a boat? And who would build it?

This was the beginning of the second phase. The native members of the council took over its direction. Not one of them thought of Bourdaroux. They gave a party on the beach at Anatonu which was as beautiful as my wedding party. The idea of a boat was greeted with cheers. Some wanted to start cutting down trees for the hull immediately. We had done our work well. We asked them what their boat would be like. They opened their eyes wide and described giant *pahis*. The young people hooted at them and talked about steel, turbines, steam, paddle-wheels, I don't know what all. A tremendous commotion ensued.

When the shouting had died down the villages decided unanimously to think about the problem and to meet again on the same beach in exactly two months.

Then the party resumed, but there was a sort of flatness which I didn't understand at first. But an hour later when I saw people slipping away one by one, furtively, I guessed the reason: They were all in a hurry to get to work.

Those two months brought quite a few tribulations in the life of Raevavae. Whereas for several years many families had built their *farés* inland, in order to take up farming or just for a change, all or almost all of these families suddenly flowed back toward the sea and the villages from which they had come. Almost overnight, for it was the rainy season, we saw plowed fields become overgrown with wild grass, roofs cave in, cattle that were yesterday domesticated revert to freedom.

The school was not spared. In all the classes the number of absentees rose considerably. It was no longer possible to give regular classes, for the attendance was constantly changing. Students would come in, ask a question, almost always a strange one, and armed with their answer, would excuse themselves and disappear without waiting for the end of class. Even at the church some members of the congregation came to ask Léné what kind of wood Noah's ark was made of and how the apostles navigated. Peyrole, Leguen, and I were always on call. As for Bourdaroux, he was constantly surrounded by a crowd of timid questioners. After asking him for his plans, I had been afraid that he would have a bad reaction to all these delays. It would have been in character. Feeling very awkward, for I was sure he thought I was crazy, I had explained my intentions to him. But he was a broken man, already sick, and he had no choice in the matter. He had listened to me in silence, and then said, "Whatever you say . . ."

His last ambition was to obey. It was almost as if he no longer allowed himself to think without permission. I found this attitude exaggerated, and it made me suspicious. I was mistaken;

he was sincere. I've never really understood him. It's too bad. Out of indifference, I left him free to do as he pleased. He wasn't made for this. But as I told you, I had long since given up responsibilities. By the time I accepted them again, Bourdaroux's game had been played, and lost.

In any case, now that he was left to himself, he kept busy making furniture, doing maintenance work at the hospital, and fashioning tools that were crude but sturdy, and he answered conscientiously, though without pleasure, all questions that were asked of him. Each village had withdrawn into itself and was in the throes of creativity. Each one was preparing its own contribution to the communal project. Those who did not participate in the work directly gave suggestions to those who did. Everyone had ideas, even the children, and the ground around the houses was covered with plans and diagrams that had been drawn on the sand with sticks. As I strolled around, people would show me things they were hiding from their rivals. Almost everywhere there was a main plan, something that might have been called the official plan, which was approved by the wisest and which was the object of fervent interest. This did not prevent the independents, the free-lancers, from privately working on their own plans on a more modest scale. Some were making drawings, which they were constantly changing to the point of madness, as they waited for the opportunity to show them. Others, a more numerous group, were building models. In Mahanantoa, where more than anywhere else the people longed to distinguish themselves in order to restore their reputation, they even built a boat a dozen yards long which resembled an ocean liner and had three smokestacks higher than a man. When it was put in the water, this vessel immediately rolled over on its side and sank, to the amusement of the spectators.

At last the long-awaited day arrived.

As soon as the sun rose, from all over the island the different villages, walking in procession and carrying their masterpieces, converged on Anatonu. The whole island suddenly hummed with activity. Everywhere there was laughter and shouting. The villages furthest away had left by torchlight. The closest ones arrived by sea, in merry fleets, with their women and children, everyone decked out in flowers. The council, which had appointed itself the jury, waited for them on the beach, surrounded by all the people of Anatonu. In the cool morning air huge fires were burning to heat up the stones that would later be used to cook the meat for lunch. For the first time in several weeks the sky was clear and a little breeze coming off the sea fringed the distant reefs with white.

Almost at the same moment all the villagers arrived, little dense and clearly distinguishable groups, the women carrying provisions and gifts, the men carrying their work on litters, like reliquaries, or pressed to their breasts, like relics.

At first we wandered slowly around to get a general impression. Everything that could conceivably be imagined was there: many canoes, both single and double-bottomed, many miniature transatlantic ships, cargo ships with derricks, a few with tapered silhouettes like warships, but also things that were square, round, slender, squat, flat like rafts or keeled like racing boats, things that had never been seen before and, although many were represented in three dimensions, difficult to imagine floating on the ocean. The most curious part was that although the exterior detail had been very carefully done, none of these designs contained any means of propulsion.

At this point I perceived a danger. Our project couldn't be carried out unless the whole island participated in it; but having worked alone, the villages now found themselves in competition. This was a state of mind which had always existed in Raevavae, but which my games and contests had exacerbated. Although I considered it a good way of bringing out individuals, I found it undesirable in the matter that concerned us and was afraid, not without some show of reason, that it would lead, if not to open warfare, at least to a kind of shabby jockeying for control.

So I proposed that the models be displayed, not by villages as they were, but by types: the *pahis* with the *pahis,* the rafts with the rafts, the sailboats with the sailboats, etc.

This idea was soon accepted, for everyone was convinced of the excellence of his own work and confident that it would eclipse all others by comparison.

At first this created a tremendous amount of confusion and Peyrole, whose mere presence had a calming effect, had his hands full. Finally we were able to judge. The people of Raevavae were totally free of vanity. In France in the old days a confrontation of this kind would have ended in a fight, would have given rise to resentments. With us these comparisons simply made certain inadequacies obvious to everyone, and showed that some designs had never gone beyond the stage of the first sketch, or even of the idea. Their creators saw this themselves, and were the first to throw into the fire, laughing, what had seemed to them perfect only a few minutes before.

After this purge, five models remained under consideration: a double-bottomed *pahi,* which was perfect, easy to make, and very easy to handle; three European boats whose smokestacks indicated that they would have to have engines; and a strange oval affair that looked a little like a swimming pool or an enormous dead body, whose greatest charm was undoubtedly its originality.

My preference, as I've told you, was for a steamship. I felt that only such a boat, with its complexity and all the problems it would compel us to overcome, could fill that symbolic role which seemed to me so important. Seeing how excited everyone was, however, I didn't think it would be wise to express my opinion. As it happened, it prevailed naturally. The *pahi* was rejected contemptuously, almost without examination. Anyone, the people around me said, could make a boat like that.

The real contest was between one of the ships with smokestacks and the strange round gondola I mentioned. This craft seemed to appeal to people primarily because it had neither bow nor stern, which would certainly facilitate changing direction. Pretending to be neutral, I trembled.

At last someone, I've forgotten who, who was laughing uncontrollably, finally succeeded in making himself understood and between fits of choking asked whether this marvelous advantage of having neither head nor tail wouldn't be a little inconvenient when one wanted to follow a precise direction.

There was a moment of dazed silence, then everyone burst

out laughing. The tub was carried to the water, and three children armed with paddles were taken aboard and instructed to steer. Since the boat wasn't caulked it would not have gone far, if it had been able to move at all. But it did nothing but go around in a circle faster and faster until it was half full, at which point it wobbled for a moment and then sank without a bubble.

So after two days of discussion a single model remained, and it was one that I found suitable.

As I read over what I have written, I'm afraid I may have put too much emphasis on the amusement that accompanied these proceedings. Don't think for a moment that it expressed contempt. It was just that the people were goodhearted, and laughed at their own mistakes. But until failure had proved to them that they were wrong, they believed in what they were doing and gave it all their attention. This must be stressed. Otherwise the effort that the whole island made over such a long period of time would be unbelievable.

50

THE PROJECT TOOK us eight years. The construction of this boat was a challenge whose magnitude intoxicated us. But it was also a folly such as I'm sure no free society commits or ever will commit.

Consider our situation, our resources. There were just a thousand of us, counting the newly born and the old. We knew our island well and we knew how to use everything it had to give us, but it didn't have everything. When it came to tools, we had little besides our own hands and our ingenuity. The tools we did have, the remaining supplies in the government warehouse, suddenly appeared to us as they were, ridiculously inadequate.

In the end we decided to build a wooden hull and to line it with sheet metal if we could. We had to choose a site for the shipyard. The most practical location was the beach at Rairua, which had direct access to deep water and was not far from the channel of Teaverua. But the big pine trees that we needed to make the timbers grew at the foot of Turivaa, at the eastern end of the island. Mai was in favor of Vaiuru, which was better situated, but whose bay was very shallow for several hundred yards. Someone suggested that we build the hull in the middle of the woods and then transport it to the sea by rolling it on logs over a road that would have to be made. In the end we decided to build it in Rairua.

Bourdaroux, without saying anything to me, closed up the former police station which he had been so proud to live in at first, and moved himself and his tools to the middle of the pine forest, where he built a small *faré*. Many men did the same thing, without hesitating.

During the first year over a hundred trees, among the most beautiful on the island, were cut down, sawed up, prepared, and carried to Rairua by long columns of men who laughed and sang under their burdens. For the keel they took a native oak, a tall, straight giant of a tree which was rolled to the sea and slowly towed the whole length of the island by dozens of canoes. Often, women and children went to see the builders and came back carrying light boards which they piled up near the big framework in Rairua.

No road was built, but when the tree-cutting was finished and the little *farés* had been abandoned, a wide, hard road, formed by the bare feet of the porters, ran across the island from east to west.

Then slowly, for the problems were infinite, the keel took its place on the beach, and there rose before our eyes the gigantic skeleton of a sea monster.

The natives were quite good at all this. But they had to live and couldn't devote themselves wholly to their passion. The work crews were constantly changing. At certain times, because the fish were running in the lagoon, or because the crops were waiting to be harvested, the shipyard was deserted. In the blazing sun the beams turned white, and then grey, and the pieces of wood scattered around added to the desolate appearance of what could be regarded as either a ruin or a promise.

While the builders were doing their part, several of Tekao's students had overcome their reluctance and approached Bourda-roux to discuss the problem of the engine. Although they had read all the books on the subject that were in the library, they had never seen what they wanted to build. Bourdaroux served them well. There's no other way to put it. This imperious man, proud of his age, his experience, and his status as a white man, listened to them, answered their questions, tested their ideas with models, and was for them the most devoted of servants or the finest of teachers, which sometimes amounts to the same thing.

By this time I was convinced that he had changed pro-foundly and tried to have a reconciliation with him. He neither rejected me nor encouraged me. The truth was that he no longer needed friends. The only thing that concerned him was his own opinion of himself. Perhaps, too, the fact that I knew about his role in the death of Dubois kept him away from me. Or maybe he just didn't like me.

He had moved his operation to Rairua when the lumber camp had been abandoned, and he hardly ever left the beach. Sometimes on Sunday afternoon he would go as far as Leguen's farm, and if Leguen was alone he would sit down for a moment and drink a glass of wine in silence, and then walk heavily home, after leaving a toy for the children.

To him more than to anyone else we owe the machinery and most of the metal parts of the ship. But it wasn't he who proposed the voyage to Rapa.

All we had found on the island was a narrow vein of iron ore and a few small beds of lignite at the foot of Mount Hiro. It wasn't enough. At one point we considered collecting all the objects made of iron and steel that we could get hold of and melting them down, but even if we had been able to spare them, they wouldn't have been sufficient.

I hunted for a solution and found one in a geography book. It said that Rapa, a volcanic island, possessed an abundance of mining resources. And Rapa was only six hundred miles away, only a little further than Tubuai, where I had landed with Tapoua and Mai when we made our voyage to Tahiti.

The natives built on their own, without our help, the big

332

double-bottomed *pahi* that I had scorned, covered it with a sturdy roof, fitted it out with a big sail, and left with a crew of ten, practically without consulting us.

For seven months there was no sign of them. Then one morning they were discovered anchored in front of Rairua. Their boat, which was loaded to capacity, had taken a beating from the sea on the homeward voyage. The crew was emaciated and exhausted. They had lost a man in Rapa, crushed in a cave-in at the foot of a mine shaft. But they had brought back coal and big lumps of iron which they had smelted at the mine in a little furnace they had improvised with the help of one of our books. Finally, they had brought with them four men whom they had found in Rapa.

Three of them were natives of the Tuamotus who had been employed by the French government to work on excavations in Rapa. The fourth was a Frenchman named Gervais who was half crazy.

According to their own account, these men were the sole survivors in a population of over three hundred persons, a mixture of Europeans and natives. At the time of the *tsunami,* they had been together in a concrete-lined underground chamber in which instruments of measurement were about to be installed in connection with French atomic tests. Everyone else had been carried away by waves, crushed by landslides, or killed by flying rock.

The four survivors hadn't been as lucky as ourselves. Rapa was a barren island with a harsh climate. The only part with trees on it was far away from the sea. They had been too weak to carry to the shore the tree trunks they would have needed to build a boat big enough for a long voyage. With no hope of escaping and no possibility of having children, they had given in first to despair, and then to indifference.

The men from Raevavae who had found them told me that they were so filthy they looked like animals. They also told me that they didn't believe all of their story, because they had noticed signs here and there on the island that led them to think that several small communities had existed recently and had made war on each other. Their own opinion was that our four survivors were the final victors of this war, and that they may have eaten their victims.

The man named Gervais, as I said, was almost in his second childhood. He trembled with fear as soon as anyone came near him, and was subject to attacks in which he became dangerous. The rest of the time he sat huddled in a corner, not moving or speaking. I had him taken to the hospital. He spent two months there during which he seemed to calm down and become less violent. Several times he was found weeping, but he would never tell anyone why. Finally one morning he was found dead. He had hung himself on his sheet.

His three companions, once they had received adequate nourishment and had taken up life in the community, blended in easily and I heard no more about them. I soon forgot what might have gone on a few years before in Rapa, and nobody ever reminded me of it. My only conclusion was that we in Rae-vavae had been very lucky.

With the lumps of crude iron that had been brought back from Rapa, and a tremendous amount of labor, the work crews succeeded in making a shaft and a propellor. They also hammered out a large number of pieces of sheet iron which were used to build the boiler and to line the sheathing below the waterline.

Finally, five years and nine months after the party on the beach at Anatonu, the ship was launched. Launched is really not the word for it. Although it was ninety feet long and almost twenty-five feet high, it was carried to the water by a multitude of ecstatic people. After that it almost sank, for everyone wanted to get on board at the same time. Finally, it was anchored a hundred yards from the beach, in a spot that was sheltered from the wind, and after it had been blessed and covered with flowers like a young bride, the crowd gathered in front of it on the sand and danced in its honor for three days and three nights.

To show that this was only a beginning, I had suggested that we christen it *The First*. As you know, in the end it was named by popular demand *The Memory of Our Fathers and the*

Hope of Our Children. You're used to it. Maybe it doesn't bother you. I must tell you frankly that I find it ridiculous.

After it was put in the water, it took us three more years to equip and finish this "memory" before we could finally put to sea.

51

DON'T THINK THAT this meant that life was suspended in Rae-vavae. We continued to come and go and tend to our business, as usual. Once the first enthusiasm had died down, no one lost interest in the project. But our passion had become more re-strained, more normal. It was understood that the island was in labor, and that we were all midwives. But birth is a simple thing, although it can be dangerous, always involves pain, and is never completely understood. Improvised crews took turns working on the boat, one group taking over where another had left off. Ever so often those who were at work would announce that an un-expected obstacle required extra hands. People would come to help out, there would be a party, everyone would feel strong and happy, then everyone would go back to his own life, until he felt the time was right to come and donate a few days or weeks to the public good.

For me, with or without the boat, life was just about the same. Together with the council I ran the government, answered questions, made improvements, settled disputes. In my leisure time I joked with the people, treated my daughter Anne like a princess because she was the prettiest blonde on the island (in fact, she was the only one), encouraged the arts of leisure, and tried to find answers to those questions which I'll never stop asking myself.

Around this time, maybe because of Toutepo, whom I'll have more to say about later, I thought a lot about God. In the last analysis, I don't believe there is a person called God. But neither do I believe that there is nothing. It seems to me that outside of matter and above it there is an invisible but coherent reality which one might as well call God. This God is deaf and has no mouth. And yet it is sometimes possible to feel his presence, to communicate with him, to become part of him. I believe that this can happen to everyone in moments of silence and equilibrium, through meditation, in the happiness evoked by the contemplation of beauty, in love, or in generosity. It has happened to me. At such times one feels that the vibration of the world is in harmony with one's own, and one senses without being able to prove it but with total certitude that one is a thousand times vaster, freer, stronger than one's own individual self.

Out of all this I have never drawn any conclusions of value to other people. My beliefs are mine alone. But stupidly, during this period of waiting, and of what I now realize was idleness that preceded our departure, I tried, not to found a religion, quite the contrary, but to help my fellow men in this area.

I decided it would be useful to build some little retreats in isolated and especially beautiful spots, not for the practice of any particular religion, but simply places where those who wished could withdraw for a moment, collect their thoughts, and meditate.

They weren't even hermitages, but rather stopping places in which to spend an hour, catch one's breath, and go on one's way. I built three of them by myself, out of stone. They were small—nine by twelve feet—and had only two openings, a low door that opened on a choice landscape, and a very small window through which the light fell on a bare wall at an angle that indicated the passing of time.

I hoped that those to whom these stopping places would be useful would discover their use for themselves. When people asked me what they were for I smiled and said nothing. I was quite pleased with myself.

A month later three families had moved in with their chickens and pigs, and were starting to clear the surrounding land.

I asked them to leave and, to avoid the same thing happening again, I asked three simple-minded old fellows whom I trusted to oversee and maintain my refuges and to admit only those for whom they had been designed.

This worked for a while. Then Léné came to see me and asked me respectfully what I was up to. My three innocent old men, perhaps overcome by the majesty of the settings, had all had revelations and were starting a new way of worshipping Kérito. Naturally they were the sole priests of this nascent religion. At first I lost my temper, then I laughed. I politely threw the old men out and told the families they could move back in. My religion was dead.

Time passed slowly. If it hadn't been for the boat, one day would have been identical to the next. The island practically ran itself. We suffered neither famines nor epidemics. We were growing old without noticing it. Oh, once in a while the face of a friend, seen from an unusual angle, in a harsh light, or in an off moment disturbed us, just as we were surprised by the appearance in every part of the island of these young people whom we had educated, who were not ourselves, but who had our knowledge, and who often took the liberty of having ideas of their own. Yes, time was passing.

Leguen's life was gently slipping away without our being able to do anything about it. He worked too hard, drank too much. In spite of the all-consuming vegetation, the heavy rains that washed away the terrain, parasites of all kinds, and the undersized animals of the island, he had worn himself out trying to recreate a countryside similar to the one where he had been born and which he carried in his heart.

Everyone loved him. He was unpretentious and kind. These are words that are often said, but are rarely true. In his case, they were true. With the natives, who had adopted him, he often argued about questions of farming or breeding. But he never hurt anyone's feelings. He wanted to explain, to convince.

"They don't know," he would say, as if he were talking about a physical weakness.

His older son is a drunkard. The other one is a good farmer. Pierrette, my godchild, is a doctor. You know her.

Peyrole was asleep. His wife had dizzy spells and agonized over her children. I have no right to blame her for the way she brought them up. But she made them miserable. And to do this, to prevail against the spontaneity and innocence of the island, she must have expended enormous quantities of intelligence and character which would have been so useful elsewhere . . .

Daniel, her eldest, was a weakling. At twenty-two he was still tied to his mother's apron strings, was afraid of the sun, hadn't learned to swim. At one time he thought he was a painter. Later he became a rather good cartographer. It was he who trained the staff of the school of geography. It was also he who made our first printing press and cut the type molds for the font of characters. But when his mother died he started to drink, and that was the end of him.

Claude, his younger brother, was completely different. He took after his father—solid, red-faced, slow, but stubborn. Until he was fifteen, he was quiet. Then he set up housekeeping with a girl, and his parents lost all influence over him. Peyrole never mentioned it to me, but I don't think he was unhappy about it. His wife was bringing up his children the way children had been raised back in Rabastens. He couldn't blame her for it. But in his heart he must have found it stupid. Claude was on the ship with us when we made our first voyage. We had had to conceal his departure from his mother. When his parents came to join us after the second voyage he found them a house and took care of them. But he never lived with them again. I don't know what became of him after that.

We didn't get any older, but one at a time, our children stopped being children. Katherine, preoccupied as she was with her work, saw this and worried about it. She knew that your father wouldn't be happy. You know that he wasn't. Out of the four full-blooded white children of Raevavae, not one did anything of importance. She was also worried about what would become of our daughter.

Little Anne was blonde, the only blonde in Raevavae, perhaps the only one in the world. She was sweet, generous, and imperious at the same time. She thought she was the daughter of a king whose touch had the power to cure the plague. As a child, she had played with the natives. As a woman, she retained a condescending affection for them. She was the only one of her kind, as her mother had been. But she didn't have me.

338

Odile Peyrole did everything in her power to get her to marry her son Daniel. Anne wasn't interested. I understand her. It would have been completely contrived. For a while she worked with her mother at the hospital. Then Toutepo started preaching, and her fate was decided forever.

52

AFTER REVEALING TARA's innocence to me, Toutepo went on exactly as before. For at least two years more he continued to go to school and to take care of my horses.

Then one day he quietly stopped working, and we almost lost sight of him. He spoke seldom, did not dance, did not play, did not look at girls. People found him boring. No one noticed him. Except for Katherine and Noémie, the only person who paid him any attention at all was perhaps your father. But I never had any inside information on this subject, and in any case your father was by then too extreme, too tormented to carry on a sustained relationship with a boy like Toutepo.

So Toutepo sat alone on the slopes of Mount Hiro, from which both good and evil have come to us, reading the Bible. I told you that one of the peculiarities of his nature was that nothing affected him that had not first been understood by his intelligence. This isn't entirely true. His life is well known. There have been numerous cases when instinctively, guided by his heart, he took action with the energy that you are familiar with.

But I still believe I'm not mistaken in saying that in spite of appearances, Toutepo is a cold person, guided by reason. The only time he gets really excited is when what he sees is in conflict with what he knows. What rouses him is not so much the spectacle of suffering or evil as the keen awareness of the outrage that this suffering and evil represent in comparison with the harmonious simplicity of his spirit. In the Bible, which he read over and over like a textbook, he found rules of conduct. To illustrate these rules, he discovered heroes. On this basis he reconstructed a world that was clear and strong, in his own image.

In his eyes, the moral nature of things is infinitely more real than their physical nature. In spite of all the respect I have for him, I have often wondered whether, as was thought at that time, he isn't completely stupid.

It was Noémie who put the Bible in his hands, it was she who for years guided him in his reading. It is fortunate that she did. I wonder what would have happened if he had not gone beyond the law of retaliation. You know: "An eye for an eye, a tooth for a tooth . . ."

He constructed himself a simple and noble world founded on the divine teachings. He contemplated it, learned it by heart, digested it, assimilated it. Without difficulty, for he is pure, he tested its strength on himself, and then one day he came down to us.

Silently he walked all around the island, observing men and women given over to lechery, children lazy and deceitful, houses in disrepair, jobs left unfinished, proofs of our weakness everywhere exposed. He was outraged, and he said so.

People listened to him because he had a gift for speaking and he was possessed by the Bible. I'm quite serious. I'm not naturally sensitive to these things, but I was moved. I can still see him, a solitary figure facing a small crowd on a big, grey beach. He had no rhetorical tricks. His voice and his gestures had the same natural beauty as his face. We couldn't help loving him, because he looked so much like what we had all dreamed of being as children.

He never asked anything for himself. Léné, who was soon convinced that he was only barely worthy to serve this inspired being, offered him the church. He accepted it naturally. And once again life in Raevavae took on a new dimension.

I remember perfectly that this happened a few months after our men had returned from Rapa. The high furnace in which they melted down the metal consumed an enormous amount of wood. For over a year we had to let it stand idle for lack of woodcutters, which delayed the completion of the boat by that long.

But at the time no one cared. After having raised us all to a fever, the boat had been forgotten by everyone, or almost everyone. In fact, under the pressure of Toutepo, the material world made of flesh and blood, stone, earth, water, and grass almost collapsed and disappeared behind the cold, clean universe of moral perfection.

Toutepo is gentle, modest, and inflexible. Alone, he is nothing, and he knows it. But God is in him. He is his voice. Because of this, he is inflexible. You know him; he's not a thundering prophet. He stands there, observing silently. Nothing escapes him. He understands everything, confessions and lies alike. He accepts them in the same spirit, he judges only actions. When it comes to these, he is made of rock. He weighs them accurately, and reads what his scale shows. He is not there to judge, but to speak. He himself doesn't count. He passes on God's opinion, no matter what the consequences. To himself or to anyone else.

Nothing touches him. Nothing could make him yield. I don't really know who he is. Once he was established at the church, he took charge of the island and turned it around. Suddenly he became the bread and water, the music and dancing of Raevavae. He didn't force anyone. But at that time his power was tremendous and his logic impeccable. Life is so simple, the way he explains it. Everything has a cause, everything has a purpose. Men need only be just and have faith in order to arrive, if not at happiness, at least at peace. How could one help being tempted?

The island just missed becoming one big monastery in which nothing counted but the service of God. I myself was fascinated, and ready to become the economic father of this new theocracy.

And then time passed. The skeleton of our boat, lying on the sand, began to attract our attention. More and more workers came back, at first proclaiming loudly that they were only doing their duty, but later to savor the taste of freedom once again.

Toutepo certainly sensed the shift, but he didn't dare or didn't choose to cast blame. He's really very honest. Monasteries are useful, but they are not made to contain an entire population. When our ship was afloat, we all sighed with relief. Our madness had passed.

It had left changes in its wake. The people of Raevavae had not become saints, but from then on they knew what a saint was. Through excess of goodness, they had discovered sin, and their neglect had taught them the meaning of perseverance. They were no longer completely those beautiful, inexhaustible animals who were once ruled by their instincts. They were ready, now, to reconquer the world.

I protected Toutepo when the tide turned. I brought him back to the forefront at a time when people were tired of him. I helped him get together the faithful souls who really loved him. I took every opportunity to show my respect for him. I knew now that he would never be completely victorious. But neither could I deny that he was useful. He let me do as I chose, without illusions or regrets. I was useful to him too, and in my own way, I served him. Neither a dupe nor a hostage, he took advantage of this without thanking me for it. He has often been severe with me. Today, age is bringing us closer together. But he doesn't approve of the role I have chosen, and looks down on me for having made such a big effort for so little.

On the twenty-fourth of March of the year twenty-one, we set sail. There were fifty of us, as we had planned, and I was the oldest.

We had confidence in our boat. To try it out as well as to get a supply of fuel, we had first made a trial voyage to Rapa with a light load. Our storerooms were full, and we had coal and provisions for a long crossing. And I didn't think that after such a long time the aftereffects of the catastrophe could pose any danger to our health.

Nevertheless, when we started to move slowly toward the neck of the lagoon and turned to look at our island, at the tiny port of Rairua and the hills covered with our people singing and weeping and waving flowers, then for a moment we cursed the victory that had given us this ship.

53

I WAS TEMPTED to cut off this narrative with that half-century-old image which I had forgotten, which I pulled out of my memory for you, and which has just awakened so many dreams.

We were young, and the world was new—oh, how new! Yes, I almost stopped without saying goodbye. I have nothing important left to tell you. Most old men talk too much. They finger words, ideas, images the way children paw objects. I don't want to be one of those old men. The rest isn't interesting. You know the official version, and from what I've told you, you can guess what has not been said. Men are both themselves and their opposite. Nothing remains clear for very long. You know that. Why should I tell you what you already know?

Nor am I going to tell you about our voyage. First, because I have written an exact account of it which you've read and to which I would have very little to add. To tell you how alone and frightened we were on that empty sea, under that empty sky, to describe to you my feelings when, in the ruins of Sydney, we discovered in the basement of that devastated bank that now famous sentence, no doubt the work of a dying puritan whose despair had made him a poet: "On this fourteenth of July, O God, men in their arrogant madness lost the world you entrusted to them . . ."; to admit that I wept, first with joy, and then with pity when, in Borneo, we came upon the first colony of survivors and saw to what extremities they had been driven by a sudden reversion to savagery—what would be the point? These are merely the impressions of a traveler. And besides, none of this is important. When I arrived in Raevavae I was the shadow of a man who had fallen into a seeming paradise. The island and I learned to live together, we became ourselves, we were born. By common consent, in friendship, by helping each other, we ceased merely to exist. We evolved. Yes, every one of us in Raevavae,

343

according to our capacities, at the whim of circumstances, transcended ourselves, without pride, but with self-respect.

For a long time we worked in silence, without being sure of ourselves, without knowing where we were going, or even if we were going somewhere.

And then we got stronger, gained confidence. So to be sure we were not mistaken, to have a proof of our new condition, we decided to build a masterpiece. Something that would enlist all our strength and intelligence, but also all our character and perseverance. With our own arms we carried wood, hundreds of tons of it. With our hammers, we pounded dozens and dozens of sheets of iron, and each blow was the hundred millionth part of our task. Twice our boilers exploded and several of us died, the victims of our ignorance. We cast our propellor in the sand and polished it by hand, and the first time we turned it on it tore out the shaft and the bearings. We labored painfully, beyond our strength, like madmen. But we worked together, and of our own free will. And we finished our masterpiece. This was the end of our apprenticeship. As chance or destiny decreed, it was also the end of our life in Raevavae. This island was our world, and the whole world. It gave us life. It taught us. When we were ready, it pushed us toward the sea and said to us, "You don't need me any more."

It was true. We had to leave. But we have done nothing since then but apply the lessons we learned there.

I know I am shocking you. For you, the world begins with yourself, with our federation of the hundred towns, with our order, our laws, with this open world which we are beginning to reconquer. No doubt you are right. I will die tomorrow. And tomorrow you will decide to live. You will have your problems, as I have had mine. Perhaps, through me, you will know what we all owe to Raevavae. But you will never feel it the way I do. The world still belongs to me, in a way. Your world is asking to be born.

But don't forget that everything came out of that black dot on the map.

Because of the Fijians, we are one people, welcoming everyone, but a people into which newcomers must blend.

Because the day after the *tsunami* there were seven hundred and eleven of us, and because we lived with that number on good terms, each of our towns has the same number of inhabitants and must send out a group of colonists to settle elsewhere if it exceeds that number.

Because in Raevavae we always lived on the fish in the lagoon, the fruits of nature, and the flesh of wild animals, because we learned there to build houses out of leaves, to wear tapa, and to eat from earthen dishes that were as easy to make as they were to break, we know nothing of luxury, economy, or unnecessary effort.

Because in Raevavae everyone was free, we know nothing of money, wages, or poverty.

We are a hundred towns, of course, but we know as little about war as if we were only one. The rare conflicts that arise between our towns are resolved by the big assembly which meets every three years, and this is enough. Its verdicts are wise, no doubt. But the fact that the inhabitants of the two communities bringing charges must all have their hair cut before they can plead their case, is enough, believe me, to eliminate a lot of petty bickering.

Each of our towns, under the direction of the two councils, that of the elders and that of the young people, lives well, and in harmony. And if our councils have only the power of giving the verdict, but not that of carrying out the punishment, which is left in the hands of the winner, this is because if I had been the executioner as well as the judge, I would not have executed Tara.

If we believe in education so strongly that we don't allow people to vote until they have completed their three years of fundamentals and then their three years of electives, but if we allow everyone to decide freely at what period in his life he will be a student, and if the elective courses include such varied subjects as basket weaving, dancing, and mathematics, this is because we discovered in Raevavae that school should only teach the basics and give people confidence.

Finally, if we make such a religion of gift-giving, if our craftsmen, our fishermen, our farmers love so much to give presents, if our poets, singers, performers, athletes, and scientists are so eager to give other people the benefit of their talents or their learning, is this not primarily because in Raevavae the gift honored the giver?

In a word, Raevavae was the egg. When you have described it and followed it to its maturity, you know almost everything there is to know about the chicken.

For your sake I have tried to break this egg and then to reconstruct it. The new version may be less beautiful, less glossy, a little irregular, a little strange, but in some way it is also simpler and easier to understand. Here it is. Take it. It belongs to you now.

And now that it is in your hands, now that I have become transparent, I can begin to take my rest.